D0115743

Drove All Night

#1 PASSING THROUGH

SARAH HEGGER

To the incredible Terry M.
Your courage humbles me.
Your determination inspires me,
and I cherish your friendship.

You can tell everyone this is your book.

Acknowledgments

This book took a while to reach release, and it wouldn't have made it without some very special people who helped me along the way. Thanks to Kristi Rose who is holding my hand through this terrifying leap into Indie publishing. How she remains patient through my barrage of idiotic questions is a mystery, right up there with crop circles. Also Tara Cromer who is a constant source of encouragement and ego stroking. You two ladies are the best and I owe you BIG TIME. It's in writing now, so I can't renege.

I'd also like to extend my thanks to the incomparable Penny Barber. There are good editors, there are great editors and then there is PENNY BARBER. And yes I did mean to put that in caps. Thanks as well to Renee Rocco, who is probably reading this as she puts my scribblings into a legible format. These covers you made for the Passing Through Series! Girl!!!!!! I couldn't love them more. It's been wonderful to reconnect with you as we both take another step in our publishing journeys.

As always, thanks to my family, particularly my husband and his constant helpful plot suggestions. His title suggestions are best never mentioned again.

And last, but by no means least, you fabulous people who make up the Sarah Hegger Collective. You keep me going.

Copyright © 2019 Sarah Hegger

All rights reserved. No part of this book may be reproduced in any form or by any means without the prior written consent of the publisher, excepting brief quotes used in reviews.

Format and cover design by: Renee Rocco

First Electronic Edition: June 2019
ISBN-13: 978-1-7329331-2-5
ISBN: 978-1-7329331-3-2

Praise for Sarah Hegger

Positively Pippa

"This is the type of romance that makes readers fall in love not just with characters, but with authors as well."
—*Kirkus Review* (Starred Review)

"What begins as a simple second-chance romance quickly transforms into a beautiful, frank examination of love, family dynamics, and following one's dreams. Hegger's unflinching, candid portrayal of interpersonal and generational communication elevates the story to the sublime. Shunning clichés and contrived circumstances, she uses realistic, relatable situations to create a world that readers will want to visit time and again."
—*Publisher's Weekly*, Starred Review

"Hegger's utterly delightful first Ghost Falls contemporary is what other romance novels want to grow up to be."
—*Publisher's Weekly*, Best Books of 2017

"The very talented Hegger kicks off an enjoyable new series set in the small Utah town of Ghost Falls. This charming and fun-filled book has everything from passion and humor to betrayal and revenge."
—Jill M Smith, *RT Books Reviews* 2017 / Contemporary Love and Laughter Nominee

Becoming Bella

"Hegger excels at depicting familial relationships and friendships of all kinds, including purely platonic friendships between women and men. Tears, laughter, and a dollop of suspense make a memorable story that readers will want to revisit time and again."
—*Publisher's Weekly*, Starred Review

"…you have a terrific new romance that Hegger fans are going to love. Don't miss out!" Jill M. Smith
—*RT Book Reviews*

Nobody's Fool
"Hegger offers a breath of fresh air in the romance genre."
—Terri Dukes, *RT Book Reviews*

Nobody's Princess
"Hegger continues to live up to her rapidly growing reputation for breathing fresh air into the romance genre."
—Terri Dukes, *RT Book Reviews*

"I have read the entire Willow Park Series. I have loved each of the books … Nobody's Princess is my favorite of all time."
—*Harlequin Junkie*, Top Pick

Drove All Night

SARAH HEGGER

SarahHegger.com

Chapter 1

At Main and Fourth, a minivan shot through the stop sign. Ben hit the lights and siren.

The minivan veered across the road and screeched to a halt at an angle from the sidewalk.

"Shit." Ben punched the brakes. Keeping his eye on the vehicle, he called it in.

Whoever drove that thing had bought themselves a couple of hefty fines. Reckless asshole. Some people should not be allowed behind the wheel.

Stepping out of the cruiser, he palmed his sidearm. The car had Pennsylvania plates. Not from around here, and driving like a crazy person. He approached with caution.

The driver's door flew open and someone leaped out.

The pale, wide-eyed woman hit the ground. Her knees smacked the blacktop so hard he winced. She threw her hands out in front of her. "Do it." The woman sobbed. "Arrest me. Take me away. Lock me up and throw away the key."

Fifteen years as a cop and this was a new one on him. Ben stopped midstride and loosened his grip on his weapon. "Ma'am?"

"I can't." Her shoulders jerked up and down. "I just can't anymore."

A rusted pickup stopped and Hank Styles hung his grizzled old head out the window. "Everything all right here, Ben?"

That's all he needed, Hank Styles playing deputy. He waved him on. "All good."

"She don't look so good." Hank leaned further out his truck. "What's wrong with her?"

It went easier if you didn't engage the conversation. "Drive on, Hank."

The woman staggered to her feet, wrists still held out to him. She took three tottering steps in his direction and collapsed.

Ben caught her a heartbeat before her head hit the road.

"Holy crap." Hank jerked his head back in. "She's dead." He rolled up his window and gunned his truck down Main.

Ben checked for a pulse and found one at her neck. Her skin felt hot and clammy. She was burning up. An ambulance, maybe?

"Is my mommy dead?" A plaintive voice came from the van.

The van door opened and Ben stared straight into hell. A boy, maybe five or six, and covered in barf blinked back at him. From the far side, a scarlet-faced toddler hiccupped and then yowled. Two older kids, wearing identical girl faces peered around the van door at him.

The smell made his eyes water; an unholy miasma of body fluids that did not belong on this earth.

The woman stirred. "Ryan?"

"You fainted." Ben hoisted her into his arms. First step, get her out of the road. "Lie still."

"Where are you taking her?" One of the girls cocked her head at him.

Ben jerked his chin to indicate the side of the road. "Stay put."

He walked around back of the minivan and set her gently on the grassy shoulder.

"Are you arresting her?" The girls moved to the other side of the van, hanging over the squalling baby, heads jammed together as they peered through the open window.

"Nope."

The woman opened her eyes, squeezed them shut, and then opened them again. "Who are you?"

"I'm the police chief, ma'am."

"My children." She bolted upright, slamming her head against his chin.

Ben tasted blood as he pressed her back down. "Lie still. You fainted."

She blinked at him, but lay back. She had brown eyes, dark like his morning coffee and huge in her pale face. When not passed out on the side of the road with sweat sliding down the sides of her face, she might even be pretty. Too thin, but real pretty.

He turned to the minivan. "Any water in there?"

"Nope." Three heads moved from side to side. The baby kept right on bawling.

Ben jerked his chin at the red-faced crier. "He sick?"

"Uh-huh." One of the twins slow-nodded. "He's got the flu, and he pooped in his diaper. Mommy didn't have any more so we were going to Walmart to get some. He's screaming coz he's got a sore bum."

Sick mum, one sick toddler, one puking boy and a set of lively twins. He weighed his options.

They didn't cover this sort of shit in the police academy, or the army, and Ben was man enough to know when he'd drifted way out of his league. He reached for his cellphone.

Ma answered on the fourth ring, sounding as delighted to hear from him as ever. "Ben!"

"You home, Ma?"

"Of course I am. It's baking day and they want some cupcakes for that fundraiser for the library. Do you think I should put sunflowers or flip-flops on the top? What with it being summer and all."

"I'll be right over."

"What's wrong?" Her voice sharpened. "Did you get shot? Are you injured?" She heaved a sigh. "You forgot to eat lunch again, didn't you?"

He had, but not his biggest concern right now. "Bringing some kids."

"What? What kids? Whose kids? Where did you find them?"

"See you." Ben hung up on her still firing questions. If he answered those, she'd only find a raft more for him.

"Ma'am?" He looked down at the woman. "Can you tell me your name?"

"Poppy." She swallowed. "Poppy Williams."

"Well, Poppy Williams, I'm gonna have to drive your car."

"Are you a car thief?" Her eyes widened.

Ben shook his head and hoisted her into his arms. She weighed next to nothing. Her sweatshirt claimed her as Property of Philadelphia University and hung on her narrow frame. He placed her gently in the passenger seat.

Her eyelids fluttered closed as she fought sleep. He'd bet by the shadows under her eyes it had been a long, long time since Poppy Williams had gotten a good night's sleep. Her fever must be knocking the crap out of her round about now.

Her eyes flew open. "My children."

"I got them." He buckled her in.

"Are you kidnapping me?"

"No, ma'am."

Her lids fluttered closed, only to startle open again. "Are you a rapist?"

"Nope." He took his badge out and held it in front of her fever-glazed gaze. "I'm the police chief, ma'am. I got you."

Chapter 2

The stink in the car had Ben driving with his window wide open and still nearly dry heaving all the way. Poppy Williams woke every now and then, and went back to sleep as soon as he assured her he was still the police chief. Eventually he put his badge on the dash right in front of her.

Ma stood on the sidewalk, hopping from one foot to the other. That was the thing with his mom. She never walked when she could run, or stood when she could bop about like a jackrabbit. Today, she wore a red T-shirt announcing to all *Police Chief's Mom*. It might put his passenger at ease.

Poppy hardly looked old enough to have four children. Her dark hair had escaped her ponytail in tendrils that stuck to her temples. He'd bet his last dime she had one helluva story.

"Who's that?" One of the twins peered out her window. Their names were Brinn and Ciara but damned if he could tell them apart. One had on a blue T-shirt and shorts, the other some kind of dress with flowers all over it.

"Is that the perp?" The older boy, Ryan, leaned forward in his car seat.

"That's my mother." He stopped beside her.

Ma frowned at the unfamiliar car, caught sight of him and beamed. She appeared at his door before he even had it open.

"Ben." Face full of delight, as if she hadn't seen him in months, and not yesterday for lunch, she kissed his cheek. "I had no idea what to make of that cryptic message."

"I need your help." He walked around the car with her tailing him.

"You're so like your father. Never use three words when one will do. I thought you were doing traffic duty today. Isn't that what you said? Yes, you did say that. You said people were speeding out of the Walmart parking lot." She paused for breath. "And they nearly hit that nice Barker boy. Isn't that what you said?" She nodded. "That's what you said."

Ben gave her a nod to cover all those questions and opened the passenger door.

Ma snapped her mouth shut. That had to be a first. She took a step closer, straightened and stared at him. "Who is that," she whispered.

"A woman."

"I can see that." She slapped his arm. "Is this her car?"

"Yup." He slid open the side door. The reek charged out to the sidewalk.

"Oh, my." Ma clapped her hand over her mouth. "Oh, my."

The baby's lip quivered, his eyes filled up, and he opened his mouth and bellowed.

Ma folded like a cheap deckchair. Her arms shot out and she unclipped the little guy. "You poor baby."

"Sean." Poppy stirred, and tried to sit up.

Ben flashed his badge. "Chief. I got this."

She settled down again.

Ma had the baby in her arms and rocked him side to side. "You poor little guy. Are you unhappy? Tell Dot what is making you so unhappy."

"He pooped," Ryan said.

The girls craned forward between the first row of seats. "And he's got diaper rash," said the one in the dress. "It makes him super cranky."

"Well, of course it does." Ma put the kid's head on her shoulder, and ran a soothing hand down his back. "Dot is going to fix that for you. Yes she is. No need to fuss." She gave Ben a reproachful glare, as if he was somehow to blame for all of it. "What happened to these children?"

He shrugged, because other than their mother losing her shit, he had no answers.

"Come on, honey." She motioned to Ryan. "You climb out here and see Dot. You look like you could use a bath."

"I barfed." Ryan nodded. "All over myself and some of it got on Sean, too."

Ma had a stomach of iron, because she took the news without a flinch. "Did you?" She held out her hand to Ryan. "How very nasty for you."

She leaned in closer to Ben and jerked her head. "Is that their mother?"

"Yeah." He unclicked Poppy's seatbelt. "I think she's sick. I didn't know what to do with all these kids if I called an ambulance."

"Sean's sick too." Dress twin bounced to the ground. Her sister followed more cautiously. "He got sick one day after we left Philly."

"Is that where you're from?" Who needed interrogation when you had a ma like his? The baby had quieted down to loud sniffles, his flushed face pressed into ma's neck.

"Yes, ma'am." Dress twin seemed to suffer from the same inability to stand still as Ma. She bounced on her toes, canting left and then right, flipping her ponytail from side to side. "Four-twelve Mifflin Street, South Philadelphia, one-nine-one-four-six."

"Oh, my. Aren't you clever." Ma widened her eyes.

"I am." Whip, whip, whip went the ponytail. "I get the best grades in my class. Even better than Randall Greer, and he's always telling everyone how smart he is. He once cried and tried to hit me when I beat him at spelling."

"He sounds like a perfectly horrid little boy." Ma leaned in closer. "I don't like people who brag. How about you?"

"Nope." She stopped and smoothed her dress. "I like this dress. It's my favorite."

"It's very pretty."

She went back to bouncing. "I'm Brinn and this is Ciara." She jabbed a thumb at her sister. "We're twins."

"I can see that."

Ben felt tired watching her.

Poppy moaned and twisted in the seat.

"Inside?" He jerked his chin to the house.

"Yes, indeed." Ma gripped Ryan's hand tighter. "Brinn? Why don't you and Ciara follow me into the house? My son will bring your mother."

"Is he your son?" Twin sets of dark brown eyes fastened on him.

"He is." Ma nodded at her T-shirt. "See, I'm the chief's mom."

"Ten-four. Copy." Ryan grinned at him. "Roger. Copy that."

"He's very big." Brinn stopped bouncing long enough to eye him up and down. "Are you sure my mom will be all right."

"I'm quite sure." Ma hustled them toward the house. "I raised him, you know, from when he was even smaller than Sean here."

"Sean's the smallest in our family." Brinn gripped her sister's hand and towed her after Ma and the boys.

Poppy opened her eyes, gazed around her in an unfocused way, and found him. "My children?"

"Chief. Got 'em." He leaned in and hoisted her into his arms. She weighed less than a bag of feed. Under her sweatshirt he could feel the hard ridges of her ribs. One helluva story.

"Put her in your old room." Ma stood in the hallway, a staff sergeant in charge. "I'm going to run a bath for Ryan here, and get this little guy changed."

"We ran out of diapers." Brinn scrutinized him carrying her mother. "Is my mother going to be all right?"

Ciara's eyes brimmed with tears.

"Oh, honey." Ma hauled Ciara in for a hug. "Mommy's going to be fine. She's a little sick is all. Ben is going to find a nice comfortable bed for her, and then we'll call Doc Cooper."

"She doesn't look good." Brinn's lip quivered.

"Nobody looks good when they're sick," Ma said. "Now, would you like to help me run a bath? Then we can all get something to eat. Would you like that? Are you hungry?"

"I want to stay with my mom." Standing rigid Brinn glared at him.

Ben tried to look nonthreatening. Also not to loom over her like Ma said he had a bad habit of doing.

"Then, that's what you must do." Ma smoothed her hair. "You go with Ben and see that he takes proper care of your mom."

The twins trailed him to his old bedroom. He nudged the door open with his foot and stepped right into his past. Ma had barely changed a thing. His old football pennant still hung above his twin bed.

"That girl isn't wearing a top." Brinn cocked her head and glared at the Miss September poster. "Is she a ho?"

"Nope." He didn't know what to say to most people. Little girls with mouths on rails made him break out in a cold sweat. "Covers?"

The twins blinked at him.

"Pull them down."

They leaped into action and he laid Poppy down. He moved to take her shoes off.

"What are you doing?" Brinn stepped in front of him.

"Taking her shoes off."

"Why?"

"Do you sleep in your shoes?"

"No."

"Figured as much."

She stepped aside, but still gave him the stink eye, just in case he got any ideas about her mother's feet. He'd leave getting her more comfortable to Ma.

Chapter 3

Ben parked outside Grover's General Store. Give a woman half a chance and she sent you to the store. Ma had given him a list long enough to make his heart sink. A rummage through the car had revealed Poppy had run out of near about everything.

How much crap could kids really need?

He preferred using Grover's to the bigger chain stores. The Grover family had been part of the community since the first wagons chased gold west. It might cost him a few more cents on the occasional item, but Grover's always stocked his favorite brand of coffee, made sure they had the candy he favored, that sort of thing. If they didn't, they'd order it for him. They did the same for everyone in town. Coming into Grover's was more like a family visit.

"Hey, Chief Crowe." Mia Grover peered over a magazine rack she was restocking.

When the hell did little Mia get big enough to see over that rack? Seemed like only yesterday he'd been taking her and three friends for a ride in the back of his cruiser around the Elementary school parking lot. "Hey, Mia." The promise of a shortcut through his list made him stop. "Get some help?"

"Sure, Chief." She went a little pink and pranced up to him. "What do you need?"

He shoved his mother's list into her hand.

Mia scanned it, and frowned up at him. "Diapers? Are you married now, Chief?"

As if he could get married again without the entire town knowing. "Nah."

Mia's face cleared into a big, sunny smile. She wrinkled her freckled nose at him. "Is this for those children?"

"Huh?"

"The orphans." Tears welled in Mia's wide, brown eyes. "So young and abandoned on the side of the road."

Ben mentally used every ugly word he knew. And he knew a lot.

She took a shaky breath. "You're a real hero, Chief Crowe. I know you don't catch murderers or drugs lords or anything like that, but someone who would take care of those poor children is an even bigger hero."

"They're not orphans."

"She abandoned them." Mia jammed her fists on her hips, crinkling his list in the process. "I know I don't have children yet or anything, but I would never do that. What kind of woman does that?"

"Mia, honey." Bart came up behind her and put his arm around his daughter's shoulders. "I think Chief Crowe is in a hurry. Why don't you help him find what he's looking for?"

She scuttled off, snagging a shopping cart on her way.

"How ya doing, Ben?" Bart held out his hand.

Bart saved the Chief Crowe for when his daughter was around, but they'd been to school together and it was always Ben when they were alone. Bart might sag a bit more than when he played tackle to Ben's quarterback senior year, but he raised great kids and ran a good store. He also made the best ribs around and didn't skimp on them at the Founder's Day town cookout.

"Good. You?"

Bart shook his head. "Hank Styles came in for his Saturday night pizza and poker game a bit earlier." He sidled closer. "Crying shame what happened to those kids. From New York is how I heard it?"

"Philly." Ben felt the slow ache in his ass that was the Twin Elks grapevine. Just once, it would be great if they got the facts even close to straight. "Philly. They're from Philly."

"Philly?" Bart whistled as if he'd told him the kids drove straight through the gates of hell with Satan riding shotgun. "Hank says the mother is—" Bart glanced around, "—a crack whore. Saw her tripping on the road and everything."

Where did he even start? "She's not a crack whore."

At least, he'd bet all the money the county didn't pay him she wasn't. The car seats had been good quality, the kind that anchored at three points.

The car, not new, but in good condition, current stench aside, and the kids were well dressed. Not pricey, citified stuff, but good quality and sensible.

"So why'd she abandon her kids?" Bart stuck his chin out, ready to argue a point he knew nothing about.

Mia passed them pushing her shopping cart, and gave him a cheery wave. "Nearly done, Chief. Just looking for the formula."

"Does Ben Crowe have a baby?" A feminine voice floated from the chip aisle.

Another woman chimed in. "No. Did he get married again?"

The ache is his ass bloomed into a need to yell or kick something, or run naked down the road waving his dick at everyone and give them all something real to talk about.

Bart gave him an apologetic smile.

The chip aisle speculators weren't done yet. "You don't suppose he and Tara are getting back together, do you? I always thought that woman needed a child."

A child was the last thing his ex-wife needed, or him for that matter, which was funny as hell because he'd gotten himself four this morning.

Mia appeared with a laden cart. "All done, Chief."

"Is Tara Crowe having Ben's baby." A third voice joined the other two speculators and Ben was done.

He paid for the groceries, loaded them up and made his escape.

Ma hung up the phone as he walked through the kitchen door. "What did you do?"

Nothing and he shrugged at Ma. No running naked, no dick waving and no fathering children. The last one of those made naked dick waving sound attractive.

The phone rang again. Ma glared at it, and went back to plating a sandwich. She put it in front of Ryan.

Ben dumped the grocery bags on the kitchen table. "Your list."

The phone stopped, and then went again. Faster than a speeding bullet went the Twin Elk jungle drums.

Freshly scrubbed, Ryan watched him with big eyes. "Who's our vic, Lieutenant?"

"Eh?" He couldn't have heard that right.

"What we got?" Ryan chowed down on a pb&j sandwich.

"The phone has been ringing off the hook." Ma collared a pants-less Sean and tucked him under her arm. She motioned Ben to hand her the diapers. "What did you say?"

He shrugged. "Nothing. I told Bart she was from Philly. And that she wasn't a drug addict."

Ryan glanced between them. "Possible ten-fifty."

Did this kid have police codes memorized?

"You said nothing." Ma expertly diapered Sean and set him on his feet again. "That's the problem. You never say anything and now I'm going to have to spend hours on the phone fixing this."

Sean toddled for the door and Ben barely managed to get it closed in time. Kid sure moved fast on chubby little legs.

"He's been cooped up in a car, poor mite." Ma set Sean down at the table. "Hand me the sippy cup."

He blinked at her.

"The cup! The one with the two handles and the spouty thingy on the top." She clicked her fingers at him.

Brinn appeared at his side, Ciara at her six, and gave him a very adult eye roll. She rooted through the bags until she found what he assumed was a sippy cup. She also handed Ma a carton of juice. "You need to water it down," she said. "My mom says it's bad for his teeth if you don't put water in it."

"Then I'll put water in it." Ma tugged her ponytail. "Now you girls sit down and Ben will make you a sandwich."

Ben would? He didn't know what kids ate. Ryan seemed happy with his pb&j so he went with that.

The girls tucked in. "You need to get us a glass of milk too," Brinn said.

Ciara whispered in her ear.

"Please," Brinn said.

Ma had the phone in one hand, pouring juice in the sippy cup with the other.

Neat invention. With the top screwed on kids wouldn't spill. He looked at the glasses of milk in his hand, and up at the girls.

"We don't need a sippy cup." Brinn grinned at him through a mouthful of sandwich. The twins resembled their mother. Same dark eyes and dark hair. Did their mother have the same sassy, cute smile they did?

"Peg!" Ma beamed into the phone. "I need to get the prayer chain activated."

God help them all. Raw fear slithered down his spine. The Twin Elks Prayer Chain could teach the CIA a thing or two.

"How's your mom?" He asked Brinn because she seemed to be the twin who spoke.

"Sleeping." Brinn drained her milk and looked at him expectantly. He should have added milk to his list at the store. Obediently he got the carton out of the fridge and refilled their glasses.

"Vic stable," said Ryan.

"Does he always talk like that?" Again he asked Brinn.

She nodded as she chewed. "He watches too many cop shows on TV. Mom wanted to move him from his daycare but all the ones closer to her work were full, and she couldn't afford the other ones."

"How do these silly rumors get started, Peg?" Ma glared at him. "No, she's sick. Well, the flu I'd say, but Doc Cooper's on his way." She nodded and made yes noises as Peg's garbled voice drifted over. "Sure, he's retired but he's only two doors over, and she has four kids with her. I think the baby has it too." More nodding and uh-huhing. "You do?" Ma put her hand over the mouthpiece. "Peg has a portable crib she can lend us, from when her grandson was last visiting." She went back to her call.

"You drive all the way from Philly?" He felt kind of low getting information out of kids, but their mother was too ill. At least, that's what he'd say if anyone asked.

Brinn nodded. "We're going to California."

She launched into some pop-type song about girls and California. Ciara joined in.

Thus ended his interrogation session. He considered Ryan.

Ryan watched him with wide eyes, jaw working on his sandwich.

Ben discarded the idea.

"If you'd make sure the true story gets around, Peg, I'd be so grateful," Ma said. "That's right, I'm making lasagna for our adult coloring night."

Ben tuned out again. The girls' singing scrambled his man-brain. Time to check on their mother.

⟡

Ma had worked another one of her miracles here.

Poppy wore an old Cougars T-shirt from his school football days. Her breathing rasped into the silent room.

Paler than the white pillowcase behind her head, she did not look good.

He put his hand on her forehead, hot and clammy.

She stilled.

He took his hand away and her eyes opened. Her fevered gaze found him. "My children."

"Are fine." He put his hand back on her forehead, and stroked his thumb over the frown lines between her big, brown eyes. "Sleep."

Perching on the window seat, he reviewed the information he had. No ring on her finger, but four kids probably meant single mother or divorced. Could also be a widow. If there was a man in the picture, he couldn't see him allowing a sick woman to drive four kids across the country. At least not any sort of man he'd call friend.

They came from Philly, so she must have been traveling for a solid few days now. He didn't imagine you made good time with kids in tow. He guessed money was tight, with what Brinn had dropped in the kitchen about affordable daycare.

Poppy, not the sort of name you heard everyday.

Ma scratched on the door. "Doc Cooper is here."

"Okay." He had a hundred things to do, not one of them sitting and watching Poppy Williams sleep, yet here he sat.

Bald, craggy, with a careworn face, Doc Cooper hadn't changed a day in the years Ben had known him. He'd pretty much looked that old since Ben had gone to him as a kid. Retired now, his son had taken over from him a few years back. Far as Ben knew, nobody really knew how old Doc was, but they all agreed on his doctoring skills. If Doc said they needed a trip to the emergency room, that's what they'd do.

"What you got for me, Ben?" He dropped his black doctor's bag on the end of Poppy's bed.

"Running a fever, seems a little delirious."

"Whelp, that baby had himself a tidy hundred and three degree whopper going on." He unclipped his bag and took out his stethoscope and thermometer. "You need to watch that. If we don't get it down, we're gonna have to take him to the pediatric unit at County General until we get it under control."

Doc examined Poppy neatly and efficiently, pausing to hum and frown every now and again. Standing up, he stripped off his latex gloves. "Whelp! She's sick all right. Running close to hundred and five so she might be drifting in and out. Lungs are clear though, which is the good news, but she's way too thin and looks plain wore out. I don't think that's helping matters."

Anger for Poppy lit a slow burn inside him. How did a woman get into this state? How come nobody was looking out for her, taking care of her, making her world a good place to be?

"The poor thing." Ma smoothed the covers beneath Poppy's chin.

"Gonna give my boy a bell and tell him what's what." Doc packed up his bag. "Pop over to the clinic, and they'll have a script ready for you when you get there."

Poppy muttered, eyes flying open. Her gaze found his and he nodded. "You're okay." Or she would be, because he intended to make it so.

Poppy closed her eyes.

"That's the best thing for her, I reckon." Doc hauled out an ancient brick of a phone. "Looks like a virus to me, but it's a doozy, so watch her tonight and the baby, and give me a bell in the morning. Let me know how they're getting on."

"We'll do that, Doc." Ma sent Ben a look that meant he would be helping. Damn straight he would be.

"Right." Doc rocked on his heels. "That's about all I can do. If she don't show signs of recovering, we'll take some bloods and poke around a bit further."

"Thanks, Doc." Ma ushered him from the room, hands fluttering. "Let me get you a slice of my coffee cake before you go?"

"Dot, I thought you would never ask." Doc's chuckle drifted down the passage.

Poppy muttered and quieted down again. Ben settled down to watch.

Chapter 4

Poppy tuned in and out. Whenever reality returned, he was there. A big man with broad shoulders and a deep, soothing voice that invited her to trust him. For some reason, she did.

The room didn't look like her room. And then she would remember being on the road, the van, Sean being sick.

Always the big man would answer her questions, telling her the kids were fine. And she believed him. Brinn's voice would drift over, and occasionally Ryan's. Once she thought she saw the girls sitting near the bed with an older woman.

She'd heard Sean cry and tried to get up to comfort him, but the big man gently pressed her back into the bed, and told her to sleep. So she did.

He brought her water when she needed it, and forced a couple of pills down her throat. Mostly he sat and watched, light from the window illuminating his broad shoulders. Eventually, the fog cleared enough for details to penetrate. She lay on a twin bed. On the wall opposite her, Miss September's boobs challenged women everywhere. A couple photos littered the bedside table. They seemed to be a team of some sort. A football pennant in maroon and a gray with a snarling cat hung above her.

A boy's room for sure, but none of the posters seemed recent.

The big man hovered over her. "You awake?"

"Yes." Her throat felt like sandpaper. He brought her a glass with a straw. Sweet, fresh apple juice filled her mouth. "Where am I?"

"Twin Elks." He put the glass down, picked up a pill bottle, and shook two into his hand. He passed them to her and brought the apple juice back. She could have downed the entire glass, but he took it away after two sips.

"And Twin Elks is?"

Somewhere beyond the room, Ciara and Brinn were singing.

"Town," he said. "Colorado."

Twin Elks, the exit she'd taken off the interstate. It seemed too much to keep her eyes open, and her lids drifted shut. She had more questions, but her eyelids weren't interested.

⦉ ✿ ⦊

Gray curls going for broke all over her head, Ma stood in the kitchen and cracked her jaw in a huge yawn.

The baby had cried a few times in the night, waking both him and Ma. Ben reckoned she'd spent most of the night up with the baby. She'd put the twins and older boy to sleep in James and Mark's old room.

Guilt kicked his ass. Ma was too old to be taking care of four children.

"You look tired," he said.

"Nothing a cup of coffee won't fix." Ma patted her hair and gave him a bright smile. "I'm sure the children will be up and looking for their breakfast."

"I can take them somewhere else," Ben said. He didn't want to but Ma hadn't asked for any of this.

"Where?" Ma gaped at him. "And why would you do that? I'll have you know Benedict Crowe, I raised five boys. There is nobody in this town who knows more about children than I do."

"You're tired."

"Of course I'm tired. The baby is restless and had me up a few times."

"More than a few."

"Okay, we had a bad night." Ma crashed a frying pan on the stovetop. "But you are not taking those lovely children and putting them in some orphanage or some such other ghastly place. I'll be fine and Peg is coming around this morning to spell me for a bit so I can put my head down."

"Peg's coming over?" He needed to be out of here by then. Peg had an endless supply of unmarried daughters, nieces and granddaughters, all of whom were the perfect one for him.

Ma winked at him. "After ten. So you can relax and enjoy your breakfast."

Wearing matching pjs with unicorns on the front Ciara and Brinn wandered into the kitchen.

"Good morning." Ma motioned them over. "Come and sit down and I'll fix you some eggs."

"Ciara prefers cereal to eggs." Brinn rubbed her eyes.

"Not today she doesn't." Ma grabbed the eggs from the fridge. "Eggs give you power."

"Morning, Lieutenant." Ryan trotted into the kitchen and sent him a chin jerk. "What's the sitch this morning?"

Ben snatched up the coffee pot and refilled his cup. He was going to need to be caffeinated for this. "Breakfast."

"Ten-four." Ryan perched opposite his sisters. "Any grub on the go?"

"Aren't you a little comedian?" Ma ruffled his hair.

"How's Mom?" Brinn propped her chin on her palm.

"She slept well." Ben could manage a straightforward question, but Ryan and his Dragnet speak, not so much.

Ciara whispered in Brinn's ear, and Brinn put her arm around her. "Ciara wants to know if Mom is going to be all right. I told her she would but she wants to hear it from a grown up."

"Doc says she has a virus." Ma put juice glasses in front of all of them. "She's sick but she's going to be fine."

Ben sipped his juice. Time to unravel a bit of the mystery of Poppy Williams and her four kids trekking right across the country. "What's in California?"

"My grandma." Brinn wiped juice off her mouth. "Mom says she has a house for us, and a job for Mom."

Ma threw him a warning glance as she beat eggs in a bowl. "Maybe we should call your grandma, and let her know where you are."

"Oh, she won't care." Brinn waved. "Grandma and Mom don't speak. There's a gaping chasm between them."

Ben so didn't like the sound of that.

❧

Poppy propped her shoulder against the kitchen doorjamb.

A gently rounded older woman was cooking eggs. Her children, all except Sean, sat at a big, scrubbed wooden kitchen table. Happy, clean and looking well.

Ryan had stars in his eyes as he stared at the big man. The police chief. The police chief who told her she could sleep because he had this. Her legs buckled a little and she leaned hard into the solid wood.

"Mom." Brinn spotted her first. "You have a virus. Doc said."

Ciara blinked at her, relief on her little face. She got up from the kitchen table and ran to her. Throwing her skinny arms about her hips, Ciara buried her face in Poppy's stomach.

Poppy gripped the doorjamb to stop from going over.

The big man was there, firm hands steadying her, broad chest providing support, and shoulders looking like they could take on the world's problems and carry them around for a bit. "Shouldn't be out of bed."

"Oh, sweetie." Frowning, the woman bustled over. She wiped her hands on a pink, frilly apron that somehow worked with her jeans and sweatshirt. "I'm Dot and you look about ready to topple over. Ben, doesn't she look about ready to topple over? You should be in bed." She turned to the big man. Ben. Chief Ben. "She should be in bed. Don't you think she should be in bed?"

"I wanted to see the children." Black spots danced in front of Poppy's eyes. Oh dear, she might faint.

Ben swept her against his broad chest. "Bed."

The word rumbled against her ear as he carried her back down the corridor. The same corridor it had taken her what seemed like hours to walk, having to stop every time she grew lightheaded.

"Sean," she said. "I need to see my baby."

"He's sleeping." More comforting rumbling through that big chest pressed against her.

She lay her head against a rock-solid bicep.

"I'll bring him to you as soon as he wakes."

Dot followed. "Perhaps Ben can take you past him. So you can see he's all right. Ben, can you take her past the baby? A mother needs to know her baby is all right."

Ben changed direction and headed to another door.

Dot darted ahead of him and opened it. She pressed her finger to her lips, and whispered, "He had a bad night, the poor little thing. But his fever let up about three a.m. and he's slept soundly ever since."

Sean lay in the middle of a twin bed, pillows propped around him to keep him from rolling off. His sweet, baby face looked peaceful.

Exhaustion dragged at Poppy. Her eyelids seemed weighted, and she tried to blink them awake.

"She's dead on her feet. Let's get her back to bed." Dot steered Ben out of the room.

Poppy wanted to stay awake and thank these people. Somehow, she'd stumbled across two of the nicest people on the planet, and they were taking good care of her children and her. She opened her mouth to thank them but it grew into a yawn.

"You rest, dear." Dot patted her arm. "You rest up. Dot is here. And Ben is here, and your little ones are fine."

Poppy drifted off knowing that Ben was here. Chief Ben was here and he had this.

When Poppy next woke, sun streamed in the bedroom window, laying bright light over an old wooden bookcase. Books jammed the shelves, and piles of books overflowed to the ledge beneath the window.

Twin Elks, Dot, Ben the police chief, and her children were fine.

Brinn chattered beyond the bedroom door, sounding excited.

Dot answered her.

She had to find out how long she'd been sick. It seemed like this morning Ben had pulled her over. The memory ripped through her in cringe-worthy detail. Dear God, could she not catch a break and have amnesia or something?

"You're awake." Dot appeared in the doorway. She held a subdued Sean in her arms. "This little guy woke a couple of hours ago. Since then, he's had some juice and some of my special eggs." She brought Sean over.

Poppy's arms went out and Dot slipped the baby into them. She clicked her tongue. "They go down so fast, these little ones. Thank Goodness they bounce back as fast."

"Mah." Sean buried his warm face in her neck.

Dot perched on the end of the bed. "Do you think you could eat something?"

Poppy surprised herself by nodding. She was hungry. "Thank you," she said. It seemed stupidly inadequate. She battled to believe people like this still existed. People who wouldn't hesitate to help a stranger in trouble. Tears stung her eyes. "For everything."

"Good Heavens." Dot patted her knee. "No need to thank us. We couldn't leave you on the side of the road like that." She chuckled, and winked at Poppy. "I don't think Ben's had a turn like that in more years than I can count. Took the wind right out of his sails, you did."

Poppy's face heated. "Did he tell you what happened?"

Dot clapped and laughed, a happy sound that had Sean lifting his head, a smile on his face. "I would have given every cent I have to see that. Now." She smoothed the bedlinens. "I hope you don't mind, but after Brinn gave us her name, we went into your phone and found your mother's number. We knew she would be worried when you didn't arrive."

Well, if they thought that, they didn't know Mom. Except Mom had changed, she assured Poppy of that over and over and Poppy desperately needed to believe it right now. "Thank you. What did she say?"

Dot frowned. "She didn't answer, so we left a message, and left this number. Told her where you were, that the children were fine."

That sounded more like Mom. Except Mom had come through for her this time, and she was being a bitch. "I need to call her."

"I'll fetch your phone." Dot stood. "Are you all right with him or do you need me to take him."

Poppy tightened her arms around Sean. "I'm fine." Then she felt like an even bigger bitch because this lady had been caring for all her children while she slept. "I just need to hold him for a bit."

"Of course you do." Dot smiled. "I was the same way with my five. Never thought they were truly safe until I could get my hands on them. I'll fetch your phone and get you something to eat."

"Thank you." Poppy said it again, because she couldn't really say it enough after what Dot had done. "I'm so gra—"

"Stop now." Dot flapped her hands. "If you feel up to it, I'll send the others in to see you. That Ciara has been so worried about you, she's not said a word since she got here."

Ciara hardly ever said a word. Poppy closed her eyes as her troubles stuck their leering heads up and grinned at her. "*Here we are,*" they whispered. "*Just waiting for you to wake the hell up.*"

Chapter 5

Dot's eggs turned out to be more than "special". Creamy, rich, perfectly cooked and seasoned to give her taste buds a party. After a small plate of those and some tea, Poppy braced to call her mother.

A case of history repeating, like her mother before her, Poppy had fallen pregnant in high school. Young, single mothers didn't have it easy and their relationship had always been rocky. It turned craterous over Poppy's pregnancy. First, Mom had wanted her to terminate and then came out vehemently against Poppy getting married. At a time when all Poppy had wanted was unconditional support, the fights had driven a wedge between them.

Mom had moved on to another boyfriend before Poppy's marriage, then another and another. They'd lost contact before the twins were born, and not reconnected until six months ago.

Wedge mending took a lot longer than wedge making. Eight years in their case.

Mom answered almost immediately. "Poppy! What happened? Where are you?"

The maternal worrying took some getting used to. "Well, first little Sean got sick, then he passed it on to me. I'm in Twin Elks."

"Twin Elks?" Mom yelled into the phone. Loud music pounded down from her end. "Where is that even?"

"Colorado." Mom's latest boyfriend was some Hollywood movie producer of classics like *Busty Ninjas III* and *House of Death II, III and IV.* Either he partied a lot or really liked to play his music loud. "Apparently I collapsed on the police chief."

"The police chief? You collapsed on the police chief?" The music dimmed abruptly. "Tell me he was hot and not some old fart."

"Well, he's big." Her memories of Ben were fuzzy. "And his mother is incredible. She took all of us in and is taking care of us."

"Huh?" Mom sounded a little hurt. Guilt over Poppy's childhood had her charging down the path to super-momdom. "How are you and little Sean? What was wrong with you?"

"Some kind of flu." That's how much she'd gathered from Dot. "But we're recovering."

Mom's tone sharpened. "But you're still coming?"

"As soon as I can get on the road."

A sigh whispered down the line. "Good. That's good, then. I have the house all ready for you."

"Thanks, Mom." Mom's desperation to make amends pressed on Poppy. She wanted a better relationship with her mother, but Mom's orgy of self-recrimination and regret could be draining.

Laughter and music filled the line. Mom laughed at something someone said to her.

"Mom?"

"I'm here." A man spoke to Mom from the other end. "Sorry, things are crazy here right now. You called right in the middle of our wrap party."

Poppy's head pounded, and she needed to rest again. "Listen, I won't keep you long. I just wanted to tell you I'll be there in a couple of days. Can you let Jarryd know so he won't think I'm slacking on the job before I've even started?"

"Sure, baby." Mom's bubbliness sounded forced. "But there really is no hurry. You stay there and get better and we'll see you when we see you."

"Mom?" That tone she recognized from childhood, the *"I'm sorry but I can't make your concert, baby. Mommy has somewhere important to be"* or *"I know I said I would buy you a new backpack, but I had some unexpected expenses this month. Mommy's got a new job, baby. She needs to look her best".* Poppy's belly clenched, but she had to ask. "Everything's still okay with the job, right Mom?"

"Everything's fine." Mom's tone gentled and warmed. "I know I let you down in the past. That's over now, baby. I promise."

Poppy really wanted to believe it, she really did, and especially since she'd bet all she had on this working out. "Great."

"The job is still there, waiting for you." Mom cleared her throat. "There is a little issue with the timing, but it's a minor thing. Tiny."

"Issue?" God, no. Poppy grew lightheaded. "Mom, I can't have issues. I packed up my children and dragged them the breadth of the country."

"I know that," Mom said. "The movie will go forward. Your job on it is guaranteed. Sometimes the money doesn't always line up as neatly as we would like. There's a small delay in the funds coming through from one of the investors."

Poppy's stomach tightened. "I packed up the children. Gave up my lease because you said there was a job. That it was a sure thing."

"It's fine, Poppy." Mom gave a nervous laugh. "I know that. I'm the one who begged you to come, to give me this chance. I'm not going to screw it up. I wouldn't have said anything about it, it's such a minor problem, only we agreed we would be honest with each other from here onwards."

"Promise me, Mom." Poppy squeezed the words past the tightness in her throat.

"I promise," Mom whispered. "I'm here for you, baby. For you and those beautiful babies of yours. All you have to do is get better and get down here."

Tears threatened. Damn flu making her feel all emotional and worn out. "So, you'll tell Jarryd I'm on the way."

"I'll tell him." Mom brightened. "This might be the best thing. You stay there until you're better, and by the time you arrive everything will be squared away on this end."

From Mom's lips to God's ears. Her vision wavered around the edges. She'd risked everything on this, not that everything was that great in the first place, but still. Poppy had packed up her children, given up her apartment, quit both her jobs in Philly for this. The job Mom promised her, a good job, an executive assistant that would pay enough money to keep her head above water. "Okay," she said.

"I love you, baby."

"Love you too, Mom." Poppy hung up. She did love her mother, but the mistrust went bone deep. Built on broken promises, changed plans and crazy whims that went nowhere. She had to do better by her kids.

Chief Ben knocked on the ajar door.

"Come in." She still couldn't look him in the eye.

He gripped a tray in one large hand. "Ma said to bring you this."

Placing the tray on the bedside table he stood and looked at her. It must be his day off because he looked more approachable in jeans and a

T-shirt, or as approachable as any man that large with rough-hewn, strong features could look. She wouldn't call him handsome, but Chief Ben had a definite something going on. A rough and ready, lay your womanly problems on my big, manly shoulders type appeal. All of which made her even more embarrassed. And why the hell was he staring at her with that inscrutable expression?

"Everything okay?" He nodded to her phone on the bed beside her.

"Fine." Really she couldn't get flakier in his eyes. She cringed inside as she pictured herself leaping out of her minivan and enacting *La Traviata* on Main street.

His constant gaze unnerved her. He had dark eyes, darker than mere brown and they seemed to see right inside her.

"It will be," she said. "That was my mom."

"In California." He handed her a napkin, a soup bowl and a packet of crackers.

"How—?"

"Brinn."

"Right." The soup made her stomach growl, and her face grew hotter.

He strolled to the window and looked out. Chief Ben blocked out most of the window with those shoulders. They tapered into a trim waist and a very nice butt. It didn't take her imagination much to dress him in flannel and toss a huge ax over those shoulders. Just her luck to make an idiot of herself in front of the best looking man she'd seen in months. Mom would be proud. Of course, Mom would have found a way to get Chief Ben in this bed with her. From the smell of the soup, it was homemade tomato and basil. "We are traveling to California."

He grunted and kept his gaze trained on something out the window. Part of her wanted to get up and see what had his rapt attention.

"I have a job lined up there. And a house." She crumbled the crackers into her soup and took a spoonful. The soup exploded on her tongue in a savory-tart medley and she barely caught her groan of pleasure in time.

Glancing her way he nodded as if he knew exactly how good the soup was.

"I was going to travel straight through because they were waiting for me to take the job, and then Sean got sick."

"And you got sick." His low level rumble could make anyone ask for a bedtime story.

"Then I got sick." They'd drifted into all out humiliation territory. "About the...thing on the road. My..."

He cut his gaze her way, face still giving her nothing.

"My..." She spooned in soup while she hunted for the right word.

"Crisis?" He lifted an eyebrow.

Poppy couldn't be certain but she thought she caught a glimmer of humor in those sin-dark eyes. "Crisis?" She rolled the word around her mind. "Is that what we're calling it these days?"

And Chief Ben smiled.

Except when a face that stern and rugged smiled, it was an Event. An Event of white teeth, crinkling eyes and laugh lines that made you want to find another joke. Just so you could launch another Event.

"I'm so embarrassed," she said, still lost in the memory of a smile that had taken over his entire being, and disappeared again.

He shrugged. "I've seen worse."

"Really?" She had the sense it didn't really come much worse, short of stopping a busload of chain saw wielding psychopaths on their way to prom. "You've seen worse than a crazy woman throwing herself on the road and begging you to arrest her?"

He propped his shoulder on the wall. "The begging was a first."

"I'll bet." She went back to her soup. "Anyway, I apologize and I thank you for all you've done for the crazy woman."

"You're good," he said. "So, you're moving closer to your mother?"

"Yup." She took another spoon of soup.

He crossed one ankle over the other. "And your man?"

Her man what? She waited for him to finish the question.

He watched her.

"No man." Poppy cried uncle first. "There is no man. I mean, there was a man. Obviously. With four children. But there isn't one anymore. He died. Dead." Aaand now the time had come to shut her mouth, but that looking thing he did got her babbling.

Down the hall Brinn called for Ciara and Ciara answered her.

"Come and sit down and have some juice," Dot said.

Ben stood there, waiting.

Apparently Poppy hadn't finished exposing her underbelly because she said, "My mom and I, we have a history."

Still, he waited.

"I mean, of course we have a history. She's my mother and I'm her daughter, so we would have to have a history. Right?"

Ben grunted.

It gave her mouth all the encouragement it needed to keep going. "In the past, when I was growing up, though, she was a bit flakey. Act first and think later, and let the chips fall where they may. So I guess you're wondering why the hell I packed up my entire life, and my kid's lives, and acted on Mom's word."

Ben folded his arms, looking like he might be holding the wall up and not the other way around.

"She's changed. It took a while but she's finally settled down. She's been involved with the same man for a couple of years now. She's happy. They're happy. And she really wants to help me. But I'm not going to take chances with my children." Her words spilled so fast, she had to stop for breath. "So when she told me about the job, I researched it and it all looked legitimate. I even got something in writing before I made a move." Poppy scraped up the last of the soup. Guess she'd been hungrier than she thought. "Still, it's Mom. Right?"

"Uh-huh."

"I'm a mother now, I can't put my children at risk. But she's sorry. It's exhausting how sorry she is. She said she regretted not being there for me when I needed her. Like when I got married, and when my husband Sean died. She wants to help me give my children what she could never give me. That's showing real remorse, right?"

Did he nod? She would take it as a nod anyway.

"Then she brings out the big guns. Says how she was never there for me as a child, how she let me down and feels like she owes me. That you can't go back in time and although she wishes she could have a do-over but she knows she can't, so this is her second chance. A way to make it all right, and be a better grandmother than she was a mother."

He shifted.

"So, she comes up with the California plan. And it looks too good to be true, so it still took me a couple of weeks to make up my mind. I mean, a new job, a great house on the beach that is mine to use until the fall. I know what you're thinking."

He lifted a brow.

"If it looks too good to be true, then it is."

"I'm waiting to hear what happened to the job," he said.

"Oh." And, yes, she could appear a whole lot flakier when he was around. Did they make a magic pill for verbal diarrhea? "Well, I called Mom and she says there's a problem. She insists it's only a tiny problem and it will be sorted out by the time I'm better. But she's her, and I'm me. I'm worried. Old habits die hard, you know? And I'm kinda used to her letting me down."

He grunted, and straightened from the wall. Grabbing the tray in one massive fist, he touched her hand. "Don't worry about that now. Just get better."

Easy for him to say. Those were not his kids playing outside.

He picked up her bowl and put it back on the tray. He handed her some tablets and juice to wash them down with. Except, he had this way of making things seem less dire.

Those bottomless eyes looked down at her. Just by standing there he pushed the darkness back. His face gentled. "Sleep."

Chapter 6

The next day, Poppy dragged herself into a shower. The effort it took to do that much almost had her crawling back into bed. Except, she didn't have time to keep lying around in bed. A stranger, an incredibly kind stranger, but still a stranger was looking after her children. Dot had even laundered all their dirty clothes, and Ben had brought the suitcases and left them in the room. Time to step up.

Things had looked bad before. After Sean died, and the lawyers told her exactly how he'd left her. Those had been dark times. Pregnant, with three kids, no money and having to sell the family home to cover Sean's debts. She'd survived that, and now she had this chance to finally turn things around. Sometimes though, it felt like she spent a helluva lot of time surviving. Ricocheting from one life crisis to another. Going to California, accepting Mom's help was a way to put them on the road to better.

After her shower she pulled on a T-shirt and some shorts. The shorts once belonged to Sean and she winched them in at the waist and safety pinned them. The T-shirt? She couldn't quite remember, maybe Sean's too.

Giggles and yells emanated from the kitchen. By the sound of it, Dot had a raucous game on the go.

Poppy stopped short at the kitchen door. There were people everywhere. Her kids sat at the kitchen table. Even Sean, who mashed his way through cheerios and banana and used both as dominant accessorizing themes.

At the counter, rock solid and familiar, Dot made coffee for the horde of women.

"There she is." Dot flung out her arms. "Come right on in, Poppy. These ladies have all come to meet you and your little ones."

All of them? Poppy's mouth went dry. There must be twenty women crammed into Dot's kitchen.

"They brought cake," Brinn said, eyes fixed on a plate of cupcakes, beautifully decorated with pastel colored frosting.

Poppy hid behind the doorjamb, hoping she didn't look too much like a refugee in her dead husband's cast-offs. "Hi."

"You come and sit yourself down." Leading with an impressive rack, a large woman bustled forward. Above a kind pair of blue eyes, her gray hair squiggled across her forehead in a tight perm. "You must be ready to fall down."

"I'm fine," Poppy said, and hoped the woman didn't put that to the test. Already her knees had turned to mush.

"Nonsense," the woman said. "I'm Peg, by the way, chairperson of the Twin Elks Prayer Chain. I would say chairwoman but we decided to go with something gender neutral. We're hoping to get some men into the group, but they're proving resistant." She pressed Poppy into the seat beside Ciara. "And this is the Twin Elks Prayer Chain."

The Prayer Chain responded with nods, murmurs and chirps.

Like an anxious squirrel a small, round woman darted forward. "We heard all about your troubles, dear."

Tuts and clicks followed her comments.

"Would you like a cup of tea?" As if sharing a joke, Dot's gaze twinkled at her across the kitchen. "You look a little overwhelmed."

"Overwhelmed?" Peg's voice boomed. She glanced at the women congregated. "Well, of course she's overwhelmed. Stand back, Kathy." She flapped her large hands at the squirrel woman. "Let's give the girl some space. She's been sick after all."

Ciara nudged Poppy. Her gaze hadn't strayed from the cupcakes.

"Do you think they're for eating?" Brinn whispered.

"Of course they're for eating." Shooting a defiant glance at her, Kathy poked her head around Peg. "I made them especially for the children."

"I made the brownies." A slim woman about Poppy's age slid around Kathy. "Children just love chocolate, don't they?" She pushed a pan to Ciara. "I didn't include any nuts, in case we had nut allergies."

"Thank you," Poppy murmured to the group in general. So many faces, most of them smiling and looking at her expectantly. Her head set up a dull throb, but she didn't want to seem ungrateful.

"Right you are." Peg resumed control. "Darla over there by the window. Wave please, Darla,"—a backlit, slim figure waved—"brought round some diapers that her kids have grown out of. And a couple of bits and pieces for your son. We run a little playgroup over at the church through the summer. Maybe the girls would like to come along and meet a few kids their age…"

Poppy tried to keep listening, she really did, as Peg reverberated through woman after woman and their offerings of clothes, toys, meals, baked goods…the list went on and on. Had she stumbled into Mayberry? Poppy struggled to absorb it all.

As Ciara went for her third cupcake Poppy caught her hand. Beside her Brinn's face had a frosting glaze around the mouth.

"Try this." A mousy looking woman pushed a teacup at Poppy. "It's Echinacea tea, and it will help you give that nasty virus a whupping."

"Put some honey in it." Peg brandished a plastic bear bottle at her.

A shadow darkened the open kitchen door and the women hushed.

"Ladies." Ben's deep voice rumbled.

A mix of "Ben", "Chief" combined with hellos filled the room. The sea of women parted for him. His dark gaze met hers as he made his way closer.

In her wavering world, Ben provided a fixed point.

"Have some coffee cake, Ben?" Peg shouldered her way forward.

"Or a cupcake?"

"A brownie, maybe?"

"You doing okay?" Wearing the tiniest of smirks he looked straight at her. Poppy nodded.

Peering into her teacup, he leaned closer.

Laundry detergent, warm, clean man and a hint of spice hit her in a gentle wave.

"It's Echinacea tea," she said.

He raised his brow. "It's kinda yellow."

Brinn leaned closer to him and whispered, "It looks like pee."

Poppy's face flamed and she glanced at the mousy woman. Fortunately, the woman, and all the other women were staring at Ben as if he was the sun around which they all orbited.

His smile grew as he and Brinn looked at each other. "How many cupcakes?"

Brinn held up a finger.

Chief Ben raised his brow.

With a giggle Brinn added a second finger to the first.

Next he turned to Ciara, who giggled and held up three fingers.

Poppy murmured a protest. Three cupcakes was two too many.

Glancing at Poppy, Ben frowned. "You look all done in."

"Everybody's been very kind," she said. Damn, she sounded like a forties matinee damsel in distress.

"Right." As he stood another hush fell over the kitchen. All eyes snapped his way. "Ladies, I think it's time Poppy went back to her bed."

"You're so right, Chief." Kathy went bright pink.

"Good thinking, Ben." Peggy's voice ricocheted around Poppy's head.

Over Peggy's shoulder, Dot caught Poppy's eye and rolled hers. Poppy swallowed her laugh and stared down at the table.

"You ready?" Ben scooped her into his arms and carried her out of the kitchen.

Poppy couldn't be positive, but she might have heard someone sigh. She definitely caught a titter.

"I can walk." A token protest, because she didn't think she could make it down the corridor, and her current situation made her want to simper and giggle. Chief Ben had shoulders wide enough to block out the room behind him, and arms that pressed rock solid into her back and beneath her knees. Her imagination took over again, adding a couple of period touches to the scene. Maybe one of those billowy white shirts, and perhaps a sword. Except Ben was more the six-guns and spurs type. Dear lord, she'd almost pictured him in chaps and nothing else.

"Reckon you can." He placed her on the bed and tucked the covers around her.

Poppy waited for it. Her eyes already drooping in a mortifyingly Pavlovian response.

His calloused fingertip brushed the space between her brows. "Sleep."

Ben got a mental hold on his balls and walked back into the kitchen. The women of the Twin Elks Prayer chain had the hugest hearts in the county, but in a troop they scared the crap out of him.

Ma sidled closer to him. "Thanks for that. She was starting to look a little worn out."

Nodding he inched toward the door. Freedom beckoned just to Peg's left.

"Our daddy died." Brinn's voice cut through the female chatter. Brown eyes huge and limpid she hung her head.

The kitchen hushed.

Ben smelled a rat and stayed right where he was.

"Did he, sweetie." Peg hauled out a chair and wedged her ample hips into it. "Did he die a long time ago?"

"Before Sean was born."

Brinn's theatrical sigh shifted his bullshit meter and Ben had a brief mental tussle with himself to intervene, and lost. The kid had mad acting skills.

"He died without having seen his baby's face." Leaving more than one teary eye in her wake Brinn met the gaze of each member of the prayer chain in turn.

Ben's eyebrows headed to his hairline and he hauled them back down.

Clucks and murmurs whispered around the kitchen.

"Oh, dear." Peg leaned closer. "What did he die of?"

"A car accident." A single tear snaked down Brinn's cheek. "My daddy died in a flaming inferno of metal."

Ciara blinked at her sister.

Gasps of horror greeted her statement and Brinn straightened in her chair.

He should stop this, but Ben hated to ruin Brinn's moment. This sort of artistry deserved the spotlight. As long as he remembered what she was capable of in case it ever turned his way.

"Mommy said we should all be brave little soldiers." Brinn sniffed. "Her heart was wrenched in two."

Little faker even managed a wrenching motion with her fists. He bit the inside of his cheek to keep from busting a gut.

Sean being almost two, and the twins no more than eight, he had to wonder how much of their father they really remembered.

Ryan sidled up beside him, braced his legs akimbo and crossed his arms. His head barely cleared Ben's belt. "Chief."

Ben uncrossed his arms, and nodded down at him. This should be good.

Jerking his head at the women, Ryan said, "Need an assist?"

Ben's grin nearly got away from him. "I got this."

At the table, Brinn stretched into her stride. "Of course, we barely remember him but Mommy made a shrine to his memory in the corner of our living room."

"Of course she did." Almost falling over the table, Kathy pushed the cupcakes closer. "You poor things to suffer such a loss."

"Thank goodness Sean was the sweetest baby." Brinn heaved a sigh and peeled the paper off her cupcake. "It was as if he sensed Mommy's woe and tried not to worry her."

Darla sniffed and dabbed at her eyes with a Kleenex.

"Thank you," Brinn whispered and bit into the cupcake. "We don't get too many treats anymore."

Marlene pushed a tray of brownies closer to Ciara. "Well, there's plenty for you here now."

"So you've been living in Philadelphia?" Peg failed at subtle.

"In the ghetto," declared Brinn.

Ma snorted and turned her back to the room. Her shoulders trembled suspiciously.

Ben dared not look at her or he'd lose it right along with her.

"The projects." Peg sniffed and scowled around the room. "Dreadful places to raise a child."

"We had to move there after the bank took our house." Brinn's lips quivered and she draped her arm over Ciara's shoulder. "My sister has not spoken a word since we saw a pimp nearly beat his girl to death."

"You don't say." Peg's cheeks grew flushed.

"Two-seventeen." Ryan nudged him. "Assault with intent to do murder."

"That was right after three children were kidnapped." Brinn paused and made eye contact with her rapt audience. "Right from the park where we played every day."

"Two-zero-seven," said Ryan.

Ben ducked his chin to his chest.

"Kidnapped?" Kathy chewed on her bottom lip. "Are you sure, dear?"

"Oh, yes." Brinn nodded. "It was in all the newspapers. Our building was featured on FOX news."

Part of him wanted to see where the little drama queen would take this next, but there was only so much he could take. He sent Ma a look.

Enjoying Brinn's performance hugely, she grimaced. "Okay, ladies. I think I need to get this lot washed up for dinner."

"We didn't even have hot water in our building," Brinn, the little grifter, kept on going.

"Shocking!" Peg reared back. "No hot water. What was your mother thinking?"

Momentarily panicked, Brinn made a startling recovery. "She tried." She managed to squeeze out another tear. "Mommy worked four jobs to get us out of there."

The mood in the kitchen switched again, and murmurs of sympathy greeted this statement.

"Brinn." Ma had to raise her voice. "Why don't you and your sister go and check on Mom?"

"But—"

"Now." Ben backed Ma up.

She hung her head and slid off her chair. Ciara followed on behind her. As they passed him Brinn peeked up and winked.

Ben jerked his head at Ryan to follow his sisters. Brinn had nearly finished him off there.

Silence reigned as the children left the room.

"Well." Peg slapped her palms on the table. "Our path is clear, ladies. We need to help that unfortunate family get back on their feet."

Mom closed the door on the last of them before collapsing against it and giggling. "That little wretch."

Ben let his laugh go and joined her. "Think any of it was true?"

"The father died in a car crash." Ma sobered and wiped her eyes. "From what Ryan has allowed to drop, they didn't see much of him. Since his death, they haven't lived in a great neighborhood."

Ben nodded because he'd seen the address on Poppy's driver's and made a point of looking it up. Definitely a rundown neighborhood, but no kidnappings or mysterious dead prostitutes reported. He'd stopped himself from looking further into Poppy Williams. If she had anything to share, he reckoned he'd give her the chance to share it with him.

Chapter 7

Poppy woke to something delicious smelling floating up from the kitchen. Already she felt much better than she had this morning.

As she walked into the kitchen, Dot looked up. "Well, hello!"

Poppy returned her greeting.

At her feet Sean raised his chubby arms and babbled happily to see her.

Poppy picked him up and inhaled his sweet powdery little boy smell. "You look like you're feeling much better."

"Uh-huh." Sean grinned at her, looking more and more each day like a little boy and less like a baby. Each child grew up faster than the one before. As much work as they were, Poppy would miss this baby stage.

"Oh, he's well on the mend." Dot smiled and turned back to making what looked like meatloaf. From scratch with all fresh ingredients. It had been too long since her kids had eaten as well as Dot fed them. Poppy enjoyed cooking but lately there didn't seem to be enough time or energy left in her day to put what her grandmother would have called a proper meal on the table. Mom hadn't been much for cooking either, and Poppy had taught herself what she could shortly after her marriage.

In the yard outside the kitchen, Brinn and Ciara chased each other with water guns. They looked so happy and carefree with the sun shining off their dark heads, dirty bare feet padding across the grass.

"I sent them out to work off some of their energy." Dot jerked her head out the window. She laughed at Brinn hitting Ciara directly in the face with a jet of water.

"Where's Ryan?" Poppy sat with Sean on her lap, but he wriggled to get free and return to a play-doh palooza he had going on in one of Dot's pans.

"He went with Ben to get your car cleaned." Dot leaned closer and winked. "I think your little one has a bit of a man crush on my boy."

Boy? Poppy nearly snorted.

"That looks good," she said as Dot slid the meatloaf into the oven. "You know, I really can't thank you enough for ev—"

"Oh, hush now." Dot flapped an oven mitt at her. "It really is nothing and it gives me a great excuse to get out of the Prayer Chain mahjong nights. Peg always wins the kitty, and I swear she cheats."

Dot might not want her thanks, but Poppy would find a way to repay her. Somehow.

Outside, one of the girls shrieked, followed by giggles.

"I do like that sound." Dot sighed, and filled up the kettle. She joined Poppy at the table. "I had five of my own you know?"

Which explained the twin beds in the room the girls used and the size of the house. "Is Ben your oldest?"

"How can you tell?" Dot rolled her eyes. "Yes, he's my first. Overdeveloped sense of responsibility and all."

Sean banged a wooden spoon against his overturned pan. Poppy went to take it away.

"Leave him." Dot put her chin on her palm. "I miss all the noise. I would have given my right arm for some peace and quiet when they were all at home. But now..." Dot sighed and peered out the open door at the twins.

They'd abandoned their water fight and gone straight for chasing each other around the garden, galloping like horses.

"I never had a girl," Dot said. "Five children, all of them boys."

"Respect." Poppy shuddered at the thought.

"And all of them within a year or two of each other."

Dear God. And Poppy thought hers were close.

"At one time I had five children under the age of eight in this house." Dot got up and put teabags into mugs.

Poppy felt guilty just sitting there. "Let me make us some tea."

Dot opened her mouth to argue and then nodded. "That would be nice."

"I would have liked a girl." Dot chuckled. "But after five tries and five boys, we decided not to risk it again."

"Maybe you'll have a granddaughter." Poppy poured water over the teabags and left them to steep.

Dot snorted. "Fat chance," she said. "Five boys and not one of them settled down."

"Not one?" Not likely if they all looked like Chief Ben. "Do your other boys live in town?"

"Nope." Dot bent over and handed Sean a plastic cookie cutter. "I have one in New York, another in Los Angeles. Those two are the closest. My second oldest is in Australia studying sharks and whatnot. And my baby works with Doctors Without Borders."

"Wow, you must miss them." It was one of those things you never really got about being a mother until you had your own children. Somehow they never grew up in your eyes, and they were grafted onto you like vital organs.

"I do." Dot nodded. "So really, it's been nice to have your four around for a bit."

Poppy finished the tea and put one mug in front of Dot. She fetched the milk and sugar and placed them on the table.

Dot fixed her tea, and then gave Poppy a penetrating stare. "I'm guessing you married young?"

"Straight out of high school." Poppy owed Dot some sort of explanation, but Sean and their marriage had never been her favorite topic. It seemed choked by one mistake after another. "I fell pregnant with the girls in my senior year."

"Ah." Dot sipped her tea.

"My mother didn't want me to get married." The words popped out before Poppy had even fully formed them in her head. "First she didn't want me to carry on with the pregnancy. I was the result of a teen pregnancy and she wanted more for me. Then, she wanted me to have the twins, wait, and see if Sean and I still felt the same way."

"Sean?" Dot waved her hand at little Sean. "Named for his father."

Poppy nodded. "Sean never got to see him. He died when I was pregnant."

"So you gave his son his name." Dot grew a little misty-eyed. "That's so very sad."

Poppy got the familiar churning in her gut. It sounded so romantic and poignant when she told people, but then she didn't tell them the rest. Sean's mother had been inconsolable at her son's death, and in her exhaustion and her nagging guilt, Poppy had named the baby after him.

There didn't seem any point in admitting she hadn't loved Sean, not in the end anyway. That along with the shock, the grief and the fear had come a guilt-ridden dose of relief. Not that he had died. She hadn't wished that on him, but that her marriage was over. If he'd lived, Poppy doubted they would have made it through another year. She had already gotten the name of a divorce lawyer before that awful last night.

Sean was dead. There was nothing to be gained by tarnishing his name with the truth.

Out in the garden a woman greeted the girls.

Dot muttered something under her breath that sounded very close to "fuck", but Poppy couldn't have heard that right. Slapping her palms on the table, Dot stood.

Poppy had never seen her anything other than cheerful, and the cold look on Dot's face disconcerted her.

Arms outstretched a woman stepped into the kitchen with a beaming smile, "Hi, Ma."

"Tara." Dot made no move toward the woman.

Poppy stared a little, knew she was doing it but couldn't seem to drag her eyes away. Tara was wow. Straight up beautiful, put together and gorgeous.

"You look great, Ma." Model-good-looking with striking eyes above cut cheekbones, Tara gave Dot a killer smile. "Are you doing something different with your hair?"

"No." Dot crossed her arms.

Tossing her long, wavy blonde hair over her shoulder, she smiled at Poppy. "Hi."

"Hi." Beside Tara's painted on skinny jeans and beautiful linen shirt Poppy was channeling her frump toad. And Tara's shoes. Poppy bit back a whimper. She might sell a child for a pair of heels like those.

Tara smelled great too, like citrus, honey and vanilla. "And you must be Poppy. I swear this town is buzzing since you arrived."

"Yes." She barely stopped herself from basking in the light like a smitten acolyte.

"Are those your girls?" Tara pointed outside, wrinkling her nose. "They're adorable."

"Thank you."

"And this little guy too." Tara crouched beside Sean.

Poppy caught her breath, but the seams on those skinny jeans held. Of course they did, because when Tara crouched nothing bulged. Poppy sucked in her stomach.

"Aren't you just the cutest thing ever?" Tara cooed.

"Ya." Sean beamed at her, clearly male in his moment of stupefied admiration.

"What can we do for you, Tara?" Dot's cool tone jerked Poppy back from the brink of her girl-crush.

Tara laughed, a low, husky noise that made Sean's mouth drop open. "Come on, Ma. Do I need a reason to come round and see you?"

Something crackled in the air between the two women, and Poppy dragged her attention off Tara's shoes and into the kitchen drama.

"I'm Tara." She turned and thrust her hand at Poppy. "Ben's wife."

"Hi." She had not just gotten a pang that might be disappointment in the midsection.

"Ex-wife," Dot said. "Tara is Ben's ex-wife."

The air sparked again as Tara stared at Dot.

Dot smirked back.

"Anyway." Radiant smile in place Tara swung back to her. Except now that Poppy really looked, it didn't quite make her eyes. "I heard about what happened." She gave another of those sexy chuckles. "In this town how can you not? Right? And I came to see if there was anything I could do."

"No, I'm fine thank you." Poppy said.

"Well, if there's anything you can think of." Tara dug in her Kate Spade and pulled out a card. "Give me a call. Anything at all. I'm not much good with children but I can so do a girls' night out, a shopping trip, lunch? Give me a call."

Palming the card Poppy thanked her. But seriously, Tara's idea of help existed in another dimension. A girls' lunch followed by a shopping trip did not even approach Poppy's priority list. Being widowed had taught Poppy to sort through all the offers of help she'd received in the days after Sean's death. On the heels of tragedy people flocked to her and the children. Most of them really meant well, but only a few delivered. As a widow you learned the hard way to sort through the Karens of this world, to find the Dots. Some people made the offer, however well meaning, but never followed through. And then others, got on with the helping.

"Is Ben around?" Tara stepped over Sean and peered through the door leading to the rest of the house.

"No." Dot blocked Tara at the doorway. "He's working."

Tara tossed her head back and laughed. "How did I know he would be?"

Dot's jaw tightened.

"Will you tell him I stopped by?" Tara cocked her head and then raised an eyebrow. "Never mind, I'll call him myself."

For a moment it looked like Dot might charge across the kitchen and scratch Tara's eyes out.

"Bye now." She waggled her fingers at Poppy. "And don't lose that card. This town can get to a girl."

As Tara's shapely ass receded down the path to the street Dot muttered, "Bitch."

Poppy almost choked on a mouthful of tea.

"I'm sorry." Dot dropped into the chair opposite her. "But I cannot stand that woman."

Poppy's phone rang and she dug it out of her short's pocket. Speaking of difficult women.

"Hi, Maura." She greeted her mother-in-law.

Ben made no sudden moves as his ex-wife swayed her hips out of Mom's house and down the walkway toward him. "Tara?"

Running ahead of him Ryan disappeared into the house.

"Benedict." Bottom lip caught between her teeth she stopped in front of him. "You're looking good."

A familiar tingle accompanied her statement. He might have messed up in every way a husband could, but the sex had always been worth sticking around for. As long as he remembered that's all it was. "And you."

Tara always looked great, which partially explained the brain shutdown that happened whenever she got an itch she needed him to scratch. That and being a dumb shit who needed to get laid more often. But being police chief in a small town didn't leave his dating vista wide open. The chief needed to watch where he took his urges because everybody else in Twin Elks sure kept their eyes on him.

She stroked his forearm with long black fingernails. "Your mother still doesn't like me."

"What are you doing here?" No denying that. Mom had been wary of Tara when they had started dating, which had blossomed into active dislike by the time Ben threw in the towel and filed for divorce.

"I came to see who all the fuss was about." Tara said it lightly enough, but once you'd lived with the woman, the brittle undercurrent rang loud as a bell.

"Huh." For a woman who liked to sleep around as much as Tara had through their marriage, her almost pathological jealousy smacked of hypocrisy.

"She's pretty." Tara readjusted the strap on her purse. "In a kind of worn out way."

"She's been sick." He could have kicked himself. His defense of Poppy would bring the Tara-tiger out.

She gave a bitchy little titter that scraped his last nerve. "But you did notice she was pretty."

"I suppose." He shrugged. "She had a problem."

She pressed closer. "And you love to rescue a girl with a problem. Don't you, Ben?"

Shit, Tara knew exactly what scab to pick at. It took a very deep breath not to bite back. "It's my job."

"Hmm." Tracing the line of his buttons with a fingernail she peered up at him. "Will I see you this weekend?"

As his wife, she'd never bothered to learn his work schedule, but now with the chance of their occasional hook-ups, Tara knew exactly what shifts he worked.

Lately she'd been pushing for more, but Ben resisted. He always felt a little dirty when he came back from seeing Tara. The emotional cocktail between them was a septic mix of guilt, anger, resentment, blame and shame. In fact, the only reason their half-assed arrangement worked was because she liked the tang of forbidden. Him? Not so much. But he did like sex, and getting it from Tara meant no expectations and no hopes raised. He'd already screwed up so badly with her, Tara no longer had any illusions about him he could shatter.

"I don't think so," he said. "Need to help Ma with the kids."

"I see." Tara's blue eyes hardened. "Must say, Ben, finding you looking after these kids is a bit hard to swallow. Given what happened."

She sashayed to her low-slung, sporty sedan and climbed inside.

So much had happened between them. A lot of it nasty. A lot of it his fault. Her infidelity might have stung more if he hadn't just about handed her into another man's bed.

He walked into the kitchen.

Poppy sat at the kitchen table, talking on the phone. Or rather listening because it seemed like the other person did most of the talking. She raised her hand as he entered.

Ben nodded a greeting.

Worn out? Tara's green-eyed monster made her blind. Sure, Poppy could do with a few pounds on her, to fill out those cheeks and put some sparkle back in her eyes. She had the sort of pretty that made a man want to sit next to her and make her laugh. When she smiled, which she didn't do enough of, deep dimples formed on either side of her wide mouth. He really liked her eyes, deep coffee brown and expressive. Those eyes had done him in when she looked up at him on the road that day. A man would do stupid things to make them go soft like they did with her kids.

Right now, her eyebrows puckered together and she rubbed the spot between them. "Yeah, I know, Maura. I was going to call you."

The voice on the other end grew shrill.

"Yup, Twin Elks…uh-huh…Colorado."

Ben pulled a beer out the fridge, and offered her one.

She hesitated and then nodded. "All right, Maura. I'll call you in a few days and we can talk."

He popped the caps on both beers and put one in front of her. Shit. His mother would have his ass, and he went to get her a glass.

"This is fine." Poppy waved off the glass, and took a deep sip. Her eyes closed, she sighed and licked her lips. "Perfect."

He dragged his eyes off her full mouth. "Bad news?"

"Not really." She wrinkled her nose. It stuck up at the end, kind of cute. "That was my mother-in-law."

"Ah."

She took another sip of her beer. "She's not happy about us leaving Philly."

He nodded. "Why did you?"

"Leave?" She was rubbing between her eyes again. "It's complicated."

"Most things in life are," he said.

"The thing is…" She made circles with the condensation from her beer on the tabletop. "I needed to get away. For lots of reasons." Jerking her head at her phone, she said, "Maura being one of those."

Sensing more was on the way, he sipped his beer and waited.

"She's very attached to the boys." An edge of old anger rode her sigh. "But only the boys. She lost her son, I get that, but mine can't replace what she lost."

"No, they can't." Yup, she'd called it all right. Her situation was complicated.

"I have to raise my children my way. You know what I mean?"

He nodded. Raising kids, he didn't know anything about. Considering how badly he'd blown his one chance to be a father, it was probably best he never try. Doing things his own way, however, that he could relate to.

"And Maura and I don't see eye to eye on how to raise the boys. It's why I never wanted to accept much help from her. It comes with strings. Heavy strings."

There she went with that spot again, leaving it red. He caught her fingers and tugged them away.

She stared down at their joined hands.

Warmth crept into his palm and tingled up his arm. He dropped the connection before he gave in to the urge to stroke.

"Sean, my husband, was her baby. I think she spoiled him. I always believed she was part of the problem." She glanced up at him. "Sorry. I don't know why I'm unloading all of this on you."

He didn't mind. In fact, he grew more curious about her as the days wore on. "It's fine."

"No, it's not fine." She got to her feet and stared out the window. "This is my problem."

Ben got the sense she had more than her fair share of those. His confusion lay in why he suddenly wanted to heft some of them around for her. Some women had this thing, this air of desperate, fragile strength. Tara was right about that. It was his kryptonite. Problem being, he sucked at the rescuing thing. Professionally he knew he was good at his job. On the personal front, his armor looked a little dented.

"Anyway." With a tentative smile she turned back to him. "Your ex was here."

"Yeah." He stamped on the sudden urge he had to overshare. For some reason he wanted to tell her about Tara. How things had been with them, not how they were now. And that was just plain dumb. "I dropped your car off with Doug," he said. "To be cleaned."

"Ugh." She did that cute as hell nose crinkle thing. "I'm not sure anyone deserves to be that unlucky."

Doug had clearly thought the same thing if the look on his face had been anything to go by. "He has big hoses."

Poppy laughed. It made his chest warm. Her laugh came from a sweet place inside. "Will you tell me where it is? So I can settle up with him."

He nodded, but hell would freeze over before he took her money. Money he would bet she didn't have a lot of, what with raising four kids on her own.

The smell of meatloaf filled the kitchen, reminding him he hadn't stopped for lunch. They sipped their beers.

Outside, Ryan babbled on to his sisters. The kid talked a mile a minute, most of it like a cop show.

"Mooom," Ciara yelled. "Ryan is bugging us."

She sprang to her feet. "I'll just…"

"Yup."

She hightailed it out the kitchen, leaving Ben staring at her round ass and wanting to punch himself in the face for doing it.

Chapter 8

Determined to stop being a parasite, Poppy got up early the next morning and had breakfast going by the time Dot emerged.

"Oh." Dot stopped and blinked at her.

Maybe Dot didn't like people messing in her kitchen. "I thought I'd make breakfast." Poppy could have kicked herself. She should have asked. "There's coffee, and...I should have checked with you."

"No." Flapping her hands Dot bounced into the kitchen. "I'm surprised is all. When you have boys, you don't expect this sort of thing."

"Oh." She fiddled with the spatula, not sure what to say next. "I made pancakes. I hope that's all right."

"That's perfect." Dot beamed at her. "Do you need me to get the children up?"

Relief making her smile back, Poppy shook her head. "Sean was still sleeping when I checked, and I think I'll leave him. Ryan and the girls are looking through that mountain of stuff your friends brought."

"They're good people." Dot poured them both a cup of coffee. "They gossip like a bunch of roosting hens, but when the chips are down, you can count on them."

"I can see that." Poppy went back to her pancakes. "I'm not used to that sort of thing. In our apartment block I think I only knew the names of the people who lived right next to me. People pretty much get on with their own stuff."

"Cities are like that." Dot poured cream into her coffee. "I like to visit, but it's always nice to come back here."

While they chatted Poppy finished making pancakes. It felt nice, easy as if they'd known each other a lot longer. Dot called the children in for breakfast while Poppy went to check on Sean.

Awake now, he blinked his big sleepy eyes at her. Poppy picked him up and snuggled him. These still drowsy, stolen moments with Sean were some of her best. Too soon children bounced out of bed, determined to spread their little wings. Ryan was still young enough for cuddles, but Ciara and Brinn always seemed to reach for each other first. At times she felt cut off from them, separate from their tight little unit.

Sean squirmed. Cuddle time over, and Poppy put a fresh diaper on him and put him down so he could get to the kitchen on his own steam.

"Did you bag the perp?" Ryan's asked from the kitchen.

"Yup." No mistaking who that deep rumble belonged to.

Poppy stopped to check her hair in the hall mirror before the kitchen. Deep shadows stained the skin beneath her eyes. Her mouth had settled into that tight groove that drew lines on either side of it. She touched the prominent jut of her clavicles. Sean's old T-shirt hung on her like a paper bag. Who was she kidding? She looked like a contender in Miss Refugee. Depressed with her reflection she slunk into the kitchen. In high school she'd been considered pretty. One of the girls everyone wanted to date.

Hips propped against the counter, Ben raised his chin in greeting. A welcome warmed his eyes.

"Hi." God, she even sounded defeated. Somewhere in the last eight years the bubbly high school senior had disappeared into this pathetic twenty-six-year-old widow with four children, no money, not that many prospects, and zero game.

The kids sat at the kitchen table devouring pancakes. She caught the maple syrup bottle before Ciara drowned hers. "Not too heavy on the syrup, you're sweet enough."

Brinn glanced up at her and smiled, then went back to her pancakes.

Ryan divided his attention between stuffing his face and eye-crushing on Ben. Poppy empathized with the urge. Hair still damp from a shower, Ben looked fine this morning. Crisp and pressed in his uniform. All ready to be rumpled up.

"Look who dropped by." Dot's eyes twinkled. She had Sean on her lap as she fed him.

Poppy got it together. That pretty high school senior didn't have four kids relying on her. She needed to buck up and find a way.

"Would you like some pancakes?" The top of her head not even reaching his shoulder she stood next to Ben. It made her feel waif-like, and a little breathless.

"No, thanks." He shook his head. "I already ate."

Her appetite gone, Poppy cleared away the pan and the mixing bowl. Ben shifted closer to her. "You got a minute."

Poppy's belly tightened as she registered his serious tone. "Umm…"

"You go ahead." Dot waved them toward the door. "After we clear up, the children and I are going to check out the playgroup." She winked at Poppy. "The twins might want to spend a couple of mornings there."

"Then, yes." Poppy experienced a growing certainty she did not want to hear what Ben had to say. She'd deal with the playgroup later.

"Why don't you take Poppy for a walk?" Dot sprang to her feet. "Take her down to the new coffee shop. It will do her good to get out."

Dot meant well, but foisting her on Ben made Poppy squirm inside.

With a shrug Ben lifted a brow in question. "Problem?"

"I'm sure you have other things to do," she said.

"Nope." As he straightened and motioned for her to precede him he seemed to take the matter as settled.

Gentle morning heat bathed the quiet residential neighborhood in clear, sparkly light. Poppy took a deep breath. No exhaust fumes, cigarette smoke or grilling residue from the greasy spoon on the corner of her street in Philly. Just the fresh scents of soil and growing things.

"Hey, Chief." Two kids on bicycles yelled as they rode past.

"Good job." Ben tapped his head and gave them a thumbs up. He caught her watching him, and smiled. "Helmets."

"Ah."

A woman knelt beside her walkway, elbows deep in dark red earth. "Ben."

Ben stopped and waved.

"Glad to see you're feeling better." The woman smiled at Poppy.

Poppy didn't think she'd seen her with the prayer circle.

"Small towns." Ben winked at her.

He winked at her. Winked. Poppy missed a step and nearly met the grass verge face-to-face. Ben caught her elbow and steadied her.

"What did you need to speak to me about?"

"Coffee," he said. By which she took him to mean that he would talk to her over coffee. A man of few words, the police chief of Twin Elks.

He looked so perfect here, as if somehow, he and the red etched mountains around them were a package deal. Tall, powerfully built and so comfortable in his place in the world. Her imagination didn't have too far to go before she had Stetson on his hand and a tin star pinned to his chest.

Dropping her chin, she hid her grin. She'd already thrown herself under the dork wagon in front of him one too many times.

A polite distance from the curve of her ass Ben's hand in the small of her back steered her across the road. He dropped the contact as soon as they'd reached the sidewalk. Poppy wanted his hand back there, only about three inches lower.

Like Dot's house, the homes on the street were big and old. Established gardens fronted the road. About halfway down the road, Poppy stopped.

Amidst an overgrown garden sat a grand old Victorian dame. Vines tangled over her porch, almost obscuring the fine scrolling and ornate pillars. Paint, now faded to nondescript, peeled and flaked over her front. Her trim must have been painted dark green many, many years ago. She rose three stories, her final front gable complete with a round porthole window.

"Winters House." Ben stood beside her.

"It's lovely." Poppy could have stood there for hours and looked. The bouncy teenager she had been had always dreamed of living in a house like this. She still spent hours on Pinterest looking at Victorian mansions.

"Needs some care." Cupping her elbow Ben got her moving again.

Poppy risked one more backward glance. "Is someone living there?

"Horace Winters." He grimaced. "Crusty old bastard, but big heart."

"Perfect." Poppy chuckled when Ben cut a glance at her. "It's perfect," she said. "The old derelict house with the grumpy old owner inside. Even his name is perfect. Horace Winters."

The side of his stern mouth tilted up slightly. Not as good as his full-scale smile but enough to cause a little shiver of appreciation. She wouldn't call Ben Crowe handsome in any sort of classical sense. His attractiveness resided more in the hard, uncompromising bone structure. He had a man's face, rugged but not pretty.

They turned onto a busier road. Squared red-bricked buildings marched in orderly rows on either side of the street. Red and yellow awnings with scrolled writing vied for attention. Quaint, Victorian looking lampposts presided over the parked cars. It was like stepping into a postcard complete with the snow-capped mountains rising in the distance. Waves and greetings were called out from both sides of the street. Ben steered her beneath a red and white striped awning and into a coffee shop with *Kelly's Koffee Klatch* painted on the window.

It was larger than it looked from the street and Poppy took a deep breath of the rich smell of dark roast. Several small tables littered the space in front of a large counter. The gurgle and hiss of a coffee machine drew her. Who would have thought Twin Elks had a treasure like this?

"Hey, Ben." A pretty blonde greeted him from the other side of the counter. "Twice in one day, it must be my lucky day."

"Kelly." Ben nodded at her. "Poppy."

"Poppy." Kelly held her hand out over the counter. Her big blue eyes twinkled at Poppy. A broad, full mouth saved her face from girl next door pretty. "You must be the mysterious stranger we're all talking about."

"I must be." Poppy returned Kelly's infectious smile.

"Good to see you're up and about." Kelly cocked her head. "Of course, now we'll all have to speculate about what you're doing with our hot lawman."

Heat flooded Poppy's face.

Raising his eyebrow at Kelly, Ben took it in his stride.

"Not me of course." She pressed her hand to her chest. Each of her nails was painted a different color. "I used to spy on Ben skinny dipping up at WintersPond, so he's lost his mystery for me."

Ben cleared his throat.

Had he gone slightly pink? Yes, he most certainly had. Poppy giggled.

Kelly propped her elbow on the counter and leaned closer. "Fantastic ass, by the way. Make sure you check that out before you leave town. It might be about all we have by way of things to see and do in Twin Elks."

"Coffee." Ben choked the word out.

"Straight up, black, and stronger than a mule's kick," Kelly said. She rolled her eyes at Poppy. "Please tell me you're going to order something that will do justice to my barista's genius."

"Latte?"

Kelly waggled her fingers at her. "Gimme more."

"Caramel?"

"Uh-huh, uh-huh."

"Skim milk."

"Keep going."

"Dash of vanilla."

"Let me put some whipped cream on that and my day is made." Kelly slapped her palm on the top of the counter.

"Done." Poppy returned her grin.

"Where the hell is my coffee?" A man yelled from near the window.

Kelly jammed her hands on her fists. "Just hold onto your fire there, Vince. I've got two hands."

"I could always go to Starbucks," Vince called back.

"Do that, my friend, and you'll find your pet rabbit on your stove. You read me there, Vince?" Kelly turned back to them. "Take a seat, your coffee will be right out."

"Not if you have it here it won't be right out." Vince, clearly, needed to get the last word.

Ben led her to a table close to the window. He waited until she sat before he took the seat opposite. "Checked on your car," he said.

"And?" Here it came, the something he needed to talk to her about.

"It's clean."

"And."

He shifted in his seat. "Don't mean to pry, but not sure how you're situated. Financially."

Damn! She did not like the way this had started. "Not great."

"I reckoned." He nodded. "Because there's an issue with your brakes. Asked them to check the car out while they cleaned it."

"I know about the brakes." Sometimes she'd give her right arm for one day without real life slipping the shank in. "I hoped they'd get me to California. The mechanic in Philly said they would."

He looked at her. "Is that right?"

"I would never put my children in an unsafe car. I mean, I know it sounds bad. Like I ignored them, but I was planning to do something about them as soon as I got my first paycheck. I just—"

"Stop." His big hand engulfed hers. "I know that."

She breathed a sigh of relief because somehow it mattered what Ben thought of her. "I have enough to pay for the brakes. But that's really going to cut into the money I budgeted to get us to California."

"Might take a day or so to get those parts in from Denver too." He pursed his lips.

Funny she'd never noticed how full they were, with his bottom lip plumper than the top, kind of sensual. And so not the point. "I'll work it out."

"You can stay here as long as you need," he said.

"My budget doesn't really stretch to a motel or anything."

"Stay with Ma."

How tempting that sounded. Stay here and lean on the big, quiet chief and Dot for a couple more days. She shook her head. "I really appreciate that, but I already owe you and your mom more than I can possible repay."

"We never asked." A frown creased his brows.

"Sorry?"

"We never asked for payment."

"I know that." She'd offended him and it was the very last thing she wanted to do. "I never meant to imply that. But I can't keep living off other people. However kind they are."

Studying her, he leaned back in his chair. "You could work."

"Where?"

"Here in Twin Elks. We're not the city, but there are always people needing a helping hand. A temporary one."

"I wasn't planning on being here that long. I can't keep living with your mother."

"Sure you can."

"I c—"

"She likes having you and the kids around."

"She likes it for now, but do you really think she's going to be so happy when I announce my children and I are staying for longer?"

He shrugged. "She gets lonely."

"Not that lonely." The trip to California had stretched her finances. She'd budgeted as well as she could but four kids on the road brought all sorts of unforeseen expenses. Mom had hinted she might stay put until the job in California opened up. A temporary job might give her that slight edge she needed. If she found something for a week or two, she might buy herself some breathing room. And if someone had a job that temporary. Her thinking carried a lot of ifs in it. She couldn't build a life for her and the children on if. "I'll think about it."

Kelly hurried around the counter with two cups of coffee, and went right past them. "Here you go, Vince. Stop bitching now."

"Love you, Kell. You know that."

"Sure you do, Vince, but it's still not getting you laid."

Poppy burst out laughing, and Kelly turned to her with a wink. "Sorry, hon, it's how I roll. I'll get to your coffee."

"If I stayed, I'd have to find something to tide me over." She couldn't believe it but she was actually considering this.

Ben raised his eyebrow.

"I pay my way," she said.

"You're stubborn." He crossed his arms.

She was stubborn? She gave his arms a pointed stare. "Uh-huh."

He rewarded her with a quick grin.

The coffee took a while longer. They drank it and left. Ben didn't talk much, so Poppy filled the silence with looking all about her. It wasn't uncomfortable though. She actually liked that he didn't feel the need to fill the quiet with chatter. She lingered a moment outside the beautiful old house, and he stood beside her and let her take her time.

As they approached Dot's house, the twins and Ryan were playing in the front yard, looking happy and carefree. She wanted to keep them that way forever. For so long they had been her sole responsibility. Dot and Ben had quietly and competently taken some of the weight off her shoulders. How did you ever thank someone enough for that?

She stopped and put her hand on his warm, hard forearm. "Ben?"

"Uh-huh." He looked down at her, waiting as she struggled to find some words.

"Thank you. For everything."

His gaze warmed and he put his free hand over hers. "You're welcome."

Heat flooded up her arm from where he touched her. She wanted to turn and thread her fingers with his.

His gaze drifted down to her mouth and back again.

Did he...could he...he couldn't be thinking about kissing her?

The air sucked out of her lungs. It had been so long since she'd experienced attraction, it took her a moment to recognize it.

He felt it too.

The air between them crackled and popped.

"Poppy." He shifted closer.

"Mom." A small body slammed into her legs. "Come and see the fort we made."

Chapter 9

The conversation over dinner went pretty much as Ben guessed it would. The moment Ma heard about the car, she tried to insist Poppy stay with her.

Poppy stood her ground. She wouldn't freeload off Ma anymore. In a way, Ben respected her for it, but her stubbornness made him want to pound the table.

The kids drooped over dinner and Poppy shepherded them all out.

The sounds of getting them ready for bed drifted into the kitchen.

"So." Ma pinned him with a look.

He had a pretty good idea where this was heading. His mom had known him since before his ass was cracked.

"You think she'll stay?"

If he had anything to do with it. "She should. Don't see the point in her running hellbent for California when she could take a week or two, get things together."

His brain stalled and refused to go any further. He didn't want to think about Poppy leaving, and that bothered him enough to slam the door on that train of thought.

"I hope she does." Ma sighed and folded her arms on the table. "She's a nice girl."

Girl? Nope, Poppy may have that sweet smile but she was all woman. It got harder and harder to not notice that. That tiny moment in the yard before Brinn had interrupted them had shaken him up.

"Ben Crowe!" Ma rapped her knuckles on the table. "Don't you just sit there with that look on your face."

"What look?" He had a pretty good idea he knew what was coming as well.

"That look." She jabbed her finger at his face. "You think I don't know what you're thinking." Not for a minute was he that stupid. "But your father was the same and I read him like a book and I read you too."

"Huh." He could see that his contribution to this conversation had ended.

"You like her." Ma lowered her voice. "You like Poppy."

"And?" Because denial was pointless.

"And?" Mom's eyes bugged. "And? What are you going to do about it?"

"Nothing."

"That's what I thought." Mom sat back with narrowed eyes.

"She's leaving."

"She says she's leaving," Mom said. "But a lot can happen between now and when she goes. Have you ever thought that fate might have dropped her right into your lap? No, you didn't, did you? And it wouldn't even cross that closed mind of yours to maybe get to know her, and see if there was anything there."

"Life doesn't work like that, Ma." Not for him anyway. He lived in the real world where he was about the worst sort of man for a woman like Poppy and her children. Besides, Poppy would be on her way as soon as Doug fixed her brakes. "She's leaving."

"Oh." Mom balled her fists. "Get your head out of your ass, Benedict."

"Eh?" That shocked him. Mom hardly ever swore.

"Tara is history. You made a bad choice and God knows, you've paid for it. But every woman is not Tara."

"I know that, I do, but I played my part, same as Tara did." Ma had never accepted his portion of the blame when it came to Tara. The night he had found out the baby was gone, Ma had held him as he sobbed, and still not one word of blame had come out her mouth. His Ma loved him like a mother should and that made her blind to his faults.

"There are decent women in this world. Decent women who would love to have a man like you by their side."

There came his cue to get the hell out. "I gotta go."

"Of course you do." Mom's wooden spoon whistled past his ear and smacked into the wall. Ben picked it up and placed it on the table.

Ma had the phone in her hand. "Peg," she said, scowling at him. "I'm going to need some help."

Ma didn't get it, and it would hurt her too much to explain it to her. Inside, where his heart should be, there was nothing left to give. Empty.

❦

Poppy stared at Doug, owner of "Doug's One-Stop Service: the place for all your car, truck, tractor, and lawn mower repairs for over sixty years."

Doug gave her an apologetic smile as he wiped his hands on a greasy rag. "My dealer in Denver needs to send to Wyoming for your brakes. It's gonna take at least two weeks to get 'em here and fitted."

Two weeks. The words shrieked in Poppy's head. She didn't have the money to put them up in a hotel for two weeks. Not even Pattersons Hotel, which advertised nightly rates from thirty-five dollars. Hotels meant eating out, laundromats and other expenses that seemed to buzz around her head like angry bees.

Dot gave her an encouraging nod.

"Sorry." Doug tucked his rag into the back pocket of his overalls. He didn't look old enough to have been providing the community's automotive repair needs for the sixty years scrawled on the wall above the open work bay. "I can try for faster but you should get settled in for a wait."

"Oh, dear." Dot patted her hand. "Why don't we take the children for an ice cream and have a chat."

Poppy wanted to scream that she couldn't afford ice cream right now, not with the news from Doug, but Dot already had the children rounded up and climbing into the car.

While she and Dot buckled them all in, Ciara and Ryan argued about their favorite ice cream flavor.

"I know it seems bad," Dot said as she pulled her seat belt around herself. She started the car. "But I had a little chat with Peg this morning and we think we have a solution for you."

"Dot." Poppy needed to say this as kindly as she could, because Dot had been unbelievable. "It's very generous of you to offer your home to us, but I really can't take it. You don't even know me. I could skip town with your television and your computer."

Dot chuckled and joined the flow of traffic down Main street. "I'm pretty sure you won't, but I had something else in mind."

"Mom." Ryan kicked the back of her seat. "Brinn says I can't have sprinkles. Why can't I have sprinkles?"

Dot winked at her. "We'll chat in a bit."

With four children, later always proved about twenty minutes after you thought later might be. First they had the all-important flavor debate, with Brinn changing her and Ciara's minds every few seconds. Then, Sprinklegate nearly developed into all-out war. Finally, everyone settled with more or less what they wanted and Dot and Poppy could chat.

"Peg and I put our heads together." Dot dug into her strawberry cheesecake in a cup. "And we have a little idea for you."

Two littles in one conversation could only mean Dot had a big plan going. "Oh, yes?"

"Well you know the big house three doors down from us. The one Ben said you liked?"

"The grand old Victorian?"

Dot grimaced. "Only not so grand right now."

"All the old girl needs is some love and attention."

"All old girls need that." Dot snickered and popped a cherry into her mouth. "Anywho, so the house is owned by an old grump called Horace Winters."

"Ben told me."

"Ben actually got that many words out?" Dot's eyes twinkled. "Now, what Ben might not have told you is that Horace is waiting to go into an assisted living facility."

Poppy shook her head. She rescued Sean's hair from the spoon he'd decided would make a great accessory.

"Up until last week Horace had a lovely gal, Hildy, taking care of him. But Hildy's mom got sick and Hildy can't stay with Horace until he goes into the facility. So…" Dot made big eyes across the table. "Horace needs someone on a very temporary basis to take care of him. Not a nurse or anything. Just someone who can cook his meals, tidy up, be a sort of glorified housekeeper."

It took a moment for the penny to drop. "You mean me?"

"Of course I mean you." Dot waved her spoon like a baton. "You could stay in the main house with the kids, and take care of Horace. That way you wouldn't be freeloading."

"Dot." Poppy steered a spoon into Sean's mouth. "That really is very kind of you and Peg but I can't move in with a stranger. Not with the children."

"That's the beauty of this." Dot flushed and leaned over the table. "Horace lives in the carriage house. The big house is totally free. You could even help him out a bit by packing up some of his stuff before he leaves."

It sounded too good to be true, and if it walks like a duck, and quacks like a duck… "I'm not sure, Dot. I really am very grateful you thought of me, but I don't know this man."

"But I do." Dot spooned up ice-cream. "And Ben knows him and can vouch for him. Plus, we live just down the road, and we will keep an eye on you."

Not convinced, Poppy concentrated on the post ice-cream wipe up.

If he spent any more time at Ma's place, he'd need to start paying rent. He didn't want to admit that Poppy kept drawing him back here, so he left that out of his thinking.

"Ben!" Ma looked up and gave him her sunniest smile. A sure sign she was up to something. "How lovely to see you."

"Just stopped in." On his way back from checking on Poppy's car at Doug's. Imagine the surprise waiting for him there. Poor Doug had held firm, but not by much. "Doug tells me Poppy's car will take two weeks."

"Yup." Ma turned and messed with the dishes in the dishwasher. She raised her voice over the racket she was making. "Apparently some part has to come from Denver. They're out of stock and it's going to take all that time."

"A Toyota part is gonna take two weeks?"

She fluttered to the cupboard and crashed plates together. Tutting, she shook her head. "Those foreign cars."

"Uh-huh." God she drove him crazy. Love her as he did, Ma made him want to kick shit. "Isn't Doug Peg's nephew?"

"You know he is." Ma had great game face, but her flush gave her away. She jammed her hands on her hips and went for broke. "What's with all the questions anyhow?"

Ben looked at her. "Ma."

Ma dropped her gaze and shuffled her feet. "The part will take two weeks to come from Denver. Doug swears to that. And Horace needs a caretaker for a couple of weeks. So it works out perfectly."

"That's how we're gonna play this?"

Ma had the audacity to grin at him. "You got that right, bucko!"

Ben stopped halfway down the garden path and suppressed a groan. His afternoon was not done with him yet.

Ryan stood next to his cruiser, rocking from his toes to his heels. "Afternoon, partner."

"Afternoon." Sometimes it went easier if you didn't fight it.

"Heading out?" Ryan stepped back enough for him to get the driver's door open.

"Yup."

"Need some backup?"

He climbed in. "Nope."

Then he did it. He made the gigantic mistake of looking at the kid.

Ryan's shoulders drooped. He looked like Ben had taken his puppy away from him.

"Shouldn't you be playing?"

Scuffing the walkway, Ryan shrugged. "Twins don't want me to play with them."

"What about Sean?"

He got a look of scalding scorn. "Sean's a baby."

"Huh." He pulled his seatbelt on. "I'm going to work."

Ryan's face lit up. "I could come with you."

"No." Damn, because now the little guy looked even more crestfallen than before. He softened his tone. "Kids are not allowed in on-duty patrol cars."

Shoving his hands in his pockets, Ryan screwed up his face as if giving this some thought. "Even if you are arresting them?"

"Okay, sure, then, but we don't arrest kids a lot."

"What about if you're responding to a two-oh-seven." Ryan cocked his head. Dark hair stood up like a halo around his crown.

"We don't get a lot of kidnappings around here.'

"Two-seventy-three-A?"

This could go on all day. "Why don't you go to the park?"

Ryan sniffed. "What for?"

"There are kids there. Playing ball and stuff." He didn't know what "stuff" entailed, but surely kids couldn't have changed that much.

Ryan dropped his chin and stared at his feet. "Don't know them."

"You will by the end of the game."

Ryan shrugged. He glanced up, face alight with hope. "Or I could come with you. I won't make any noise, and if anybody asks I can tell them I'm under arrest."

"No." Just when he thought he couldn't feel any more like a dick, Ryan sniffled and swiped away a tear. "I tell you what."

Up came his little face.

"You can ride with me to the park."

"And do what?" Ryan narrowed his eyes and shoved his hands in his pockets.

"We can see if there are any kids there you want to play with."

"Then what?" Clearly, he wasn't going to let Ben pull a fast one on him.

"You play."

"And if they don't like me?"

That stopped him in his tracks. "Why wouldn't they like you?"

"Because." Another shrug.

He'd never make it to work at this rate. Ben climbed out the car and opened the back door. "Does your mother know where you are?"

Ryan shot into the seat and clipped his belt before he replied, "No."

Breathing deep, Ben stomped back up the pathway. Not wanting to take his eyes off Ryan, he opened the door and yelled, "I'm taking Ryan to the park."

"That's great," Ma called back.

Poppy appeared in the hallway, her cheeks flushed. Damn woman got prettier every time he ran into her. "You don't have to do that. Don't you have to get to work?"

"Doesn't matter." And suddenly it didn't. "I can call in and tell them where I am."

She chewed her lip, undecided for a moment. "Did Ryan nag you?"

Ryan slunk down in the backseat of the cruiser. "Nah." Ben couldn't snitch on the little guy. "I asked what he was up to."

"Still." Poppy had her maternal evil-eye on the top of Ryan's head. "You don't have to take him to the park."

"The park?" Ma appeared like magic, almost vibrating with excitement. "What a lovely idea. I'm sure everyone would love a trip to the park."

The trap snapped shut around him, and Ben had to smile at her ingenuity. Ma thought fast on her feet.

"Girls!" Ma yelled. "Wouldn't you love a trip to the park with Ben?"

"Ben?" Brinn's voice floated in from the back yard. "Is Ben here?"

Twin sets of footsteps clattered their way.

Poppy had gone all shades of red. "Really, I don't want Ben to have to—"

"Give up." Ben leaned close enough to whisper in her ear. The scent of lemon and honey hit him like a jab to the gut. "And I really don't mind."

"Really?" Her big eyes provided the knockout punch completing the one-two to his senses.

"Really."

Half an hour later Ben pulled up to Winters Park and unloaded four kids, their mountain of stuff and Poppy.

As it stood a short way from the office, he drove past the big, central park at least twice a day. Bordered on one side by the old town hall it stretched down to Riddler's creek on the one side and gradually faded into a set of hiking trails on the other.

Plenty of people milled about on this warm evening. His arrival with Poppy and the kids was well noted by all. Heads craned to get a better view. A couple of women stopped their power walking long enough to hold a whispered emergency conference at the sight of him with Poppy's kids. He couldn't have made a bigger deal of it if he'd hired a sky writer.

The twins immediately headed off for the children's playground.

Pushing Sean in a stroller Poppy followed. She wriggled her fingers at Ryan. "Come on. Let's go play."

"Ben and I are going to play." Ryan pressed against Ben's leg. He gripped a handful of Ben's pressed pants and clung.

Ben suppressed his wince and motioned Poppy on ahead.

With Ryan between him and the driver's seat, he grabbed his radio. "Four fourteen this is five twenty-two."

"Hey, Chief." Ronnie, his regular dispatcher, eighty if she was a day, wheezed out a chuckle. "Thought I might be hearing from you."

Huffing, Ryan shook his head. "Breaking protocol."

"Ronnie, listen up. I'm down at Winters Park. Call my cell if you need me."

"Right you are, Chief." Ronnie snickered. "Looks real good on you, Chief. You're a regular family man now."

Ben dropped the radio back in its cradle. A crap load of responses came to mind, but he bit them back as Ryan continued to clutch his pants and stare up at him with the sort of hero worship that made him want to squirm.

"Look." He pointed to a group of boys doing something that involved a ball, lots of running and even more yelling.

"Shouldn't we..." Ryan made a circular motion with his arm. "Patrol the park."

"You see anything that needs patrolling?"

Ryan squinted and raised his hand to shield his eyes from the setting sun. He pointed to an elderly man sitting on a bench and reading his newspaper. "Possible three-ninety over there."

The last time Dave Mills had been drunk was Christmas, and even then it had been at a party. "I reckon not."

Holding Ryan's hand he propelled him toward the group of boys. The closer they got the more Ryan put the brakes on until he stalled them both.

Poppy looked over from the playground and waved. She had on another man's T-shirt and a baggy pair of shorts. Sunlight backlit a mouth-watering figure Ben wanted to see a lot more of. Feeling like a dog, he waved back before dragging his gaze back to Ryan "What's up?"

"I don't want to go over there." Thrusting his hands behind his back, Ryan took a step back.

Well, damn. The little guy looked like he might burst into tears at any moment.

Ben strolled a wide circle around the playing boys, coming up from another direction.

Eyes on the boys, expression half-hopeful, half-fearful, Ryan trailed along behind him.

Growing up with four brothers, Ben had never had any issue with approaching strange children. Most of the time it was in an effort to get away from his younger brothers. Looking at Ryan reminded him of other kids Ryan's age. Kids who hung around and watched while the rest of them played. "You let me know if you want me to introduce you," he said.

Ryan nodded, still staring at the other kids.

Ben propped his shoulder against a nearby lamppost and waited.

Taking a couple of steps closer, Ryan stopped and glanced back at him.

Ben nodded. He was right here, and he would stay here.

Ryan took another few steps and then hunkered down.

Ben willed one of the boys to look over and see Ryan. Maybe run up and invite him to play.

Over on the playground, Poppy crouched beside Sean as he played in the sand box. The twins seemed lost in their own world, clambering up and down the jungle gyms and chatting to each other.

Ciara only ever spoke to her sister.

Ben kept waiting to hear her say something to her mother, or one of the other kids. But no, when Ciara wanted to speak she whispered in her sister's ear.

A shout went up from the boys. The ball had landed close to Ryan.

"Throw it," one of the boys yelled and waved. "Throw the ball."

Ryan stood slowly and glanced at him.

"Go ahead." Ben motioned the ball.

Ryan trotted to the ball and picked it up. He stared at it in his hand for a moment before throwing.

The ball lolli-popped to the ground a few feet in front of him.

Ben winced. The boys all groaned. A couple of them laughed and pointed at Ryan.

Face red, Ryan scuttled back to him. His jaw wobbled as he tried his best not to compound his humiliation by crying.

Ben had an almost overwhelming urge to march over to the other kids and teach those little shits to laugh at someone else. But kids were kids.

Right there he made himself a silent promise. By the time he left Twin Elks, Ryan would have the best arm of any of them.

Chapter 10

Poppy distracted Sean while Doc Cooper examined him. An old hand at young children, Doc Cooper got the examination over with quickly.

"Whelp!" He clicked his bag clasps shut. "Little man looks fighting fit again. What about you?"

Under that sharp gray gaze, Poppy suppressed the need to fidget. "I'm fine."

"Any headaches?" Doc rolled down his cuffs and fastened them. "Fever?"

"Not anymore."

"Hmm." He stared at her. "If that changes, you get Dot to give me a bell."

"You know I will." Dot hovered in the background.

Doc's eyes twinkled as he grinned at Dot. "I look forward to that."

Going pink, Dot rolled her eyes and flapped her hand at him. "I've got some banana bread, fresh out the oven."

"Toss in a cup of coffee and I'll be right there." Doc winked at Dot.

"Oh, you!" Dot went even pinker and scuttled out the room.

Poppy dressed Sean and set him on the floor. His chubby legs took him out of the room after Dot. "Doh."

"Well, hello, Sean." Dot's voice drifted down the passage. "Are you here to keep Doc Cooper in line?"

"Doh?" Sean giggled.

"As if he could." Doc's chuckle turned roguish,

Poppy hesitated to join them in the kitchen. She didn't know what was going on between Dot and Doc, but she intended to give them time to find out.

Instead, she called her mom.

"Baby girl!" Mom answered almost immediately. "Is everything okay?"

"Yup." Another of Dot's boys must have occupied this room. Sport's posters plastered the walls, mainly hockey, but whoever had lived here before was an equal opportunity sport's lover. "The doctor was here this morning and cleared Sean and me."

Mom took a breath. "That's great. So, when were you thinking of setting off?"

On the bookshelf, a jumble of trophies made a metallic skyline against the books. Dot didn't speak about her boys much, but Poppy knew she called all of them, often. "There's been a bit of a snag."

Mom's phone crackled as she moved. "Oh?"

"The brakes on my car are shot, and they need to be repaired."

"Oh."

Poppy didn't know how her next statement would be received. This new version of her mother wasn't as predictable in her reactions as the old. "And apparently it's going to take two weeks for the part to get here."

"Two weeks." Mom sputtered.

Poppy jerked the phone from her ear at Mom's volume. "That's what they tell me."

"How can it take two weeks?"

"I'm not sure." In the back yard, Brinn and Ciara had a tea party going on the grass. Dot must have set that up for them. "Probably a small town thing."

"Huh." Mom didn't have any experience with small towns either. "Are you going to wait for it to be repaired?"

"I don't really have much choice. I need my car."

"Yes, you do." Mom stayed silent for a moment. "Will you be able to stay with Dot while you wait?"

"She offered." Because Dot had the biggest heart in the world. "But I really don't want to impose on her.

"No, you wouldn't." Mom chuckled. "Do you need money for a hotel or something?"

Poppy squirmed inside. The habit of hiding her situation from her mom out of ridiculous pride too ingrained to be overcome quickly. "I'm not sure. Dot said there might be an opportunity for me to stay here as a sort of housekeeper to some elderly man. Apparently he only needs someone for a week or two. It would give us a place to stay, and mean I didn't freeload off Dot."

Mom's tone sharpened. "What old man?"

"I don't know him." Mom's protective streak also took some getting used to. "But I thought I might check it out. What with the job there being delayed and everything."

"I could send you money," Mom said. "I don't have much, but I have enough to tide you over." She took a deep breath. "I would say come right away, but you need the car and..." More crackling as Mom moved around.

Mom always fidgeted when she got nervous. Poppy's gut tightened. "And?"

"Well, the plan was always for you to use this house here as a base while you got set up. But with the funding for the movie being delayed, it means we aren't leaving for Europe as soon as I thought we were."

"Is the house going to be a problem?" Poppy might as well take it all on the chin at once.

"No," Mom shrieked. "There is no problem. When we go to Europe, the house is yours. You could come now, but the car and...well, Jarryd isn't used to children." As she rushed to explain, Mom's voice grew breathier. "And you know how people who don't have kids get when they're around kids. And you have four kids."

Poppy wanted to trust Mom, she really did, but things like this didn't help. "You're saying it's better if I stay here?"

"I can send you money," Mom said. "And it's only short term."

"No." Money, never a problem until it was. She still wished she'd paid better attention to finances when Sean was alive. "Let me meet this elderly man and then we can talk further."

"Okay." Mom sounded relieved. "But if it's not going to work out, we'll make a plan. I can send you money for a hotel, or I can talk to Jarryd."

They chatted a bit more, then Poppy hung up. She and Mom had always pretty much lived from paycheck to paycheck. When she'd married Sean, she'd thought that was all over. Sean's parents weren't wealthy, but they had a lot more than Mom, and Sean always seemed to find money like it magically dropped into his hands. Except, not so much magic as creative accounting, which all caught up with her after Sean's death.

Grabbing an old receipt and a pencil from her purse, she did some quick calculations, and then some slower calculations. The numbers didn't change. Paying for the brakes and spending more time on the road added a burden to her already strained finances. When you had money, more always seemed to magically appear. When you didn't, that necessity that cost a buck fifty inevitably cost a buck seventy five, plus tax.

In the garden, Brinn yelled. Head bobbing, Brinn gestured, while Ciara stuck her chin out and frowned.

Needing to head the girls' fight off at the pass, Poppy walked into the kitchen.

Dot looked up. "Is everything all right?"

Doc had gone. "Yes." Poppy managed a smile. "But it looks like the girls are about to get into it."

"Really?" Dot peered out the kitchen window. She shook her head, sending her mop of gray curls quivering. "Well they look to have sorted it out now."

Sure enough, Brinn and Ciara were chatting again.

Dot loaded coffee mugs into the dishwasher. "Is there something else bothering you?"

"No." Digging her nails into her palms to stop herself from whining Poppy shook her head. She couldn't afford the luxury of despair. After the brake repairs on the van, she could make it to California but a motel here in Twin Elks would wipe out any contingency. As four young children pretty much defined contingency, she said to Dot, "I've been thinking about the Horace Winters thing."

"Oh." Dot's face lit up. She glanced at Poppy and her face fell. "Don't feel pressured or anything. You know I would love to have you all stay here."

Dot's kindness made her want to cry even more. "I know that."

"But I could have a chat with Peg and see what we can set up."

"I'd like that." Poppy grabbed a cloth and wiped the table. At this stage she had very little to lose.

Peg did whatever Peg did, and Poppy and the children followed Dot up the road to Winters House later that evening.

Columbine grew through the rickety picket fence, poking its cheerful head into her path. In the waning light, Winters House reared dramatically against the twilight with a twinkling light beside the garage the only sign of life.

Brinn pressed closer to her. "This place is creepy."

"No, it's not." Poppy infused some cheer into her voice. "It's just old." And creepy as hell with those dark shadows on the porch, and the dark windows leering at them.

"It's fine." Dot creaked the garden gate open. "The house is lonely. It hasn't had anyone live in it for a long time. A house needs people in it."

Herding the children through the gate and ahead of them Dot touched Poppy's arm. "Now, Horace can be a bit...testy."

That didn't sound good. Not at all. Poppy nodded. "Should I leave the children out here with you?"

"Oh, no." Dot skipped over the lawn toward the garage. "He likes children. It's only big people he gets a bit tricky with."

Double great and the buck seventy-five rule in action. Poppy trailed in her wake. The garden needed some serious attention. Someone had created a circular rose garden at some point. The central sundial canted like a drunk, choked by a necklace of nettles. The roses twined in a snarl of deadwood, thorns and blooms, but it must have been beautiful back in its day.

A narrow path beside the garage led to a wooden door.

Dot got them all in front of it before banging on the door. "Horace? It's Dot and I brought Poppy and the children for you to meet."

From the other side of the door a man asked, "Who?"

"Poppy." Dot yelled louder. "Remember. Peg spoke to you about her."

"Stop yelling." The door jerked open. A backlit figure stood in the doorway. "And I don't need to be reminded about conversations I had just this afternoon. I told Peg I was fine."

Poppy was frankly relieved. Horace sounded altogether too grouchy to have around her children.

"Dark as sin out here," he said and clicked on a light.

Poppy blinked in the sudden illumination.

"Well, you're not fine." Dot crossed her arms. "You can't manage here on your own and Hildy's not coming back."

Horace Winters looked like he'd been sent over from central casting for the role of the mad professor. A fringe of white hair stood up around his liver-spotted pate. Bent over, he only barely reached Poppy's shoulder, and his beady eyes fastened on her now with a glare that made her shiver. His scowled deepened. "Damn interfering woman."

Not sure who the damn interfering woman was, Poppy touched Dot's arm. "It's fine. Let's not bother Mr. Winters any longer."

"These your kids." Horace ran his beady gaze over the twins, then Ryan and finally Sean, who she'd propped on her hip.

"Yup." Dot rocked on her feet. "That's Ciara and Brinn. Brinn's in the dress. Next to them is Ryan, and the one in Poppy's arms is Sean."

Horace snorted and tugged the sides of his ratty green cardigan around himself. "Nice looking kids."

"Thank you," Brinn said. She took a step closer to Horace. "We're very well-behaved as well."

"Is that so?" Horace wheezed. It took Poppy a moment to realize he was laughing.

"Oh, yes." Brinn's ponytails whipped with her vigorous head nod. "You kind of have to be when there's four of you."

"Your mom beats you into shape, does she?"

Ryan gasped and shook his head.

Brinn grinned at Horace. "All the time." She giggled. "With a great big stick. With thorns on it."

"I can see that." The corner of Horace's mouth lifted. He swung his razor gaze back to Poppy. "So, Poppy Williams, you best come in and tell me your story."

Poppy had no intention of doing that, but Dot beamed at her and tugged her into the house. It smelled like dust and old fried onions.

"I live in here now." Horace made a vague waving motion. "The old house is too big for me."

"And the stairs bother his hip," Dot said.

Horace scowled at her. "You gonna tell this story?"

"If you don't." Dot poked his shoulder. "Now stop being a grouch and let's see if we can help each other out here."

Modern furniture fit like a bad hairpiece in the wainscoted splendor of the carriage house. Scarred wooden floors looked like nobody had given them some polish love in a while. A television blared in what must be the sitting room.

Horace limped to a remote and snapped it off. He jabbed his thumb at the couch. "Sit."

Clutching Sean on her lap, Poppy sat.

Squeezing into her as close as he could Ryan stared around him with huge eyes.

Brinn looked around her with interest while Ciara studied the photographs cluttering up a seventies style plexiglass coffee table.

Horace shoved his leg out in front of him and lowered himself into an armchair kitty corner from the couch. "Got a bad hip."

"He's had it for a while." Dot settled like a roosting hen onto the other armchair. "But he won't have it fixed."

Horace scowled at her.

Dot winked back. "You don't scare me, Horace Winters."

"More's the pity." Horace turned back to Poppy. "Peg says you're stuck here for a week or two. Something about your car."

"That's right." Poppy handed her phone to Sean to keep him happy. "Doug says it should take about two weeks to repair."

"Huh?" Horace pointed at Sean. "Let him run about. Nothing in here I care about that much anyway. Plus, Dot can keep an eye on him while we chat."

Poppy wasn't at all sure she wanted to have this chat anymore.

"Cookies keep him occupied." Brinn leaned closer to Horace. "They're good for keeping all children quiet."

Horace barked out his wheezy laugh. "You're a sprightly little thing aren't you?"

"Maybe." Brinn frowned. "Depends on what sprightly means."

Chuckling Dot got to her feet. "Come on." She wagged her fingers at Ryan. "Let's see if Horace has something yummy in his kitchen." She motioned for Poppy to give her Sean.

Reluctantly Poppy handed her safety blanket over.

Dot winked at her. "He's not as bad as he looks."

For Poppy to give this serious thought he'd have to be a lot better than he looked. Then again, she was fresh out of attractive options, and he was nice to the children.

"Gonna level with you," Horace said. "Only need someone until the first of the month. That's when a place opens for me at Golden Oaks." He snorted. "Why have they always gotta give these places such lame names."

The name was kind of lame and Poppy shrugged. "That's the assisted living place?"

"Yup." Wincing, Horace shifted his leg. "My daughter doesn't want me living here alone anymore. Says I can't manage on my own."

"What do you say?" Poppy struggled to get a read on how Horace felt about the move.

"She's not totally wrong." Horace grimaced. "Place has gotten to be too much for me. Needs a lot of energy to keep it like it should be kept."

Hence the mess in the garden and the need for repairs to the house.

"It's safe enough" Horace jerked his thumb toward the house. "I have a structural engineer check it out once a year." He stopped and stared at her. "You gonna say something?"

"I'm not sure." Mentally Poppy tugged on her big girl panties. "What is it exactly you need from someone?"

"Keep an eye on me." With a grimace Horace adjusted his leg. "Keep this place clean, cook my meals. Don't need anyone to wipe my butt or anything."

Poppy flushed. Horace didn't hold back. "Would we be able to stay in the house?" Even if it was only for two weeks, she did like the idea of living in such a grand old dame.

Horace huffed. "I told you it was safe. Not thirty seconds ago. Might be a bit dusty and the furniture came with Noah's arc, but you should be comfortable enough."

From the kitchen, happy shouts must have meant Dot had unearthed something the children fancied.

"Just until the end of the month?" She couldn't believe it, but she was giving this serious thought. They would be living in a separate house from Horace, and one thing she could do was take care of people. Ben vouched for Horace. Dot vouched for Horace, and lived only three doors down.

Horace nodded. "Don't need anyone after that."

"And I need to get to California." She'd lived in Philly with four kids, working two jobs she hated to keep them fed. If she could do that, how bad could one elderly man be?

Horace raised his wiry brow at her. "We got a deal Poppy Williams? You live in the house, watch out for me. I cover expenses while you're here and we part ways at the end of the month."

Poppy held out her hand. "We share expenses and we've got a deal Horace Winters."

Chapter 11

It didn't take much to transfer their belongings from Dot's house to the old mansion. As Dot helped them pack their suitcases and make the three-door pilgrimage the next morning Poppy still had her misgivings.

The porch groaned as Horace limped over to the front door and opened it.

The door creaked its protest.

Before she stepped inside Poppy stopped a moment to admire the beveled stained glass inset on the front door. Two steps into the house, and her feet jammed.

Heavy dark-wood wainscoting sucked up all available light. Dust covers shrouded pedestals on either side of an imposing wooden staircase.

Dot nearly ran into her back. "Dear Lord."

Dear Lord was right and Poppy wanted to back right out.

Elaborate filigree work, liberally festooned with cobwebs, adorned the walls and ceiling.

Ryan sneezed. "It smells funny in here."

"It's the dust." Dot stamped on the ornate gold and red oriental carpet. A small cloud of dust had already dulled her patent leather ballet flats. "Did Hildy ever do any cleaning in here?"

"Not so as I can tell." Horace's face was drawn into sad lines as he studied the hallway. "She sure was grand in her day."

Maybe that day had come and gone thirty years back.

Horace cleared his throat. "Hildy spent most of her time in the kitchen."

He led the way past the staircase down a narrow, dark hallway. As he opened the swing door into the kitchen, light flooded the hallway.

At least the kitchen had escaped the dust storm in the hallway.

It was like stepping back in time. Massive arched windows faced the back of the property and captured all available light. Subway tiles, their grouting dark with age, marched floor to ceiling over every wall.

"Cool." Brinn poked her head inside the opening housing a range that must heat the entire kitchen during winter. "Is this like an olden times oven?"

"Yup." Poppy ran her fingertips over the chipped and scarred surface of the farmhouse sinks. Probably put in long before they'd come back into fashion. They looked old but clean.

Dot sidled up to her and whispered, "You can always come back to my house, you know?"

"No, it's fine." Crazy as it was, the kitchen gave her hope. Straight out of her dreams, albeit an older, tarnished version, this kitchen called to her. On that range she would have the time to put together the sort of meals she'd always wanted to make for her children. Not only whatever she could afford or the best she could do in the time she had. At the scarred, sturdy central wooden kitchen table she could see the children clustered with cookies she'd baked and glasses of milk.

Fighting for supremacy with the ancient fixtures stood a stainless steel Sub-Zero fridge.

Ryan opened the door and peered inside. "There's no food in here."

"That's because there's nobody here to eat it." Horace jerked his head at the fridge. "Hildy said I needed to put it a new fridge."

Ciara ran to the windows and peered outside. She whispered to Brinn by her side.

"Is this all your yard?" Brinn gaped at Horace.

"As far as you can see." Horace joined them at the window. "Beyond those trees is a stream." He pointed. "We used to go fishing there when I was a boy."

Pressing closer to the smudged window pane Ciara gasped. She whispered something to Brinn and pointed.

"What is it?" Poppy came up behind them. Overgrown and in serious need of mowing the lawn stretched away from the house and ended in a thick stand of aspens. Flashes of water caught the morning sunlight between the ghostly white trunks. She curled Ciara's pigtail around her finger. "It's just the stream catching the light."

The entire house made her think of gothic ghost tales.

Ciara stared at her. A strangely adult look that said Poppy didn't get it at all. Turning from the window Ciara investigated the rest of the kitchen.

"Microwave over here." Horace stumped to a dresser stacked high with crockery and cookware. "Hildy wanted one of those too."

"Are you sure you want to stay?" Looking around her with a grimace, Dot bounced Sean on her hip to keep him happy. "You don't have to do this, you know? Peg never said it was this bad."

"Look, Mom." Ryan had a door open to a narrow set of stairs. "A secret stairway."

"Servants stairs," Horace said. "From back in the day. Leads to the top floors."

"Can we go?" Face alight with delicious possibility Ryan inched into the stairwell.

Why not? Poppy nodded. "Let me go first."

The servant's stairs were cheap, painted wood and wound up through the dingy stairwell. At the top, a handsome oak door opened onto a landing. More heavy dust shrouded Victorian furniture hulked in the jewel-toned light.

Crowning either end of the landing two floor-to-ceiling Cathedral stained glass windows cast their multi-hued light across the polished wood of the floor and wainscoting.

"Oh, my." Dot expressed Poppy's thoughts perfectly. Oh, my, indeed.

Brinn turned in a slow circle. Green, blue, and red muted flashes of light painted her upturned face.

It was like stepping into a fairytale.

A stately old grandfather clock, presently silent, presided over the space.

"Horace, the first one, commissioned those windows for his wife. He wanted her to feel like she lived in a garden all the time." Nostalgia softened the craggy lines of Horace's face.

A trickle of excitement ran through Poppy. The dust and cobwebs could be swept away, and for two weeks she could play princess in this old house. "It's beautiful," she said, but the words were woefully inadequate.

Horace huffed. "Four bedrooms on this floor." He jabbed his thumb at the four closed doors flanking the landing. "Two bathrooms. Not pretty but the plumbing works." He opened one of the doors on the right. "Hildy used this room."

Poppy could see why Hildy had chosen it. An octagonal window seat occupied one of the house's four turrets and faced the back garden. A perfect place for whiling away time with a book.

"Look at the bed." Brinn stood in wide-eyed admiration of the huge four-poster, complete with ornate floral drapery.

The furniture alone must be worth a fortune.

Poppy was sold before she saw the ancient claw-foot tub in the bathroom. But that sealed the deal.

All four bedrooms had a turret window seat, to the children's vocal approval. The rest of the floor needed a good clean, but other than that was fine.

Dot's eyes sparkled as she scrutinized the rooms. "A dusting and some clean bed-linens and these will be just the ticket." She ran her hand over a mahogany dresser. "Somebody took good care of all this wood."

"House has been in the family since the first Horace came over here with the gold rush." Horace tugged the dust shroud off a beautiful old rocking chair.

Ryan stared at him. "What's a gold rush?"

"A long time ago, people came to Colorado to get rich on gold." Dot put Sean down on the window seat.

"Did other Horace find it?" Ryan skipped over to Horace.

"Nope." Horace dropped the dust shroud on the floor and tugged another from a handsome matching dresser. "My great-great grandfather discovered that men who chased gold needed supplies. He set up a general store for those chasing down the shiny dream."

Ryan's face fell. "He discovered a store?"

"Something like that." Horace smiled. "It made him enough money to build this house and bring his sweetheart over from England."

"Girls." Ryan pulled a face. "He should have rushed for gold."

"There's more upstairs." Horace jabbed his thumb at the ceiling. "But I'm all done with stairs for the day."

"Right." Dot whipped her cell out. "I have some calls to make." Perching beside Sean on the window seat she punched numbers. "Why don't you take Ryan and the girls up and explore," she said to Poppy. "Sean and I will keep an eye on old Horace here."

"Less of the old." Horace lowered himself onto the bed and stretched his leg out with a wince.

Dot shook her head. "You need to get that hip fixed and maybe I wouldn't call you old."

"You need to mind your own business." Horace glared at her.

Dot laughed. "Where's the fun in that." She shooed Poppy with a wave. "Go along then. I need to activate the prayer chain."

Poppy led the twins and Ryan up a narrower staircase, just as grand as the one from the entrance hall but on a smaller scale.

The kids lost it on the top floor, almost levitating with excitement. Two smaller bedrooms led off from a central sitting room. Porthole windows gave the entire floor a nautical feel.

"Ciara and I can sleep in here." Brinn dashed between the two bedrooms. Clearly intended for children, this floor must have housed the nursery. Narrow brass beds, two to a room, with more homely furnishings. "Ryan and Sean can have this one."

"I don't like this one." Ryan trailed after her. "It's dirty. And I don't want to sleep with Sean. He cries."

"Sean will sleep with me." Poppy had serious misgivings about all the stairs and Sean's need to explore. "You should all pick a bedroom on the other floor."

"No." Brinn jerked to a stop in front of her. "We don't want to. We want to stay up here."

"On your own?" Poppy had visions of dragging herself up these stairs as night fears crept in.

Face alight with wonder, Ciara whispered in Brinn's ear.

"We won't be alone," Brinn said. "And we'll have each other."

"I think you'd be better off downstairs." The size of the house made her want to keep the children closer.

"Please, Mom." She got it double-barreled from two sets of brown eyes. "We won't be scared," Brinn said.

"I tell you what." Poppy entered negotiation mode. "Why don't you stay up here for one night and see what you think in the morning." She'd lay money on them not making it through the night. Still, sometimes an option beat a flat-out no, and she'd have beds ready for them on the floor below anyway.

"And if we like it, we can stay." Brinn frowned.

Poppy let her have that ground. "If you like it, you can stay."

"I want to stay up here," Ryan whined.

Brinn stamped her foot. "You can't. This is our space and you said you didn't like it up here."

"No, I didn't." Ryan stuck his chest out. "I said I didn't like that room. I want to stay up here."

"It's our special place." Brinn slung her arm over Ciara's shoulder. "You can't be here. Tell him, Mom."

"M-o-o-m." Ryan tugged on her shirt. "That's not fair. How come they can have a special place and I can't?"

Brinn and Ciara wore matching mulish expressions.

Ryan wore his full-on pleading face.

"Ryan, it's a long way from me up here," she said.

"Yeah." Brinn pushed forward, arm still around Ciara. "You're a baby and you need to stay near Mom."

Sometimes, you wanted to slap duct tape on your children's mouths. Let the mommy police lock her up and throw away the key for that one.

"Am not." Ryan's lip quivered.

"Well, now." Dot appeared at the top of the stairs with Sean climbing in front of her. "Isn't this a perfect space for princesses and fairies?"

With a big frown, Ryan opened his mouth and shut it again.

Sean toddled forward, eyes laser-locked on an old rocking horse beneath the window.

"Why is it for princesses and fairies?" Ryan crossed his arms and glanced about.

"Oh, I don't know." Dot shrugged. "That's the first thing that came to mind when I came up here."

"It's for pirates," Ryan said. "Those are pirate ship windows."

Dot screwed up her face as she examined the windows. "Do you think so? I thought fairy castle."

Doubt flickered across Ryan's face.

Blessedly, Brinn kept her mouth shut.

Dot shrugged. "But then, what do I know? I thought the room next to the one your mom is going to take looked like the X-Men mansion."

"I'll sleep there," Ryan said.

Dot spoke boy and Poppy almost kissed her.

"So." Dot rubbed her palms together. "The prayer chain is on its way. All except Linda because they always have a family lunch on Sundays."

"Prayer chain?" Poppy flickered back to the kitchen full of women, all talking at once.

"Uh-huh." Dot dragged her forefinger through a line of dust on the bannister. "If you're going to sleep here tonight, we have to get it all ready for you."

"We?" People were actually coming out on a Sunday to clean a house for a stranger and her kids? Poppy's head nearly exploded. "Call them back, Dot. They can't do that."

Dot gaped at her. "Why not?"

"Well…because…it's Sunday and they don't know me. Nobody does that, and I can't repay them. No, Dot, you have to call—"

"Poppy." Dot grabbed her shoulders and gave her a small shake. "Breathe."

Poppy breathed. It didn't help.

"This is Twin Elks," Dot said. "This is how we do things here." She clapped her hands. "Now. I think we should start in the kitchen." She waggled her fingers at the twins. "You girls can tell me what you think we need to do down there."

Poppy picked up Sean and followed Dot down the stairs. She'd landed in a parallel universe. There could be no other explanation.

Chapter 12

As the prayer chain moved through the rooms like a cheerful, chatty army, Poppy wandered around Winters House feeling superfluous. Housework never made her as chirpy as it did the prayer chain. She had a meeting at the kitchen table with Horace about what he liked to eat, and drew up a shopping list.

He offered her the use of his old boat of a Cadillac. After some trouble getting the car seats situated she and the kids set off, inching their way down the road. The car made her nervous. Bigger than your average tank, the Caddy hunkered down on the road. The children loved it, getting lost in the novelty of window winders and pop open ashtrays.

Following Dot's directions, she eventually pulled up in front of Grover's General store and parked. She breathed a big sigh of relief they'd made it in one piece.

"And hello and howdy to you." A balding, potbellied man wearing an apron bustled toward them the moment they entered the doors. "You must be Poppy and I'm Bart." He pointed up. "Grover. Bart Grover. Now how can we help you?"

"Ah?" Under Bart's keen brown gaze, she produced her list. "I'm here to get some groceries."

"Then you came to the right place." Bart chuckled. He made a sweeping motion to encompass the children. "And who are these little people?"

"Brinn and Ciara. They're twins." Like it wasn't obvious, but Bart's unrelenting attention threw her off her game. "And this is my son, Ryan." She bounced Sean in her arms. "And this is Sean."

"Hello there." Bart shook each child's hand in turn. "Now, let Bart find you a cart to make the little guy more comfortable."

Before she could reply, Bart skipped off, and returned pushing a cart with a child seat near the push bar.

"Mia." Bart pirouetted with one hand raised. "Come on over here and help Miss Poppy find what she needs."

"Oh, that's okay." Poppy felt the reins of her shopping trip getting snatched out of her hands.

"Nonsense." Bart spun back. "We pride ourselves here at Grover's General Store on enriching your shopping experience." He leaned in close enough for her to get a waft of Old Spice. "Shopping with little ones can be so wearing on the decision maker."

A teenage girl with sandy hair and the same brown eyes as Bart hurried toward them. "Hi." She grinned, displaying a full rack of braces. "I'm Mia." She pointed up. "Grover. If you'll give me your list, I'll get that done for you."

"No, really." Poppy tucked her list behind her back before Mia could snatch it out of her hands. "I'll just wander around. Find what I need."

"Oh." Mia's face fell.

Bart drew himself up tall. "Well."

"But Chief Crowe let me get all the stuff for you last time." Mia's bottom lip trembled. Her large eyes took on the wounded doe look.

"Then by all means." Poppy knew when she was beat. "I would love some help."

Bart gave a trembling sigh. "That's better."

"Follow me." Mia perked right up, and spun on her heel. "First let's get the heavier items for the bottom of the cart." She studied the list, nodding as if she approved. Halfway down, she stopped and raised an eyebrow at Poppy. "Prune juice?"

"Um…it's for Horace. Horace Winters. I'm going to be looking after him until—"

"Righty-ho." Mia waggled her head and giggled. "I know the kind he likes too."

The boat chugged to a stop outside Winters House about an hour later. Her U-Haul sat in a patch of long grass between the ivy-covered garage wall and a split pole fence. Somebody must have moved it from Dot's.

Nearly every window of Winters House gaped wide open to the warm afternoon air. From the number of cars still parked in the street, the prayer chain must be hard at it. The weight of their kindness pressed down on her. How could she ever thank them for all the hard work?

As Poppy unbuckled Sean and hoisted him out the car, Dot appeared on the front porch. Beaming from ear to ear, she approached them in her water splotched "Mom's Law" T-shirt. "There you are. Bart called to let me know you were on your way home."

"Dot." Ryan ran up to her. "Mia gave me this sucker." He pulled it out of his mouth and held it out.

Dot dutifully inspected the sucker. "That was very nice of her. Did you say thank you?"

"Yeah." Ryan nodded. "And she said I was so good I could come anytime I wanted."

"Isn't that nice." She smoothed back a hank of Ryan's sweaty hair, and smiled at the twins. "Hello, girls. Did you get a sucker too?"

Brinn and Ciara nodded.

"We've got your bedrooms all cleaned out." Dot leaned down, hands on her knees to go face to face with the twins. "Kathy even found some pretty covers for your beds. Want to come and see?"

Ryan screwed up his face. "What about my room?"

"We're done in there too." Dot held out her hand to him. "You should come and see as well."

Sean squirmed in Poppy's arms. "Doh!"

"And hello to you too." Dot danced over to Sean and held her arms out to him. "Do you mind?" She waited for Poppy's nod before she took him. "Dot missed you." She buried her face in Sean's neck and made him giggle. "Yes, she did. Dot missed you."

Poppy grabbed armfuls of grocery sacks from the Caddy's trunk and walked them into the kitchen.

Ben stood from a crouch in front of the range. Dressed in cargo shorts and a T-shirt, he looked more casual than she'd seen him before. He smiled. "Hey."

Boy, oh boy. That. Smile. Poppy locked her knees before they buckled. Dirt streaked one lean cheek and her fingers twitched to wipe it off. Touch.

"Hey." A wash of shyness hit Poppy and she kept her face hidden in the grocery bags.

Ben's big hands appeared and plucked groceries from her arms.

"I can—"

Ben put them on the table. "Are there more?"

"Yup." Poppy got between him and the door. "But I can get them. Really I can."

"Uh-huh." He walked right past her and out the kitchen.

Poppy trailed his lovely ass all the way to the Caddy. "You don't have to do this. I'm sure you're busy, and they're only groceries. I unload them all the time at home. In fact, I didn't even have to put them in the bags because Mia—"

Ben turned and she nearly plowed into his chest. "Breathe."

Poppy breathed. One breath and then another. Then she took a few more breaths because Ben leaned into the trunk and grabbed the remaining bags. Muscle bunched beneath his T-shirt, and the hem rode up and gave her a happy snippet of tanned, slim waist.

Back into the kitchen they went with Ben leading and Poppy following. He pulled milk out of the first bag.

Poppy reached her limit. Leaping in front of him, she put her hands out. "Stop."

Ben cocked his head and waited.

With a bit of effort she wrestled the milk out of his hands. "No," she said. "I can put the damn groceries away. All day I've done nothing but watch other people work around me and I can't do it anymore. Dot, the prayer chain, Bart, Mia, they're all doing everything for me and being so kind." Tears crept into her eyes and she had to blink them away. "And I know they are being super kind, but I don't know what to do with that. They don't even know me. How can I possibly thank these people for all they've done? And just when I think that, they start doing more stuff for me."

Ben touched her cheek. "Poppy."

"What?" She ducked her head to hide the stupid tears.

He lifted her chin and forced her to look at him. "Don't cry."

"I can't help it." Her voice wobbled like a stupid girl's. "All this niceness is making me feel awful and I know that makes me the most horrible person in the world. I should say thank you and be grateful, and I am grateful…"

"Poppy." His dark gaze touched her face like a whisper. "They know."

"Why are they doing these things? They don't even know me."

Ben grinned. "For Ma."

"For Dot?" She'd missed something. The same something that gave Ben a naughty twinkle. And, holy hell! How did anyone keep a thought in their head when he bent that look on them? Tough man, with a wicked gleam equaled hormone overload. This from a woman who'd pretty much thought her hormones gone forever.

"Ma wants you to stay." His mouth kicked up in a wry smile.

"Why?"

"She's matchmaking."

Was Ben blushing? "Matchmaking? With who?" The truth hit her like Horace's Caddy in free fall. "Oh, no. Oh, my God, no. No." Words failed her and she shook her head. "They can't think—oh, dear God. This is so embarrassing. I'm so sorry. I never meant to—no. This is terrible." Poppy ran out of steam

Ben raised his eyebrow. "You about done?"

Poppy nodded, because she couldn't find the right words to express all she had going on inside her.

His warm palms cupped her face. "Listen up."

With dark eyes in the uncompromising beauty of his face, he had her undivided attention. "I'm listening."

"Nothing is broken here that can't be fixed." He pressed his lips to her frown.

Poppy's mind emptied, the breath left her lungs in a whoosh. Somewhere deep inside, her rusted girls parts gave a dull *ka-chunk*.

Hands still around her face, he pulled away. "You're all right, Poppy Williams."

Ben left Poppy unpacking groceries. Before the prayer chain buried the Williams family in kindness he needed to have a word with Ma. But Horace first. Ben liked most people in this town, including Horace Winters. Knowing Horace and his peculiarities, Ben tracked him down to the carriage house.

Television blaring, Horace was hiding out with a baseball game.

Horace looked up from his tatty red armchair. "You here too."

"Yup." Ben took a seat on the sofa. "Ma wanted me to check the old range is working."

"Interfering woman." Horace stared at the television. "She could have asked me and saved you a trip over."

Ben raised his brow and stared at Horace, because Ma may be interfering, and nobody knew that better than he, but she deserved respect. "What did you say?"

Horace opened and shut his mouth. "I supported your promotion to chief, you cocksure sonofabitch," he said.

Ben knew better than to take offense. Doc had him on the strongest meds he could, but the old bastard didn't want the surgery that would take the pain away. Besides which, Horace was Horace, and had pretty much been in a crappy mood since his wife left him thirty years ago.

Point made and Ben nodded. "About Poppy."

"What about her?" Horace turned in his chair and flung his arm over the back. "You got a little twitch in your pants for her?"

There were days, like right now, when Ben wished he'd taken a job in Denver. "Seriously, Horace?"

"No offense." Horace went red.

"She's got her hands full."

"And?" Horace's face got all cunning and knowing. "You came over here to warn me to be nice to your girl. Is that what you're doing, Ben?"

It was exactly what he was doing, but Horace already looked smug enough. "Don't give her a hard time."

"Or what?"

"Or I might give you a hard time."

"Hah!" Horace jabbed a finger at him. "You can't do that. That's police brutality."

"Not yet it isn't"

Horace huffed and turned back to his ball game. "Hear tell, you've got a thing for our Poppy." He dragged out the syllables of her name. "Like taking Poppy to the park with her kids. Regular Sir Galahad now aren't you?"

"You can be a good guy, Horace. Be that guy for Poppy." He'd lived in this town all his life. Nothing should surprise him anymore and the gossip certainly didn't. But the surge of pure anger that followed it was new. He wanted to tell Horace to shut the hell up, along with all the other sticky beaks in Twin Elks.

Poppy was a nice woman, and he liked her kids. A nice woman having a hard time at the moment. Okay, and she was really pretty and the way she opened her mouth and vomited words was straight-up adorable. But still. Everyone had their noses in her business. Making insinuations like they knew her. He spun on his heel before he did or said something he'd regret.

"Not gonna answer that?" Horace taunted.

"Horace?" Poppy tapped on the open doorway. She had a plate with a sandwich in one hand, a glass of juice in the other. She raised them and shrugged. "With the house so busy, I wasn't able to make much more than a sandwich, but I thought you might be hungry."

Horace scowled. "What's on it?"

"Um." Poppy peered at the sandwich. "Ham, cheese, tomato, lettuce. If you don't like that I can make you another."

Ben looked at Horace. Hard.

Horace forced a smile. "My favorite."

Chapter 13

Poppy turned full circle and still couldn't quite believe she stood in the same house. The prayer chain had ruthlessly rooted out any sign of dust, dirt or debris. Someone had even managed to clean the grout between the kitchen tiles.

She had a plan now, and that always made her feel better. It wasn't a great plan and she hadn't extrapolated her options all the way through, but at least it was something. Until things in California were settled she could stay in Twin Elks and not keep living off Dot's charity. She had two arms, two legs and aimed to use them.

A lack of formal education narrowed her job prospects down to those things other people, more educated people, weren't prepared to do. After the financial mess Sean had left behind, she'd abandoned her pride years ago.

"Right." She faced off against the old range. "You and I are about to be best friends."

Several YouTube videos on how to use the range later, she managed a put a roast chicken with green beans, carrots and mashed potatoes on the table. She made up a plate for Horace and asked Brinn to take it to him.

Pulling Sean's high chair up to the table, she got him settled. Next she seated Ryan and Ciara at the table. The kitchen table in the middle of this glorious old kitchen. A table she could pretend belonged to her and her family, even if only for a little bit.

Mellow light cast a soft glow over her children, the air redolent with the scents of the meal she had cooked for them. At eighteen her dreams had centered around going to college, changing her mother's legacy and building a successful career for herself. Now, this was her dream. And it was a good one. More than anything she wanted a safe place for her family, good food to fill their bellies, and a sound roof over their heads.

Face intent on the tray she had clutched in her hands Brinn minced through the kitchen door.

"Didn't you take that to Horace?"

"Yup." Horace limped in after her. Sniffing, he stared over Poppy's shoulder. "Um…I thought I might eat in here." He cleared his throat. "With you. Save the little ones from carrying heavy trays back and forth."

"Okay." Poppy made a place for him beside Ryan. Except, this was his house and she shifted his placemat to the head of the table. "You should sit here."

Horace dragged it back to beside Ryan and lowered himself onto the chair. "Here is fine."

"Horace." Brinn gave him a menacing look. "You need to take your elbows off the table."

Poppy opened her mouth to stop Brinn.

Horace got there before her. "Huh." He lifted his elbows and looked at them. "You are so right there, Miss Brinn."

Poppy spent most of the night walking between the girls' room on the floor above, Ryan's room beside hers, and checking in on Sean in her room. She couldn't settle. The old house creaked and groaned around her. The furniture loomed dark and large in the moonlight filtering through the windows.

Even at night, the stained glass cast subdued colored light over the wood floors. She sat cross-legged in a pool of soft pink and listened. A dog barked somewhere in the neighborhood. Crickets rose and fell in a shrieking chorus in the bushes.

A strange feeling filled her chest. She pressed her palm against her breastbone, half expecting it to warm her hand. Peace. She felt at peace for the first time since she'd read that pregnancy test all those years ago.

Peace.

She caught a couple of hours sleep before dawn, when Sean woke her and she started her day, tired, but still feeling good.

Poppy was cooking breakfast for Horace and the children when Dot popped her head over the kitchen half-door.

"Doh!" yelled Sean, pumping his chubby fingers from his high chair.

"Hello there, my darlings." Dot bounced into the kitchen. She grabbed Sean's fingers and made a huge show of pretending to nibble on them. "I came to see how you all slept. Were you all right in this big, old house by yourself?"

"We were fine." Poppy poured Dot a cup of coffee and put it on the table in front of her. "The children slept well."

Dot gave her a sharp glance.

Poppy should have known better than to think Dot would miss the implication in that statement.

Dot cuddled a sleepy Ryan. "How are you and Horace getting on?"

"We're getting on fine." Horace stomped into the kitchen and took the same seat as he had the night before. "What are you doing here?"

"Drinking coffee." Dot twinkled at him. "Actually Peg was on the phone first thing. Wants to know if the children would like to go around to playgroup this morning."

"Playgroup?" Brinn and Ciara exchanged excited glances.

"Organized by a bunch of clucking chickens," Horace muttered.

With his spoon halfway to his mouth Ryan stopped. "They have chickens there?"

Dot and Horace chuckled.

"No. They don't have chickens there." Poppy put French toast on the table. So far she and the range were getting on great. "I'm not sure I can swing into town and dump my children on strangers."

"Strangers. Pfft." Dot sugared her coffee. "It's run by the prayer chain, and some of the women who helped you clean the house yesterday will be there. Everyone takes turns in watching the playgroup for a few hours. Except the working moms, and they get a free pass because we all know how that can be."

"So, I drop the children off and then go and watch the playgroup?"

"Yup." Dot sipped her coffee. "There's a roster you fill in. Of course, nobody is going to say anything if you don't take a turn."

"To your face." Horace tucked into his breakfast. "They won't say anything to your face, but you can bet your name will be burning up the wires from one end of town to the other."

"We don't—"

Horace snorted.

"Okay." Dot shifted in her chair. "There might be a little chatter when you're not about."

Ciara whispered in Brinn's ear.

Brinn leaned forward. "Can we go, Mom? Can we?"

Situations with strange children never bothered the twins. Maybe because they always had each other. "I'm not sure. If I can't take a turn watching the group, then it would be unfair to leave you there for the morning."

"Once you've fed me, you can do what you like." Horace cut Ryan's French toast into smaller squares for him.

"Please." Brinn and Ciara gave her the eyes.

"They'll be quite safe," Dot said. "And I can take Sean while you drop the others off."

"No, that's fine." With the kids in playgroup, she'd have time to get Horace's cleaning done. "He can stay with me."

"Oh." Dot's face fell.

Poppy felt like she'd kicked Dot. "Unless you want to take him."

"I really do." Dot's face lit up. "It's been such a long time since I had a little one in the house, and it doesn't look like any of my boys are going to change that in the near future."

Poppy hesitated. The time to herself would be nice, but she didn't want to impose, and she didn't know how the children would react to a playgroup full of strangers.

Right on cue, Ryan's lip trembled. "I don't wanna go."

"Ryan!" Brinn scowled at him. "Of course you want to go."

"No, I don't."

"You do." Brinn gave it all her enthusiasm as she beamed at him. "You really, really want to go."

Ryan shoveled up French toast. "Don't."

Ciara groaned.

Brinn glared. "Just because he doesn't want to go, why does that mean we can't go?"

"It doesn't." Dot put her arm around Ryan. "If your mom says it's okay, you girls can go to playgroup and Ryan, Sean and I can spend the morning together."

Dot looked so genuinely thrilled by the idea that Poppy found herself nodding. "Okay."

While the girls got their shoes on Poppy cleaned up after breakfast.

Dot finished her coffee, tried to help Poppy clean, and went away laughing as Poppy shooed her out.

Poppy got Sean's bag ready while she smeared sunscreen over everyone. She dropped the boys off first.

Dot had some baking plans for herself and the boys.

Poppy wished her luck with those.

"I'll bring the boys over when we're done." Dot waved her off.

Then Poppy and the twins set off walking to St. Stevens. Another beautiful Colorado day surrounded them. A gentle morning breeze cut the building heat and made the walk pleasant.

"Morning, Poppy. Girls." A middle-aged woman nodded to them from behind a bush she was trimming.

"Morning." Poppy nodded. She thought Dot had called the woman Holly, but she didn't want to chance getting it wrong.

A pickup truck rumbled past. The grizzled old driver raised a hand in greeting.

"Do you know him?" Brinn turned and watched the pickup putter down the street.

"No." Poppy had to smile. "That's how things work here. People are friendly."

"Huh." Brinn and Ciara exchanged a glance.

St. Stevens sprawled over a wide, green swathe of lawn. A low-slung, angular building that gave off a seventies architectural vibe. Poppy followed the sounds of children around the side.

Fencing separated a child's play park and kept all the children inside. Children of all ages crawled over the wooden play sets. Opening the gate, Poppy ushered the girls in ahead of her.

"Hello," said a woman about her age. The one from that day in Dot's kitchen who'd baked the nut-free brownies.

"Hi." Poppy kept a hold on Brinn's hand. Already the twins squirmed and wriggled to join the shrieking swarm of children around them. "Dot said I could come around about the girls joining the playgroup."

"Of course." The woman held her hand out. "I'm Robin, by the way. We met at Dot's house when you were ill."

"I remember. Hi, Robin." Poppy shook her hand.

"You brought your twins." Robin beamed down at Brinn and Ciara. "How lovely."

"We wanted to play." Casting her gaze at her feet Brinn scuffed the grass. "We just wanted to play with the other children. What with being new to town, and not having any friends."

Poppy wanted the earth to open up beneath her and swallow the three of them. Brinn had the victim look down pat. A nasty sensation that this wasn't the first orphan Annie Brinn had pulled snaked through Poppy.

Face softening, brown eyes brimming sympathy Robin went down like a felled tree. "Of course you do." She patted Brinn's shoulder. "You poor things. You run along and play with the other children." Robin leaned closer to Poppy. "She told us how things were in Philly. It must have been awful for you."

"Er…yes." A heart to heart with Brinn loomed in Poppy's future. "Dot said there was a volunteer list where I could sign up to take my turn."

"Right inside." Robin brightened. "Let me show you where it is."

Poppy followed Robin into a church hall where more children played, supervised by a scattering of what Poppy assumed were mothers.

"Did you bring a snack?" Robin waved to a couple of the mothers.

"Um…no." Damn. She should have thought of a snack.

"Oh." Robin's face fell. Then she perked right up again. "Well, never mind. Most of us have a little something extra." She squeezed Poppy's shoulder. "For those less fortunate children."

Oh, Miss Brinn had some explaining to do. "I'll make sure I bring one next time."

"You don't have to." Robin flushed. "We can help you out."

"No, it's fine. I really can bring a snack."

Lips pursed, Robin paused and studied her. "Only if you're sure you can."

"I'm sure." Outside, Brinn had climbed to the top of a wooden fort, the little faker. "Now, where do I sign up?"

Robin led her to one corner of the hall, where a desk and small filing cabinet sat. The woman behind the desk also seemed familiar. In fact, this one had helped clean Winters House yesterday.

"Hi, Poppy." She hurried around the desk. "It's Kathy."

"Kathy." Robin took hold of Poppy's arm. "Poppy is here to sign her girls up for playgroup."

"Great." Kathy rubbed her hands together. "We need to do a little bit of paperwork. For the county." She rolled her eyes. "But then we'll be good to go."

"Poppy doesn't have a snack," Robin whispered.

"That's fine." Kathy shot her a quizzical glance. "We have plenty of moms who forget or leave them at home. Families have troubles here in Twin Elks too." With a kind smile, Kathy squeezed her arms. "We raise our children like a village here. None of that…unpleasantness."

Poppy might have to eat her young. She certainly understood the urge to do it. "I need to sign up to take a turn watching the playgroup."

"Ah." Kathy bustled back around the desk and consulted a desktop calendar. She frowned and hummed. "How are you for July?"

"July?" Poppy nearly laughed. "I won't be here in July. We're leaving at the end of the month.

"Really?" Kathy cocked her head.

"Yes." Poppy took her arm back from Robin. "We really are only passing through. If that's going to be a problem for—"

"No." Kathy rushed around the desk. "No, no, no. Not at all."

Robin frowned down at the calendar. "But the rules are that every moth—"

"I know the rules, Robin." Kathy's voice took on an edge. "I made the rules, remember?"

"Ye-e-s." Robin stared at Kathy.

Kathy stared right back.

"Oh?" Robin went wide eyed. "Of course you did. Yes. Silly me." She tittered. "We'll take your name and you can be an alternate. In case someone can't do their turn or something."

"Is that okay?" Poppy didn't want to upset the system, and there was clearly something going on between Robin and Kathy.

"That's perfect." Kathy nodded and smiled.

"Perfect." Robin grinned.

"Well, okay." Poppy filled in a form for each child. Pretty standard stuff about allergies, and a waiver for the group. "I'll pick them up before one."

"Perfect." Kathy grinned.

Robin beamed. "Perfect."

Lingering in the playground Poppy watched the twins play. Already they'd infiltrated a group of girls around the same age. She'd have to talk to them later. Not only about Brinn's theatrics, but also about this stop in Twin Elks being temporary. Poppy didn't want them getting attached.

Standing outside St. Stevens she experienced the strangest sense of having nothing pressing to do, and nobody demanding her time. She needed to get back and do some cleaning for Horace, but she had hours left of her morning. Letting curiosity drive her, she wandered onto Main street. Maybe she could pick up something for Horace to have with his midmorning coffee.

Despite its charming facade, Main street told a slightly different tale. One in four of the stores were either boarded up or displayed "For Rent" signs. The big chain stores on the far end of Main must have been difficult to compete with. She found herself in front of Kelly's and popped in for a coffee. The giddy freedom of being able to order, pay for and drink a cup of coffee while it was still hot, almost went to Poppy's head.

Again this morning the coffee shop bustled. A few faces she'd seen before when she visited with Ben.

Kelly ran back and forth behind the counter.

Poppy sat at a stool near the coffee machine and waited.

"Hey there." Kelly glanced at her. "Poppy, right?"

"Right."

Kelly tapped used coffee grounds into the garbage. "Skim milk latte, caramel, with a dash of vanilla?"

"Right." Poppy was impressed. "You remembered."

"It's my one and only party trick." Kelly winked. "You want whipped cream today?"

"Sure." Because why not. It was a whipped cream sort of feeling to be sitting here like a normal adult.

The door opened and a couple walked in. They came to the counter and placed their order.

Over the hiss and gurgle of the machine, Kelly stared at Poppy. "Word around town is you're shacked up with old man Winters."

"What?" Poppy flushed.

The new couple gaped at her.

"No, I'm working for him." Her face might catch fire at this rate. "I'm taking care of him until he goes to an assisted living facility."

Kelly grinned and winked. "Just messing with you. How is the old fart?"

Waiting for her response, the couple stared.

"Good," Poppy said. "His hip acts up."

"Ah." The man of the couple nodded. "Needs a hip replacement."

The woman shook her head. "Too stubborn."

"Or too scared his daughter will sell the house out from underneath him if he goes into the hospital." The man took his coffee, handed the woman hers and they left.

"The one who wants him in assisted living?" Poppy turned back to Kelly.

"Yup." Kelly grabbed a stainless-steel jug and stuck it under the frother. "Hold that thought," she yelled as the machine drowned them both out.

While Kelly spooned milk onto the cappuccino Poppy waited. Maybe she should ask Horace about his daughter.

Kelly pushed two cups across the counter. "Coffee's up!"

Two older women came and collected their cups.

"There you go." Kelly put her latte in front of Poppy. "Horace's daughter is a real piece of work. Lives in Denver and only comes down here when she wants something."

"Kelly, where's my coffee?" Vince yelled.

Kelly grimaced. "I'm gonna kill him." She glared at a man in a ball cap over by the window. "This isn't your house, Vince. You don't get to yell orders at me like you pay my salary."

"I pay for my coffee." Vince stretched back in his chair.

Wow. For a quiet town Twin Elks had its fair share of hotness.

Long, lean and muscled. Vince pushed his cap to the back of his head and grinned at Kelly.

"Remind me to charge you double." Kelly jabbed her finger at him.

"I'd gladly pay double if it got me my coffee faster." Vince winked at Poppy

Kelly stayed hectic the entire time it took Poppy to drink her coffee. She bought a couple of scones for Horace and left.

Poppy swung the gate open on the rickety old hinge. Just inside the gate, crabgrass pushed through the cracked walkway. Poppy leaned in and tugged it out. Another patch grew out the side of the walkway, encroaching on a bed. Weeds choked the entire bed, so she didn't know why she thought this one would make a difference, but she tugged it out anyway.

"What the hell are you doing?" White hair making a puffball about his head Horace stood on the porch.

Poppy waved her crabgrass like a truce flag. He could be pissed that she'd been gone too long. "Um...I just pulled this out."

"You pulled out my flowers?" Favoring one leg and doing a jerky swing with the other Horace limped toward her. "You put those back."

"It's crabgrass."

"I don't give a royal shit what it is, put it back." He leaned heavily on the railing as he took the four steps from the porch to the walkway.

Wow! No wonder Horace didn't have anyone taking care of him. If she was Horace's daughter she might also stay away.

Anger building with each step Poppy strode into the kitchen.

They had an arrangement here, and that didn't give him the right to speak to her like he wanted. If this was going to work, she and Horace needed to get a few things straight.

Chapter 14

Poppy took the scones she'd picked up in town to the carriage house and knocked on the door. Difficult men, one thing she'd sworn off since Sean's death.

Horace called for her to come in. Scowling at the TV he sat in his lounger.

Poppy put the coffee on, and arranged the scones on a plate. She could do this. Calmly, rationally and firmly draw a boundary around his behavior. After Sean's death she'd sworn to herself to speak her truth. Even to crusty old men.

Horace's television program blared loud enough for her to hear it from the kitchen.

She walked into the sitting room and snapped it off.

Horace glared at her. "What?"

"I thought I might do the cleaning in here now," she said and took a steadying breath. "But first, we need to have a talk."

"Women." Dropping his chin Horace crossed his arms with a huff. "Always with the talking."

Poppy might not have much, but she'd taken too much crap from Sean during their marriage to accept it now. "You were rude to me earlier."

"I know." Horace cleared his throat. "Sorry."

Poppy had a moment of vertigo. All armed for a fight, his easy capitulation caught her off guard. "Is it the weeding you didn't like or something else?"

"If you wanna weed, then weed." Horace picked up his remote. "It was something else."

"Okay, then." Feeling a bit cheated out of her righteous indignation Poppy stood there a moment. "Do you want to talk about it?"

Horace looked at her with horror and snapped the television back on. "No."

"All right then." Poppy retreated to the kitchen. "I'll get your coffee, then do the cleaning."

Horace turned the volume up.

"You know." Poppy turned back before she entered the kitchen. "I'm only here for a short while, but if I do something wrong, tell me. Politely."

Horace grunted.

Boundaries. They worked. Who knew?

Ben had no good reason for pulling up to Winters House in the middle of the afternoon. On his way to do one of his occasional checks on the abandoned warehouses at the end of Main street, he was driving right past. If you discounted the quick left, then right he'd taken to drive right past.

Poppy sat in the shade of an aspen with Sean plucking at the grass beside her.

Ryan popped into his path. "What's the sitch, Lieutenant?"

"Chief," Ben said. "I'm the police chief."

"Right you are, Chief." Ryan gave him a jaunty salute. "That's wa-a-ay better than a lieutenant."

Damn, where did this kid get this stuff from?

Folding his arms, Ryan gave a chin jerk. "Twins are getting a little restless. Need watching."

"Ten-four." Damn. Kid had him speaking this way now.

As he approached Poppy, Ryan fell into step with him.

She looked up and smiled.

His chest did a weird twist thing, and warmed. Poppy had a beautiful smile, and it used her entire face.

"Chief Ben." Brinn's brow furled as she and Ciara swaggered up to him. "You need to talk to my mother."

Ciara folded her arms.

"Is that right?" He glanced at Poppy. Talking to her was no hardship.

She closed her eyes, took a deep breath and stood. "The girls don't think they should go to the church playgroup."

"Huh." Twin sets of eyes fastened on him, demanding his agreement. He had no opinion because he had no idea why this was his problem. Still, he could find out a few more details. That wouldn't hurt anyone. "Why?"

Ciara whispered furiously in Brinn's ear. Brinn nodded, and made affirmative noises. "Ciara says that we don't know anyone there. And we won't get to know anyone there because we're leaving. They will think we're strange and nobody will want to be our friends. Then—"

"Stop." Ben's head threatened to explode. He had no idea how to deal with kids. "You went today?"

The twins nodded.

"Did you have any fun at all?"

A slow second nod.

"Maybe you should give it a chance before you decide you don't want to go." It sounded like the sort of thing Ma would have said to one of her boys.

"Good job." Ryan gave a firm nod. "That's what Mom said."

"Huh." He glanced at Poppy. "Everything else okay here?"

"For the most part." Poppy gave him a look of approval with her melting brown eyes that made him feel about ten feet tall. She shrugged and ran her fingers through the long grass. "Horace and I had a bit of a thing this morning, but we got past it. I think."

"A thing?" For some reason that released a minor shit storm inside him. Part of him wanted to pound his chest and declare he would take care of her. Jesus! It didn't get more asinine than the idea of him taking care of a woman. Just ask his ex.

"Not a big thing." Poppy rescued a beetle before Sean put it in his mouth. "He got a bit grumpy with me, but he seemed to get over it fast enough."

"Ben!" Wiping her hands on a drying cloth Ma appeared on the porch. "This is a nice surprise."

Was she living here now? Seems she was here about as often as he was. Ma had on a bright pink T-shirt with "Chairperson" scrolled across the front. Ben had no idea where she got them all, and he'd given up asking what the writing meant a long time ago. "Ma."

Instead of her usual kiss for him, Ma motioned the kids. "Come on, Dot has your snack ready."

The twins and Ryan scampered after her.

"She came around about thirty minutes ago and offered to make their snack." Poppy frowned and propped Sean on her hip. "I feel like I'm taking advantage of her."

"You're not." Ma had the biggest heart in the world, but that didn't make her a pushover.

"Still." Poppy bent and gathered up Sean's toys.

He got the feeling Poppy hadn't had a lot of help. Maybe ever. He had so many questions, but he didn't want to frighten her into her shell by asking them. "You didn't have anyone back in Philly?"

"You mean help." Her gaze grew guarded and she looked away from him. "Not really. And what I did have was complicated."

Her answer raised more questions, but Poppy would share when she felt ready.

"Thank you." She straightened, Sean on her hip, her other hand full of toys. "For what you said to the girls. I wasn't making much headway."

He hadn't done much, so he shrugged it off. "The thing with Horace."

"Yes." Poppy cocked her head.

"He's been alone for a long time."

She snorted. "I'm not surprised. What with the way he yelled at me."

As she walked to the house he fell into step beside her. "He got that way when his wife left."

"His wife left him? I assumed she had died."

"Left him. Thirty years ago."

Poppy gaped at him. "Thirty years ago and he's still not over it." She hitched Sean higher. "Did he get grumpy after she left or was that the reason she left?"

"After." Horace would rot before he told Poppy anything. Stubborn and proud to a fault, Horace hated sharing what he saw as his failure. Ben had that in common with the old man. "He loved her. More than she loved him."

Poppy's big brown eyes grew soft. "That's sad." She sighed and looked around her garden. "Sometimes being married can be the loneliest place in the world."

True that. Ben took the toys from her hand and followed her and Sean into the kitchen

❤

It never ceased to amaze Poppy what a difference a couple of days could make in an eight-year-old's life. Two days at the church playgroup, and Brinn and Ciara hurried her through breakfast.

Ryan, not so much. She'd taken him to playgroup with the girls on their second morning. When she'd picked them up in the afternoon, the mothers running the group said he stuck pretty much to himself.

"Good morning." Dot bent and kissed Ryan and then Sean on the head. "How are my lovelies this morning?"

Dot popped around every morning and took Sean with her when she went. Her excuses ran the gamut from his recent illness to feeling responsible for Poppy working for Horace and therefore being duty bound to help out.

When she cooked breakfast Poppy now included her.

Not a ray of morning sunshine, Horace sat huddled over his cup and waited for his breakfast. He nodded his thanks as Poppy slid a plate of eggs in front of him. Grumpy he might be, but Horace was easy to feed. He ate anything and often came back for more.

Next, Poppy filled a mug, added cream and two sugars and put it in front of Dot.

"Thank you." Dot beamed at her as if Poppy had solved all of Dot's life problems with that one cup of coffee.

The way Poppy saw it, it was the least she could do. With things the way they had been with her mother, having another woman around for support and company took some getting used to, but in a good way.

"Finish your eggs." She caught hold of the car Ryan rammed into the side of the milk carton.

He threw her a reproachful look and shoveled another mouthful. "Do I have to go?"

"Yes." She scooped up Sean's scattered Cheerios, and gave him some cut up fruit to gnaw on.

Humming some unrecognizable tune, Sean rocked from side to side in his high chair.

"Ciara and I have a friend." Brinn spread two inches of jam on her toast. "Her name is Rebecca, but everyone calls her Becky."

"Oh, yes?" Poppy moved the jam out of her reach.

She'd never really gotten on with other girls. Sometimes it seemed as if she didn't speak girl and the list of rules around being with others of her gender seemed too much trouble to navigate. The twins didn't have the same problem. Of course, they always befriended people as a two-man team.

Poppy half-listened to a recitation of Becky's finer points, and a criticism of her pink running shoes. She tipped more eggs onto Horace's plate.

Since Sean's death, she'd regretted not having a close female friend. She'd missed having much friendship at all. As if the condition was in some way contagious people tended to avoid a young widow. As for male company. Suffice to say, not a lot of men were keen to date a woman with four kids.

Ciara whispered to Brinn.

"Ciara and I are going to play school with Becky," Brinn said, a layer of jam coating her mouth. "Only Becky doesn't want to be the dad, but I said she must because her hair is the shortest."

"I see." Dot cradled her coffee mug. "You know, not all boys have short hair, and not all girls have long hair."

"Long hair on a man." Horace jabbed at his eggs with his fork. "Man needs to show respect for himself and others. Cut his hair. Shave."

Dot chuckled. "You're a dinosaur, Horace."

"Like Ben. Ben has short hair and no beard." Brinn glanced at Poppy. "But it's not about hair." She turned back to Dot. "It's about rules. You need to have rules."

"You do?" Dot raised her brow.

"Sure." Brinn nodded. "Otherwise...total chaos."

Poppy nearly choked around her mouthful of coffee.

With a careful nod Dot took it all in. "I can see how total chaos would be a problem."

"Especially in a school," Ciara said.

Poppy froze, then forced herself to relax. Ciara hated it when she made a big deal of her rare utterances. She did speak, just not all that often and lately, hardly at all.

Fork midway to his mouth Horace glanced from Poppy to Ciara. He took a breath and carried on eating.

Dot nodded, and sipped her coffee. "Especially in a school."

Horace and Dot had handled Ciara like pros and Poppy wanted to cheer. Instead she turned and put the breakfast dishes in the dishwasher.

"Okay, shoes on," she called. Although this took much less time than it used to, someone was always missing something.

"I don't want to go." Ryan dragged his feet to the backdoor. "And I don't have any shoes."

"Where are your shoes?" Poppy walked past Dot to reach him.

Dot held out a hand and high-fived her with a wink. Yes, it felt great to start the day with Ciara speaking.

"Dunno." Ryan shrugged. "I think the dog next door ate them. Or maybe this is a two-eleven and we need to call Ben."

"We're not calling Ben." Poppy stamped on the tingle of excitement the idea of calling Ben caused. Ben owed them nothing. Not one more second of his time. He'd already done so much for them.

"I don't think we need Ben for this," Horace said. "Especially since your thief hid your shoes under the sofa in the den."

Poppy fixed her son with a stare. "Go and fetch them." She turned to the twins. "Girls, get your teeth brushed."

Dot watched them clatter out of the kitchen. "You know, Ryan could always stay with Sean and me."

"Dot, I can't possibly ask you to watch two of them. Besides, Ryan will get used to the playgroup. He'll have a friend by the end of the week."

"You didn't ask." Dot got up and refreshed her coffee. "I offered, and I like having him around. He's a lively little thing. But you're his mom, so the decision is yours."

Ryan slunk back into the kitchen and threw puppy-dog eyes at her. "That place is like juvvie."

Dot gave her the same eyes as Ryan. "You aren't going to send Ryan to juvvie?"

"You may as well give in." Horace stood. "I've known the woman since she went to preschool, and she'll only keep at you until she gets her way."

"True." Dot chuckled.

Whispering to each other and giggling, Brinn and Ciara ran back into the kitchen.

"Okay." Poppy gathered up her purse and handed the girls their snack. "Ryan you can stay here with Dot today. But—" she held up a finger "—if you don't behave, you'll have to go to playgroup. And this is just for today."

It was hard to tell who was more delighted by her change of mind, Ryan or Dot.

"We'll take Sean to the park," Dot said. "He likes it there. Remind me to take some bread so we can feed the ducks."

"Roger that." Ryan beamed at her.

As if the weather was colluding to create paradise in Twin Elks, another warm, clear Colorado day greeted them as they hit the sidewalk. Still early enough for a light, fresh breeze to cut the heat, it made for pleasant walking. Brinn and Ciara walked on slightly ahead of her. Occasionally Brinn would toss a comment back at her, but for the most part they spoke to each other.

"Morning, girls," Peg boomed from her garden. She waved her hose. "Gonna be a hot one. You girls got sunblock on?"

"Yes." Poppy answered for the girls.

"Ciara and me like Horace's house," Brinn said, over her shoulder.

"Me too." Poppy couldn't let the girls get too attached. "But it's not ours, and we will find our own house in California."

"We know." Brinn and Ciara clasped hands and started one of their songs. She vaguely recognized it as a Disney tune.

Dave Mills stopped on his morning power walk and smiled at the twins. "That's a nice, cheerful thing to hear first thing in the morning. How are you, Poppy?"

"Good, thanks, Dave." It still weirded her out a bit how friendly people were. Dave could talk a hole in her head, so she hustled on with a smile.

"Do you like Horace's house?" Brinn took her hand.

Jumping over the cracks and lines of the sidewalk Ciara kept a few steps ahead.

"I do," Poppy said. "I like old houses. I can imagine all the things that went on in them over the years."

"Is it old?" Eyes intent on Poppy as she waited for the answer, Ciara turned and walked backwards.

"It's very old." Poppy widened her eyes. "More than a hundred years old."

Both girls looked impressed.

Ciara went back to her skipping game.

"I like to think of all the people who have lived there before. What they wore, what they did, that sort of thing." Sean hadn't liked old things. Used, he'd called them. When they bought their first house together, a small starter condo for their young family, Sean had bought it right off plan.

Poppy had dragged him around many of what he called thrift store houses before giving up and letting him buy a new house again. When the bank repossessed the house they'd lived in before his death, Poppy had not been sorry to see it go. An ultra-modern, slick palace of chrome, steel and cement. Looking at the house objectively, it had been lovely, but it had never felt like a home to her. No, if she pictured home, she pictured something like Winters House.

"You know, girls." She let her imagination out to play. "If it was a hundred years ago, we might be sitting on the porch swing and spending all day watching the birds."

"All day?' Brinn scrunched up her nose.

"All day." Poppy mimed fanning herself. "I might get up to get some more lemonade, or I might call for someone else to get it for me."

Brinn grinned. "Who would make our dinner?"

"The cook." Poppy wafted her hand. "Please don't bother me with kitchen stuff now."

"Or Dot." Brinn nodded. "Dot's a good cook. She could make our dinner."

"Dot has her own house." The children had all grown fond of Dot very fast. It was hard not to fall in love with Dot.

"But that one's plenty big enough for Dot to live in it with us," Brinn said.

"And Ben." Ciara kept her head bent, checking the sidewalk for cracks.

"Yeah." Brinn cut her a crafty look. "Ben could come and live with us."

It didn't take a genius to see their little heads working. "I don't think Ben would want to come and live with us. I'm sure he has a very nice house of his own." Time to get them off that track. Still, she could picture Ben with his back propped against a post, his long legs stretched out on the porch top step. "I would have a different color paint in every room."

"Some could be pink." Brinn swung their clasped hands. "Maybe even different kinds of pink."

"Maybe one could be pink," Poppy said. Brinn would paint the entire world pink and cover it in sparkles if she could.

"And blue," Ciara said.

Happiness blossomed inside her and Poppy didn't even bother to hide her smile. Since Sean's death, Ciara had been disappearing further and further into her relationship with her sister. But this morning—it hurt even to hope—but this morning she'd not only spoken, she'd engaged. "We could definitely have a blue room. Maybe we'll even paint blue on the outside of the house."

"And pink." Brinn frowned. "If she can have blue, then I can have pink."

"Okay." Poppy tugged the pigtail nearest her. "We'd paint one half of the house pink and the other half blue."

"What about Ryan and Sean?" With a giggle Brinn peered up at her. "Sean's favorite color is orange, and Ryan's is green."

"I thought Ryan's was blue."

"That was last week," Brinn said. "And now he likes green and yellow. Like the green and yellow on Ben's chief car."

Ah, she might have seen that one coming.

"Well then." Poppy tapped her chin as if giving it some thought. "We'll have to divide it into quarters. One pink, one blue, one orange, and one green and yellow."

Brinn pulled a face. "That would look weird."

"True," Poppy said. "But it would be our kind of weird."

Ciara took her hand. "We have the best kind of weird."

Chapter 15

By the following Monday Poppy had the day's routine down pat. She fed the horde breakfast, after which Dot took either Sean or Sean and Ryan with her. Some days Ryan went to playgroup, others he went into all out rebellion. A mother of four learned to pick her battles.

Then she and the twins, and sometimes Ryan, walked to school. She always stayed a moment to chat with whichever moms were on duty that day, and then came her favorite part of the morning, coffee at Kelly's.

After coffee came the housework for her and Horace, but the break with Kelly helped brace her for it.

"Hey, girl." Kelly popped her head around the coffee machine. "You're late this morning."

"Sorry." Poppy climbed onto her regular stool. "Kathy was at playgroup this morning and needed a rundown on everything the children and I have been doing."

Kelly rolled her eyes. "She's good people, Kathy. Married to a complete asshat. Grumpier even than your Horace."

"Speaking of." Poppy made sure nobody was close enough to hear her. "What's with him and the ex-wife?"

"That story is going to need my full attention." Kelly shook her head. "Saddest thing for old Horace."

Damn. Now she felt bad for every nasty and semi-nasty thought she'd ever had about Horace and his bad temper.

"Kelly," Vince hollered. "I can see my life passing before my eyes here."

"Want me to speed that up for you?" Kelly frothed milk and drowned out any possibility of Vince making a verbal comeback.

One of the great things about Kelly was that she knew the lowdown on everyone in town. Kelly had grown up here, gone to college in Boulder, but returned here after a failed marriage. Kelly opened up about everything but that marriage.

"So, Horace's wife." Kelly got back from slamming Vince's coffee on his table. "Naomi." Kelly rolled the syllables of the name around her mouth. "Some blue-blooded princess he met in Boston."

"I would have thought Horace would marry a local girl." Poppy sipped her latte and sighed with pleasure. Kelly had an honest-to-God coffee superpower going on.

"As did every pretty young thing in Twin Elks." Kelly settled on the other side of the counter with her own cup of coffee. "To hear my grandma tell it, there was quite the dust up for old Horace in his day."

"I can imagine." One of Poppy's forays through the house had unearthed a drawer full of old pictures. They all had frames and hanging wire, so Poppy presumed they'd hung on the wall at some point. She'd like to pluck up the courage to ask Horace if she could hang them again. But then she wouldn't be here long enough to appreciate them and for now, she was content with winning the battle in the garden. "Horace was quite the looker in his day."

"Uh-huh." Kelly wiped foam off her top lip. "And rich. Grandma says the Winters family have always been loaded."

"Is he still?"

"Oh, yeah." Kelly nodded. "Don't let the crusty old sweaters throw you off. Horace could buy and sell most of this town."

At least the sweaters weren't crusty since she'd been doing the laundry. "And his daughter never comes to see him?"

"She blows through every two years or so. Mainly to check if he's still breathing and if she can cash in on her inheritance."

That was sad. Loneliness clung to Horace, and he lit up when her children were around. For all his gruffness, he wasn't a bad man. "So why did the wife leave?"

"According to grandma, she was a total bitch, and nobody but Horace was sad to see her go." Kelly grinned. "But then again, that could be because Naomi beat my grandma to Horace."

"Was Horace mean to her? Naomi, I mean."

"Quite the contrary," Kelly said. "Even grandma admits that Horace was totally in love with that woman. Treated her like gold. Did anything he could to make her happy. Again, according to grandma, that was a lost cause from the get go."

"Really?" She had already formed an entirely different scenario in her head. One involving a doormat of a woman who finally left her no good spouse. Silly Poppy! That sounded a lot more like her story.

"Totally." Kelly rolled her eyes. "The woman could spend money like nobody I've ever seen. Mind you, she wore the most kick-ass shoes." Kelly got a dreamy look on her face. "I wanted her shoes."

"Ben said she left about thirty years ago."

Kelly frowned. "Yup, sounds about right. I was much younger when she left, but it caused such a scandal in this town. It's all my mom could talk about with the other moms. Naomi left and took their daughter with her."

A customer came in, and Kelly got up and filled their coffee order.

"See you, Kelly." Vince got up to go.

"Not if I see you first, Vince," Kelly yelled back. She pointed as the door shut behind Vince. "There's another one married to a total bitch. But our Vince is one of those good guys." Something lurked at the back of Kelly's comment, but before Poppy could delve any further, the coffee shop door opened.

"And speaking of bitches," Kelly muttered before pasting a syrupy smile on her face. "Hey, Tara."

Tara peeled her designer shades away from her eyes and catwalked to the counter. She looked incredible in a pair of jeans Poppy wouldn't have squeezed into even pre-baby days. Tanned bare shoulders gleamed above a diaphanous tank. "Kelly." Tara smiled. "And Poppy. Great to see you again."

"Uh-oh," Kelly whispered so only Poppy heard. "Brace for it."

"Ben didn't tell me you were working here." Tara plunked a killer purse on the counter. "I'll have an Americano, Kelly."

"I'm not." Poppy tried to keep it neutral but Tara got her hackles up. "I pop in on my way back to Horace's."

"Ah, yes." The hard glitter in Tara's eyes made Poppy a little nervous. "I heard you were babysitting the town hermit. How's that going?"

"Fine." Poppy shied away from sharing any Horace details with Tara.

Kelly scooped the grinds for Tara's coffee. "Can I get you anything to eat?"

"Oh, God, no." Tara laughed. "When Ben says he likes me out of these jeans better than in them, he means he'd like to take me out of them. Not me bursting out."

"One Americano." Kelly slapped the coffee on the counter. "To go."

"Thanks, Kelly." Tara slid her bag over her shoulder and pursed her bright red lips. "Did I see Vince leaving? You know Chelsea is one of my best friends." She flashed her white teeth in a feral smile. "I would hate to have to tell her you two were still hanging onto that old high school flame you had going." Her laugh could have cut diamonds. She swept Kelly with an even harder gaze. "Not that Vince would, of course."

"Of course." Kelly beamed back. "You have a nice day now."

"I always do." Tara smirked. Waggling her fingers over her shoulder, she sashayed out with her coffee. She stopped with the door held open. "And Poppy, I'll get Ben to set up a time when we can have you over for dinner."

Tara shut the door and strolled to her car.

Poppy didn't get it, and she hated how much she didn't want to get it. "I thought Tara and Ben were—"

"Divorced." Kelly slammed coffee grounds into the trash. "Yeah, they are. The only one who doesn't seem to think so is Tara." Kelly cackled as she cleaned around the coffee machine. "She came in here, special like, to pee all over Ben's leg in front of you."

"But why?" Heat crept up her face. Okay, she found Ben attractive. That seemed too tame a word. She found him very attractive. Disturbingly attractive and her rusty bits had definitely woken up around him, but she hadn't shared that with anyone. Dear God, did Ben know she had a bit of a thing for him?

"Please." Kelly rolled her eyes. "You and Ben together all the time. Him playing happy families with you at the park. Things get around. Tara must not have liked what she was hearing."

"You said they were divorced."

"And they are." Kelly grimaced. "Word has it that Ben has visited his ex a couple of times. Outside of regular hours." She leaned over and patted Poppy's arm. "But I'm sure it's just sex. After what Tara did to him, no way he's going back there for anything other than an oil change."

Poppy wasn't proud of her insatiable need to know more, but she couldn't stop herself. "What did she do to him?"

"Oh, boy." Kelly hauled the tray of brownies out of the display case. "That one is a real piece of work. It's only because Ben's the kind of guy he is that he didn't lose his shit."

She itched to ask again, but that might make her look too eager, so Poppy sipped her latte.

Kelly cleared her throat and raised her brow.

Poppy looked at her, and her face flushed. Yeah, she was a master of subterfuge. Check out the poker face on Poppy.

"Ben was away, doing one of his tours of duty. Tara loved being married to the hometown hero. Especially when it meant she could get her a little something-something on the side."

"What?" Poppy grabbed a brownie. "She was unfaithful to him?"

"Yup." Kelly hoisted herself onto a stool behind the counter and bit into her own brownie. "Story goes she had more than one indiscretion."

"Wow." Poppy's heart ached for Ben. She knew exactly how much that sucked.

With a grimace Kelly said, "Of course everyone felt sorry for her after she lost the baby."

Poppy's stomach knotted. "Ben and Tara lost a baby?"

"To hear Tara tell it, only she lost the baby and Ben was to blame." Kelly shook her head. "Only thing is, I was around then, and I'm not so sure there was a baby."

"Really?" Faking pregnancy was a new level of nasty as far as Poppy was concerned. "Surely not."

"Only Tara knows for sure." Kelly shrugged. "But rumor around the time she fell pregnant was that things with her and Ben were rocky. Apparently he found out about all her special friends while he was serving. Then suddenly she's pregnant and everything is okay again. Ben's by her side."

Poppy felt disloyal snooping like this, but no way she could stop herself from asking. "What happened?"

"Ben starts talking about going on another tour of duty." Kelly propped her hip against the counter and folded her arms. "Tara freaks the hell out. Loses the baby due to the stress of Ben leaving. He quits the army and we have a new chief of police."

"Wow." Poppy had no idea what to say to that.

"Yeah, wow about covers it." Kelly huffed. "I dunno. It just all seemed too convenient. And Ben, being the original good guy, totally believes her story." Around a mouthful of brownie, Kelly made a face. "That's the part that pisses me off. Nice guy like Ben. Just about every single woman in this town committing minor crimes to get him to come around."

"Huh." Poppy needed to digest that.

"So, what's your story?" Kelly went for a second brownie. "What brings you collapsing into our hot police chief's arms?"

"A bunch of stupid decisions." Poppy tried for a light shrug. So many bad decisions that talking about them stuck in her throat.

Kelly tilted her head. "Hit me with one. I bet I've got one to match it."

Oh, Kelly was so on. "I got pregnant in the summer break before my senior year."

"That's pretty good." Kelly twirled a strand of hair around her finger. "I finally got my V card punched in my senior year by the school big mouth. Ended up all over the school and the town. With pictures."

"Yikes." Poppy took a second brownie. "I married my baby daddy."

Kelly frowned, tucking her legs up on the stool. "And this is bad because?"

"He was the male version of Tara."

Stopping with her brownie halfway to her open mouth, Kelly gaped. "But you have four kids. I'm assuming with the same man."

"Yup." She might as well tattoo stupid across her forehead. "Ryan was a reconciliation after I caught him the first time. Sean came after a last ditch couple's therapy attempt. Big Sean never met little Sean." Poppy drank her latte. She'd said about all she could without having to rehash the night of Sean's death.

"Not gonna lie to you." Kelly dusted brownie crumbs off her shirt. "That's gonna be hard to beat."

Poppy laughed. The total lack of judgment from Kelly made her feel like less of a failure.

"Okay, I think I can get close," Kelly said. "I let the guy I loved more than anything go because I was too proud to tell him the truth. Now he's married to an unrelenting bitch, while I serve him coffee every day."

Outside the store, a pickup chugged into life and eased out of the service station.

Inside, the few customers left murmured over their coffee while she and Kelly sat in a brooding silence.

So many decisions she could have made differently. Ultimately she had the children from hers, and nothing could ever make her regret that. Not the two jobs she'd worked in Philly to feed and clothe them, and not the hours spent before his death waiting for Sean to come home, wondering where the hell he was and who he was with.

"So, Poppy Williams." Kelly stood. "What happens in California?"

"That's a good question." Her sigh built in her belly and she released it. "I'm hoping the house pans out, and then I can take the summer and figure out my next step. One thing I do know is that I can't go back to Philly."

"I'll drink to that." Kelly held up her coffee mug.

Poppy clinked hers against it. "To the future."

"The future," Kelly said. "And while you're thinking about said future, you might consider there are worse places to be stranded than Twin Elks."

The front hall made a perfect place for folding laundry, and Poppy had a bunch of it to fold. Four children plus her and Horace made for a lot of dirty clothing. The staccato tick of the grandfather clock on the upstairs landing kept her company as she upended her clean laundry onto the floor.

Happy and tired from a busy day the kids collapsed into bed each night. Even Sean slept through the night here. Sleeping kids meant a sleeping mom, and catching up on sleep had improved her outlook a hundred times.

For once things didn't look impossible. Even the delay in getting to California had a silver lining.

A boot scuffed on the porch, followed by a soft knock.

Poppy opened the door to Ben.

"Hi." It must be the fright of finding a tall man lurking on her porch that triple-timed her heartbeat. Such a liar, and not even a very good one.

Ben nodded. "Can I come in?"

"Sure." Poppy led him into the clothes-strewn front hall. Now he must think she was a total slob. "I'm folding laundry." She grabbed a handful of T-shirts and put them back in the laundry basket. "I don't normally throw clothes all over the floor. But the floor's clean and it makes a great space for…"

Ben crouched, picked up one of Ryan's dinosaur T-shirts and folded it. He pulled another from the pile and executed another three-second fold.

"Wow." Poppy sank back down to the floor. Should she really let him sit here and fold laundry with her? "You're good at that."

He flashed her his sudden smile. "Army."

"Okay." Poppy upended the basket again, so she could put the ironing in it. The conversation with Kelly made her feel a little awkward, like she'd been spying on him or something.

Ben held up a yellow T-shirt with a big pink daisy on the front.

"Ciara's." Poppy pointed to the small pile of Ciara's stuff.

"Kids sleeping?" Ben folded three shirts to her one, and made sure they went into the right piles.

"Yes." Poppy separated a pair of Horace's pants. He always argued with her that they didn't need ironing, but for as long as she and the kids lived here, and she took care of him, the man was going to wear pressed pants.

Ben dropped Horace's button-down into the ironing basket. "Heard Tara came by the coffee shop."

"Ah." Poppy's cheeks heated and she got very interested in folding Brinn's dress. "She came for coffee."

"Uh-huh." Ben shifted closer to her. "Tara multitasks. She say anything I need to apologize for?"

"Um." God, she really didn't want to get into this, because Tara hadn't really said much of anything. More like toss around a couple of heavy-handed hints. "She said you liked her out of her jeans." Why had she said that exactly? Floor, open and swallow her whole.

Up went Ben's eyebrow.

"It was a joke. She was joking." Not able to face Ben, Poppy leaped to her feet and gathered up the neat piles of folded clothes. "She was making a joke as Kelly made her coffee. And she does look very nice in her jeans. Nobody could blame you for liking her in them. Or out of them. I mean, and it's not only the jeans. Tara is a beautiful woman. I'm sure she looks great in all sorts of clothes. Skirts!" Time to shut the hell up. "I bet she has great legs."

The grandfather clock chimed ten. Poppy knew this because she counted all ten in the excruciating silence that followed her outburst.

"She say anything else?" Ben stood and stopped right in front of her.

He towered over her in a way that made her want to climb him. Poppy clasped the clothes to her chest before she gave in to the temptation. "Only that you would invite me to dinner. You as in she and you, would invite me to dinner."

"There is no me and Tara." Ben's face was unreadable, but his tone on that was definite.

"Oh." Before more inane babbling came out she bit down and kept her mouth shut.

"Hasn't been for a long time." He moved closer, cupping the side of her neck in his big palm. His eyes warmed like a slow-rising sun.

Poppy wanted to press into Ben's strong, warm clasp. "It really is none of my business."

"Looks like Tara made it your business." His voice grew deeper, raspier.

Her pulse thrummed loud enough to drown out her good sense. This close Ben was all heat and hard man. "Why is that?"

"She's jealous." Ben dipped his head. His breath brushed her lips.

His mouth was on hers before her brain had even processed the intention. Firm, full and hot enough to melt her knees. He caught her bottom lip between his for a moment and then he straightened again. He brushed his thumb over her cheek. "And I reckon she's got good reason to be jealous, Poppy Williams."

Poppy stood there, stupefied as he walked out the door and shut it on a soft click behind him.

Holy cow! Poppy gave her jelly-knees a break and sank to the floor. Ben Crowe had kissed her. Okay, not a hot, wet and heavy bedroom sort of kiss, but definitely nothing fraternal. The kiss was more like a statement of intent. "Holy. Freaking. Cow."

Chapter 16

Ben crouched in front of the storm culvert. The stray had worked itself so far back all he could see was iridescent eyes.

Ryan squatted beside him. "What do your reckon, Chief? What's our play?"

He'd dropped by to check on Ma and ended up with his miniature deputy. The call about the stray had come in as he tried to tell Ryan that he really couldn't come with him that day.

"We need to get him out," Ben said. That evening, he intended to dig up a ball from when he and his brothers used to play and teach Ryan some normal boy skills. Maybe say hi to Ryan's mother as well.

Definitely say hi to Ryan's mother.

"Gonna pop a cap in its ass?" Ryan peered up at him.

"Nope." He bit down hard on his back teeth to stop the laugh. "And don't say ass."

"Ten-four." With a wink, Ryan tapped the side of his nose.

Ben stood half expecting Ryan to tell him he was *too old for this shit.* "Stay here and keep your eye on our...vic."

Ryan beamed a huge smile at him. "Roger that, partner."

Ben walked back to his cruiser and pulled out the lunch Ma had slid into the passenger seat. Didn't matter how old they got, Dot would feed her boys. With his four asshat brothers on different parts of the globe, he got all the mothering for five kids. He grabbed the ham sandwich and returned to the culvert.

Face tense, eyes on the dog, Ryan hadn't moved. "Got my eye on the vic."

"I can see that." Ben crouched beside him and tore off a bit of sandwich. "Let's see if he's hungry."

"I'm hungry," Ryan eyed his sandwich.

"Then, we'll get you something to eat as soon as we're done here." Ben tossed a bit of sandwich into the culvert. "Now stay very still and quiet. We don't want to scare him."

The stray inched closer to the bait, grabbed it and darted back again.

A little closer to the open end this time, Ben dropped another piece.

The stray went through the same routine, but didn't dart as far back this time.

"That's it," Ben crooned. "I know you're hungry, boy, and I can fix that for you."

"What if it's a girl?" Chest over knees Ryan crouched.

"I don't think it matters too much. It's the quality of my voice that does it."

"Huh," Ryan said. Then he gentled his pitch. "There's a good dog. Come on then. Come and see Ryan and Chief Ben."

The stray's ears flickered, as it glanced at Ryan and then back to him.

Ben dropped another lure.

Ryan kept right on crooning.

The dog took it and stopped and stared at them, glassy eyed.

"Give him more." Ryan nudged him.

Ben did as he was told.

"Yummy, yummy ham," Ryan wheedled. "I like ham, boy. Do you like ham?" Eyes fever bright, he glanced at Ben. "It's working."

Letting Ryan take the lead, Ben dropped back on his haunches. "Keep talking to him. Keep feeding him the sandwich. Let him know he can trust you."

As Ryan worked on getting the stray out the culvert Ben almost held his breath. Ryan's entire being seemed focused on the dog. If ever a kid needed a win, it was this one. Poppy was a good mom, impressed the hell out of him and Ma, but she was one woman with four kids and not enough money to go round. For as long as they stayed in Twin Elks, Ben wanted to take some of that load off her slim shoulders.

Beneath his green and red striped T-shirt, Ryan's shoulder blades poked out, like small, breakable wings. Softly so as not to startle him Ben laid a hand across them. The boy's fragility and vulnerability made him want to step between Ryan and the world.

"He's coming." Ryan's cheeks flushed. "Come on, little guy." Ryan kept on dropping bits of the sandwich. When it looked like he'd run out of bread before the dog made it out, Ben handed him the cookies Ma always put in for him, because she knew about his sweet tooth.

Ryan frowned at Ma's best oatmeal and raisin. "Are cookies good for dogs?"

"I think we can risk it." God, he liked this kid. So eager to grab onto life and run with it.

Black nose working the air, the stray finally poked his head out the culvert. "Easy," Ryan whispered. "Don't scare him."

The little guy looked like he'd been living on the streets for most of his short life. Tan coat matted and patchy in places, and skinny as a toast rack. Huge paws stuck on the end of his legs like doorstops. Little guy wouldn't stay that way for long. "I'm gonna pick him up," Ben said.

He didn't want to explain dog bites, possibly rabies, to Poppy. Sweet as honey she might be, but he could picture her going all mama bear on his ass. Actually he could picture her going all amazon on his ass, except that image did a whole lot more for his libido. A libido that had gotten a lot more chatty since he'd kissed her.

The puppy squealed as Ben grabbed him.

"Don't hurt him." Tears flooded Ryan's eyes.

"I'm not hurting him." Ben tucked the puppy next to his heartbeat. "He's scared."

Shifting from one foot to the other, Ryan frowned at the puppy. "What should we do with him?"

"Vet." Ben's sensible side prodded him toward the pound, but with the way Ryan's big, brown eyes loved on the puppy, he couldn't do it. Looks like Ma had another surprise coming her way. Fortunately, the mother of five boys knew how that went. Especially Gabe who would bring home anything that breathed and nurse it back to health. He sure could do with Gabe now, but his brother had gone to Australia two years ago. Seemed the great white shark needed Gabe more than the animals of Twin Elks. He wrapped the puppy in his jacket and settled him with Ryan in the backseat.

Cara Addison was a newbie. Meaning anyone who'd lived in Twin Elks less than twenty years. She'd appeared and bought up the old vet practice a couple of years ago. Along with every other man in Twin Elks, Ben had tried to date the statuesque brunette, but so far, no winners. Hindsight being what it was, he was glad she'd turned him down. He liked her quiet manner with the wicked sense of humor that peeked around her seriousness every now and again. She also played pool like a hustler and they'd become friends.

He'd called ahead and Cara was waiting on the sidewalk for them as he pulled up.

"Ben." She greeted him with her big smile, which always seemed to come out of nowhere. "What have you got for me?"

Ben opened the rear door of the cruiser and Ryan edged out with the puppy clutched to his chest. "We rescued him," he said. "I think you should take a look at the vic."

"The...er...vic?" Cara glanced at Ben.

"Yup." Ben jerked his head at the puppy.

"Bring him in." Cara hustled up the steps into the low, rambling seventies concrete block that housed the animal clinic. "I'll take a look at your vic and tell you the sitch."

Ryan beamed at her back. He glanced up at Ben. "She's good people, I can tell."

The puppy needed feeding and a bath, which Cara saw to. He also had some skin irritations that she gave them medicine to treat. She estimated the little guy at around six months and gave him his shots. When Ben tried to pay her, she waved her fee. She looked down at Ryan instead. "You pay me back by taking good care of him."

As they drove back to Ma's, Ryan sat quietly in the back of the cruiser. "Ben?"

"Uh-huh."

"Do you like dogs?"

"Sure."

Ryan pressed his cheek to the puppy's head. "I like dogs."

"Dogs are good." Ben kicked his own ass for the problem he'd created. Boy plus dog could only add up to trouble.

"Ben?"

"Uh-huh."

So softly, Ben had to crane to hear it, Ryan whispered, "I can't have a dog."

In trying to help Poppy out, he'd given her an even bigger headache. Judging by the size of the puppy's paws, a very big problem. Shit! He deserved to have his ass reamed over this. "That's okay. Ma loves dogs." And cats, rabbits, baby birds, and even a raccoon on one memorable occasion.

Picking up his phone to give Ma a heads up, he saw he had missed three calls from her. Sticking in his earpiece, he returned her call. Three missed calls made his nape prickle.

"Ben! I've been calling and calling you."

He knew right away something was up. "What is it?"

"It's the girls." Ma sounded strangled, like the time Mark had got himself caught out in a massive thunderstorm. "The playgroup called, and they've disappeared."

"Fu—"

Ryan's head shot up.

"I'm on my way to you now. Tell me more when I get there."

Fuck, fuck, fuck! Ben's heart hammered away in his throat. His hands grew slick on the steering wheel. The traffic on Main street crawled along. Probably something to do with the blow out sale going on at the department store. Screw it! He hit the lights and siren and stepped on the gas.

Ryan perked up. "Oh, man! Punch it, Chief."

Arms wrapped around her chest, watching for him, Mom stood on the sidewalk outside her house.

As much as he wanted to yell for answers, he got Ryan and his new friend out first.

"A puppy?" Ma glanced at him and raised her brow. "A big puppy."

He had nothing. "We found a stray."

"Ben said you would like him." Eyes huge and pleading in his pale face, Ryan hugged the puppy.

Ma's face softened. "I love dogs. Why don't you take him inside?" She stroked Ryan's hair. "Find him one of those plastic bowls under the sink. I'm sure he's thirsty."

Ben's bad feeling blossomed into low-grade panic. For Ma not to say something about the dog meant this could get bad.

Ryan disappeared around the back of the house.

"Tell me," Ben said.

"The kids were playing in the church garden." Ma tightened her arms around herself. "They let them do that if it's a nice day. Anyway, when they went to call them in for a snack, the girls weren't with the others."

"How long?"

"An hour, at most."

"Okay." Ben's heartbeat dropped back to normal. An hour meant no panic yet. "Have you called Poppy?"

"The playgroup called Horace's but there wasn't any answer. I wanted to speak to you first. I'll run over there now, but Horace plays that television so loud, he can never hear the phone." Ma shivered despite the day's heat. "Poppy goes to Kelly's sometimes in the morning."

Ben trotted back to his cruiser. "I've got this."

Ma followed him to the cruiser. "I'll get the prayer chain going. Make sure people are on the lookout."

He nodded. "Can't hurt."

Flipping the light and sound show off, he drove to Kelly's place. He didn't want to scare the crap out of Poppy arriving like the cavalry.

"Hey, Ben." As he entered, Kelly gave him her wicked smile.

Poppy turned and smiled at him. "Hi." The smile slid from her face. "What is it?"

It never got easier to be the bearer of bad news. Ben didn't think she needed him dragging it out. "The playgroup called Ma. They said the girls weren't with the other kids."

"Shit!" Kelly grabbed hold of Poppy's arm.

Poppy paled, and went still. Then she went into action, grabbing her purse from under the counter, she stopped right in front of him. "Let's go find them."

"They can't have gone far." Kelly trailed them. "It's a small town, somebody must have seen them."

Vince stood up from his table by the window. "I'll get some of the truckers I know looking out for them as well."

Poppy dug her cell out. Three missed calls, all from the church group. Not only had she been sitting here while her girls went missing, she'd had her phone on silent.

Ben gave in to his desire to touch Poppy and gripped her shoulders. "It's only been around an hour. Can you remember what they were wearing this morning?"

Poppy closed her eyes and frowned. "I can't…"

"Take it easy." He rubbed her arms. "Breathe and think."

"Pink." Poppy's eyes flew open. "Brinn was wearing a pink sundress with white flowers. I remember because she insisted on wearing her old sneakers with it. Ciara is in a My Little Pony T-shirt and green shorts."

"You got that?" Ben looked at Vince.

Vince nodded and headed out.

"Let's go to the church first." Ben helped Poppy into the car. "Maybe they've gotten one of the kids to tell them something."

She nodded and hugged her purse to her chest. Damn, she'd gone so pale he was worried she might pass out.

He touched her knee. "We'll find them. I got this."

The mothers running the church group had disintegrated into panic. Thank God, Peg had arrived and seemed to be bringing order back to them. When they pulled up, she strode to the cruiser.

Poking her head through the open window, she patted Poppy's shoulder. "The good part about living in a small town is that there are not many places for them to go," she said. "One of the girls saw them walking together toward Elm." She pointed to the road Poppy must have walked with the girls.

"Could they have gone home?" Ben dialed Ma as he asked.

Poppy's thumb went at the strap of her purse like she wanted to wear a hole in it. "Maybe. But they liked it here. Why would they do that?"

"Ben?" Ma picked up immediately. "Any sign of them?"

"Nope."

"I've knocked on Horace's door, and the main house. No answer. I'm going to search the garden," Ma said.

"We're on our way." He said goodbye to his mother and got the car moving. He would drive the way the girls might have walked. Brinn and Ciara were bright kids. He couldn't see them setting off without a destination in mind. "Can you think of anywhere they might have gone?"

Poppy shook her head and craned out the window.

Ben eased slowly down Elm. Nothing on either side of the road. He stopped every few hundred feet for them to get a good look around.

He took a right on Oak. Traffic got a bit busier and he hoped like hell Poppy had taught them road sense.

Ma stood on the sidewalk waving her arms.

"Stop!" Poppy leaped out the car before Ben had fully stopped.

"They're here." Ma pointed to the tangled perimeter of the garden. Down near the river, almost completely concealed by overgrown bushes stood an old gazebo. With two dark heads.

_____ ❤ _____

Poppy didn't know whether to shake the life out of them or hug them. In the end, she grabbed both girls, pulled them in tight and yelled, "What were you thinking? You never go off on your own. Ever. You know that."

Eyes huge in their pale faces, Brinn and Ciara stared at her.

"We wanted to play in the garden," Brinn said. "We walked home. We were going back for snack time."

Poppy nearly lost it. There was so much wrong with that statement, she didn't even know where to start. And they'd taken years off her life in the last ten minutes. "What?"

Ben arrived behind her.

"You wanted to see the garden?" Hysteria made her voice shrill. Poppy tried to haul it back down again but the inner shriek wasn't having any of it. "You are never to wander off without telling an adult. You know that. Haven't I told you that again and again? I could—"

"Take it down." Ben cupped her nape.

She nearly ripped his hand off. "Don't tell me to take it down."

Carrying a pitcher and glasses on a tray, Horace shuffled down the garden. "What's all the yelling about?"

Her girls had gone missing and Horace had been making lemonade. Poppy dug her nails into her palms. "We tried calling you."

"I was outside." Glasses clinked as Horace limped up the gazebo steps.

Ben took the tray from him. "Girls went missing from playgroup."

Horace stopped and drew his craggy brows down. "They did?"

"You didn't think it was strange they were home early?" Poppy tried to reason herself down. The girls were fine.

Horace shrugged. "Nope."

Poppy turned back to Brinn. She couldn't deal with Horace now. "What are you doing here?"

Brinn sniffed. "Ciara wanted to see Cecily."

"That's what they told me." Horace stuck his chin out. "I didn't know they'd run away."

"We didn't run away." Ciara spoke in her quiet, gentle voice, glancing between the adults as if she had no idea what all the fuss was about. "We wanted to see her. We were going to go right back."

Teachable moment. Poppy recognized it, tried to calm down and had to take ten steps away. Why did teachable moments nearly always mean overcoming the gut-grinding parental knee jerk?

"Nothing wrong with that." Horace scuffed the dirt. "Good for kids. Sunshine. Garden."

Poppy saw red. She really did, like a film dropping over her eyes. Horace wanted to give her parenting tips. "There is everything wrong with it if they disappear without telling anyone."

"Huh." Horace sniffed. "You girls should have told your ma where you were going."

Irrationally she wanted to smack him for saying exactly what she had said. "Could you just…not?" She turned to the girls. "Get inside. We will talk about this when I've calmed down."

"But mo-o-om." Brinn gave her the Bambi eyes. "We just got started, and there's so much more to do."

"Now." Why was everyone looking at her as if she was the bad guy? Sean used to do this to her too. Always Sean got to be the parent with the huge, elaborate gifts. Like the air rifle when Ryan turned two, or the motorized car when the girls turned four. Poppy got to be the bitch who returned them.

Brinn stuck her lip out and jammed her hat on.

"She'll be here when you come back," Horace said. "You talk to your ma. Talk to her real nice because you gave her a bad scare today."

What a pity Horace hadn't thought of that before the girls had shaved a couple of years off her life. A tiny part of her brain kept trying to tell her to chill. The girls were fine. They'd been here all along. In the lexicon of bad outcomes, this was a win. They hadn't even been gone that long.

Since the day they were born, the children had been her responsibility. Her sole responsibility. And that part was calling the shots right now. Poppy marched the girls across the long grass toward the house. She had more to say to Brinn and Ciara, but she would lose the audience first.

"You know"—Horace raised his voice—"they had the good sense to come back here."

"Stay out of this, Horace." She grabbed little hands and tugged the twins closer.

Horace blinked at her. "What did I do?"

"You never told me they were here. You have my cell number. Why the hell didn't you call me?"

"They're not my responsibility." He limped into his house, and slammed the door behind him. Peeling paint flaked to the ground.

"Bye, see you later," Ciara whispered and waggled her fingers at an overgrown patch of columbine.

"Are we going back to playgroup?" Brinn tugged on her hand. "Can we, Mom?"

"I'm not talking about this now. You've broken a very big rule today, and we'll talk about that first."

"Horace should have called you." Ben trailed them into the kitchen. "But you're phone was on silent, Poppy. Even if he did, you wouldn't have known."

Her rational brain tried for a takeover but it wasn't happening. "Yes, he should have. And you can bet I'll be talking to him later." Poppy pointed to the girls. "Upstairs."

"Why are you mad at Horace?" Defiant to the end but with enough self-preservation to keep her distance, Brinn stuck her chin out but edged away from Poppy at the same time.

"When I leave you somewhere, you stay there until I, or someone I trust comes to get you." Poppy took her anger out on the door, yanking it open. She motioned up the stairs. "You're both in a timeout."

Brinn dragged her feet in protest.

Ciara's bottom lip quivered.

"Poppy," Ben said. "They're fine."

Didn't he always have that inscrutable look on his face? She hated not being able to read him. Conscious of their avid audience she lowered her voice and stepped closer. "They left the playgroup without telling anyone. They could have been anywhere. Gone anywhere."

"But they didn't," he said.

"They broke one of the first safety rules." She wanted to shove him and see if that would get any reaction. "I can't let that fly. What happens next? I hand them both a pair of scissors and tell them to run?"

"Poppy—"

"No." She didn't want to hear it. The same thing had happened with Sean. She tried to put some rules in place, and Sean blissfully trampled all over them and took the kids with him. So what if they ate candy for dinner? What did it matter when they went to bed? Who cared what they watched on television?

Ben looked down at her. Still, silent, and judging, and it cut right through to the bone.

Because when Ryan had puked his guts out in the middle of the night from too much candy, Sean was not the one wiping his face. Or when Ciara woke up screaming from a nightmare, Sean had kept right on sleeping. When she'd battled for three weeks to get Ryan to sleep in his own bed, Sean hadn't cared. Because Sean had been in someone else's bed at the time.

And then he died, and left everything in her hands. What right did Ben have to judge her? He didn't even have kids. In fact, he spent his entire life holding other people at arm's length, and now he called her unreasonable. Thought she should lighten up.

Poppy needed to walk. She spun about and stomped back into the garden.

He came after her. "Poppy."

"No." She yanked away from his light grip on her arm. "You don't get to tell me how to raise my children. You don't get any say in how I do that. Not unless you want to help me with it every day. Do you?"

"I didn't say that."

"Of course you didn't." She wanted to do something really immature like shove him. Hanging on by a thread and probably only because Brinn and Ciara were peering out their window, all eyes, she walked away. She stopped, not done yet, and marched back to him. "Children disappear every day never to be heard from again. You should know that." She poked his hard chest. "You don't even have children, and now you're the expert. I am so tired of people telling me how to raise my kids. You have no idea how tired of that I am."

"I didn't—"

"You didn't have to say anything. I can see it on your face. I can see what you're thinking."

"No"—he took a deep breath—"you really can't."

She waited for him to say more. Of course, he didn't, because Ben never said enough of anything. He never told her about Tara, and that dumbassery that he kept doing with his ex. When he wanted to kiss her, he went ahead and did and then left. Did he ask her out? Say something? No, Ben stood there. Just like he was doing now.

"Ugh." The garden was too confining and she flung open the garden gate and marched out. Her feet slapped the sidewalk. People couldn't wait to share their opinions with her. She should do this or do that. But not one of them were walking in her shoes.

The cruiser pulled up beside her. Ben had his shades on and the window down. "Get in."

"No." Poppy quickened her pace.

"You gonna walk?"

"What do you care?"

The cruiser crawled along beside her.

She passed an elderly couple walking their dog. They openly gaped at her and the cruiser.

"Drive."

"Poppy."

"Just. Drive on."

He did.

Chapter 17

Poppy stormed around the block until she had it under control. As she walked, reason crept in. First, she felt foolish for her behavior and right after that guilty.

Nobody in this town had done anything else but go out of their way to be nice to her and her children. Horace had had no reason to think the girls might have skipped out on school. In fact, he had been busy taking care of them when she tore a strip off him.

And Ben...

God, she had been the worst kind of bitch.

When Poppy slunk back into the house, Dot sat at the kitchen table peeling potatoes.

"Hey." Dot put her peeler on the table. "I thought I'd get dinner started for you. The girls are upstairs, Sean is having a nap and Ryan is watching television."

"They scared the life out of me." Her anger had cooled enough to get her voice down to inside level.

Dot went to work on a potato. "I imagine they did."

Poppy nodded. The hot day had left her thirsty so she filled a glass from the faucet and drank it.

The scrape of Dot peeling filled the silence.

"Ben tell you anything else?" Like how she'd yelled at Horace, yelled at him and done a good impersonation of a crazy person all around Twin Elks.

"Ben?" Dot snorted. "Please. That boy of mine doesn't say much of anything. You might have noticed that."

"We had...words."

"Uh-huh." Dot dropped her skinless potato into a pot of water at her elbow. "I figured as much."

"Actually, I had words and he pretty much put up with my crazy." Not much got past Dot. "Thanks for starting dinner."

"No problem." Dot pushed a second peeler toward her. "Why don't you help me peel?"

Poppy jerked a chair out and threw herself into it. "I can't believe the girls did that." She grabbed a potato. "And I can't believe I behaved like that. It's no excuse but Maura, my mother in law, was always telling me how to parent the children. Always criticizing the way I did things."

"Parenting is always easier when you're doing it to someone else's kids." Dot grabbed another potato and peeled. "Your girls they did wrong, leaving like that." She shook her head. "Kids! They'll take something into their heads and suddenly all the rules you've been cramming in there fly right out."

"They know better." Gripping her potato Poppy squirmed at her earlier tantrum. She knew better too.

"My boys did the same a time or two." Dot chuckled. "Once Gabe saw a hurt cat, and he followed it clear to the other side of town. It took us all day to find him, and when we did, he was sitting under this tree waiting for the cat to come down again."

"What did you do?" Better than all the walking in the world was Dot's easy manner.

"Yelled," Dot said. "And then yelled some more. Dragged his butt home and then burst into tears."

The pressure in Poppy's chest eased a little. "Did you punish him?"

"Damn straight I did." Nodding, Dot dropped her finished potato in the water. "They've got to understand that there are some rules that can't be bent even a little bit."

"Should I let them go back to playgroup?" She gave up pretending to peel. Dot lowered her hands to the table. "That's up to you."

Just like fixing her behavior was also up to her. Time for the adulating portion of the day. "I should talk to Horace. I had no right to yell at him."

"I can tell you that for all his faults, Horace Winters is a good man," Dot said. "He wasn't thinking today."

Poppy snorted. Her level of anger had been so out of whack with what had happened and now she needed to make things right again. "They weren't even gone for that long."

"How long is long enough?" Dot picked up the potato Poppy had abandoned. "I don't think there's any right time to be scared when your kids are involved."

Now Dot was trying to make her feel better, and that made it worse. "I overreacted."

"Maybe a little." Dot chuckled. "Horace is not used to children. And even when his daughter was around, he didn't get much of a chance to be her daddy."

"Kelly told me his wife left him."

"That woman." Dot grabbed the pot of potatoes and slammed them down on the stove. "She came from *Boston*." Dot made Boston sound like Sodom and Gomorra. "She didn't like small town living. No idea why she married Horace, but she did."

Dot stared out the window. "She was real pretty though. Wore the most beautiful shoes." She shook her head and opened the plate under the pot. "Anyway, you would think she was the first woman to have a child, the way she was with Claire. Always picking at Horace about what he did wrong. Poor man couldn't do a damn thing right. Then she ups and leaves him and takes their daughter with her."

Now she felt even more of a bitch. "Why did she leave?"

Dot shrugged. "Said she couldn't stand living here anymore. Anyway, she filled Claire's head with all sorts of rubbish about Horace. Turned Claire against her dad."

Dot was such a nice woman, she might not believe bad of someone she knew. "What sort of things?"

"How he kept control of money. Deprived her. That sort of thing." Dot came back to the table and sat. "Anybody looking at that woman knew she wasn't on a budget. Still doesn't stop Claire from floating into town whenever she needs money." She patted Poppy's hand. "All I'm saying is that Horace made a mistake. So did your girls, and it all turned out okay in the end."

Guilt gave her a shove. "That's what Ben said."

Dot cocked her head and studied her. "And I'm guessing not much else."

Poppy laughed. God, Dot knew her son well.

"His dad was the same," Dot said. "Never could get more than a couple of words out of that man. Sometimes it was like playing twenty questions to get a simple answer out of him." Shaking her head, Dot laughed softly, her expression wistful. "Near drove me to drink it did. Ben's always been like his daddy, but it got worse after he left the army."

"I took my anger out on Ben." Making her confession Poppy felt small and unworthy.

"He's got broad shoulders." Dot chuckled. "Why don't you go and talk to him, honey? Make peace."

Hoping for a reprieve she said, "I don't know where he is."

"Down by the gazebo," Dot said. "With the girls playing there today, he wanted to make sure it was safe."

Poppy really didn't know what to say to Ben, because having faced down an hysterical mother with control issues, did he run for the hills? Nope. He spent his free time making the garden safe for that same mother's children.

Maybe she could wing it and see what came out. Super call considering her past success with winging it; winging it had seen her married to a boy-man who didn't want the responsibility that came with marriage and kids. That might be her first in on this conversation. Comparing Ben to Sean didn't make sense. Ben and she weren't married and the kids weren't his. Ben and Sean shared about as much in common as a Ferrari and a Prius. Although she got a bit fuzzy on who was the Ferrari and who the Prius.

You could call Sean the Ferrari, all flash and speed and in no way a family ride. Which would make Ben the Prius, and that so didn't fit. Maybe a new Prius, like the one in the Super Bowl ad. But really he was more like a big old pickup…and she was mentally babbling because she felt stupid.

Ben had his back to her as he adjusted a floor board. On a peg hung his uniform button-down, which left him stripped to a ribbed, white undershirt that really shouldn't have worked on anyone, but hugged every ripple and hard swell of muscle on his back like it was molded on.

Her mouth dried up.

He looked at her, silent, waiting, face so carefully blank it made it hard to recover from the hotness factor.

"Um…so…what you doing?" She totally wussed out.

"Fixing the boards." He stood.

She stepped closer, her shoulder brushing his. Heat came off him in mind-emptying waves. He cradled a piece of wood in his big hands. "How is it? Safe?"

"Not bad." He pounded an upright with the heel of his palm. "Couple of loose boards, but I'll fix those."

"You really don't have to."

"I know." Ben picked up a hammer from a toolbox near his feet.

Time to get to it. "Could we talk?"

He looked at her and waited. Of course he did.

"About this morning."

Up went his brow.

Funny but she was learning to translate those things. This one meant, *over to you, June.*

"The girls should never have pulled their disappearing act."

He nodded.

"They scared me to death when I couldn't find them. We've been living in Philly, and you tend to panic when your children go missing in a city."

His silence encouraged her to take it further.

"And it's a bit more complicated than that." She never spoke about this stuff. There had never been anyone to listen. "They've been mine for so long. I've been their only parent. Even before Sean died. I have to protect them. Nobody else is going to do it. They're my children."

Ben stepped closer. Face softening, he cupped her nape. "Poppy."

One word and she dissolved like a sugar cube. "I'm sorry for being such a bitch."

He tugged her into his chest.

Right where she wanted to be and Poppy sunk into the comfort. His skin pressed warm against her cheek. God, she wanted to lean into his strength and stay there. "I panicked and I guess I don't take too well to other people making suggestions. I just want to keep them safe."

His big hand rubbed her spine.

"I get so scared sometimes. When Sean died and I found out there wasn't any money, I lay on my bed after the funeral. Everyone thought I was grieving, but I wasn't." She peeked up to see how he took that.

Ben waited.

"I was angry. So angry with Sean for dying on us. My children were in danger and I didn't know how I was going to manage."

"But you did."

That was a good one. "I managed so well, Ryan ended up talking like a police series. I had to leave him with the man upstairs sometimes. Thank

God he was into cop shows and not something else. The twins spent too much time at school. Too much time. But between my job at the supermarket and waitressing when I could get it." She shrugged. "Ciara doesn't speak, and that's on me too. I made such a screw up of this motherhood thing."

"Poppy, honey. Don't say that." As he held her at arm's length, his dark gaze roamed her face. "You're incredible." His big roughened hands cradled her face. "Brave, strong and..."

The way he looked at her released a swarm of butterflies in her belly. "And?"

"Beautiful." His hands tightened on her face. "So fucking beautiful." His head dipped.

Hot and intent, his gaze fastened on her mouth.

Why would a man like Ben want to kiss her? Twice. Hair scraped back in a ponytail, with her wearing Sean's reject T-shirt and no makeup, nobody could find that sexy.

His mouth touched hers.

A soft brush of his firm mouth over hers and then he pulled back. Like he had the other night and she wanted more. Poppy the woman woke up with a primal hormonal bellow, which she fortuitously kept inside, and wrapped her arms around his head. She went onto her toes and pressed her mouth back where it wanted to be so bad it shot through her on a sweet ache that wasn't going to be happy with a chaste peck.

Ben froze.

Shit, had she gone too far?

Then his lips moved beneath hers, firmer and surer.

Poppy had no idea how she'd gone so long without feeling this alive. Her lips parted on a soft moan that came right from her core.

Ben slid his tongue deep into her mouth, definite and commanding. A deep groan rumbled through his chest.

Poppy's nipples paid immediate attention.

He tasted like man, of musk and spice and heat. His hands spread over her lower back and brought her flush with his big, hard—and getting harder—body.

She melted into him. Woman to man, soft to hard, curves to ridges. Her senses leaped into overdrive. The gazebo smelled like wood and sunshine. She tangled her fingers in Ben's silky hair.

Sinking deep into her with each hard thrust of his tongue he surrounded her.

She wanted him to lower her to the floor. For his thighs to shove hers apart and to thrust right into where she throbbed. Her neglected body wanted the promise implicit in his kiss, and wanted it right now.

Ben peeled his mouth from hers. A flush rode his cheeks and his gaze had gotten hotter. "We need to stop."

"Why?" She didn't want to stop until she didn't ache anymore.

Ben jerked his head. "Ma."

"Ben." Dot's voice, and coming closer. "I've made dinner if you're interested."

Ben snatched his shirt off the peg and shrugged into it. With a wry grin he arranged the shirt tails over his crotch.

Still high from the kiss and feeling alive to her toes, Poppy laughed.

Ben gave her a quick, hard kiss. "Later."

Heart pounding, sweating like he'd run a marathon Ben jerked awake. He pushed his sweaty hair off his face. He wasn't in his bedroom. So where the hell was he?

Ma's sitting room.

The dream had him all turned about. He hadn't had one of those in years. He forced his cycling mind to slow and fill in the blanks. He'd stayed for dinner at Horace's then Ryan had grabbed his attention and had him explain the intricacies of football. Hell, he'd missed most of the game, but at least Ryan was taking an interest in something other than *Lethal Weapon*. Now Ryan had taken to slapping his palms together and grunting "Omaha."

After walking Ma home, he must have fallen asleep on the couch. Ma must have put a blanket over him. He checked his watch. A little after midnight.

Dropping his legs over, he pushed the blanket aside. When he'd first gotten stateside the dreams had come almost nightly. He eased the crick in his neck from the awkward angle he'd fallen asleep at.

PTSD was not something you screwed around with, and he'd gotten the help he needed. The therapy had helped, and bit-by-bit he'd found a new base of normal. As he got better the dreams came less and less often. He tried to think when he'd had his last one.

Couldn't do it. Certainly sometime around his divorce. Tara, the miscarriage and that ugly mess had sent him back to his screwed-up place for a while.

He wished he still smoked.

A light shone from the kitchen and he went toward it. A glass of water would fix the dry mouth.

Except Ma sat at the kitchen table. She glanced up, and gave him a chipper smile that stopped short of her eyes.

"Ma?" He grabbed a glass and filled it.

Tugging the sides of her robe close together, Ma dropped her chin onto her palm. "You have a dream?"

No point in lying to Ma, and Ben nodded. But Ma needn't think he hadn't caught her quick deflection. "What are you doing up?"

"Couldn't sleep." Flapping her hand she forced a laugh. "It happens when you get older."

"Uh-huh."

"You and Poppy looked to have patched things over." Ma huffed. "Poor girl. She got the fright of her life today."

"Yup." If you waited Ma out, her mouth couldn't resist the temptation.

"Got me thinking about Gabe and that time he disappeared." Ma sighed. "You boys. You sure kept me busy with the way you would rocket from one load of trouble to the next."

"You heard from Gabe?"

"He emails me." Ma got up, filled the kettle and put it on the burner. Then she sighed. "He loves it over there."

If you asked Tara, she would tell you Ben didn't have a sensitive bone in his body, but Ma's melancholy filled the kitchen enough to have him take notice. "You miss him."

"I miss them all," Ma said. She fetched a mug and put a teabag in it. "The house is so quiet without you all here. I've enjoyed having Poppy and the little ones fill it with noise and mess again."

Yeah, his brothers needed a kick up the ass. Most of them only called home once a month or so.

"You were out cold." There Ma went with her deflection again. "I decided to leave you there. Are you going to do anything about the dream?"

"If I get any more."

"Okay."

Ma's sudden backtrack made him even more resolved to talk to his brothers. As a rule, Ma didn't know the meaning of backing off, which meant she had to be hiding some major hurting. "Thanks for the blanket."

"It's the mom reflex." She poured hot water into her cup. "Do you want to tell me what's going on with you and Poppy?"

Reason number two for getting his brothers to pay more attention to Ma.

Chapter 18

The next morning Ben dropped in to see Ma first before he made good on his promise to Ryan. Tired and grumpy after a bad night, but he'd made a commitment and he'd stick to it.

Ma didn't hear him come in, and neither did Doc Cooper, because they sat heads together at the kitchen table. Cheeks flushed, Ma giggled at something Doc Cooper whispered in her ear.

"Coop." Ma slapped his hand, and giggled again.

Ben's toast rose up and jammed in the back of his throat. Ma looked like a sixteen-year old girl with all the giggling and blushing. "Ma."

Jumping like guilty teenagers they turned and stared at him.

"Ben." Ma's chair toppled over she got up so fast. "I thought you were going to take Ryan out and play football with him this morning."

"I am." Ben gave Doc Cooper a hard look. The non-verbal "I'm watching you," man-to-man.

Yeah, Doc got the message. He stood and shoved his hands in his pockets. "Morning, Ben."

"Morning." What the hell was Doc doing whispering in Ma's ear like that? Any vague thought of scoring breakfast off Ma vanished. "I'll see you later, Ma." Later when Doc had gone home and they could talk.

Trailing him out the kitchen, Ma touched his arm. "Ben?"

Half-apologetic, half-defiant, Ma's look made him feel like the parent. He didn't want to deal with what he'd seen, so he shrugged her off. "Gotta go. Later."

Face alight with eagerness Ryan rushed out the door as soon as Ben got to the Winters mansion. "You came."

"Yup." His day off and he planned to spend it teaching a six-year old how to play football. He had not planned to spend it thinking about Ma and a man. Any man. Nothing against Doc Cooper, but Ma had been alone since Dad had died. He'd never even seen her flirt with another man, and that's what he'd caught an eyeful of this morning. He bent and laced Ryan's sneakers. "Come on. We can throw round back."

Like he'd seen heaven Ryan eyed the football under his arm. "Can I hold it?"

He handed the ball over.

Flushed, Ryan ran his small hands all over the pigskin as if he wanted to press it deep into his brain.

As they cleared the side of the house, Ben's nape prickled with the knowledge that Poppy was inside. Had she spent the night thinking about that kiss? He had. How good she tasted, how right she felt and, even more disturbing, what the hell he intended to do about it. The sensible answer should be nothing, but his humming libido didn't think much of that approach.

"You gonna throw it?" Head cocked, Ryan stared up at him.

Back to reality with a jolt. "Stand over there."

"Omaha!" Ryan trotted about five feet away from him.

Judging by his last throw at the park, Ben left him there. He didn't want to kill the little guy's enthusiasm before they even got started.

Ben tossed a lollipop at Ryan.

Ryan stared at the ball, blinked and got one right in the face.

Shit!

Bottom lip quivering, Ryan kept on blinking.

"You all right, bud?" Ben held him by the shoulders.

"Ye-e-s." Ryan snatched up the ball and handed it over. "Again."

Hands tucked into his pockets Horace lurked in the carriage house doorway. "That's it, Ryan," he called. "You got this."

Wiping his nose, Ryan nodded at Horace. "I'm tough."

"You sure are." Horace gave him a mock salute.

"Right." Ben tried to infuse as much faith into his words as possible. What the hell did he think he was doing anyway? The nearest he got to kids was work related and then they all stared at him half-afraid. "Keep your eye on the ball."

Ryan frowned, grit his teeth and nodded. Little guy would give himself a headache if he kept that up. "Hit me."

"Ready?"

"Do it."

Ben lobbed another one at him.

Gaze fixed, Ryan tottered back, stumbled and lurched two steps forward. But he caught the ball.

"You did it." Ben nearly launched into a victory lap.

From the carriage house, Horace whistled and hollered. "Atta boy."

"Now, toss it back." Ben waggled his fingers.

Still frowning, Ryan hauled back and launched the ball. It made a wobbly spiral in the air and punched into Ben's gut. He got his hands around it just in time.

"Whoa." Horace limped over the grass toward them. "You been eating rocket fuel for breakfast."

"No." Shaking his head, Ryan flushed and giggled. "But I did eat all my oatmeal."

What do you know? Ryan could throw.

Ben tossed the ball back. It slipped through Ryan's arms and dribbled on the grass. Catching? Not so much.

"Never mind." Horace motioned the ball. "Pick it up and toss it back."

Poppy appeared on the kitchen porch. The breeze draped her oversized T-shirt across her breasts, which might explain why Ryan's throw bounced off the side of Ben's head and set his ears ringing.

Eyes huge, Ryan clapped his hand over his mouth.

"Ha!" A wheezy laugh came out of Horace.

Poppy's sweet laugh rippled over the yard.

"No worries." Leaving his dignity in the crabgrass, Ben picked up the ball. That's what you got for staring at the girls on the sidelines. He tossed the ball back to Ryan.

Perfect catch.

Ryan took three giant strides back. "I'm going to throw again."

"Do it."

"Are you watching this time?"

"Yup." Other than his peripheral vision that stuck on the flash of yellow that meant Poppy stood watching them.

Ryan fired the next one hard enough to rock him back.

Sarah Hegger

Ben forced his head back in the game. Unless Poppy-obsessing had fried his brain, Ryan had one helluva arm on him.

He exchanged a glance with Horace, and got a lifted eyebrow back. Nope his brain worked fine, Horace had seen the same thing.

"Go a little further back. Let's see what you got," Ben said.

The twins shoved past their mother into the yard.

"Can we play?" Brinn bounced on her toes. "Can we play?"

A waft of honey and lemon warned him Poppy had moved closer. "Let Ryan play, girls. Why don't you play something else?"

"There's nothing else to play." Brinn made it sound like her world had ended.

Ciara gave great sad face alongside her.

"Well..." Damn, the women in this family could tie a man in knots.

"Nothing to do?" Poppy put on a thinking face and tapped her chin. "Let me see. What do we do with girls who have nothing to do?"

Ciara's face lit up on a delighted gasp.

"No, Mom." Giggling, Brinn took a couple of steps back. She shook her head slowly from side to side. "No, Mom."

Poppy shrugged. "I think I'm gonna have to."

She lunged and the girls went squealing across the grass.

"Are you gonna throw?" Ryan's voice cut in.

"In a minute."

Carefree, laughing, long legs flashing as she chased her twins around the yard, this was Poppy as he'd never seen her.

From the porch, Sean bounced and squeaked.

God, what Ben wouldn't give to see Poppy play more often. Sunlight danced off her dark hair, but nothing dimmed the light that shone from inside her. She caught Ciara and tickled her.

Ciara laughed so hard she snorted.

"Ben." Ryan tugged at this shirt. "Stop watching the girls and throw the ball."

Across the yard he caught Horace's eye. Horace raised an eyebrow at him. So busted.

"Okay." He pointed further down the yard. "You and your bionic arm get back there. Let's see what you got."

A car door opened and shut out on the street.

Ryan tossed a perfect spiral across the yard, and Ben took a moment to admire the beauty of the thing.

Poppy and the twins dropped on their backs on the grass chatting about something that seemed to demand a lot of giggling.

A curious lightness filled his chest. The sort of feeling he hadn't had since before his deployment. The sun shone brighter, the grass looked greener, even the gentle breeze played perfectly into the summer morning.

The garden gate screeched open and a woman said, "Hello?"

Horace scowled. "Who the hell are you?"

Poppy froze. Praying like hell she's misheard she rolled onto her side.

Maura Williams stood by the side of the house, her shirt artfully tucked into her knee-length khaki skirt, hair perfectly arranged around her skillfully made up face. Maura had brought reinforcements. Looming above her, tall and dark, with the same blue eyes as his late brother stood Finn.

Horace slipped back into the carriage house, slamming the door behind him.

"What a strange man." Maura lifted her brow as she watched Horace leave.

Breath coming short and fast, Poppy took her time getting to her feet. She couldn't believe Maura and Finn were actually here. Finn she'd always liked, but she'd been locked in a battle for ground with Maura since Sean had first introduced them.

"Grandma," Ryan yelled. "Uncle Finn. Watch me throw this football."

"Be careful, Ryan." Maura stepped to the edge of the walkway.

Trying not to drag her feet like the twins were, Poppy approached them.

Ben appeared at her side, and slid his hand beneath her elbow.

"Poppy." Finn jerked his head. He wasn't as pretty as Sean had been but Finn was bigger and more rugged.

"Finn." Poppy had more time for the oldest Williams brother than the rest of the family and she managed a genuine smile.

"Ben!" Ryan trotted up. "Aren't we going to throw the ball some more? I want to show Finn how good I am."

Ben put his hand on Ryan's head. "In a minute. Why don't we say hello first?"

"Dear God in Heaven." Maura pressed her red-tipped fingers to her mouth. She charged down Sean, who toddled across the porch. "Sean? My baby."

Poppy lurched. Every maternal instinct screaming to get to Sean before Maura did. It took everything she had to stop the reaction. Maura meant well, and she certainly loved the boys.

Face almost as unreadable as Ben's, Finn gazed her way.

Cuddling Sean as if she couldn't let him go, the look of raw agony on Maura's face hit Poppy hard. Maura had lost her son, and probably her favorite son at that. There couldn't be anything more painful than losing a child.

"Finn Williams." Finn held his hand out to Ben.

"Ben." Ben shook. "Ben Crowe."

"How've you been, Poppy." Finn bent and kissed her cheek. "You look great."

Did she? Right now she felt like she'd been hit by an eighteen-wheeler. "So do you."

Finn did look good. More relaxed than when she'd last seen him. Then again, she'd last seen him at the lawyer's office as the details of Sean's will were read. Neither of them had expected what the lawyer had to say.

"Mom?" As always, reluctant to approach Maura, Brinn pressed close to her leg. Which is why Poppy's sympathy always stopped short. Maura's grief was like a still-bleeding wound, but she saw nothing of Sean in his daughters.

"Brinn?" Finn cocked a dark brow. He made a big show of thinking. "No. Ciara?" He put his hands on his hips and shook his head. "Definitely, Brinn."

"Or maybe Ciara." Brinn rolled her face into Poppy's side.

"No, I'm Ciara." Ciara clapped her hands over her mouth and giggled.

They remembered. So did Poppy. Finn wasn't a bad guy, and certainly much more reliable than his younger brother had been.

"You girls wouldn't be messing with your old uncle Finn, would you?" Finn crouched eye level with the twins.

"Mom said we should respect old people," Brinn said, with a wicked lilt.

"Brinn." Like she'd been sucking lemons, Maura's mouth puckered up. "That's no way to speak."

"Mom." Finn frowned. "She's just teasing. And because of that"—he sighed—"I'm going to have to punish her."

"No!" Brinn squealed and dashed into the yard.

Ciara grinned and quivered as Finn pounced.

Upending her over his shoulder, he chased after Brinn.

"Well, now." Flushed and panting, Dot arrived.

Poppy guessed Dot had seen the car pull up. This being Twin Elks, Dot would probably be expected to report back to the prayer chain on the visitors.

Dot laughed as she watched Finn horse around with the twins. "Why don't we all go inside and visit a bit."

Ryan stuck close to Ben, one arm wrapped around Ben's thigh.

"Hello, Ryan." Maura smiled at him. "Have you got a kiss for grandma?"

Ryan shook his head.

Maura stiffened. The look she gave Poppy as she followed Dot into the house promised a reckoning.

Ben cupped Poppy's elbow. "Okay?"

"Not really."

He squeezed as if to tell her he stood beside her and motioned her to precede him.

Thank God for Dot as she carried them all over the awkwardness of sitting on opposite sides of the sitting room. The air between them swirled with unspoken words and accusations.

Still hanging on to Sean, Maura looked around with her lip curled in distaste. No, Horace's house wouldn't pass the Maura inspection because it didn't look like it was waiting for the photographer from *Better Homes and Gardens* to appear.

Fortunately, Dot had an endless supply of small talk to fill the uncomfortable silences. But even she was running out, when Finn came in with a twin under each arm and dropped them on the floor.

Wedged into the same armchair, Ryan stayed glued to Ben's side.

The twins immediately clamored for Finn to play some more. "Later, chickens." He cupped Ciara's chin. "I think I'm going to rest my old bones and have a drink first."

"The girls have grown," Maura said.

Brinn fidgeted with her dress.

Sean fussed for Maura to put him down.

Maura bounced him and murmured, trying to get him to change his mind. Not having any of it, Sean whined a protest.

"He wants to walk," Brinn said, face a mixture of longing for Maura's approval and the need for her attention, even the negative kind.

Sean squawked and Maura put him on his feet. He immediately toddled to Poppy.

Finn took a seat on the sofa next to his mother.

"Good drive?" Ben shifted.

"Uneventful," Finn said. He cleared his throat. "Some roadwork coming out of Denver."

"Ah." Ben nodded.

"Uh, uh, uh." Arms extended, Sean demanded Poppy pick him up.

Ciara whispered to Brinn.

"Well!" Dot beamed at everyone. "Isn't this nice."

Finn laughed. A deep boom that echoed around the room. "I'm sorry." He rubbed his chin. "We should have called before we arrived."

"I have a right to see my grandchildren." Maura glared at him.

And there you had it. Poppy tamped down her knee jerk reaction.

"Come on, Mom." Finn shook his head. "We arrived here without any warning." He looked at Poppy. "I'm sorry, I wasn't thinking."

"We wouldn't have to have traveled all this way if Poppy hadn't disappeared." Maura dug in her purse and found a packet of Kleenex.

"I called you before I left." Jaw so tight, Poppy barely managed to get the words out. She had called Maura and left a message. And okay, it had been a little cowardly not to tell her in person. But sitting right here, now, Maura dabbing at her perfectly made-up eyes was the reason she'd cut and run.

"Come on, girls." Motioning the girls, Dot stood. "Let's go and find some of those cookies you baked with your mom. Come along, Ryan." She waggled her fingers.

Ryan got up and followed.

Silently asking if she needed him to stay, Ben looked at her.

Poppy shook her head. "Could you take Sean?"

Nodding, he rose, took Sean and followed his mother and the children into the kitchen.

And Poppy sat alone with her in-laws in Horace's sitting room.

Maura went to an antique dresser, and shuddered. "How old is this thing?"

"Victorian." Poppy had no idea but she guessed most of the furniture had come with the house.

"And you live here?" Eyes wide, Maura crossed to the ornate, carved mantle. "God, this stuff must give the boys nightmares."

"Mom." Finn's voice rumbled a warning.

"It's temporary." Poppy hated that she felt the need to explain herself. "My car needed some repairs, and we had to wait. Dot, the lady you just met, arranged somewhere for us to live."

Sniffing, Maura poked at a stuffed armchair. Horsehair stuffing crinkled beneath her fingers. "Does this town not have a decent hotel?"

Opening her mouth to explain further about her money situation, Poppy stopped. Money had long been a bone of contention between her and Maura, one of them anyway. When Maura lent money, it came with a string of conditions.

"There was a job for me in California," Poppy said. "And a nice house we can use for the summer."

"You had a job." Spinning to stare at her, Maura drew a shaky breath. "And a perfectly fine apartment."

"Fine? That apartment was far from fine." Finn cut a hard look at his mother. "Let's not go there, shall we?"

"It's not my fault." Maura jerked. "I told her she could come and live with me. But she didn't want that."

Finn shook his head and stared at the ceiling. "And she goes there anyway."

Poppy didn't have to let this dissolve into an argument. "Maura, you and I wouldn't—we can't live in the same house together." It had been bad enough with Sean acting as occasional buffer. Without him, Poppy couldn't see herself living under the constant arc of Maura's disapproval. The "helpful" suggestions that never ended. After Sean's death, it had only gotten worse. Maura stomped over any tentative boundaries Poppy put in place. Especially when it came to Ryan and little Sean.

Visits that didn't include the girls, gifts for the boys and helpful suggestions on how to raise the twins, until Poppy thought she might go mad trying to run interference and keep her troubled family floating. Mom's offer had come as Maura started murmuring about lawyers. Poppy didn't think Maura had a hope in hell of getting any of her children from her, let alone separating the family and giving Maura just the boys, but why wait around and find out? Not when the rest of their existence teetered on a vortex of crap anyway.

Finn stood. "I think we should go." He held a card out to Poppy. "We'll be in town for a couple of days. Here's my cell number." The lopsided grin he gave her reminded her of a time when he'd been in her corner. "In case you forgot it."

She should have stayed in contact with Finn.

Chapter 18

Maura fallout started the next morning when Ryan discovered the gifts Maura had left for him and Sean. For the girls, Maura left a small bag of candy each.

As Poppy put the embarrassing deluge of boy gifts away, Ryan followed her around objecting in a low-level whine.

Watching with wise young eyes that had seen it all before, Brinn and Ciara ate their breakfast.

"But they're mine." Ryan trailed her as she went to get Sean up. "Why can't I have them?"

Because your grandmother is out her tiny mind didn't seem the most appropriate answer. "Ryan, you need to get dressed."

"I want to play." He stuck his little boy chest out in a perfect imitation of Ben that almost made her smile.

"We haven't got time to play right now." Taking a whinging Sean out of the crib, she gave Ryan the eye. "Please go and eat your breakfast."

"I hate cereal." Ryan plopped on the floor.

Poppy stepped over him on the way to change Sean's diaper. "You don't hate cereal."

"I do. Grandma makes pancakes every morning. Why can't you make pancakes every morning?"

Damn! He had the whole manipulation thing down pat. Poppy breathed deep.

Squirming, Sean threw himself to the left.

She caught him and brought him back before he rolled off the bed.

Sean kicked his legs and yelled, "Nooo."

"Come on, baby. Let's get you changed."

"No." Sean's leg lashed out and smacked into her belly.

"Mooom." Brinn yelled. "Can I have the candy from the bag Gran brought?"

Baby four made for wicked diapering skills, and Poppy got the tabs fastened on Sean's fresh diaper. "No you can't."

"You're so mean." Ryan's bottom lip quivered. "You won't let anyone have any fun."

"No, no, no, no, no." Not wanting his pants on, Sean twisted like a pretzel.

Fine. No pants. Poppy picked him up.

"Grandma gave those toys to me. I neeeeeed to play with them," Ryan said.

A crash came from the kitchen, followed by a loaded silence. Then Brinn and Ciara started arguing.

Poppy hot-footed it with Sean tucked under her arm and Ryan's sniveling in her wake.

"I didn't do it." Pointing at Brinn, Ciara stood on her chair. "She did it."

A smashed glass lay on the floor, while milk seeped away, making runnels in the tile grout.

Brinn headed toward the broken glass with a roll of paper towels.

"No." Poppy headed her off. Broken glass and little fingers, a nasty combination. "Ciara go and change your shirt. Brinn, can you take Ryan into the other room?"

"Can we have then candy then?" Brinn handed her the paper towels.

"No." Some days it seemed the only word to come out of her mouth. "Ciara walk around the other way."

"Dear God." One hand over her mouth, Maura appeared in the open kitchen doorway.

The timing was so perfectly evil, Poppy almost laughed.

"Do you know there's broken glass on the floor?" Maura gave her a judgy look. "I'm sure I don't have to tell you this, Poppy, but you really shouldn't let the children near broken glass."

"Gam!" Sean beamed at Maura.

"Hello, darling." Maura grabbed his fingers and kissed them. "How is Gran's sweet boy? You should ask Mommy to get you dressed."

Not even eight in the morning and Poppy wanted to go back to bed and pull the covers over her head. "What can I do for you, Maura?"

"I thought I might take the boys for the day." Maura side-stepped the spreading milk.

"Hello, Maura." Dot stepped into the kitchen.

Like a magic fairy, and Poppy wanted to hug her.

"Dot." Maura straightened her shoulders and stuck her chin out. "Gosh, but you start visiting early in this part of the world."

"Early birds. That's us. No sense in wasting this beautiful day in bed." Dot grinned. "I came by to pick-up the boys for the day."

"Are we going with grandma?" Ryan hit the kitchen at a trot.

Dot caught him before he reached the milk puddle. "Mom's just talking about that now." She took the paper towels from Poppy and picked up glass shards.

Glaring defiantly at Maura, Brinn stood in the doorway. "I'm going to my playgroup." She grabbed Ciara's hand. "Ciara is coming with me."

"Are you ready to go?" Poppy sensed Maura, a glowering presence at her back. "If you are, can you wait outside for me?"

The twins skirted the mess.

Ciara whispered in Brinn's ear.

"Because she didn't ask us," Brinn said.

It hit Poppy dead center in her heart. She didn't spare Maura the glare as she turned. "You should have called and we could have discussed something."

"Will you make me pancakes, Grandma?" Ryan turned soulful eyes to Maura. "I haven't had any breakfast and you always used to make me pancakes."

"Of course, darling. Mommy should gave given you breakfast by now." Maura patted his head. "But how about grandma takes you out for breakfast?"

Sean squawked.

Poppy loosened her grip around him. "I'm afraid you'll have to do pancakes another morning." Maura knew she should call first. Boundaries. "Now, I have to get the girls to playgroup or we'll be late."

"What sort of playgroup?" Maura frowned.

"It's run by local mothers at the church." Poppy snatched up some paper towels and went to help Dot mop up the mess. "Another morning, you are welcome to take the boys."

Maura's low-heeled pumps slid into view as Poppy mopped. "Poppy, please don't be like this. I've come all this way to see them."

Dot glanced at her, nodded and stood. "You could always stay here with me and visit with the boys. If that's okay with Poppy."

"Can we have pancakes?" Ryan went for the kill.

"No." Dot tapped his nose. "But you can have some of Dot's super-eggs."

"He prefers pancakes." Maura folded her arms.

"I'm sure he does." Dot beamed at her. "But pancakes don't make a boy grow big enough to be a police chief."

Ryan's battle played over his face. But Dot so had his number. "Eggs." "Please?" Poppy stared at him.

Giving her his best smile, he settled at the table. "Please, Dot."

"Have you eaten, Maura?" Dot grabbed a pan and clunked it on the range. "Perhaps you'd like to have breakfast with the boys?" She looked at Poppy, silently asking for permission.

Poppy nodded. There really was no way to pay Dot back for all she'd done and continued to do.

"You go along." Dot flapped her hands at Poppy. "The girls are waiting for you. Maura and I will have a lovely morning with the boys."

There came the promise, Dot had this and she wouldn't be leaving her post. "I won't be long."

"Say hi to Kelly for me." Dot herded her out the door. Outside she threw Poppy a naughty grin and rolled her eyes. "Wish me luck."

"Thank y—"

Dot jammed her fists on her hips. "Now, I know you're not going to start all that thank you rubbish again."

"You're right, I'm not." Poppy gave her a quick hug, because how the hell could you not? "I'll pour you a great big glass of wine when I get back."

"Now you're talking." Dot said with a light hip-check. "Now, come here, girls, and kiss Dot goodbye." She leaned down to eyeball the girls. "And no more going off on your own. I want to hear you say yes, Dot."

"Yes, Dot." Brinn grinned.

Dot fixed Ciara with a stare.

Ducking her head, Ciara whispered, "Yes, Dot."

"Come on, then," Poppy said. They'd have to hurry. Not that anyone would bitch, but Kathy had this way of checking her watch.

"Aren't you forgetting something?" Dot raised her eyebrows.

Poppy went through her mental check. Purse, shoes, girls, lunches. "No."

Laughing, Dot held her arms out for Sean. "How about I take him?"

The twins seemed to forget the Maura put-down in their enthusiasm about teasing her about forgetting she had Sean in her arms. All this time, even when big Sean had been alive, it had been her and her children. In a ridiculously short time, Dot had become a support system. The throb of gratitude took her by surprise. When you held on so tight for so long, you forgot what breathing space felt like. Like when you gripped a rope so tight your fingers ached when you finally let go.

As part of their morning ritual, they stopped at the garden gate.

Ciara waved at the rose garden. "Bye. See you later."

"Wait up." Cane in one hand, Horace hobbled out of the carriage house.

Damn. In all the morning's excitement, she'd forgotten his breakfast. "I'm sorry," she said as he approached.

"Eh?" Stopping, Horace frowned at her. "For what?"

"I forgot your breakfast." She looked down at the girls, and weighed her options. Still, Horace housed them and in exchange all he wanted was someone to cook and clean for him, and he really kept himself pretty tidy. "Sorry, girls. We need to get Horace some breakfast."

Horace snorted. "Never mind about that. I saw Dot in the kitchen and she can whip me up something." He tapped Brinn's shiny sneakers. "Nice shoes."

"They sparkle." Brinn stuck one foot out.

"They sure do." He winked at her, then looked at Poppy. "And a man can eat cereal for one morning. I wanted to ask about your visitors."

"They won't be staying at the house." She assured herself as much as Horace.

"Huh." With his keen gaze, Horace always saw too much. "Like that, is it?"

He had a sadness about him that spoke to Poppy. "Unfortunately, yes."

"Whelp!" He rubbed the head of his cane. "You can't always choose family."

"No." Poppy needed to get going.

"Um." Horace hobbled into her path. "About the other day? With these two."

"Oh." She hadn't spoken to Horace about it since then. As if they'd tacitly agreed not to mention her yelling at him. "I'm sorry I yelled at you. I was completely out of line."

Snorting, he tapped his stick on the sidewalk. "Should have called you."

From the garden birds chattered and gossiped. As it passed, a car slowed down and the driver waved.

Poppy didn't recognize the driver but waved anyway. "It really should be me apologizing to you."

"Sure." Horace nodded. *Tap, tap, tap* went his stick.

"Well… I need to get the girls to playgroup."

"Thing is." Horace sniffed. "Got to thinking. Not all that good with children, the taking care of them part."

That took the wind out of her, and she managed a barely coherent noise of it's okay.

Horace looked her dead in the eye. "You're a good mother, Poppy Williams. You love your kids and you do your best by them. Don't ever forget that and don't let anyone else make you doubt it."

It almost surprised Poppy into hugging him. "Than—"

"Don't make a big production out of it." Horace wacked a weed with his cane. "Maybe we could have a picnic when they get home. In the garden."

Brinn clapped and bounced. "Yes, Horace, we could have a picnic in the garden."

What a faker. Under that crusty old exterior beat the heart of a truly kind man. "That sounds great. I'll be by in a bit to get your laundry."

He scowled at her. "Make sure you do." Clearing his throat he hobbled away to the kitchen. "Laundry doesn't do itself you know."

"He's not really angry," Brinn whispered.

Short on charm, but long on loneliness, something she knew a lot about. "I know."

The tight Maura-shaped knot in her middle unraveled a bit more as she and the girls walked to playgroup. Her dark, grimy little Philly apartment was a long way away from the bright, sunny day all around them. People saw her here. She had a face and an identity. It had been too long since she had felt that way.

She stopped at the playgroup to apologize for the twins' disappearing act. Peg waved her on with a snort.

The coffee shop buzzed with activity when Poppy opened the door. Avoiding Maura was as good an excuse as any to stop and spend some time with Kelly.

"Hey, girl!" Kelly yelled.

"Poppy." Vince called. "Thank God. Tell your friend I want my coffee."

Kelly's head appeared around the side of the coffee machine. "Got naked pictures of you, Vince. Never forget it."

"Shit, Kelly. I was four." Vince ducked his head.

"Naked is naked, Vince." Kelly grinned at Poppy. "Tough crowd this morning."

Climbing onto her usual stool, Poppy let the morning rush ebb and flow around her. When she got a chance, Kelly would bring her coffee. With Dot on Maura duty, Poppy couldn't stay too long.

Mid-froth Kelly tilted her head. "You okay?"

"Fine." For the moment. "Why?"

"Didn't want to say anything before." Kelly laughed. "But you don't normally wear *Hello Kitty* socks."

Poppy followed Kelly's pointed look to her feet. Sure enough, Ciara's cheerful hot pink *Hello Kitty* socks stared up at her. "Maternal hazard."

"Well, hello there." Kelly had her extra-flirt voice on.

Poppy turned.

"Hi." Finn stood behind her. "I came to find you."

"Nah, you don't want her." Kelly propped her elbows on the counter. "She's got four kids. Too much hassle."

Finn's gaze strayed to Kelly's impressive cleavage.

He totally deserved to flounder, but Poppy rescued him anyway. "He already knows I have four children." She stepped closer. "Kelly, this is my brother-in-law, Finn Williams."

Finn dragged his attention to her. "Got a minute?"

"Sure she does," Kelly said. "It'll give me a chance to make you a cup of coffee that'll convince you you've been wasting your life away waiting for me."

"I look forward to that." Finn grinned.

And he really did have a great smile. The sort of smile she'd seen the girls melt for. Wicked, direct and a shot of adrenaline straight to the ovaries.

Kelly's mouth dropped open. That would teach her. Poppy wanted to giggle as she led Finn to a quiet table in the corner.

Knees knocking the table, he folded himself into the chair. "Again, sorry for the surprise appearance yesterday."

"A little warning would have been nice." Things between her and Finn had always been okay. Maybe because he hadn't been around that much.

"Yeah." He rubbed his neck. "But I really wasn't sure you might not run."

Straight to the point, and that deserved honesty in return. "You might be right. Though in fairness, I wasn't so much running as escaping."

He nodded. "So, what's the plan now, Poppy?"

Technically she didn't have to answer that, or any of his questions. Sean had died before she discovered her fourth pregnancy. They were no longer related, but this was Finn, and he'd extended the only helping hand she'd gotten from the Williams family. "When my car's ready, and my mom has things settled, we go to California."

Kelly arrived with the coffee. Had she tugged her shirt lower? "Anytime."

Finn watched her flounce back to the kitchen. "Your friend?"

"Yup." How long since Poppy had been able to say that about someone.

"What's wrong with your car?" Finn blew on his coffee before sipping.

"The brake pads needed replacing."

Blinking, he put his cup down and adjusted it. "You still drive that Toyota?"

"Uh-huh."

Finn's look went from confusion to outrage to disbelief. "How can that take longer than a couple of hours to fix?"

Several days into accepting that she'd been skillfully outmaneuvered into staying, Poppy laughed. "Apparently it takes two weeks in Twin Elks."

Clenching his fist, Finn's face tightened. "That's ridiculous. You should take—"

"It's okay." She put her hand over his fist. "Things work differently here, and my mom was relieved to have a little extra time on her end."

Flipping his hand over, Finn captured her fingers in his. "The thing is, Poppy." He shifted and cleared his throat. "The way Sean left things with you was totally shit. I guess I wanted to come here and see if you were okay."

Finn had left as soon as Sean's will was settled. Poppy didn't know exactly what he did, but it involved the armed forces, and lots of unexplained absences. When he'd been around though, Sean had stayed closer to home. Or got better at hiding his extra-curricular excursions. Finn had no compunction in telling his younger brother when he had screwed up.

"I'm doing better," she said. "Things in Philly were not so good."

"And my mother didn't help." Finn nodded. "Look, I get how she is. I really came by this morning to tell you that." He finished his coffee. "I want you to know, I'm not here to make things worse for you, Poppy."

"Eh?"

He grinned. "I'm on your side."

"Wow." It's about all she had. "I didn't expect this."

Finn grimaced. "Yeah, and that's part of what I want to fix." He stood. "I should go and rescue Dot from my mother."

All long-legged grace, Finn strode out of the store.

"So." Kelly nudged her. "That's your brother-in-law. Anything like your husband?"

"No." Poppy found a smile. "And that's a good thing."

Chapter 20

When Poppy picked the twins up from playgroup, they chattered all the way down the road to Horace's. Clearly feeling much more optimistic about their afternoon than she did.

Ben texted her to let her know he would bring the boys by Horace's because Dot had a meeting. A longer voice message from Dot filled in the blanks. She and Maura had taken the boys to the park, followed by ice cream. The message sounded cheerful, so Maura hadn't dented Dot's perpetual optimism. Poppy got the feeling Dot didn't allow anyone to do that to her.

Doing his best not to look like he'd been waiting for them, Horace stood by the gate, wearing a large, straw hat with the brim unraveling.

"Hey, Horace." Brinn pranced down the sidewalk when she caught sight of him. "I'm hungry."

"I made you lunch." Horace hitched his ratty old trousers. "But you're going to have to sit down and eat like a civilized person.

Brinn beamed up at him. "I can do that."

"You made lunch?" Surprise stopped Poppy moving for a moment.

"Yup."

"Thank you."

Horace nodded back. "You're welcome. I'm not completely helpless."

Ciara smiled at him and wandered into the garden. She moved straight to the overgrown Victorian rose garden and stood with her head tilted.

"What are you doing, sweetheart?" Poppy tried to see what held Ciara's attention.

Ciara waggled her fingers, then turned back to the gazebo. The secretive smile she gave creeped the hell out of Poppy.

"What do you keep looking at?" All Poppy could see what the rose garden with the dilapidated sundial.

"Ben," Brinn shrieked. "Mom, it's Ben."

Sure enough, it was Ben pushing open the front gate and strolling her way.

Poppy's heart did an annoying little excited leap. Since that kiss he took up even more mental real estate. She blamed it on the lack of any sort of sexual activity, and she meant sexual activity of any sort, for so long she might as well have been on a desert island.

Ben gave her his lazy smile.

Ryan ran up to her. "Nana bought us ice cream and a new kite."

Poppy gritted her teeth, but along with the other gifts, she was going to have to bite the bullet and say something to Maura. Again. Which Maura would conveniently ignore. Again.

Sean toddled to her and headbutted her legs. He held his arms out. "Uhp."

How would she greet Ben if there wasn't anybody around to see? She'd walk right up to him and slide her hands up that broad chest. Curl her fingers in the shorter hair at his nape, and slam her mouth over his.

"Mom." Ryan tugged on her shirt. "You're not listening to me."

No, not a word because some part of her brain was still rolling around the grass wrapped in Ben's strong arms. "What is it?"

"Horace says the sandwiches are ready, and I'm hungry."

"Ma said Sean is about ready for his nap," Ben said.

"Okay." Poppy caught the faint waft of the no-nonsense spicy aftershave Ben favored. "I hope we're not keeping you from anything important."

"No." He touched the base of her spine, shepherding her toward the children.

Good thing he didn't have more important things to do, because she really wasn't sorry. Not even a tiny bit. "Would you like to stay for lunch? Horace made sandwiches."

"Sure." With his dark gaze, heavy and intent on her, they might be the only two people in the world.

Sean whimpered, growing heavy in her arms. "I'll put Sean down."

"I'll give Horace a hand."

Dragging herself away from Ben, she took a grouchy Sean upstairs and put him down in his travel crib.

Joining everyone in the garden, Poppy had to compliment Horace's sandwiches. Tuna salad and egg salad, cheese and ham, and some mystery mix involving peanut butter that the children devoured. He'd even arranged them on a platter and set out a table under the gazebo.

After lunch, she left the children in the shade of a cluster of quivering aspens and indulged her need to look around Horace's garden. Perhaps Ben would even join her. Bigger than it appeared from the road, around back it sloped down over three acres to a busy river. Larger trees dominated this side of the garden. A trellis sagged above the back porch. Heavy honeysuckle vines rioted over it and threw deep shade onto the porch.

She stood at the top of the garden and let her imagination wander. She would plant a bed almost entirely of lavender to attract the hummingbirds. Maybe mix it with Mexican sage and columbine. She didn't know enough about which plants thrived there. If this was hers, she'd do her research, make sure she planted with the environment in mind and created a self-sustaining space. A long time ago someone had tried to take advantage of the natural rock formations and create beds. Bit by bit her imagination reworked it until it spread its splendor beneath the graceful old trees.

Maybe a garden seat, definitely a bench or two. A small herb garden would guarantee fresh herbs for all the home-style cooking she would do on the kitchen range.

Her fingers itched to burrow in the soil. Below the warmer soil on the surface, it would remain cool no matter how hot the day. Even in Philly she'd tried to nurture a couple of African violets in her window. But to have something like this. Her heart ached with the need to plant things, love them, bring this perfect space back to thriving life, filled with bugs, birds and growing things.

"Hey." Ben joined her.

"Look at it." Her full heart demanded she share. "It's glorious."

Ben grunted.

Poppy had to laugh. Not being in her head, all he would see was the current wreck. "I could work magic in a place like this."

Ben looked at her. His gaze warmed and he held out his hand. "Show me."

"The children?" From behind them Ryan shrieked with delight. He waved his shirt over his head and charged the twins.

"Horace has 'em. Show me what you see."

His hand warm in hers, Poppy led Ben around the garden. It didn't seem strange talking to him about what she saw. He didn't laugh at her ideas, or try to change them. He listened. So she talked some more, and included the house and how she'd always dreamed of owning a place like it. The connection flared live and bright between them. She stopped midway through outlining her plans for the porch.

The look on Ben's face dried up her thoughts. He looked hungry, and her need surged in response.

Ben sure as hell hoped Poppy going quiet and blushing meant the same thing was happening in her mind as his. "Poppy?"

She stared down at the ground. "Give me a minute."

He gave her a minute.

Then she said, so soft he nearly didn't catch it. "I'm having inappropriate thoughts."

"Shame on you, Poppy." Like she was his true north, he closed the distance between them. His laugh built in his chest and he leaned into her, nuzzling the tasty curve of her neck. "And with Horace and the kids so close."

"I blame you." Shifting her head, she gave him the space he needed.

Needing to taste, he sucked on her silky skin. "And how's that?"

Poppy giggled, quiet and smug, like she knew the effect she had on him and delighted in her power. "It's probably the handcuffs."

Whatever it was, it worked for him. "It's later, Poppy." Ben dipped his head, clamoring for a taste of her. Her lips trembled beneath his and he took it easy. As much as he wanted her, he needed her to be onboard with this.

Poppy moaned and opened her mouth beneath his.

Ben let go and went after what he wanted. She tasted so sweet it shot straight to his cock. Against him she pressed small and delicate and round in all the right places. He molded his hands to her back. No bra. And he was in so much trouble. Kids and Horace here, right now, and much too close.

She gave a soft whimper as he ended the kiss. The sort of noise that made him want to yell to hell with it and lay her down in the tangled grass. He needed her to open her eyes before he lost the few good intentions he still had. "Honey?"

Her eyes blinked open—soft, sweet and ricocheting his desire back at him.

"We can't do this here," he said.

She flushed and tried to step out of his arms.

Ben tightened his hold on her. There was only so far he would go in the name of good sense and she felt perfect against him.

"You're right." She rested her palms against his chest, burning right through his shirt. "It's been a while."

That gave him an embarrassingly he-man rush that didn't help his situation. "How long?"

"Not since I fell pregnant with Sean." She dropped her head on his chest. Her hair smelled like fruity shampoo.

Almost three years. Poppy needed a man to stand at her side, a man to help her raise those kids. His track record with forever truly sucked. He'd failed his ex and he'd failed his unborn child. As much as she turned him on, this wasn't a game.

Poppy watched hesitation wash across Ben's face. She wanted to take the words back. Yup, nothing sexier than a woman with four kids who hadn't had sex in so long she could technically be classified as a re-virgin. She needed some distance. Like maybe a hole to hide in.

She stepped away from him.

Ben's arms clamped her closer to him. "Poppy."

How the hell did he manage to convey so much with one word? "I know." She couldn't look at him. "Stupid thing to say. For once, I don't want you to say anything."

He muttered something and tucked her under his chin.

Goddammit and didn't she want to stay here for the next thirty years or so. Ben had this way of shattering the isolation chamber she'd been walking around in since Sean's death. "It was just a kiss."

"No," he said.

She was going to need a bit more than that, which probably meant she was SOL.

"It was a kiss that we both know leads to a whole lot of trouble," he said. "I want you, Poppy. In a bad way. But the things you need...I don't know if I can offer those."

She nearly nodded, and then she let his words sink in. "What is it you think I need?"

"Security." He shrugged. "Permanent."

Up until ten minutes ago she would have agreed with him. But when other girls were getting dressed up and hitting the town, she had been home with twin girls. Other girls kissed frogs, got their hearts trampled on by players, while she raised children. Maybe, just once, she could have a taste of what they'd had. "Eventually, yes," she said.

Ben looked at her, his gaze intent and searching.

"But this." She motioned between them. "This doesn't have to be that. I'm leaving as soon as my mother gets her stuff sorted. I've had permanent, Ben. I've had married. I've had widowed. What I've never had is something for me. Something that's about scratching an itch."

He frowned. "Poppy, don't take this wrong way, but I really don't think you're that sort of girl."

She had to laugh. "But that's just the thing. How do I know that? I'd like the chance to find out."

"Shit." Dropping his arms, Ben stepped back.

As new experiences went, his rejection sucked. "It's okay. You're not up for that. That's fine. I—"

"Stop." He cupped her nape. "I'm standing here with a woman I'm hot for and she's offering me no-strings sex. You're going to have to give me a minute with that."

Was that what she offered? Poppy shrugged. Yes. It sounded a lot like it. No-strings sex, when all she'd ever had was lots of strings sex. Sex with four little consequences. What would it feel like to have the other kind? She really, really wanted to find out.

"Tell you what." Ben pressed his forehead to hers. "You think about this a bit more."

She'd thought about it. "I—"

"Think," he said. "And make sure you're good with it before we take this any further."

"I don't need to—"

"I want you, Poppy, make no mistake about that." His breath brushed her lips. "But I want you to be sure you know the score before we go there."

He took her hand as they walked back to where Horace was watching the children play.

She was sure, but now wasn't the time to convince him of that.

The front gate clacked shut and Maura charged into the garden.

"Where's Poppy?" She gathered Ryan close to her.

The twins stopped playing and stared.

"What the hell are you doing?" Chin thrust out, Horace got to his feet. "Coming into my garden and making all this noise

"What are you doing with these children?" Snapping her fingers, Maura turned to the girls. "Come here, girls."

"Why?" Brinn scowled.

"Because I said so." Maura's voice rose to a shriek. At this rate she'd bring the neighbors running and wake Sean up.

"Damn." Ben shook his head.

Poppy stalked the distance that separated her from Maura. "Stop it." All eyes swung her way.

"Stop it, Maura. You're upsetting Ryan."

Ryan slid away from Maura and hid behind Poppy. "Why is grandma so mad?"

It was a very good question, and Poppy stared at Maura, waiting for the answer.

"Poppy." Maura patted her hair into place. "I was driving past and I saw this...man with the children. Where were you?"

"This is his home." Poppy wanted to smack her. The children had been having such a lovely afternoon. It seemed too long since she'd seen them relaxed and happy, playing in the sun. Okay, Horace would have failed charm school, but he'd made a place for the children in his home and he'd only been sitting in the shade and watching them play.

"I really am struggling to understand this." Maura smoothed her skirt over her hips. "You can't get away from Philadelphia fast enough, where the children have family who love them. Then I find you handing the children off to anyone."

Ben stiffened and opened his mouth.

Poppy motioned him back. This was her fight and also not the right time to have it. "You are so out of line right now, Maura."

Maura's mouth dropped open. "They're my grand—"

"And they're my children." Poppy was so damn tired of biting her tongue. She'd moved across the country to get away from this, and Maura had chased her down. "That means I get to decide what I think is best for them. We'll talk about this later."

"But I—"

"Later." Poppy took a deep, calming breath. "Girls, get your stuff together. Ryan, can you help Horace and put the cups back on the tray."

"I'll do that." Maura gathered up cups.

"No," Poppy said. "I asked Ryan to do it."

"What the hell, Mom." Finn stalked into the garden.

Ben stepped in front of him, back tense. "She's got no business speaking to Poppy like that."

With a curt nod, Finn glanced around Ben at Poppy. "I'm sorry. She got out the car before I could stop her."

"I am entitled to do what I think is right." Maura drew her shoulders back.

"Not if that upsets the children," Finn said. He stopped and looked at the house. His expression softened. "Damn, it's a beautiful house."

"It's my house." Horace limped to the gazebo. "And it's time you took your mother out of here."

"Right." Finn cupped Maura's elbow. "Come on. You've done enough."

"I'll see you out." Ben looked determined to make sure that happened.

He followed as Finn led Maura out of the garden. The pall Maura had left behind her stayed.

Looking suddenly exhausted, Horace ran a hand over his face.

Poppy took the tray from him. "I'll take that."

"I can manage," he said with a glare.

"I'm sure you can." Poppy sidestepped him. "But this way we'll have enough cups left for tomorrow."

"Bossy woman." Horace limped along in her wake.

The house smelled of beeswax and aged wood. Mellow sunlight filtered through the paned windows and created patterns on the wooden floors. It filled Poppy with an immediate calm.

Horace stamped to a kitchen chair and sat with a groan. "You wanna watch that one." He jerked his chin to outside. "She's a bitch. Reminds me of my daughter. Never shy to stick her oar in where it's not wanted."

Cursing himself for being all kinds of a fool, Ben drove past Horace's house later that night. Poppy had more crap in her life right now than she knew what to do with, but his dumb head got stuck on their kiss and wouldn't budge.

Arms wrapped around her knees she sat on the top step of the porch.

She looked fine. Sad and pensive, but fine. He should keep going and see her another time. He parked and climbed out his cruiser.

Poppy looked up and smiled, as if she'd known he would come. "Hey."

"Hey." He sat next to her on the step. Her shoulder brushed his. "You okay?"

"No." She shook her head, her cloud of dark hair moving like liquid silk. She smelled of chocolate and kid's bubble bath. Not a scent he'd ever think of as sexy, but it crept beneath his skin on a slow burn.

"She's part of why you left Philly." He took her hand and laced her fingers. He no longer questioned his need to touch her. He just went with it.

Her hand drowned in his. Nails cut short, slight roughened edges from where she worked with them constantly. A real woman's hand. The sort of woman a man could put his faith in.

"Partly." She leaned into him. "She started making these veiled threats about trying to get custody of the boys."

Ben didn't have words for that kind of stupid, so he grunted. Damn woman couldn't seriously think she had any chance of that. "You're a good mother, Poppy. Anyone with half a brain can see that."

"I've been sitting here feeling sorry for myself," Poppy said.

"Yeah?" Bound to happen with all the crap going on in her life. He rested their hands on his thigh.

"I've also been thinking about my mom. She was right about so many things, and I wouldn't see it at the time. I decided to marry Sean and nothing and no-one was going to stop me."

"You were eighteen." He didn't know anyone who made good decisions at that age.

"I know I was young," she said. "But even after that. I knew Sean was messing around right from the beginning. And instead of doing something about it then, I pretended it wasn't happening."

"I know how that is." Ben nodded. The signs had been there for him to see with Tara. He'd chosen to ignore them. Maybe if he'd paid a bit more attention to his wife, she wouldn't have tried to find it outside of their marriage. Who was he kidding? "Doesn't excuse what they did though."

"No, it doesn't. But what I don't get is why I then went on to have another two children with this man who couldn't keep it in his pants." Poppy snuggled closer like she needed his warmth.

Ben put his arm about her and drew her into him. She fit beneath his shoulder like their shapes had been molded for each other. Which got him thinking about other ways they might fit. He should move away and get his head out of his pants. He didn't.

"But now you have Ryan and Sean," he said. "Can't regret that."

"No, I don't." Her hip pressed against his. The curve of her breast brushed his side. "The children are what has made all of this bearable. If not for them, I might have folded into a ball."

He doubted that. Soft and sweet as she was, Poppy's backbone ran pure steel through her. If she made a promise she would stick to it. Like her wedding vows.

"And because of them, I really need to get it together," she said. "I was stupid to pack up like I did and trust in my mother. I put my need to make peace with her above my kid's needs. I'd be truly screwed if it wasn't for you and Dot."

Funny, because he felt like the lucky one. She and the kids had crashed into his life and forced him to move in a different direction. Tara had called him a few times now, and it wasn't coincidence that he'd left those calls unanswered. He didn't need that toxic shit between them in his life. Not when he'd gotten a taste of sweet. His sweet wouldn't last, because Poppy was passing through but at some point he'd decided to take what he could while he could.

Poppy sighed. "What I need is a plan."

Ben tightened his grip. "Well, stay here until you make one."

They sat there in silence as a big, yellow moon rose in the sky.

"Mom!" Brinn yelled from inside the house. "Do I have to take a bath?"

"Every night." Poppy sighed and got to her feet. "We have this argument every night. You would think she'd know the answer by now." Her smile took any sting out of the words. She jabbed her thumb at the house. "I should go."

"Yeah." Ben stood. She should go before he kissed her. Again. She looked all in and he didn't want to rush her into bed with him. And he should go before he ignored all his noble intentions.

"Good night." She closed the door on her beautiful smile.

Leaving Horace's house, Ben made his next stupid decision.

Sydney at the front desk of the Patterson Hotel gave him the right room number and before he could reason himself out of it, Ben pounded on the door.

Finn yanked it open. He quickly covered up his surprise with a smirk. "I'm surprised it took you this long."

"May I?" Ben gestured for Finn to let him into the room.

Finn opened the door wider.

Patterson Hotel had long since drifted into country shabby, but it was clean and they made a good, hearty breakfast, if you weren't too fussed about the state of your arteries. Finn looked like he didn't have much to worry about in that department.

"Just come from Poppy," Ben said. "She's upset."

"Sure she is." Finn nudged the door shut. He snatched up an open beer from the table. "Want one?"

"No." The guy played it cool, standing there watching Ben like he knew something. "Get the feeling your ma has been doing a lot of that."

"I get the feeling you're right." Finn sipped his beer, then dangled it by the neck between two fingers. "Unfortunately, I was not always here to stop it. But I am now."

The challenge rang in the air between them. "And why is that?"

"I care about her." Finn straightened. "My brother was a stupid shit and an even worse husband. He didn't treat her right."

"Is that why you're here?" Ben shifted his weight. Finn was a big guy, and he looked like he knew how to handle himself.

"In part." Finn drained his beer and put the bottle back on the table. "I should have stuck around longer and made sure she was all right."

"Yeah, you should have." But Finn need not get the idea that he could make up for lost time now. "What are you doing here?"

Finn stiffened. "I don't see who you are to ask me that."

Stalemate. Finn returned Ben's stare without flinching.

"If you're telling me there's something between you and Poppy, I could maybe understand this. But"—Finn shrugged—"as it is, I don't see you making any claim on her, and those are my nephews and nieces."

Ben sensed the things Finn didn't say hanging in the air between them. "And?"

"And they need protecting." Finn crossed his arms. "They need somebody who gives a shit what happens to them. Someone to be there for them. Someone in their corner. You that man, Chief Crowe?"

"I'm a friend." Ben's nape prickled. He didn't like where this headed.

"Really?" Finn sneered. "And while you're busy teaching Ryan to throw a football, making nice with their mom, driving the girls all over town—you ever think that maybe they're seeing you as a permanent fixture in their lives?"

Damn. Finn had him there. Ben's gut tightened. He'd seen the look on Ryan's face and had been ducking thinking about consequences.

"Didn't think so." Finn looked smug. "Poppy's a beautiful woman. But when you're looking into those big, brown eyes, you might want to remember she's a package deal."

Chapter 21

As Poppy picked them up from playgroup the girls danced out to her, faces flushed, almost levitating with excitement.

"Say we can go." Brinn pranced from foot to foot. "Just say yes."

Poppy glanced at Peg for an explanation.

"Town Founder's day," Peg said. "We make a bit of a big deal about it. The kids have been making decorations for the dance that night."

Brinn twirled on one foot. "I want to go dancing."

"Dancing." Ciara sighed.

"I don't know." Damn Poppy hated being caught wrongfooted. Kelly, who she relied on for town gossip, hadn't said a word about any Founder's Day.

"They have a parade and everything." Hands clasped under her chin Brinn grew starry-eyed. "We're going to walk in the parade as well. Miss Peg promised."

"Girls, I don't know if we're still going to be here." Someone had to be the voice of reason. Bad luck the role always fell to her.

The light in the twins' eyes dulled.

Ciara dropped her head.

"It's this Saturday." Peg patted her shoulder. "I'm sure you can stay that long. Right?"

Under the death stare of Peg and the combined hopes and dreams of her twins, Poppy caved. "Sure." Where was she rushing off to anyway and

Horace hadn't made any noises about needing to move into his assisted living facility.

Brinn's chatter filled the walk home. What would she wear? Did Poppy think it was a problem that she couldn't dance? Did Poppy think anyone would ask them to dance?

Horace stood at his garden gate. "Poppy."

"Horace."

"Guess what." Brinn flipped her ponytail from side to side.

Horace harrumphed. "I never could."

"We're going to the dance." Brinn threw her hands into the air and twirled. "We're going to dance and dance and dance."

"Is that so?" A rusty smile crept over Horace. "I'm sure you'll be the prettiest girls there."

"Really?" Brinn eyed him suspiciously. "Because Maddison is very pretty, and she's going. She has golden hair like Rapunzel, only not so long."

"Golden hair." Horace rolled his eyes. "Who wants plain old gold hair when you've got hot chocolate hair?"

Brinn giggled and patted her hair. "Uncle Finn says we have a touch of the black Irish."

"Lemonade?" Horace glanced at Poppy. "With strawberries."

Apparently he'd been busy again. She should be doing this for him, but Horace got such a charge out of making things. "And mint?"

"Is there any other kind?" Horace snorted as he opened the gate and ushered them inside.

Plant clippings scattered the pathway.

"You've been hard at work," Poppy said. With his bum hip, gardening must be excruciating. "I could help you with this."

"Why would you do that?" Horace stumped across the clippings.

"I don't know." Poppy suppressed the urge to stick her tongue out at him. "It must be your innate charm."

"I'm not paying you extra," Horace said.

"You're not paying me at all." Poppy put a little spring into her step.

The kitchen was lovely and cool after the noon heat.

"Hello all." Dot arrived with the boys. Her eyes lit up. "Ooh, lemonade. How lovely."

After greeting the boys, Poppy got busy with lunch.

Dot settled herself at the kitchen table with a glass of lemonade.

Out the window Poppy eyed the choked garden that was begging her to break it out of its weed prison. After lunch she might spend an hour or two on that.

"Mom." Ryan finished gulping lemonade and wiped his face with his arm. "After lunch I'm going to throw a football for you. I can throw it forever."

"Nobody can throw that far." Brinn snorted

Glaring at her Ryan said, "I can and I'll show you too. You're a girl, you don't know anything about football."

"I know more than you." Brinn stuck her tongue out. "Mom, tell him girls know as much about football as boys."

Poppy passed around bowls of pasta and placed a platter of fresh veggies within easy reach of the children. Not that she had any great expectation of the carrot sticks going down big with the under ten brigade.

"Oh, veggies." Dot gamely led the way.

Ryan, Ciara and Brinn blinked at her and tucked into their pasta.

Once lunch was finished, and the dishes put away, Horace loped off for a nap, and the rest of them followed Ryan outside, where he insisted he would show them his throwing skills.

Backing away from them, face twisted with concentration, Ryan sent the ball sailing into the air.

Poppy didn't know anything about football but that looked like a good throw to her. It arced through the air and slammed into the neighbor's fence. She clapped and made a fuss.

"Well done." On a blanket in the shade of the quivering aspens Dot clapped from beside Sean and the twins.

Sean barely looked up from driving toy cars along the lines of the quilt. A far cry from the miserable baby, nose streaming, who had clung to her every morning in Philly.

Poppy sat down beside him and earned herself a slobbery grin.

Dot opened her eyes wide and gasped as the twins told her all about the dance. "A dance? Imagine that."

"Yes." Brinn nodded. "And we are going to go and dance."

"Well." Dot cocked her head. "What else would you do at a dance?"

"Oh, Dot." Brinn giggled. "You're so silly."

Ciara sidled up to Dot. "I don't know how to dance."

"Poppet!" Dot cuddled her close. "Of course you know how to dance. Everyone does. And Dot here is going to remind you how it's done." She ducked her head to Ciara's level. "Did you know I'm a champion dancer?"

Ciara shook her head.

"Good because I'm not." Dot chuckled. "But I know enough to show my girls how it's done."

"What will we wear?" Brinn joined Ciara with a frown.

"Girls you have lots of dresses." Not quite true, but Poppy felt sure she could find something in the back of her Uhaul. She was the master of necessity.

Brinn crossed her arms. "No, we don't."

Dot perked up. "Then we'll have—"

"No. Thank you very much, Dot. They have lots of dresses." This was exactly what she knew would happen if the discussion started in front of Dot. Honestly, she loved the hell out of Dot, but any excuse to spoil the children and Dot was there.

Dot raised her brow.

"Seriously, they'll be fine." Poppy put a bright smile on it because Dot had that militant look in her eye.

"What dress will you wear?" Brinn chewed her lip. "You don't have any dresses."

Dot's ears pricked.

"I'll wear my jeans." Poppy smiled. "I'm not really a dress sort of girl anyway. I'll wear jeans and a nice top."

Dot snorted.

Poppy pinned her with a stare. "No."

Dot smirked.

With days full of sunshine and running around in the garden, Poppy welcomed bedtime now. After their dinner and baths, the children went to bed without complaints, and took all of five minutes to fall asleep.

Leaving the twins and Ryan in the kitchen with milk and cookies, she took Sean upstairs to start the bedtime routine. She had him stripped down to his diaper when the doorbell rang.

"Mom?" Brinn yelled up the stairs. "Someone's at the door. Can I get it?"

About to say no, Poppy stopped herself. Already her city living cautiousness had receded. "Check who it is first."

"Okay." Brinn clattered out of the kitchen stomping on the wood floors like she outweighed a sumo wrestler.

Putting Sean on her hip, Poppy moved to the top of the stairs so she could hear better.

"It's a lady." Brinn called up. "Can I let her in?"

"Do you know her?"

"No." Brinn appeared below her and peered up the stairwell. "But she looks like you."

It couldn't be. Could it? Poppy's stomach bottomed out. So many calls and texts but she hadn't been face to face with her mother in years. She joined Brinn in the front hall and opened the door.

Holy crap. It was. "Mom?"

Finally, Poppy understood the idea of getting caught in a timewarp. Looking more like her older sister than her mother, slim as ever, long brown hair halfway down her back, Mom stood on the porch. "Poppy Princess?"

The name made Poppy flinch, too many bad memories associated with it, too many slurred calls from Mom as she entertained a new boyfriend. "Hi, Mom."

"I should have called." Mom fiddled with her purse strap. "I would have called but I wasn't sure what you'd say if I called first."

She looked so uncertain and vulnerable, Poppy melted. "I would have said yes."

"Really?" A smile lit Mom's face. She had a beautiful smile that dared you not to smile back.

"Are you my other grandma?" Brinn stared up at Mom.

Looking down, Mom opened her mouth and shut it again. When she looked at Poppy tears glistened. "They're so big."

"We grow," Brinn said. "We kids grow all the time. Like weeds."

Mom pushed her fingers against her mouth.

"Come in."

Facing each other across the entrance hall, the tick of the grandfather clock loud, Poppy had no idea what to say. When people had history like her and Mom, bitter history, sad history, there was so much that needed saying that getting started seemed impossible.

"Is that Sean?" Mom put her hands halfway up and dropped them again.

Poppy led Sean nearer. "He likes people, he'll let you hold him if you like."

"Really?" Mom wrinkled her nose like an excited girl. "Come on, Sean." She wriggled her fingers. "Come to…Grandma."

Brinn tugged Poppy's shorts. "Is that really my other grandma?" The hope on her face nearly killed Poppy. So far, grandmas hadn't been all that Brinn dreamed they would be.

"Of course I am." Mom touched her cheek, then her head. "Could I have a hug?"

It was hard getting through the bedtime routine with her mother there. The children were fascinated by her, and bedtime ended up being a lot later than usual.

Eventually Poppy turned the twins' light off.

Ciara was out already, and Brinn still fighting a losing battle.

Ryan slept flung across his bed, and in his travel crib, Sean looked like a plump, rosy angel.

In the kitchen, Mom wandered around touching things. She turned when Poppy got back. "All down?"

"Yup." Poppy hunted a bottle of wine, and poured them both a glass. Their conversation might need it. She took the seat opposite Mom. "How are you?"

Looking closer, she saw subtle signs of aging, fine lines around Mom's mouth and eyes. Her mother had always been younger than other people's mothers. And more beautiful, and more in demand by everyone else's dad.

"I'm good." Mom sipped her wine. "I wanted to..." She cleared her throat. "I was worried about you."

The look of challenge on Mom's face almost made Poppy laugh. She looked so fierce as if daring Poppy to refute her statement. Younger Poppy would have used the vulnerability against her. "I'm fine. We're all fine. We're actually more than fine. The people here have been so kind."

"And the house?" Mom stood and touched the surface of the dresser. "This furniture is incredible."

"I think it's mostly original," Poppy said. "Horace lets me stay here in exchange for cooking meals and cleaning for him."

Mom raised her eyebrows. "And you're okay doing that?"

A hot surge of irritation shot through her. Menial tasks had always been beneath Mom. "I got the best part of the deal."

"Yes, of course." Mom cleared her throat. "I didn't mean it like...I'm glad you found somewhere you like."

The awkwardness stretched between them. "It's fine. I do like it here and the children are very happy."

"Great." Mom's smile was a bit too bright. "That's really great."

She moved around the kitchen before coming back to the table. "I can't stay long. It's getting late and I want to get back to that hotel."

The way Mom had said "that hotel" made Poppy glad she'd ended up at Horace's. "Is Jarryd with you."

"Um...no."

All of Poppy's alarm systems triggered. She knew that face. It was the one that meant the latest romance was in trouble. "Everything all right with Jarryd?"

"Not really." Mom surprised her into silence. Normally chirpy declarations and assurances followed. "We haven't broken up so everything with you is still fine but I'm a bit angry at him to be honest."

"Oh?" The honesty thing was new as well.

"You know I've been talking about us going to Europe to find a director?" Bracelets clinked as Mom waved her hand.

"Yes."

"Well, the plan was always for me to go with him. But now he's talking about going on his own." Mom grimaced. "I was so mad I had to get away from him before I said something stupid."

"And you came here."

"I was also worried about you." Mom looked so sincere Poppy believed her. "But the two seemed to fit so neatly together, that's what I did."

Not liking the idea of Mom alone in a crappy hotel Poppy was tempted to invite Mom to stay at the house. But she really did have to clear it with Horace first, and she wanted to take a day or two and see how she got on with this new version of her mother. "I'm glad you came."

"Me too." Mom smiled and sipped her wine. "It seems…quiet here."

"I think it's nice." Poppy kept her defensive mechanism under raps. "It's peaceful here. Calm."

"A little too calm for me." Mom gave a brittle trill of laughter. "I need a lot more action, I'm afraid."

"You probably won't be here long," Poppy said. "My car has to be ready any day now, and I'm sure Jarryd misses you while you're away."

"Maybe." Mom wrinkled her nose. "But I really like him, Poppy." Mom's shoulders drooped. "I mean I really, really like him. Like maybe I love him like him."

"I hope it works out for you." She meant it too. Mom had sounded happier with Jarryd than any of her other boyfriends.

"Well." Mom got to her feet. "It's late and I'm sure the children tire you out."

Poppy followed her to the door. She wanted to say so much, but the words wouldn't come. She didn't know where to start. "Will I see you tomorrow?"

"If that's okay with you?" Mom looked wistful.

"That's more than okay." She pulled Mom into a hug. "I think it's time you got to know your grandchildren."

Ben arrived on time. He'd made a promise and he knew Ryan would be waiting for him to show up.

Sure enough, the kid stood on the sidewalk shifting from one foot to the other, the football clutched beneath one arm.

Ma joined Ryan as Ben parked and climbed out. True to form, she handed Ben a small cooler. "I thought you boys might need some snacks."

"How's our dog?" Ryan peered at Ma.

With a wink, Ma grinned at him. "He missed you and Sean this morning."

"Poppy here?" Ben tried not to sound too eager.

Ma gave him a look. "No, she's gone to have coffee with her mother."

"Mother?"

"Indeed." Ma looked some more. With Ryan rubbernecking the entire conversation he'd have to wait for more details. But he had no doubt he was going to hear it, and there was a lot of hearing to do.

"Are we going now?" Ryan tugged his sleeve.

Ma waggled her fingers. "Have fun. The girls and I will bake some cookies for when you get back."

Ben took Ryan back to Winters Park. As if he'd taken a snapshot of their last visit Dave Mills sat on his regular bench reading the paper. A group of young moms gossiped and drank coffee as they kept an eye on their toddlers. The same boys were kicking a ball around.

Ryan hopped out and stood, staring at the boys.

"Come on." Ben put a hand on his shoulder.

"Morning, Chief." Looking up, Dave nodded. "Who you got there?"

"Dave this is Ryan Williams."

"Poppy's boy?" Dave lowered his paper and stared at Ryan. "You here to play some ball?"

"Yup." Ryan fiddled with the ball. "Ben is teaching me how."

"Whelp!" Dave shook his paper. "You got yourself the best teacher there. Young Ben had one heck of an arm on him when he was a nipper. Ran like he had a coyote on his butt as well."

Ryan giggled and peered up at Ben. "Really?"

"Maybe." Ben said goodbye to Dave and steered Ryan toward the large, open field where the boys were playing.

"Hey, Ben!" Terri Laird waved. "Will we see you at the dance on Saturday?"

Ben nodded.

"I'll be there, too," Ryan said.

Terri winked at him. "Then you be sure to save me a dance."

"Will do." Ryan gave her a jaunty little salute.

They walked past the playground to the field.

"Ben?"

"Yup."

"Why do women like dancing so much?" Ryan glanced at him.

Ben huffed a laughed. Damned if he knew. "They just do. A clever man dances with his lady."

"Why?"

Danger loomed ahead, the sharp rocks and dizzying precipices of talking boys and girls with a six-year old. "You ready to play?"

"Sure am." Ryan bounced. "And afterwards you can tell me more about girls and dancing."

Not freaking likely, and so way above his pay grade. He motioned Ryan to stand back. "Eye on the ball."

"Got it." Face serious, gaze locked on the ball like his life depended on it Ryan braced.

"Hey." Finn strolled up to them. In jeans and a T-shirt, he looked more like the sort of man Ben would have befriended. The kind of easy guy that fit in with Twin Elks like he'd been born here. "Saw you from the window of the hotel."

Ah, yes. Patterson Hotel was one of a row of original town buildings facing the park.

"Uncle Finn," Ryan yelled. "I'm over here. Ben and I are going to play ball. You wanna play?"

Finn glanced at him.

Ben shrugged. Free park, free country.

"Sure." Finn trotted into position. "Show me what you got, bud."

Ben looped a ball to Ryan.

Ryan snatched it out of the air, turned and torpedoed it at Finn.

It hit Finn in the chest and he only managed to get his hands around it. "Holy shi—hell!"

Totally childish, but Ben enjoyed the look of surprise on Finn's face.

Finn tossed him the ball.

Ben caught it and sent it back to Ryan.

This time Finn took a good five strides back before Ryan fired another spiral his way.

Finn looked at him, and mouthed, "Damn."

Ben could only nod, because damn about covered it. Ryan had a cannon of an arm on him.

"Hey, Chief Crowe." Tyler Frankel, and his posse of ball playing kids, stood next to him. "Are you playing with him?"

"Yep." Ben caught and tossed the ball back to Ryan.

This throw went wide of Finn, but Finn back-pedaled, leaped and grabbed it out of the air. Uncle Finn had some moves as well.

"We could play." Tyler watched him take the catch.

The posse nodded.

"Here." Ben handed the ball to Tyler.

Tyler threw the ball to Ryan. Kid had nothing on Ryan.

The posse fanned out across the play area.

Finn took another catch from Ryan and handed the ball to a kid by his side.

Ben stepped back and watched the magic happen.

Ryan tossed to Tyler, who dropped the catch.

"You can throw." Tyler blew on his palms and shook them. "Cool your jets." Tyler glanced at Finn. "What's his name?"

"Ryan."

At a nearby bench Finn joined Ben nodding to the playing boys. "That's a good thing you did there."

Ben grunted, because no doubt Ryan needed to spend more time with boys his age.

"Poppy did her best." Finn stretched his legs out. "But my brother didn't give her any help."

"Why was that?" Ben didn't know if Finn would even reply, but he didn't like asking Poppy about her husband. He hated that look she got in her beautiful brown eyes—kind of empty.

"Spoiled," Finn said. "Sean was a spoiled son of a bitch who never gave a crap about anyone but himself."

Ben nodded because he had a brother like that.

"I loved him." Finn leaned his elbows to his knees. "I miss him like hell, but my brother had a lot of growing up to do."

Ben sensed more to the story.

"Shit always came easy to Sean." Finn said, lacing his fingers together. "He was a sickly kid and my mom tended to baby him. He sure as hell wasn't ready to step up and be the sort of husband and father Poppy needed."

The boys had stopped tossing the ball and were now doing a sort of running tackle game that involved a lot of high-pitched yelling.

Ryan's face glowed.

"Mark, my second youngest brother is like that." It seemed right to share back. Finn's pain and anger sat in the taut lines of his shoulders. "Big shot hockey player now."

"Yeah?" Finn glanced at him.

"Everything always came easy to Mark. He's never had to step up, so he doesn't."

Finn shook his head. "How many brothers?"

"Five of us."

Finn raised his eyebrows. "You the oldest?"

"Yup."

"The responsible one." Finn gave a dry chuckle. "Curse of the oldest child."

Curse maybe, but Ben wouldn't have it any other way.

Chapter 22

Poppy had a devil of a job holding Brinn still long enough to brush her hair. Both girls vibrated with excitement as she got them ready for the Founder's Day Parade. They'd never been part of an event like this. Just another thing her children had never had.

Dot corralled Ciara and managed to tie yellow ribbons around her ponytails. They each wore a bright yellow T-shirt with a big smiley face on the front. Brinn paired it with an orange floral skirt that she wouldn't be talked out of. More sedate, Ciara had opted for a pair of denim shorts.

Even Sean had caught the excitement in the air, and bounced on his diapered butt.

Ryan ran up and down the passage giving them a running time check.

The girls needed dropping off before the parade started. Poppy had volunteered to help with all the children. A decision she already regretted. If her four were this excited, God alone knew what would be happening at the gathering point.

"Why can't I join in the parade?" Ryan asked for what must be the hundredth time.

"Because you didn't want to be a part of the play group." Brinn smirked at him. "You didn't want to come and now you can't parade."

Ryan's lip pushed out. "That's not fair."

"It totally is." Brinn tossed her ponytails about. "Tell him, Mom."

"You will watch the parade with Dot and grandma Maura." Poppy dodged the issue altogether and then played her trump card. "And Uncle Finn."

"Uncle Finn's coming?" Ryan perked right up.

"Where else would he be?" Dot ruffled his hair. "Now go and put your shoes on."

With Dot's help, getting children ready to go out no longer seemed such a daunting task.

Ben would be working. The whole of the Twin Elks police force worked on festival days. Ben had even gotten four additional officers from the county sheriff to bolster his force. Dot told her that on festival days the level of drinking rose right along with the stupidity level. Of course, most people in town knew who to keep an eye on, but Ben always played it safe. Last year one of the Gresham boys had decided it would be a good idea to add their ATVs to the parade, which would have been fine if they hadn't also thought to throw firecrackers into the crowd.

Finally they got all four kids loaded in Poppy's newly fixed van. God knew how they'd gotten the stench out, but it smelled nearly new. The engine purred to life. It had never sounded this good, and she needed to call for the invoice. Doug had waved her off with some story of not being up to date on his paperwork.

At the gathering point on the high school football field, Peg had things well in hand. Standing with her clipboard in one arm, and a whistle around her neck, she herded kids, their parents and anyone else who got close enough, in the right direction.

"Poppy!" She boomed. "Glad to see you. Gather up the yellows would you."

Poppy gathered as many yellow T-shirted little bodies as she could find.

"I'll see you after." Dot took Sean from her and guided Ryan ahead of her with promises of something sugary and not normally allowed. "Have fun."

Fun? Maybe not, but it made her feel like a real mother to do things like this with her children. More like all those TV commercial mothers and less like her rolling train-wreck of a reality. To one side, the high school band drowned out all conversation as they warmed up. Finally they got all the yellows with the yellows, the greens with the greens and the blues with the blues. Except for Maddison, who was a blue but insisted she wanted to walk with Ciara and Brinn. Even Peg decided to count it as a win and the parade set forth.

As parades went, Macy's organizers had nothing to worry about, but it seemed like the entire town turned out to wave them on. Twin Elk High presented their prom king and queen on the back of a hot pink convertible. The elementary school had kids dressed in Founder's day outfits, interspersed with Batmen, Spidermen, Captain Americas and a good sprinkling of fairies and princesses. The high school marching band did a fairly good job of keeping the tunes recognizable. The fire department dropped in behind, lights flashing from their three fire trucks. Then came the brightly colored floats of the Lions Club, local businesses, and the 4H club on horses.

In the middle of the yellows, Brinn waved to the crowd like visiting royalty. Ciara bobbed along next to her, smiling shyly at the cheering crowds.

On the sidelines, Dot had Sean in her arms. Ryan sat on Finn's shoulders. Even Maura cracked a smile as they passed.

Poppy teared up and then felt all kinds of stupid. People took stuff like this so for granted. Little slices of happy and normal that her kids didn't have enough of.

Mom stood next to a beautifully dressed, handsome man and gave the girls a jaunty wave.

Her companion never looked up from his phone. Not even when the fire trucks whooped their sirens. That must be Jarryd. A ten second sighting of him already had Poppy's hackles up. The look of perpetual boredom on his face made her want to smack it off for him. Yeah, the parade was hokey and small town but it had a definite charm as well, if you unbent enough to go with it.

Poppy shook off her irritation. God knows when she would get to spend another day like this one. She wasn't about to waste it on Jarryd and his cynicism. Besides which, Jarryd had agreed to having her and the children in his house while he and Mom went to Europe. She downgraded him from jerk to aloof.

Ben passed her a couple of times, looking solid, dependable and ridiculously handsome in his uniform. On one of his passes, he caught her eye and winked.

Poppy wanted to giggle like a girl. Already she recognized more faces in the crowd than she'd known on her block in Philly.

Horace stood on his own, leaning on his cane and scowling. He gave the girls a little finger salute as they called out to him.

Kelly stood with her mother and her brother and yelled out Poppy's name.

Neighbors, people who came into the coffee shop, moms from playgroup, and members of the Twin Elk prayer chain, all met her eye and waved and smiled.

The parade wound through town and ended at Winters Park. Local businesses had set up stalls in one area, alongside residents who had a dizzying variety of talents from glassblowing to baking and everything in between.

Dot and Sean already had a picnic table waiting for them. They ate sandwiches and brownies under a bright summer sky. The air filled with mingled scents of barbeque, sun block, cotton candy, and popcorn. Kelly joined their picnic with her family. Horace drifted past, got chatting with Dot and ended up staying for the entire day.

By the time Poppy loaded the children into her van at the end of the day, they were all feeling as tired and hot as Sean. Home for a nap.

Getting a cranky Sean out the car and down for a nap took the patience of both Poppy and Dot. The twins collapsed in front of the Disney channel. Ryan gave it a valiant effort but fell asleep on the couch halfway through the first show.

A shower and a half hour with a book loomed in Poppy's future.

Dot followed her down the hall toward her bedroom. "Um...Poppy? About tonight?"

Did Dot want to stay in? The woman was amazing the way she took care of the kids all the time but it had to get tiring for her.

Shifting from foot to foot, Dot blinked at her. "Now don't be mad."

"I won't be mad." How could she ever be mad at Dot? Then again, not many good surprises started with those words either.

"You know we were talking about the dance?" Dot plucked at her *If You Think The Police Chief's Tough, You Should Meet His Mother* T-shirt.

Poppy did the Ben thing and waited.

Tilting her head, Dot avoided making eye contact. "Well, I got to thinking that it must be a long time since you've been able to get prettied up and go out."

It had been a long time. The sort of long time that got too depressing to sit down and calculate. "Yes."

"And you're such a pretty girl, I couldn't see you go off in a horrible dress, or another pair of jeans that are too big for you."

And she knew exactly what Dot had done. "You got me something to wear. Something pretty."

"Not that I thought there was anything wrong with what you normally wear." Dot held her hands up like she could fend off any mad from Poppy.

Only Poppy wasn't feeling mad. Embarrassed, a bit, because nobody liked looking like such a pauper the neighbors pitied you. Guilty because she didn't want Dot spending her money on her. But over and above that, Poppy felt like she wanted to hug Dot and keep on hugging. Whatever Dot did was motivated by her immense kindness, and she had given Poppy so much more than a dress. She'd given her permission to be a woman again. It took her a moment to get past the lump in her throat. "You got me something to wear."

"I did." Dot squared off. "And I know you said I mustn't and you didn't need anything, but I don't care." She tossed her head. "I like you, and I want you to go out tonight and have fun. Dance with a handsome man, maybe have one or two glasses too many. In fact, I insist on it."

"You gave me my Cinderella moment." Poppy wanted to crumple into a bawling heap. Too pregnant and too miserable to want to party with kids her age she hadn't gone to her prom. Her wedding had been a quick affair at the Williams' house. She'd worn a dress of her mothers and fought nausea throughout the ceremony. Talk about your omens.

"Don't cry." Dot leaped forward and wrapped her arms around Poppy. "It's nothing fancy or anything, just a pretty dress. And maybe some shoes."

The familiar Dot scents of honey and vanilla wrapped around her. When had Poppy last felt pretty? God, she couldn't remember. Sean had hooked up with his first extracurricular months after the twins were born. Still struggling with the baby weight, Poppy had somehow convinced herself that it was her fault. Then Ryan came along shortly after, and Sean had disappeared more and more from their lives with each passing day. A last ditch effort had given her baby Sean. Between Sean's traveling and other women, the woman in Poppy had gone into hiding.

Not since eighteen had Poppy felt pretty. She didn't even know if she had it in her anymore. Pretty involved more than a dress and some shoes, it was an attitude. Pretty girls carried themselves differently, spoke with confidence, walked like they knew people admired them. Could she be that girl again?

"Sweetie." Dot smoothed her hair back. "It's just a dress."

"N-no it isn't." Poppy tried to get it together but it was an epic fail as a new stormfront blew in. "It's about so much more than a dress."

Dot cuddled her. "It always is, darling. It always is."

Chapter 23

Feeling as shy as a freshman at her first homecoming, Poppy, with Dot's help, herded the children into the barn-like town hall where the dance was being held. Brinn pranced around like a show pony in her dress. Even Ciara looked smug about her new jeans and pretty shirt.

Ryan, as always, wanted to be where the action was. "Do you think Nathan will be there?"

"I'm not sure." He'd been firing names at her since they left the house and Poppy struggled through the blur of faces that made up the group of boys Ryan had played with at the park.

"I think there's a good chance," Dot said, smoothing his cowlick back. "Nathan's parents always come."

"What about Tyler?" Ryan scrutinized Dot.

"I can't say I know any Tyler." Dot got him by the shoulder and steered him into the hall.

"Tyler," Ryan said it louder this time. "You know Tyler. He has brown hair, and he likes Batman."

Dot gave it some thought. "Brown hair and batman?"

"Uh-huh." Ryan nodded. "And he is about so tall."

"Batman, brown hair and a little taller than you?" Dot spoke fluent boy.

Brinn slipped her hand into Poppy's. "You look pretty, Mom." She examined Poppy from head to toe. "You're going to be the prettiest mom there."

She'd settle for a girl who looked nice. "Thank you, darling. You look pretty too."

"I know." Brinn nodded. "I brushed my hair again and again to make it shine. I brushed Ciara's too."

Not happy about being confined, Sean squirmed in his stroller.

"Uh-uh, Sean." Ciara wagged a finger at him. She pushed the stroller into the hall.

Someone—Poppy suspected Peg—had transformed the hall with balloons and streamers. Colored lights lit a dance floor already filled with people, young and old.

Brinn grabbed Ciara and ran for the action.

Poppy went after them, but Dot stopped her. "They'll be fine. Everyone knows who they are."

Brinn joined a group of girls their age and tugged Ciara into the group. Her girls were busting moves over there. Their sheer joy in dancing beamed out of them as they went at it with a lot more enthusiasm than skill.

She waved to a few familiar faces. Across the dance floor, talking to a man who had his back to her, was Ben. Dressed in jeans and a white button down he gave her a whole other reason to feel shy. Good Lord, that man had it going on with his long legs and spectacular ass.

He looked around suddenly, caught her eye and froze. An appreciative grin spread across his face.

As far as Cinderella moments went, Ben played his role like a champion.

Poppy smiled. Okay, she might have put a tiny hair toss in it. When a girl wore a red halter dress that flirted above her knees, and heels that made her legs look long, hair tossing kind of went with the territory.

Ben raised his brow. Challenge accepted. His gaze roamed her from head to toe, and back up again. Across the room he gave off enough heat to melt her joints.

"Oh, my." Dot giggled. "That went better than expected."

God. Dot had watched her eye-hump her son. Ew! Poppy jerked her attention away from Ben.

"Evening, Dot. Poppy." Doc Cooper looked dapper this evening in a sports jacket and pressed pants, hair neatly combed.

"You look dashing, Coop." Dot smoothed Doc's lapel.

From five feet closer now, Ben watched Poppy, his gaze hot and hungry.

Doc went pink and cleared his throat. "I've never seen two prettier girls."

Locked in Ben's dark, sensuous gaze Poppy let them chat.

Dot nudged her. "Coop and I are going to dance."

"Fine." Suddenly she was alone.

Ben stalked across the remaining distance. He took her hand and looked his fill. "Poppy."

The way he loaded her name with all he hadn't said sent a shiver down Poppy's spine.

He drew her forward to the dance floor. Pressing a hand to her spine he took her other hand in his.

Warm, hard and strong, Ben pulled her closer and Poppy's head spun. And he really knew what he was doing around a dance floor. Evading a middle-aged couple, he steered her into the open.

"Dancing lessons." He grinned. "Ma insisted."

"Dot did well." Poppy relaxed into his effortless lead.

Ben spun her out and drew her back against his big, warm body. His breath stirred her hair. "You look beautiful."

"Thank you." She didn't want to question it, so she relaxed into it. Things could get a lot worse than dancing with a handsome man who made your heart skip a beat.

In Ben's arms she wasn't the responsible Poppy, the worried Poppy, the always one step behind life Poppy. Her skirt flared each time he twirled her. She was just a pretty girl in a red dress dancing with a man she really, really liked.

The music changed pace, and Ben slowed their steps. He drew her closer to him.

Poppy rested her head against his shoulder.

His arm tightened about her back, his grip on her fingers enfolded her hand.

She had no idea what the song was. Everything in her focused on Ben. God, to stay like this forever…

Ben's breakfast was interrupted by his ex-wife pounding the door. Because she'd developed the habit of letting herself into his house he'd changed the locks a couple of months after she moved out. Originally, he'd bought the land on some dream of building a family home for him and Tara and their kids, and much later their grandkids to enjoy the beautiful hikes all around them.

Pity Tara thought his dream sucked.

After his divorce, he'd moved out of their condo and into the cabin on his land. It wasn't much, but then he didn't need a whole helluva lot.

"Are you going to let me in?" Tara peered at him and did some dumb eyelash thing that used to make him go all horndog. It had worked a treat when he was eighteen. The sort of look you learned to dread when you lived with Tara every day, because it sure as shit meant she wanted something.

Ben threw the door wide.

She slipped past him in a heavy waft of spice. Poppy smelled of kids and flowers, fresh, light and real. Tara smelled like trouble, and he had an inkling of what this was about. He'd pretty much taken a bullhorn and announced his interest by dancing with Poppy last night.

"Great, coffee." Tara helped herself, and looked around. "Are you ever going to do something with this dump?"

He poured himself a cup of coffee and waited.

"I don't understand how you live like this," she said.

No, she didn't and Ben wasn't going to waste his breath trying to make her. She made his space feel tainted.

"So." Tara dabbed the corners of her mouth with her thumb. "I hear you put on quite the show last night."

Was he clairvoyant or what? At this point his contribution to the conversation was mute, so he shrugged.

Tara glanced at him. "I hear your new friend made quite a splash in her red dress."

Splash? Nah, that was Tara's territory, but Poppy had looked beautiful enough to make any man sit up and take notice. And they had noticed. All around the barn last night, masculine glances had tracked Poppy.

"Ben." Tara clanked her mug onto the counter. "Are you going to give me a hand here? I'm trying to have a conversation with you."

"I'm not sure what you're doing, Tara," he said. He knew for damn sure he didn't want this conversation.

"I want to know about her. Poppy." She screwed up her mouth as if the name tasted bitter. "Everyone says you have a thing for her."

"Huh." Yeah he had a thing for her. A thing that grew each time he saw her. His inner schoolboy snickered.

"Well?"

"Well what?"

"Do you?" Tara clinked her fingernails on her mug. "Do you have a thing for this Poppy?"

"I don't see how that's any of your business."

Tara gaped. Making a visible effort to get her shit together she snapped her mouth shut and picked up her coffee. "It is as long as you're sleeping with me."

"Was." He made sure to state the word clearly. "Was sleeping with you. That hasn't happened in a long while now."

"Not since she came to town anyway."

And a little while before then, but he knew better than to point it out. Tara would launch off in another direction if he gave her the chance. He wanted this conversation over. Now.

Tara ducked her head and examined her fingernails. "Are you sleeping with her?"

No way he intended to answer that. "We're done here."

He took her cup and put it in the sink.

"Ben!" All angry eyes and flushed cheeks Tara glared at him. "I have a right to know."

"No, you really don't." He motioned toward the door. Today's plans did not include his ex-wife.

"This is because of Dave, isn't it?"

Dave? Oh, that Dave. The man she'd been fucking while he was on a tour of duty. "This has nothing to do with him." He gave her shoulder a gentle nudge toward the door. "And nothing to do with you either."

"So that's it. Just like that." Tears filled Tara's eyes. "After all this time. After all we've been through. We're done."

"Tara." He took a deep breath and tried to make it as gentle as he could. "We've been done ever since you climbed into another man's bed. We've been using each other for convenience. I never asked you for exclusive, and we both know you haven't been."

"I never—"

"Tara."

She dropped her gaze.

He didn't need her protestations of innocence, because they really didn't matter to him.

"I'm sorry." She pushed away from the counter. "How many times do you want me to say I'm sorry?"

He so couldn't have this conversation again. It's not that he'd suddenly discovered forgiveness. He simply didn't care anymore. Whatever happened from here, he'd finally cut those nasty tendrils.

"You'll regret this, Ben Crowe." She stalked away from him. With the door held open, she whirled. "When she leaves, don't think you can come crawling to me and I'll take you back. You go this time, you stay gone."

Ben sipped his coffee. "Fair enough."

Poppy slept late the next morning. Tired from their night out, the kids all slept in. She stumbled into an empty kitchen sometime around eight, and put the coffee on. She welcomed the quiet, and a few moments to live through last night again.

Ben had danced one song after the other with her, until Finn had cut in. Twin Elks would no doubt be buzzing this morning. She'd spent the rest of the evening with Dot, and Kelly joined them. Still, the chord between her and Ben remained taut. Wherever he moved in the room, she sensed him. She had only to look up, and he had been watching her.

Things had gotten complicated. Poppy poured herself a cup of coffee. Outside a beautiful day lit up Twin Elks. Clear blue skies over a rich canopy of green invited her to come and play. It had been too long since she had played. But the look in Ben's eyes promised a very grown-up sort of game. A game she'd almost forgotten how to play. She sipped her coffee. Did the parts all still work after four children?

The bigger question, was it irresponsible for her to want to take something for herself?

Yeah, she'd heard the motivational speakers same as everyone else, but it got a little harder to apply those things in real life. She and the kids would leave Twin Elks for California soon. When Mom got Jarryd to see the Europe thing her way—and she had no doubt Mom would—Poppy was out of excuses to stay.

Did she really need one? Living in Twin Elks was peaceful. Warm.

A jogger padded down the street. Poppy recognized him from Kelly's coffee shop—regular coffee, two creams and no sugar.

Finn's rental car pulled up outside the house and Finn climbed out.

Poppy breathed a sign of relief when Maura didn't.

Finn spotted her standing in the kitchen and waved as he jogged up the walkway. "Hey."

"Hey, yourself." Although Sean had been the better-looking brother, he'd never had much of the magnetism Finn radiated.

His serious face split into a smile. "Is that coffee?"

"It sure is." Poppy got him a mug and poured for him. Like Ben, Finn took his coffee straight with no frills and no fuss. She put it down in front of him.

"Did you have fun last night?" Finn took a cautious sip.

"I did." Poppy couldn't stop the smile that crept over her face. "And the kids had a great time too."

"It's okay, Poppy." Finn studied her. "You're allowed to have a good time."

"I know that." His perception made her squirm.

Finn lifted his brow.

"Okay, maybe I don't know that. I have this idea that if I take my eye off the kids for a minute something awful will happen." She turned away from his keen gaze.

"That's inevitable." He joined her at the window. "Sean left everything in your hands, and now that he's dead..." Finn shrugged. "Actually, that's kind of what I want to talk to you about."

"Sean?"

Finn tended not to talk too much about his younger brother. He and Sean had tangled in a couple of knock-down, drag outs, often about Sean's treatment of her and the kids.

"Sort of." Finn motioned the table. "Do you think we could talk? Alone."

"Sure," Poppy said. Finn always looked serious, but he looked a bit extra serious this morning as he turned his mug in rings on the table.

"The kids might wake up soon," Poppy said.

"Yeah." Finn straightened. "Best thing to do is sac up and get this done." He glanced at her. "Do you think you could sit down?"

"Sure." Poppy perched on the edge of her seat. Finn's mood made her jumpy.

"So, things with Sean, they weren't great. For you." Finn cleared his throat. "Actually Sean screwed up as far as you and the kids went. Mom didn't help with the way she let him get away with everything. First off, I want you to know how sorry I am that I didn't hang around and do more for you."

The exact opposite of his younger brother. Poppy caught Finn's hand across the table and squeezed it. "You weren't married to me. I wasn't your responsibility."

"Then." Finn almost barked the word. "I wasn't married to you. Then." He shoved back his chair and stood.

Poppy didn't know what to say. She refreshed her coffee, because she had the feeling she might need it.

"I'm screwing this up." Finn rubbed his hair. "The thing is, Poppy, I would like to be there for you now."

That meant more than she could say. The children loved him and Finn's calm sensible manner kept them grounded. "And you will be."

"Not as much as I could be." Finn strode closer to her. "Listen. Just hear me out before you say anything. Can you do that?"

She got the sense that whatever he said was pretty much going to render her mute anyway, so she nodded.

"I want to take care of you. You and the children. They're my blood and it's not right that you have to struggle like you do to get by. I can change all that."

"We do fine." Please don't let this be a lecture on child rearing. So far, Finn had been on her team.

"I know you do." He gripped her hands. "You need someone to share the burden with you. To be there through the good times, the school concerts, all of that. I can be that person, Poppy."

"Wha...?"

"I can be that man for you. And I want to be."

Poppy's spine crumpled under the weight of his inference. She slumped in her chair and stared at him. "What are you saying?"

"I'm saying that I think we should get married." Finn cleared his throat.

Okay. She couldn't have heard that right.

"I know you don't love me." Finn crouched at her feet. "And it may damage my chances but I'm not in love with you either. But you're a good woman, a great mom. You're beautiful and funny and so capable you scare the crap out of me sometimes. I like you, Poppy. I respect you. Marriages have been built on less than that."

She opened her mouth and shut it again. The words rioting around her head refused to stay in an order that would come out of her mouth comprehensibly.

"I know this has probably taken you by surprise."

Poppy laughed because talk about your understatements. "Why would you want to marry me?"

"I'm never going to get married otherwise." Finn stood and stared out the window. "Love and marriage are not for me. But I love the kids, and I can give them a good home. Give me a bit of time and I think I can make you happy too. Happier than you are right now."

That wouldn't be too hard. Other than these last weeks, when happy had kind of snuck up on her. "Finn you can't mean any of this."

"But I do." He leaned his hips against the sink. "I'm not a rich man, but I make good money. Enough for the kids to have everything they need, and maybe a little bit of what they want on top of that. As for the sex thing, we could take that slowly and see what happened."

Poppy studied Finn. Really studied him as a woman studies a man. She'd never been blind to that smoking hot body. Not as handsome as Sean but still a very attractive man. Except, she did not have those feelings for him. "Finn." She picked her words carefully. "I don't—"

"Don't answer right now." He shoved his hands into his pockets. "Give it some thought and you'll see that it's not as crazy as it seems. I already love Sean's kids as if they were mine. You and I get along. We have the same values. We could make a go of it."

The thing is, it wasn't the craziest idea Poppy had ever heard. Certainly made more sense than two eighteen-year olds trying to make a go of it as parents when one of them hadn't even finished high school.

Poppy closed the distance between her and Finn. Her head barely reached his shoulder. Cupping his cheeks she really studied him. Black Irish all the way through with those incredible blue eyes in his chiseled face. God, the man sold himself short. "Finn," she said. "You are one of the best men I know. I don't know that many. Two by last count. What do you want to marry a widow with four children for? Especially a widow you don't love."

"I love you, Poppy." Bless him, but he managed to keep eye contact through that.

"You love me like a brother does, Finn." Beneath her palms, his jaw clenched. A wicked light lit his eyes.

"I dunno, sweetheart." A crooked, too-charming smile crept over his face. "There was nothing fraternal about seeing you in your red dress last night." His arms came around her and tugged her flush with him. "Look, I know you think this is crazy and you're probably right about that. But think about it, and know that if all else fails I'm your backup."

"Finn." She didn't know whether to shake him or hug him. "You're nobody's backup plan."

"Am I interrupting?" Ben stood in the kitchen doorway.

Poppy jumped out of Finn's hold.

Finn tightened his grip on her hips and kept her there. "Hey, Ben."

Ben glared at Finn.

Finn raised a brow.

Poppy swore she heard swords and armor smashing together.

"Okay." Using Finn's chest as leverage she shoved herself free. "Finn just came around to talk to me."

Ben cocked his head. "Talk?" He bent down and dropped something on the porch outside the door then strode away.

Poppy went after him.

Sean's cry stopped her at the kitchen door. She hesitated and lost her opportunity as Ben climbed into his car and drove off.

Dammit. Finn could have corrected Ben's assumption, gone to get Sean, whatever. Instead he stood with his hips against the sink and smirked.

"What?" She stomped past him to get Sean.

"You know what." Finn trailed her. "What are you doing with Ben, Poppy?"

"I'm not doing anything with Ben." Not anymore anyway. The look on Ben's face had carved itself across her mind. You had to know it to spot it because Ben played his emotion closer than a tick. She'd hurt him. Fuck! Her mind did a reflexive, watch-the-kids recoil at the swearing.

Cheeks flushed with indignation, arm stretched out, Sean stood in his crib.

Poppy cuddled him awake.

Finn propped his shoulder against the doorjamb.

Sean needed a diaper change, and by the look on Finn's face he'd caught a whiff of the problem.

"This is the reality of kids." It was a bit petty, but he could have let her go before Ben got the wrong idea. "It's not all picnics and trips to the park."

He shoved his hands in his pockets. "I know that, sweetheart."

Finn wasn't the problem here. Taking a deep breath Poppy let her irritation go. She needed to sort this out with Ben because they couldn't keep going on like this. Someone was going to get hurt. "Do you want to stay for breakfast?"

"Sure." He smiled and pointed at Sean. "Want me to handle that."

For an evil moment she almost let him do it. "No, that's fine. Why don't you go and see if you can get the others up?"

About the time the food hit the table Horace stomped into the kitchen. "What's on the porch?"

"I don't know." Poppy tried to peek around the doorjamb and ladle eggs onto Horace's plate at the same time.

"Hey!" Horace righted the pan in her hand.

"Sorry." Poppy gave up on the thing Ben had left and carried on with breakfast.

Finn stayed for breakfast and left shortly after Horace.

Poppy settled Ryan with his Legos. The twins headed outside to hold a fairy tea party.

"Did I miss breakfast?" A tired and rumpled Dot ambled into the kitchen. "Darn."

Poppy poured her a cup of coffee. "I can make you some eggs if you like."

Dot shuddered. "No, thank you. The coffee will be fine." She took a fortifying sip and then sighed happily. "Did I see Finn here earlier?"

"Yup." Despite knowing how crazy Finn's idea was, and it really was, some part of her could see the appeal. With a man like Finn she would never have to worry about so many of the things that kept her up at night. He would make sure food hit the table, shoes found their way onto little feet, and he would be there for her in ways Sean had never been. But he didn't love her and she didn't love him. Did a single mother of four really have the option of not settling?

"That's a big sigh," Dot said.

Busted. Poppy tried not to look guilty.

Sean wriggled and Dot put him down with some plastic cups and a bowl to bang. He got right down to it.

The desire to talk it out overcame her. Poppy poured them both a coffee and took the seat opposite Poppy. "Finn came by to talk to me about something."

"Did that something have to do with Ben?" Dot's gaze fastened on her.

As sweet as she was, not much slid past Dot. "Sort of."

"Tell me."

"Finn asked me to marry him."

Dot sucked in her breath. "Wow." She took a sip of her coffee and replaced the cup carefully on the table. "What did you say?"

"I said no." Because there really shouldn't be any other answer. But Poppy couldn't ignore the small part of her that was so goddamn tired of the day-to-day struggle. Here in Twin Elks it had gotten too easy to ignore the everyday reality of her life, but she really couldn't afford to do that. "He doesn't love me. Or at least, he's not in love with me. But he says he will take care of the kids and me."

"I'm sure he would." Dot fiddled with her cup. She shot to her feet. "I get it, sweetie, I really do," she said. "You have four children and they're all you think about day in, day out. My husband was a good man but he wasn't the sort of dad you see these days." She paced the length of the kitchen, grabbed up some sugar and thumped it down on the table.

Poppy ducked out of Dot's path.

"He never did school pick-ups, took the kids out for the day without me, all those sort of bonding things you see dads doing today. He was always there for birthdays, sports days and special occasions, but child rearing fell very much on my shoulders. Tim provided, and he did it well."

The sort of father Poppy had imagined as a child. Gruff, but loving, and a solid dependable figure in her life.

"Finn would provide," Dot said. "And he would do a great job of it. I've watched him since they arrived. He's the responsible kind. If he said he would marry you and take care of you and the kids, then that's what he would do. But here's the thing, Poppy." Dot grabbed a cleaning cloth and attacked the table. "Marriage is hard. I don't have to tell you that. No matter how in love you are going in, it's tough and it tests you in ways you can't imagine. You know this."

Poppy nodded. When she'd married Sean, she'd been pregnant and scared, but also so dazzled by the handsome, sweet-talking boy who had gotten her that way. She'd had some girlish notion that once the ring slid on her finger the happily ever after part would take care of itself.

"Answer me this." Dot shook with the force of her table cleaning. "Why are you going to California?"

"Mom has—"

"More than that." Dot brandished the sponge at her. "Why are you really going?"

"To give us all a better life."

"Exactly." Dot slammed the sponge into the sink. "You want something different for you and those great kids of yours."

"But I'm not naive enough to think it's going to be easy." California couldn't solve all her problems. Geography could only do so much, and she had to build their new life herself.

"And a man like Finn could make that all go away." Dot snatched up a spray bottle and got going on the countertops. "He could be the answer to all your problems. But think ten years down the line, Poppy. Think about getting into bed every night with that man. Imagine what it's going to be like when you have a fight about something one of the kids does, or because you're late on the mortgage payment. What then? Is there enough between you to carry you through that? Because that's life."

"I said no to him." Poppy winced at the sullen tone in her voice.

"But you're still giving it serious thought." Dot pinned her with a no-bullshit stare. "You're looking at it and seeing it as a way to make the bad thing go away. And it might, but it might make the bad thing even worse."

Poppy deflated. She had no business even considering Finn's offer. "You're right."

"Just think about what I've said." Dot took her hands between her wet, soapy ones. "If you still decide that marrying Finn is what you want to do, I'll support you."

Except, Dot wouldn't be around forever. In fact, Dot would probably not be around come the end of the week because it was time to move on.

Dot bustled around her kitchen. "Was Ben by earlier?"

"Um, yes. He came by when Finn was here." No way she would tell Dot how that had gone down.

"It thought I recognized the old picnic basket I used to use with the boys," Dot said.

The thing Ben had put down on the porch earlier. Ben had brought the picnic basket, which could only mean he meant for them to share it together.

Poppy went onto the porch and flipped open the basket. A picnic for two complete with a bottle of wine and glasses. Damn! For two. He'd come around to take her on a picnic and found her cuddling Finn in the kitchen. Ben had even remembered her favorite cookies. Poppy packed things back in the basket. She needed to find him.

"Dot, do you think you could watch the children for a bit."

Dot grinned and winked. "All day if you need it. Go."

Chapter 24

Poppy relied on her GPS to find Ben's house. Typical of Ben, he lived a few miles past the edge of town. Ben valued his privacy so much she checked the GPS constantly to make sure the rutted road she was on was the right one.

She stopped the car outside a neat wood cabin. Fronted by trees, the cabin faced a breathtaking view of the low-lying south range.

Ben appeared in the door and stood there doing his looking thing.

Poppy hopped out of her car. "Hi." Her voice came out all peppy and silly. Not the best start. She opened the back and wrestled the basket out. "I found this on the porch."

Striding toward her Ben nodded then took the heavy basket out of her hands.

Not knowing what else to do, she followed him to his front door.

He disappeared inside with the basket.

Poppy entered and shut the door behind her.

The cabin was simple and rustic with only the most basic furniture. The view out the back took her breath away. Soaring tree dotted crags dissected a lavish blue sky. Ben had his own small slice of heaven in his house.

Standing there, she had no idea what to say and Ben's silent presence nagged at her.

Of course Ben didn't help much. He placed the basket in the kitchen and stood there. Looking.

Go big or go home. Poppy took a deep breath. "You brought that by this morning."

Ben nodded.

"You were thinking we could go on a picnic? You and I?"

Ben crossed his arms.

"The thing is. I would really have liked that." If he spoke occasionally this would be so much easier. "I didn't know Finn was coming around." His silence made her nervous and her mouth dried. "Could I have a glass of water?"

Ben turned and opened a cupboard beside the sink. He poured her water from the faucet and left it on the counter.

Poppy approached the kitchen like she might a spider nest.

Hard to read at the best of times, Ben had his full shut down mode going.

Sipping her water she tried to formulate her thoughts.

With his plain blue T-shirt stretched to capacity over his chest it made it harder to get her thoughts in order. He totally rocked his shorts. Slim hips, with long, muscular legs dusted with hair. His feet were bare.

"What you think you saw in the kitchen. You didn't see that," she said.

Ben approached her. "Why are you here?"

"You brought us a picnic." Poppy focused on the slight rise of his nipples through the T-shirt. Ben this close set her teeth on edge. "If Finn hadn't come around, I would have gone on that picnic with you, and you wouldn't be mad at me now."

"Is that the only reason you would have gone on a picnic with me?"

"No."

"Why else?" Close enough for her to touch Ben moved right into her space.

Poppy surrendered and touched the hard swell of his pectoral. "Because I wanted to go on a picnic with you. Because I still want to do that."

"Poppy." He covered her hand with his. "Tell me what I saw in the kitchen."

"Finn says he wants to marry me." He deserved her honesty.

Ben tensed.

"Not because he loves me, but because he wants to take care of me."

Beneath her hand Ben's chest rose and fell.

"He's a good man. He would take care of you and the kids," he said.

"I know that." But Finn didn't make her knees turn to water. Finn's chest beneath her hand didn't demand she spread her fingers wide and stroke. "But it's not a good enough reason to get married."

"You turned him down?"

"I turned him down."

Ben gripped her hips and pulled her closer to him. Closer still until she rested her cheek on his chest. Hard everywhere they touched. Poppy closed her eyes and fell into sensory overload.

Radiating warmth, Ben smelled of laundry detergent, spice and clean man. His arm wrapped around her and held her against his heat and power.

"Poppy," he whispered, a husky note stroking over her senses. "I'm not sure what we're doing."

"Me either." As she shook her head, her hair swished against his T-shirt. "But I want it."

"Is it enough?" He pressed his cheek to her head.

"I don't care." Standing here with Ben, like this, she only knew she wanted. Wanted right to the heart of herself. "I've been responsible for so long, Ben. I've done the right thing for so long. Right now, I don't care. I just want this. I want you."

"One more time, baby." His lips skimmed her temple. "I need to hear you say this is okay one more time."

"This is perfect."

As much as her girl bits were singing the halleluiah chorus at finally ending their dry spell, nerves snuck around the edge. Some men—Sean, because Sean represented the sum total of her sexual experience—came at you like a freight train.

Ben framed her face with his hands, gazing at her as if looking for the secret to life. He skimmed his lips over her brow, breathing in the scent of her hair. "Beautiful Poppy." Soft kisses on her cheekbones to the corner of her mouth. "Sweet, beautiful Poppy."

Talk about feeling worshipped. Still, that nerve thing kept her halfway between advance and retreat.

He pulled back and stared at her. "What is it?"

"Nothing." She plastered a chipper smile on her face. "This is fine. It's good. It's great."

Ben raised a brow. "Uh-huh. You changed your mind?"

"No." Not changed her mind precisely. "Umm, it's been a while."

His hands tightened on her face. "I know. You told me and that's a long time."

"Tell me about it." Nerves aside, this thing with Ben felt so right. "And it's not that. Well, not only that."

Chuckling he clasped her nape. Long fingers stroked the lines of tension, and played along her scalp. "Is this where you tell me about your weird fetish?"

"There was only Sean," she said. "Before. He was my first and my only. I don't have much experience at this."

He dipped his mouth closer to hers. "Experience is not what makes someone good at this."

"Pretty sure…" Full sentences danced out of her grasp. "…not right."

His lips brushed hers. "No, this is something that's all about letting go enough to feel." He sucked her bottom lip into his heated mouth. "Being able to relax and reach for what feels good."

"I—"

His tongue slid into her mouth, opening her up for his kiss. Sean had kissed like it was a smaller step to a much more important goal. Ben explored her mouth like he had nothing better to do for the rest of his life.

Her eyelids drifted shut trapping her in a bubble of intimacy.

Ben's tongue coaxed hers into action. His groans encouraged her to explore like he was. One kiss bled into another, growing hotter more intense.

She clung to his waist to keep herself anchored. Her back hit the countertop. Somehow he'd moved her backward.

Time stopped, measured only in the pant of their breathing, the slide of their tongues. Until it wasn't enough anymore. Needing to touch, she slid her hands under his shirt. Hot, silky muscle flexed beneath her fingers.

He kept his hands on her scalp, giving her silent permission to take this at her pace, explore at her will.

Pressing her breasts into his chest she slid her forearms up his back. The smell of him, the taste and feel of him, all swirled around Poppy in a sensual high. She'd had four children and never come close to experiencing the need building inside her. His shirt impeded her progress and she tugged at it.

Ben broke away from her. He fisted the back of his T-shirt and pulled it over his head.

Some women went their whole lives without being offered the treat presented her. Ben was beautifully put together. She traced the firm swell of his pectoral muscles. Dark brown nipples tempted her, and she ran her nails over them.

Ben groaned and dropped his head back, presenting her the powerful column of his neck.

She could do anything. The heady power of it hit her hard. Pressing her mouth to his neck, Poppy slid her hands, fingers splayed, down the most perfect set of abs in the world. Her greedy touch found the dip of his obliques and pressed. She undid the button to his shorts and slid the zipper down.

His skin tasted salty.

Holy shit, Ben was commando under those shorts. His hard cock brushed the back of her fingers as if demanding its share of the attention.

Poppy wrapped her hand around him, and stroked.

His shorts dropped to the kitchen floor.

Ben hissed. "Shit, Poppy." He grabbed the bottom of her shirt and hauled it over her head. Gripping her hips he lifted her onto the counter. "Now it's my turn to play."

He stepped between her spread thighs, his gaze lingering over her breasts and down.

Poppy sucked in her belly. Four kids left their mark on a girl.

"Fuck." Ben cupped her breasts.

Heat shot straight to her core and Poppy arched into his touch.

"You drive me crazy." Touch gentle, he slid calloused hands around her and released her bra clasp. Her breasts spilled out and he cupped them.

Hair dark against her pale skin, Ben lowered his head and took first one nipple and then the other into his mouth. He sucked her deep, using just the edge his teeth to create the most perfect friction.

Slowly, reverently he worshipped her breasts until she was wet and aching and arching into each pull of his mouth. His hands dove into the back of her jeans and grabbed her ass. He pulled her against the hard ridge of his cock.

"Yes." It hit Poppy right on the sweet spot. This is where she needed him, hard and demanding against her.

Ben rocked his hips against her.

Poppy nearly came from that alone. Needy and primed she followed the drag and pull he initiated.

Ben pulled back. "We're going to need to get these off."

Her jeans, at least two size two big, slid right off her hips and sighed onto the floor.

He stepped back and looked at her. Standing naked with his cock jutting and his gaze eating her up he was sexy enough to have her squirming on the counter.

He covered her mound with one huge hand. His thumb found her clit and brushed.

Even through her panties it made her whimper.

His long fingers slid beneath the edge of her panties.

Poppy held her breath, so desperate for the touch he teased her with. She needed his mouth. Catching him by the nape, she dragged his mouth to hers.

This kiss was hot, wet and dirty, as Ben ate into her mouth. His tongue thrust possessively, his breathing harsh through his nose.

And, holy crap, those fingers found each sweet spot and stroked and petted.

He used his chest to press her back. The counter on her back was shockingly cold against her heated skin. Poppy hissed in a breath.

Ben yanked her panties down her legs and spread her thighs wider.

A moment of self-consciousness hit her and Poppy tried to tighten her thighs.

Ben shook his head. "Don't cheat me of this, baby. Let me look at you."

Oh, God, with that tone he could ask her for anything and she'd give it to him.

He crouched at her feet.

Shit, shit, shit. Was he going...holy shit...he did!

His mouth scorched her.

Poppy reared up.

Ben's big hand on her tummy pressed her back down.

This man didn't have rush in his vocabulary.

Poppy's orgasm hit her almost embarrassingly fast. If it hadn't rendered her so completely sated, she might have given a shit.

Ben stood and looked at her lying on the counter. He picked her up like she weighed nothing. "I think we should change venue for the next part."

Poppy wrapped her thighs about him and monkey clung. He must have moved, because next thing she felt the soft yield of a mattress beneath her back.

Ben rose above her with his elbows of either side of her. "You still with me?"

"Uh-huh." She did what felt right and arched into a stretch. "But right now I feel...great.'

"Good to know." He grinned and ducked his head.

With his infinite patience, Ben started all over again. Soft kisses that drugged her into compliance. He explored her body and awoke a deeper, aching need in her. A need that wouldn't be satisfied until she had him buried deep inside her.

With the edge of her desire sated, she melted into the heat Ben created around her.

She wrapped her thighs around him and pressed her needy core against his cock.

He pulsed against her.

"Now, Ben."

"Yes, ma'am." He leaned over and grabbed a condom from his nightstand.

Watching him sheath his cock was one of the sexiest things she'd ever done. His hands on his cock sent lust humming through her. Maybe one day he would do that for her, pleasure himself while she watched.

Fisting the base, he pressed his cock into her, moving slowly and carefully until he was deep inside her.

Poppy writhed beneath him. She needed him to move, to help her find the completion building inside her again. If he took his time now, she might hit him. Poppy dug her nails into his ass. "Ben."

"Baby." He rose onto his hands above her. "I've been wanting this for too long to rush now."

Well, okay, when he put it like that.

Ben withdrew and drove home.

How the hell had she gone without this for so long? Except it had never been like this, not even in those heady early days with Sean.

Ben made love to her with his entire being. Attuned and watching her for cues, he quickened his pace, and found the perfect angle to send her closer to the edge.

His face tightened. Sweat slicked both their bodies.

Poppy came slow, sweet and devastating.

One thrust and he followed her over.

Ben dropped his weight onto her.

He was heavy but Poppy loved it. He surrounded her, their bodies slick everywhere they touched. He panted against her ear. The harsh rise and fall of his chest echoed through her torso. Poppy closed her eyes and wrapped her arms around him.

He raised his head, his dark eyes grave and searching. "Hey."

"Hey yourself." She couldn't stop the huge smile that spread over her face. "That was incredible."

He actually blushed. "I try my best."

It was so damn adorable, especially after everything they'd done. "That was your best?"

"Problem?" Up went one eyebrow.

"Not sure." Poppy made a meh face. "You might have to give me your best a few more times before I can judge."

"Hell, woman." He dropped his forehead against hers. "You're going to have to give me a minute or two."

"Okay." Poppy stroked his back from his shoulder blades to the arch above his fine ass. "But only a minute or two."

With a bark of laughter, Ben slid away from her. He dealt with the condom and then rolled back toward her. He tucked his arm beneath her head.

Poppy found the crook of his shoulder with her cheek and snuggled there. Ben kissed the top of her head. "What time do you need to get back?"

"Soon." She wanted to shove back at reality trying to make itself comfortable in their moment. "I left your mom with the kids."

"She really doesn't mind you know." His deep voice rumbled through her ear. "She loves having them around."

"Still, I can't take advantage of that." She spread her hand over his chest, because she could.

Ben grunted.

So, non-verbal Ben was back.

"Are you laughing?" He raised his head to peer at her.

"You don't speak much do you?"

He rolled her onto her back with a big grin. "Words are overrated."

Poppy took the walk of shame in broad daylight. Close to noon, she'd crawled out of Ben's bed and made her way home. Did it still count as a walk of shame if you weren't wearing your dress from the night before? Did it count if you weren't really ashamed? Not having done this ever, the finer points escaped her. She'd showered at Ben's house to avoid the questions when she got home.

Her body twinged in places she'd forgotten about. The other side effect of not having done this in a while. Her fat grin might be another. As she walked into the house she found Maura playing blocks with Sean in the lounge and her high popped.

"Hi." She kissed the top of Sean's head and took a moment to draw in the baby smell.

Maura's face was glacial. "Hello. I came around but you weren't here."

"No, I wasn't." She didn't have to explain herself to Maura. "Is Finn here?"

"No." Maura handed Sean a larger red block. "He had some things to take care of."

Her relief felt a bit like a betrayal but she couldn't face Finn now. "Where are the others?"

"Dot took them to the store to buy some baking things." Maura corrected the block order for Sean.

"Nah!" Sean knocked the blocks over and put them back the way he wanted.

Maura frowned. "Shouldn't he be able to do this by now? My boys could do this before they spoke."

Of course they could. Poppy took a deep breath. Maura's boys could probably have built the Eiffel Tower out of matchsticks by Sean's age. "He'll get it when he's ready."

"You have to take care of their early development." Maura tried to guide Sean to put the blocks in ascending order.

Poppy winced. Sean didn't like people interfering in his games.

Sure enough, Sean swiped the blocks across the rug. "Nah! Nah! Nah!"

Maura would learn, and in the meantime Poppy could do with a cup of coffee. "I'm making coffee," she said. "Can I get you one?"

"I don't drink coffee." The glare Maura tossed her could scald ice. "It interferes with my sleep."

"Okay." Poppy picked up Sean's sippy cup to refill in the kitchen.

She put the kettle on, then diluted apple juice with water for Sean.

"Where were you?" Maura followed her to the kitchen and stood in the doorway, taut and unhappy.

For a tempting moment, she almost told Maura exactly where she had been. Instead she attempted a light shrug. "Out. I had a few errands to run."

"You were with him weren't you?"

"Who?" Guilty heat crept up her cheeks and made a liar of her.

Maura sneered. "You know who. The same man you made a fool of yourself over at the dance."

Wow. Maura didn't pull any punches. Then again, she never had. Maura had never been able to keep her opinions about Poppy to herself. Why did Poppy do Sean's laundry that way when he preferred his socks folded this? Did Poppy not know Sean liked something green with every meal? Had Poppy made sure the children went to the right preschool, the same one Maura's boys had attended?

"I'm frankly surprised that I have to tell you these things." Maura took the sippy cup, removed the lid and refastened it. "Towns like this one thrive on gossip, and you putting on a show with the local police chief will set them all off. Did you even think how this would effect your children?"

"No." Because she hadn't. As gossipy as Twin Elks was, Poppy didn't see what she did with Ben as anything but her business. Both of them were single, consenting adults.

Maura gaped. "Well, you should have. I came around this morning to talk to you about it and I find you gone and the children in a stranger's care. The least you could have done is make sure they were safe and with family before you went whoring off."

Everything inside Poppy stilled "Did you just call me a whore?"

"No, I was pointing out your behavior." Maura took a step back.

"By what right." Poppy put the mug down before she cracked it. "Who are you to come here and say things to me like that?"

Maura stiffened. "I have every right. You gave me that the day you married my son."

"Your son is dead." The words clunked through the heavy kitchen atmosphere. "If you ever had that right, you lost it the day he died."

Maura paled. "And you're happy about it. You're happy my Sean is dead."

"No, I'm not." Aware of baby Sean in the next room Poppy lowered her voice. "I never wished that on him, but I am glad I'm out of that marriage."

Going even paler, Maura hissed in her breath. "How dare you?"

"I dare that and more." If Maura felt no need to watch what she said, Poppy didn't either. "Sean didn't want to be married. He made that clear every time he left me alone with his children so he could go off and have one affair after another."

"And whose fault is that?" Maura clenched her fists. "He never wanted to be married, and especially not to you, but you trapped him. You got yourself pregnant and trapped him."

And there it was. The truth between them laid bare. Poppy let it hover before her. A strange dispassion settled over her. Truer words had Maura never spoken. No, Poppy hadn't trapped Sean into marriage. He'd been her first lover, and she had fallen for one of the oldest lines in the book. The one where he said you couldn't fall pregnant from not using protection this once.

In Maura's reality none of that mattered. All she saw, all she had ever seen, was an adored and indulged son who got himself into trouble. It was much easier for Maura to believe Sean the victim than face the truth about her child. Sean was reckless, impulsive, irresponsible and indulged, and if Maura faced that reality, it demanded she face her accountability. Like the son she'd raised, Maura had no intention of doing that. How Finn had emerged from the same mother defied understanding.

"You are the children's grandmother." Her voice came out cold, calm and crisp. "And you have an important part to play in their lives." She stalked closer to Maura.

Maura backed up a step.

"But that doesn't and has never given you the right to speak to me like you do. You have no right to criticize me and call me names. I'm not going to threaten you with not seeing the children, because I'm not going to stoop that low. But things are going to change or you can forget seeing them without me being there."

Maura trembled, her face tight and pale. "They are my grandchildren."

"But first they are my children and I will raise them the best way I know how. If you want to be a meaningful part of their lives you are going to have to learn how to watch your mouth around me." This had been building for far too long for Poppy to be able to stop now. "I am also done with you ignoring the girls and playing favorites with the boys. If you want to be a part of your grandchildren's lives, you are going to have to learn how to be a part of all of their lives." She dragged needed breath into her lungs. "I am more sorry for you than I can say that you lost your child. As a mother I can think of nothing worse, but that does not give you the right to replace him with my children. And it certainly does not give you the right to treat me like crap."

"How dare you." Shaking, Maura snatched her purse from the table. "I'll make you sorry you ever opened your trashy mouth." She slammed the door behind her so hard the key fell out of the lock.

Poppy stood in the kitchen trembling with the force of emotion raging through her. So many different feelings that they fought for space inside her.

From the other room, Sean burbled as he stacked his blocks without interference.

The door opened and Dot and the other children walked in.

Dot took one look at her, and shooed the children into the other room. "Go and watch cartoons for a bit. I'll call you when we're ready to bake."

Ryan stuck his lip out. "But you said—"

"I know what I said and now I'm saying this." Dot got them settled and came back. She led Poppy to the table and pressed her into a chair. "Tell me."

In disjointed sentences Poppy managed to get enough of the story out for Dot to grasp the gist.

"Ah." Dot fetched a bottle of wine from the fridge. "I think we need something a bit stronger than coffee right now."

"But it's only lunchtime." Poppy had no idea why she protested because she wanted that wine bad.

"It's after four o'clock somewhere in the world." Dot poured and pushed a glass toward her. "I had a feeling this was coming."

"Then you knew more than me." Poppy took a hefty swig of wine. "After she called me a whore, my mouth opened and it all came pouring out."

"Well." Dot clinked glasses with her. "I think it was a long time in coming, and I'm drinking to that."

God, she adored Dot. From somewhere Poppy found the humor in the situation. "She's furious with me."

Dot snorted. "That woman is angry with the world." She grinned. "And I don't like her."

Chapter 25

With a head full of Ben, Poppy needed to find her happy place with her hands in the dirt. So she bundled the kids out the door and went to find it. She and the kids dropped by Horace's with some cookies.

"I'll come outside for a bit." Horace sniffed the cookies like they might contain arsenic. "I've nothing better to do."

"Will you make lemonade?" Ryan studied him. "Because weeding deserves lemonade."

Ryan was giving Brinn competition in the smart mouth thing, and Poppy really needed to get on that. Later. When she could summon up the patience for the conversation that would ensue. Raising kids to think for themselves had some cons.

It didn't help that Horace gave a crusty bark of laugher. "I'll make lemonade." He ruffled Ryan's hair. "But only if you ask nicely."

"Please, Horace, would you make us some lemonade?" Ryan had the whole big-eyed thing down pat.

Brinn joined him with a cheesy grin. "Please, Horace, nobody makes better lemonade than you."

Ciara echoed Brinn's grin.

Horace rolled his eyes. "You're all too clever for your own good." He limped further into the garden. "You get yourselves busy and I'll see what I can do."

If ever children needed Super Nanny, it was hers.

Poppy explained to the twins which plants to pull and which to leave. Brinn and Ciara really got into the gardening thing. Ryan, not so much. Making boats out of leaves was much more his thing. Sean just liked getting stripped down to his diaper and running around in the sun. Poppy slathered sunblock on every available bit of child skin. She and Sean had a bit of a power struggle over the hat, which she won.

The tangle of emotions caused by Ben and her foray into no-strings sex eased as she worked. She'd gotten exactly what they had both signed on for. No need for residual tendrils of longing, and wanting more. It probably had more to the sudden breaking of her dry spell than emotional attachment anyway.

Horace hobbled toward the house. His limp seemed worse today. What the hell, she could keep an eye on the children from the kitchen window. Poppy braced for the acerbic rejection. "Want some help?"

Grimacing, Horace nodded. "Suit yourself."

To give in without more lip meant he must be in a lot of pain.

"Girls, keep an eye on Sean and Ryan, I'm in the kitchen over there," she said

"Okay." Ciara already had dirt on her face. They had about ten minutes before the novelty of weeding wore off.

Horace sat at the kitchen table, barking instructions while Poppy made the lemonade. As she suspected, it tasted so good due to the generous application of sugar.

"How was the dance?" Horace stretched his bum leg out with a wince.

"It was fun." Poppy added plastic cups to the tray with the lemonade. She cut up some fruit and cheese for a snack.

Outside the window, Sean sat next to Ryan, happily crushing boats as Ryan made them. As Ryan seemed to think it as funny as Sean did, she left them to it.

Brinn had her head down in the flower bed.

With her back to the window, Ciara seemed to be chatting to the air.

"Who the hell is she talking to?"

Poppy hadn't realized she'd spoken aloud until Horace harrumphed. "That would be Cecily."

"Who's Cecily?"

"That depends." Horace looked smug. "Tell me something, Miss Poppy. Do you believe in ghosts?"

Poppy went cold and then warm. Horace was messing with her. He had to be. "No."

"Then it doesn't matter who Cecily is." He jabbed his thumb at the tray. "Are you going to add any meat to that?"

"I don't know." She kept her eye on Ciara. "Am I going to add meat?"

"Of course you are." Horace slapped the table. "Growing bodies need meat to make them strong."

"I know about twenty vegetarians who would disagree with you." She got busy on some cold cuts. "How's your hip today?"

Horace scowled. "We can be friends, girl, as long as you don't start nagging me about my hip."

Damn, she wanted to keep going, but that would make her a little too much like Maura. "Fair enough." Then, with no idea why she brought it up, she said, "I had nasty fight with Maura this morning."

"That bitch who came here the other day?"

"That's the one."

"She reminds me of my daughter." Horace fiddled with the head of his cane. "Never knew a woman more determined to rule the world and everyone in it her way."

"Maura lost a son." And why was she defending her exactly? "I think it scarred her."

Horace cackled. "And she was all sunshine and roses before he died, right?"

"Umm...no." Poppy arranged the cheese and cold cuts on the platter. If Maura had been there, she certainly would have rearranged them. "She never liked me marrying Sean. She believes I trapped him into marriage."

"Did you?"

"No." She hadn't even wanted to get married after she found out she was pregnant. Of course, her mother's opposition had driven her right down the aisle with Sean, and ignoring her screaming instincts.

Horace grunted. "Then, that's all that matters. Even if you did, nobody could blame you. Raising kids is hard enough, not many would want to do it on their own."

"My mother wanted me to terminate the pregnancy." Maybe if she and Mom could have calmed down enough to talk this through rationally, things might have been different.

Rubbing his thigh, Horace glanced at her. "Wasn't her decision."

"No, it was mine, and I don't regret the decision I made."

"So, what's eating you up?" Horace had his keen gaze on her face.

"I was thinking that maybe if I had spent less time crying and fighting with my mother, things might have been different."

Horace snorted. "No point in doing that. First off, it's past and we don't get to rearrange it. Second, we don't get to go back and change one thing only. You know what I think?"

She really did want to know. "What?"

"We all talk about changing something in our past like it's an isolated incident. Time doesn't work like that. You go back and change one thing, and it will have a ripple effect and change a whole lot of other stuff. We are where we are." He shrugged. "Some of it good, some of it bad, but it is what it is, and we are exactly where we should be."

Wow! Philosophy from Horace. "That's deep, Horace."

"And you've got a smart mouth." He heaved himself to his feet. "Now let's get out there before your kids destroy my garden."

"I'm hot." Brinn collapsed on the grass under a large aspen. "I can't weed anymore."

"There you are." Mom waved at them from the gate. "Can I come in?"

Horace scowled at Mom. "Am I running a hotel here?"

But Horace had a slight flush on his cheeks even as he scowled. Yup, Mom had that effect on men.

"Wow! That's some gardening you have to do there." Mom opened the gate and tripped into the garden. She shaded her eyes and examined the house. "Someone should totally buy it and fix it up. It's a wr—"

"Mom." Poppy needed to get a word in before Mom really put her foot in her mouth. "This is Horace Winters. He owns the house. It's been in his family for generations."

"Gosh." Mom turned her starlet smile on Horace. "That is wonderful. I'm Heather."

"You don't look old enough to be anyone's mother." Horace responded like every other man on the planet to Mom's charm.

Mom giggled, so intrinsically female it made Poppy feel like a troll. "I can assure you I am. Old enough to have grandchildren, in fact."

"If I hadn't seen it with my own eyes, I wouldn't have believed it." Horace winked.

Yes. Horace. Winked. At her mother. All her childhood, Poppy had watched this song and dance. Prettier than everyone else's mother and a lot younger, Mom had always created a ripple amongst other parents. Mothers resented her, and dads couldn't get close enough to her.

Mom tapped Horace's arm. "You're a riot. I can see why Poppy loves it here so much."

"Grandma." Brinn sat up and waved. "We're over here."

"Hey, my darlings." Mom walked to the girls and sat cross-legged between them. She could pass for eighteen from behind, and not much older than that from the front.

Poppy caught Horace staring at her. His faded brown eyes bore a weight of wisdom and experience in them. They stripped Poppy of her pretenses, so she shrugged and called the children for their snack.

Mom nibbled on a cracker. "Carbs." She moaned around a bite. "I can't tell you how long it's been since I've had carbs. Anyway." She poured herself a cup of lemonade. "I need to talk to you about California."

Poppy froze in the act of pouring lemonade for the children. This had better not be heading where she thought it might. "What about it?"

"We need to take off soon, and Jarryd needs me to sort out the details for the house." She took a small bunch of grapes.

Poppy handed Sean a piece of cheese. "The house is still available?"

"Absolutely." Mom smiled. "So Jarryd changed his mind about taking me to Europe."

Jarryd hadn't stood a chance. "When do you leave?"

"As soon as we get back to California." Mom stared at Sean mangling grapes. "Is he going to eat those?"

"When he gets them mushy enough."

"So, while he's here, Jarryd would like to meet you. Go over some things with the house and give you the keys." With a slight shudder, Mom averted her gaze from Sean,

Poppy almost didn't dare ask. "And the job?"

"Will start as soon as we get back from Europe," Mom said. "In the meantime you can stay at the house, hang around on the beach, and get yourselves settled." She turned to the twins. "Wouldn't you like that? A house right on the beach."

Ciara whispered to Brinn.

"We like the beach," Brinn said, and looked at Poppy. "But we like it here better."

"Of course you do." Mom twinkled at Horace. "With such a lovely house to live in, but I promise you you're going to love living close enough to hear the sea at night."

Ryan's lip quivered. "But if we're there, we can't be here."

"That's right." Mom glanced at Poppy and frowned. "But you were only ever passing through Twin Elks."

That did it. Ryan opened up like a faucet. "But I don't want to leave here. I want to stay with Dot and Horace." He hiccupped a shaky breath. "And Ben is teaching me to play football."

"But, sweetie." Mom blinked at him. "You were always coming to California."

"Mo-o-om." Disappearing face first in Poppy's belly, Ryan wailed. "D-don't wanna leave."

Shrugging, Mom gave her a helpless stare.

"Hey." Poppy turned Ryan's face to hers. "It's okay, sweet boy. We spoke about this, remember?" She wrapped her arms about him and rocked. God, she hated doing this to him. She could never have guessed Ryan, all the kids, would take to Twin Elks like they had.

"But that was before we liked it here." Brinn's lip quivered.

Ah, hell! Here it came. Momentary panic swept over Poppy.

"And Cecily." Face grave, Ciara pointed at the garden. "That was before Cecily."

Mom clambered to her feet. "Umm…I think…I'll go." She scuttled off before Poppy could even nod.

"Now then." Horace cleared his throat as he patted Brinn and Ciara on the shoulder. "That's a lot of noise on such a lovely day. You'll scare Cecily away."

The girls stared at him, even Ryan quieted in her arms. For her part, Poppy dearly wanted to know who the hell Cecily was.

"I think you'll like California," Horace said. "I like it there just fine. In fact, I'm retiring there."

"What's retiring?" Using Poppy's shirt as a Kleenex, Ryan peered at Horace.

"Living large." Horace winked at him. "Getting other people to do everything for you, so you can sit on your keester all day and read a book."

Crisis diverted, for the moment. Poppy dreaded the upcoming scene with the children. She didn't blame them. There was a lot about Twin Elks to like.

Chapter 26

With the kids going to bed without much fuss, Poppy found her nights free. At first, she'd taken full advantage, caught up on TV series she'd heard other people talking about and read some of the large collection in Horace's library. A real library, all oak paneling with a huge desk facing walls lined with bookshelves begging for someone to get comfy in one of the big leather wingbacks and read.

Too restless to settle, she poked around the library looking for a distraction from her conversation with Maura and the battle looming with the children. Things had gotten complicated fast, and when you added her growing feelings for Ben into the mix her thoughts nearly drove her nuts.

Sitting at the desk, she pulled a pile of paperwork toward her. With Horace leaving in a few more days, she'd do him a favor and clear some of the clutter. Old bills and junk mail didn't keep her mind from dwelling. She'd half expected Ben to come around today, which was stupid because the man had a job, and an important one and he'd already spent more time with them than she could expect. And then there was Finn and his offer.

As much as she agreed with Dot that marriage to Finn shouldn't be an option, the practical side of her, coincidentally the same side of her that put food on the table, kept mulling it over.

At the bottom of the paper pile, she found a couple of items dated earlier this year. Those she sorted into piles for Horace to take a look at. Bold scrolling script caught her eye. *Golden Oaks Assisted Living Centers.*

And right below that with a picture of a lovely stone house surrounded by green fields it said, *Where your loved ones are our priority.*

The facility in California Horace was going to. As she put it in the pile for Horace three bold-typed words leaped out at her *failure to respond.* That sounded a bit threatening and Poppy skimmed the letter.

Poppy stopped skimming and read. Each word. Then she read it again.

"Damn." Her voice sounded eerie in the silent house. Horace hadn't responded to the offer of a place, and they'd written to inform him his place had been filled. No need to jump to conclusions. Except, and this is the thing that made her stop and read a third time, for a man who was supposed to be moving on in a few days, Horace looked very comfortable. No bags had been packed. He hadn't even asked her to get his laundry ready.

The deadline on the letter had passed three days ago.

Deciding to speak to him about it in the morning, Poppy finished tidying the paperwork and took a long soak in the massive tub upstairs before bed.

The next morning, she dropped the girls off and came straight home. Dot had already taken the boys, and Poppy knocked on Horace's door.

"You're early." Horace yanked the door open. "Don't you usually have coffee with Blondie in the mornings?"

"Yes." Now, standing there, Poppy grew uncertain. Maybe she should leave things alone. This wasn't really any of her business. But she liked Horace, despite his permanent grouchiness, and she needed to know what would happen to him when she left. "I need to speak to you about something."

Horace scowled and stomped to his recliner. Springs creaked as he threw himself into it. "I suppose you're leaving."

"In a day or two." Poppy handed him the letter. "I found this last night."

Glancing at the letter, Horace sniffed, but he was also not looking at her. "So?"

"Is it what I think it is?" She sat near him on the sofa.

Clicking off the TV, Horace turned to her. "Are we playing word games now?"

Spend enough time with anyone and you got to see through their bluster. "Do you have someplace to go when you leave this house? Isn't your daughter taking it over?"

"What's it to you?" Horace turned on her and glowered. "You're leaving. It's nothing to do with you."

"Horace." He was right, she was leaving but she really didn't want to think of him here, all alone. "I want to know you're going to be all right."

He barked out a laugh. "Like you care."

"I do." Who knew she'd end up caring for him?

Crossing his arms, he averted his gaze. "I'll be fine."

"Does your daughter know?"

"I'm tired." Horace clicked on the TV. "I think you should go now.

"Hora—"

"Go."

Outside his door, Poppy hesitated. Not ready to tell Dot and unleash hell on Horace, she walked to Kelly's.

Kelly heard the story and gaped at her. "You are kidding me."

"Nope." Poppy needed to move. Slipping behind the counter she stacked clean cups on top of the coffee machine. "And I'm pretty sure his daughter has no idea."

"Horace is a stubborn old fart." Kelly shook her head. "I can't say I'm entirely surprised."

Poppy managed a tight laugh. "What should I do? The logical thing is to let his daughter know and let her handle it. But..."

"But Horace and she don't exactly get on." Kelly pulled a face.

"And I can't leave him in that house without anyone to take care of him."

"Well, you can," Kelly said. "It's not like you're related to him, or have even known him for long enough for anyone to expect you to take care of him."

"I can't." Poppy knew all that. She'd gone over it in her head during her soak in the tub last night. "I like him."

"Poppy." Kelly covered her hand. "He's not your responsibility."

"He has to be someone's."

The bell over the door jangled and they looked up.

Kelly groaned, and Poppy did too, only inside where nobody could hear.

Tara sauntered in looking amazing in a body hugging blue maxi dress. If Poppy tried to wear that, she'd look like she was playing dress up in her mom's wardrobe.

"Hi." Tara snarled more than smiled.

Poppy's hackles rose.

Hands on her hips, Kelly nodded at Tara. "What can we do for you?"

"Just coffee, black." Tara patted her svelte curves. "Have to watch the weight."

Kelly busied herself making Tara's coffee.

"So." Tara leaned her elbows on the counter and looked at Poppy. "I hear you had a good time at the dance the other night."

Kelly glanced at Poppy, and then Tara. "You didn't go?"

"No." Tara chuckled. "Those dances are not my thing. It's all very charming, but when you grow up here…" She made a face. "Ben's quite the dancer. But then you know that, don't you, Poppy?"

Poppy felt like she had been dragged up in front of the whole class. "Um…sure."

"Dot made all her boys take dancing lessons when they were small." Tara smiled, all teeth and no happy. "Ben hated those lessons."

"Here you go." Kelly thunked Tara's coffee on the counter.

"Of course it came in very useful on our wedding day." Tara sipped her coffee and moaned. "Kelly, you make the best coffee."

"Thanks." Kelly crossed her arms.

Tara had a way of putting you on the defensive. Poppy shoved her hands behind her back before she copied Kelly's posture.

"Speaking of marriages." Tara grabbed a paper napkin and dabbed at her mouth. "Rumor has it your in-laws are in town."

As a segue, it was pathetically thin. Poppy couldn't wait to hear where it went. "Yup."

"I hear your brother-in-law is hot." Tara giggled and looked coy. "Not that I'm interested in other men."

Kelly snorted. "Seriously, Tara? Hot new guy in town. I'd have thought you'd get right on that."

Tara threw her a death stare. She recovered quickly with another girly smile. "Why eat out when the cooking's good at home."

Knowing Tara was full of crap didn't quite stop Poppy's urge to puke.

"That's not the way I hear it," Kelly said. "If I believed all the gossip I'd heard, I'd have to say that you ate out a lot. Rumor has it that you got bored with home cooking."

"You shouldn't believe everything you hear." Tara glared at Kelly.

Kelly glared right back. "Neither should you."

"Really?" Tara stared at Poppy. "So it's not true that your in-laws are here to take you back home with them?"

"No." Was that what everyone was saying?

"That's a pity." Tara sipped her coffee. "Because a woman alone with four kids could use all the help she can get. The way I heard it was your brother-in-law, Finn—" Tara cocked her head. "It is Finn isn't it? Apparently the way Finn was watching you and Ben the other night has got people talking about how maybe he'd like to take over where his brother left off."

Poppy's head whirled. She had no idea how Tara came by her information. If Tara had come to this conclusion, it could mean other people had too.

"Of course, that's gossip." Tara's face was tight with bitchiness. "But if it was true, I'd snap that offer up, Poppy. Not many men would want to take on another man's children. Especially not four of them."

"Coffee's on the house." Kelly stood between Tara and Poppy. "And I'm using my right of admission. Get out of here, Tara."

"I'm going," Tara said, raising her voice as she walked away. "Ben's not the paternal type Just thought I'd give your new girl a friendly warning. Ben didn't even want his own children. I can't see him taking on someone else's."

As Tara shut the door behind her, the doorbell jangled again. She strolled across the parking lot and climbed into her car.

"She's full of shit." Kelly shook her head. "You really must have kicked over a hornet's nest to bring her out to warn you off."

Ben and Dot had been so kind to her and the children, made her feel welcome and wanted. Tara's crap really didn't bother her that much, but it did bring unwelcome thoughts with it. Somehow she had allowed their kindness to sneak past her caution. She'd relaxed her guard around them. The other night with Ben had proven that. Ben had burrowed beneath her skin. Sure, she dressed it up as wanting to experience some of the things she'd missed out on, but the truth was far more dangerous. She liked Ben, a whole lot. In a different world, where she didn't have children, she might be even thinking relationship. Ignoring her reality, she'd leaped into bed with Ben, forged a connection she had no business messing with.

"Poppy?" Kelly stood in front of her. "Don't let Tara get to you. She only came here to mess with your head."

Poppy laughed, but none of it was funny. "It worked."

Chapter 27

Two days later, Poppy stepped in as a replacement and ran the church playgroup with three other mothers. They included her in their conversations, but clearly knew each other well. It left her with far too much time to think. She volunteered to supervise the finger painting in an effort to get out of her head.

Amongst purple, green, red and yellow paint smears going nearly everywhere, she lingered on the dull resounding question of what she was she going to do about Horace. For three days she'd done nothing, existed with Horace pretty much like they always did but with her pretending to know nothing.

On top of which, it was time to face that her excuses to stay were embarrassingly transparent. They went something like: everyone had been so kind, how could she refuse when Kathy asked her to step in with the playgroup? She could delay her departure one more day. Besides, it gave her another day to speak to Horace.

That and Tara's visit made one thing abundantly clear. She was in deep with Twin Elks and she needed to get out before she got in any deeper. Before she admitted how much it bothered her that Ben hadn't called.

She grabbed a chubby fist covered in paint and wiped it before the child could suck on it.

"Snack time," one of the mothers announced.

It took all four of them to clean hands and faces and get thirty children seated in front of slices of watermelon.

"Hey." Donna, dark-haired and younger than the others, joined her as Poppy poured juice into plastic cups. "You look after old man Winters, don't you?"

It yanked Poppy out of her head. "Yes. Why?"

"I saw his daughter earlier." Donna pulled a face.

That couldn't be good. If Horace carried a cell she would have texted him.

Rachel and Anna, the other two young moms sidled closer, faces alight. "You saw Claire?" Rachel shook her head. "I can't stand that woman."

"Me neither." Anna distributed juice cups. She looked at Poppy over the children's heads. "You know about her, right?"

"Dot might have mentioned something," Poppy said.

"Last time she came here Mr. Winters ended up at the medical center." Anna frowned. "He thought he was having a heart attack. Turned out to be stress, but still…"

The date on the letter! When they failed to get anything from Horace, the facility must have contacted his daughter. Well, that was one decision made for her. If his daughter was here, then she could deal with Horace.

Only that still didn't sit right. Horace hid a lot behind a crabby exterior and one of those things was a big, kind heart.

"What's she doing here?" Donna handed out napkins to the kids.

"Who knows?" Rachel shrugged and rescued a cup before it could go over. "But she and Tara Crowe are still tight."

A sick feeling churned in Poppy's stomach. Had her friendship with Horace ended up causing trouble for him? Was the daughter here because Tara had been telling stories? No doubt about it, Tara would not be sad to see the back of Poppy and her children.

"Hey!" Donna squeezed her arm. "Are you okay? You look really pale."

"I'm fine." Poppy tried for a smile. Unconvincing if Donna's smirk was anything to go by.

Anna sidled closer and lowered her voice. "Tara's a bitch. She loves making trouble."

Rachel snorted. "Especially when it comes to Ben."

Poppy wanted to run and hide. As the other three women looked at her she felt stripped to the bone. They knew all about her and Ben. Or at least made an accurate guess. She was so damn stupid. She should never have danced with him like she had the other night. Never have allowed him to be seen with her and the children as much as she had. With the whole town watching them, she had opened him up to gossip.

"Tara threw him away like old garbage," Anna said. "Now you come to town and she's threatened.

"Totally." Rachel nodded. "He likes your kids. He takes care of them. And you're pretty." She giggled. "The way he looked at you at the dance. Whew!" She fanned herself with her hand.

The other two giggled.

Donna nudged her and waggled her eyebrows.

Poppy did her best to join in. They were trying to be nice to her, trying to show their support, but each word drove her guilt deeper. She'd put Ben, and now Horace, in a horrible position.

Poppy waited until all the children had been picked up before she left the church hall. Donna, Anna and Rachel helped her clean up.

Sean had dropped off to sleep, so tired he didn't even stir as she loaded him into his stroller.

Ryan had a Play-Doh dog in his fist, and chattered about showing it to Ben when they got home.

Except not their home. She'd dragged her children into this and now she needed to separate them. God help all of them with that. How did you persuade your children that leaving a place was a good idea when your hankering to stay was part of the problem?

As Poppy let the children in the garden gate, the front door opened and a woman stormed out. Tall, blonde and effortlessly stylish in jeans and a draped top, she stopped when she saw Poppy.

"Hi." Not sure what else to do, Poppy gave the woman a little half wave, which was so dumb it made her teeth hurt.

"So you're her?" The woman shut the front door and stalked closer. She was attractive rather than pretty with strong, aquiline features and piercing green eyes. "I'm Claire."

"Hi." She'd already said that. Poppy dragged in a breath and tried to get a hold of herself. Claire was intimidating the hell out of her. "I guess you've been to see Horace?" So lame, because what else would Claire be doing here.

Claire frowned. "You know about Golden Oaks?"

"I found out three days ago."

Gazes keen and curious, the twins and Ryan watched the conversation like a tennis match. Sean squirmed in his stroller, pumping his legs because he wanted to get out.

"Talk to him." Claire's glare could have scalded. "Talk to the stubborn old bastard and make sure he calls them."

Poppy trod carefully. "He won't listen to me."

"He doesn't listen to anyone." Claire sneered. "But he needs to go into that home and now. I have plans for this house that don't include him." With that she brushed past Poppy. Stopping with her hand on the gate, she spoke over her shoulder. "And don't get any ideas about that house. It's mine. I earned it."

Damn! Claire Winters was everything Kelly and Dot had said about her and more.

"Who is she?" Ryan chewed on his lip as he watched Claire get into a low-slung sedan.

"Horace's daughter." Poppy unclipped Sean and let him out of his stroller. He immediately climbed the porch steps.

Brinn sighed. "We don't like her, and neither does Cecily."

"Who is Cecily?" Poppy let Claire go for a minute.

Ciara smiled at her. "Our friend."

Poppy waited but the twins followed Sean into the house.

Claire had stormed out of the main house, so Poppy guessed her best chance of finding Horace would be inside. Outside the kitchen Poppy hesitated, not sure whether to intrude or not, and then made her decision. Horace was her friend. She pushed open the door.

Hunched over the kitchen table, Horace looked gray and battered. He glanced up. "You saw her?"

"As I was leaving."

"Is he all right?" Brinn frowned at her.

"I think he's a bit upset." Poppy smoothed wayward hair from Brinn's face. "Maybe you guys can do something quietly while I talk to him?"

"Sure." Brinn and Ciara nodded.

Ryan peered into the front room to their left. "Can I watch TV?" Always one to want the TV on, Ryan was pushing his luck.

"Okay," Poppy said. "But just this once."

"Cool." Ryan grinned and scampered into the front room.

Poppy settled the children in front of cartoons and went back to the kitchen.

Horace hadn't moved. "Did you call her and tell her?"

"No." Poppy moved to the fridge and pulled out a lasagna she'd made the night before. "I was not sure what to do."

Horace nodded.

"Are you hungry?" She slid the lasagna into the range.

Horace gave her a wan version of his usual scowl. "No, but don't fuss."

"Don't growl." She pulled up a chair opposite him and took a seat.

"Did she talk to you?" Horace folded his hands on the table.

"Yes." Poppy kept it light. "She wants me to talk to you about Golden Oaks."

"Of course she does." Horace stretched out his bum leg. "I'm messing with her plans for this place."

Poppy didn't know what had happened between Horace and his daughter. There could be more to this story than she'd heard, so she trod carefully. "Can I ask you why you didn't take the place?"

"I don't want to go." Horace slammed his palm on the table. "I never wanted to go to that damn place, but Claire found it for me and tried to shove me into it."

"Why?"

Horace gave a dry, bitter laugh. "My daughter hates me."

"Surely not." Poppy had been angry with Mom at times, but she'd never hated her mother.

Horace stared at his hands. "She hates me because her mother hated me. But like her mother, she enjoys my money, and comes here often enough to make sure I haven't given it away to someone else."

"Have you?" Knowing Horace it seemed a fair question.

He laughed, more genuinely amused this time. "Not yet." He sighed and looked around the kitchen. "I grew up in this house, you know?"

Poppy nodded.

"And my father before me, and my grandfather." He settled back in his chair with a misty expression. "My great-grandfather built it for his young bride. She only lived in it for a few years before she died young."

What a sad story. Poppy tried to picture the house as it would have appeared to a young Victorian bride. It must have been a dream home.

"My great-grandfather, also a Horace by the way, put his heart into every stone in this place. My grandfather said they were very happy here until his mother died. She loved the house."

"What happened after she died?"

Horace shrugged. "Nothing very dramatic. No tragic suicides or anything like that. Old Horace grieved for a time, but eventually married a very nice woman to help him raise his young son. They never had any kids, so my grandfather was pretty much a spoiled little shit."

"And?" Poppy leaned her elbows on the table, as fascinated by the look on Horace's face as his story. Pride, love and history were all written across his craggy features.

"My grandfather had the money gene," Horace said. "Ended up buying up or starting most of the businesses in this town. We had Winters Mercantile, Winters Bank, Winters Supply and Feed, Winters Haberdashers and Ladies Emporium. He even got the local school started."

"Winters School?"

Horace chuckled. "How did you know?"

"So he must have married."

"He did. My grandmother, Clarissa. They say she was a helluva girl. They had six kids in all, the oldest being my father. By the time he retired my grandfather had seen the writing on the wall and diversified the family money. He kept enough of his capital in the town to keep it alive, but he knew times were changing."

"Just how rich are you, Horace?"

He stared at her. "Rich enough for my daughter to pretend she doesn't hate me to get her hands on my money. And she hates me a lot."

"Tell me about your dad."

"Dad never worked a day in his life." Horace shrugged. "He didn't have to. The house always passes to the oldest child and he got that. Plus my grandfather pretty much made all his kids rich by the time he died. Dad just farted around managing the family trust, and occasionally showed up to board meetings."

"Are you an only child?"

"Yup." Horace massaged his leg. "But I have more cousins than any man needs." He shrugged. "And of course, you will have heard my story."

Poppy nodded. Maybe one day Horace would tell her the full story.

"Now we come to the sad part." Horace stared out the window. "You see my daughter doesn't think of herself as a Winters. Hell, she even took her mother's maiden name after the divorce. Mathews." He snorted. "Claire Mathews. Her mother and I—" Horace grimaced. "We screwed up our marriage badly enough, I didn't want it to screw her over too, so I let it go. I supported them." He rapped the table. "Don't you make any mistake about that. A man supports his family."

Poppy had never thought otherwise for an instant.

"Now, Claire Mathews, who is too proud to call herself Winters but not too proud to take the Winters money wants to tear this house down and sell it to a condo developer."

"What?" Poppy couldn't believe anyone could consider destroying such a beautiful old place. Yes, it needed a lot of work, but under a loving hand, the old girl could be sparkly again. The heating bill would be murderous, but it would totally be worth it. "I always dreamed of a house like this." Poppy laughed at her younger self. "When I was younger I even had a collection of magazine pictures of houses just like it that I kept in a scrapbook."

"I wondered about that." Horace smiled. "Not many pretty young things want to live in a place like this."

Poppy snorted. "Don't flirt with me, Horace. I'm a respectable mother of four."

"You should be so lucky." Horace pulled himself to standing and clomped over to the fridge. He hauled out a couple of beers and thumped them on the table. With a deft wrist flick, he had the cap off one and then the other. "I need a drink."

"Is it good for you?"

"Don't mother me."

"Cheers." Poppy clinked her bottle against his. "Surely if you speak to Claire, explain what the house means to you, she will keep it."

Horace sipped his beer and made an "ah" of enjoyment. "It wouldn't do any good. Claire wants to tear down any memory of her life here and her sperm donor."

Poppy wrinkled her nose. "Don't say sperm, Horace. It grosses me out."

He chuckled and sipped his beer. "So, tell me your tragic story. You're all frowny and wrinkled, so don't even bother saying its nothing."

As they were sharing, Poppy told him about Finn.

"Don't marry the brother," Horace said. "You'll only end up resenting each other. He may be all noble and stoic now but what happens when he meets a girl he can love. Or you meet someone?" Horace waggled his eyebrows.

Poppy sighed. "I know. Finn is a great guy though."

Horace grunted and sipped his beer. "You could stay in Twin Elks, you know? Get yourself a job, a house. Cost of living is a lot lower than California."

"Doing what?" Poppy pulled a face. "Once you leave I have no place to live."

"You have skills. You could find something else," Horace said.

"Like what?" Poppy didn't really want to have this conversation. Talking about Horace's problems made hers seem smaller. "My only skill is being married and raising kids, and my dead husband wouldn't even rate those as much of anything."

Horace made a rude noise. "Your ex sounds like an asshat."

"That pretty much sums it up." Poppy had to laugh.

"What about our handsome police chief." Horace pinned her with a stare. "And don't even think of telling me you're not doing the nasty with him."

"Seriously?" Could a face get hot enough to explode? "You can't say things like that."

"I'm old." Horace grinned. "I can say whatever the hell I like."

True that. Poppy shrugged. "It's complicated."

"Complicated?" Horace slammed his beer bottle on the table. "I'd like to find whoever first said that and beat the crap out of them. No shit it's complicated. You got a man, you got a woman, and you got the sum total of both their lives sitting between them. Of course it's complicated. And it always was."

"Okay then." Poppy squirmed in her chair. That had cut her down to size.

"Relationships are complicated." Horace pounded the table. "They always are and they always will be. Now give me something better than that."

"I have four kids."

Horace nodded. "This is true, but you have four great kids who would pour more love on the lucky man who got them than any man deserved."

Tears stung her eyes. That had to be the sweetest thing Horace had ever said to her. It might be one of the sweetest things anyone had ever said to her.

"You did good with those kids, Poppy." Horace jerked his head toward the front room. "The only person who's not sure of that is you."

"Ben doesn't want children," she said. "He didn't even want his own."

Horace gaped at her, then his face creased into a grin that became laughter. "Oh, I hear Tara coming out of your mouth now. Ben didn't want children with his faithless whore of an ex. But when she got pregnant he manned up and got himself ready to be a father." Horace kept on chuckling. "And the only person who really believes she was pregnant is Ben. You must have Tara wetting her designer pants right about now."

"I don't know about that." Gorgeous, put-together Tara in the red corner. Poppy the walking train wreck in the blue. The walking train wreck with four children. Great children.

"And you're never going to know unless you give it a chance." Horace tapped his fingers on the table and scowled at her.

"What?"

"I'm thinking."

"Does it hurt?"

"Yes." Horace chuckled. "Actually it does, but it's not me it's going to hurt."

"I'm hanging on the edge of my seat here." Poppy smiled back at him. She really did like this crusty old coot.

"Get us another beer and I'll tell you."

"You a rowdy drunk?" Poppy did as she was told, because this was the best she'd felt all day. She gave them to Horace to do his cool trick with the caps.

"You love this house, right?"

"Yup."

"If you owned it, what would you do with it?"

Poppy looked around her. "No offense, Horace, but it needs a lot of work, and that's what I'd do."

"So buy it from me." Horace shrugged.

Poppy snorted beer through her nose. It took a while to clean herself up. "If I had the money, I totally would."

"How much money you got?"

"In total?"

"Nope." Horace shoved her purse across the table. "On you. Right now."

"Horace." Poppy grabbed her purse before it ended up on the floor. "Are you having a senior moment? Do I need to call someone?"

"How much?" He scowled at her.

Poppy dug out her wallet and opened it. "I have thirty-two—nope." She found another single. "Thirty-three dollars and some change."

"Count out the change."

"You're having a breakdown, aren't you?"

"Count." Horace pounded the table.

"Keep your pants on." Poppy upended her change compartment and counted. "Four dollars and fifteen cents."

"So you have thirty-seven dollars and fifteen cents?"

"Yup." Poppy gathered up her change and put it away.

"So here's my suggestion." Horace leaned forward and grinned. An expression that reminded her of Golem and not in any way that was good. "I'm going to sell you my house for forty dollars. You have to come up with another two bucks eighty-five."

Chapter 28

Still in a daze Poppy put the children to bed. She and Horace had argued in circles until she had ended it by calling the children for dinner.

Horace insisted he wanted to sell her the house for forty dollars. Forty dollars. She couldn't let him do it. The house was his history, his family story. As well as being worth so many thousand times more that it hurt her head to think about it.

But she did think about it, too. Some venal part of her brain kept insisting that she grab onto this incredible opportunity and run with it, which showed what a really horrible person she could be. The incredible house, her dream house, and on all that land for the princely sum of forty dollars. Life didn't toss many opportunities like that at a person. As in, maybe none.

It was wrong though, taking advantage of Horace's grief and anger over his relationship with his only child. Despite how twisted Claire's intentions for the old house were.

The whole situation made her sad. Families got angry with each other. They said things and did things and allowed those things to drive a wedge between them. Time went on and the wedge became the new normal. It's not that she believed you had to love your family because you shared the same blood. Some people got born into a crappy gene pool. However, other people, people like her, allowed pride and shame, anger and disillusionment to widen the gap until it spread like an aching chasm between them and their family.

Ben wasn't much of a drinker, but every now and then he liked to occupy a barstool at *The Bugling Elk*.

Trying to recreate his pub from back home, an English immigrant, Warren Watts, had established the bar back in the sixties.

Despite the name, it had about as much charm as a used gum wrapper. A mash-up of English pub meets American small town bar that didn't work for anyone other than the locals. But the beer was cold, and Warren's daughter, Maddison, ran it in a low-key way that suited his mood right now.

Three days since he'd last seen Poppy, warm, sweet and naked in his bed. Three days, nine hours and around twenty-two minutes. He knew this because he'd spent every one of those three days, nine hours and twenty-two minutes resisting the urge to be with her. She was leaving. He needed to remember that.

Maddison slid another beer in front of him and he nodded his thanks.

Since his last deployment ended, he'd watched the drinking. The need to drink until you fell into a dreamless sleep had lured him too damn close to the point of no return particularly over the time when Tara had lost their baby. His counselor had given him other ways of managing the stress, and he preferred using those. But some nights, he wanted a beer and enough noise around him to keep him out of his damn head.

He hadn't slept well in weeks. The dreams had crept back with enough regularity that sleeping became a vicious game of Russian roulette. He'd called his counselor and had a session scheduled with her next week. It happened, she had said, the important thing was to get to the root cause and move on.

Yeah! Except he had the nasty feeling he understood the root cause here and it didn't sit well with him.

"Hey." Finn bellied up beside him. "Feel like some company?"

Not at all, but he shrugged for Finn to take the seat anyway.

Finn ordered a beer with a Jack chaser and looked around him. "This is…interesting."

Warren Watts had maintained to his dying day that Elvis lived, and the bar screamed his Elvis fandom loudly. The pride of old Warren's collection, the white spangled suit in a glass display case hanging on the wall behind the bar. Nobody had the heart to tell Warren that Elvis would have had to be about five two to fit into the suit. Warren believed *The King* had made the yellow sweat stains under the armpits and it made Warren happy to do so.

He and Finn drank their beers, both of them keeping an eye on the baseball game playing on the small screen to the left of Elvis's suit. Actually Ben couldn't tell you who was playing.

"Bad day?" Finn jerked his head at Ben's beer.

Ben liked the guy, so he said, "Bad night."

"Ah." Finn took his chaser and motioned for another one. "Dreams?"

"Yup."

"You gonna get that checked out?"

"Already done."

"Good."

Ben eyed Finn's chaser and abandoned the idea. "How many tours?"

"A few too many." Finn sipped his beer. "You?"

"Same."

They went back to drinking and not watching the ball game.

Finn had something on his mind, and Ben got the feeling this meeting hadn't just happened. He waited, because Finn would get to the point when he was ready.

Finn shifted. "So, Poppy."

Ah, here it came, and he'd guessed right. Finn had that responsible thing Ben admired in another man. A man like Finn took care of business, whatever business needed taking care of. Because of that he stayed quiet and let Finn say his piece.

"I asked her to marry me," Finn said.

The bar blurred and shifted around Ben. He knew this already but hearing it confirmed gave him the weirdest sensation of a creeping numbness moving up from his toes. Kind of like he was turning to stone inch by inch.

Finn stared at him, a direct challenge. Then he shook his head. "She said no."

Ben breathed again.

"I don't love her." Finn moved his shot glass around the condensation ring on the bar. "I mean I love her like family, brotherly type love. Poppy is good people. But I'm not in love with her."

Ben nodded. He didn't trust his voice, or the raging need to take Finn apart.

Smiling into his beer glass, Finn said, "I tell you this in case you are interested. Or might be feeling some of the non-brotherly love yourself."

After the other night it seemed stupid to keep telling himself that this thing with Poppy would go away. He'd scratched the itch and the itch only grew bigger and bigger until he spent too many hours thinking about how to get Poppy back into his bed again. "Why do you want to marry her?"

"It feels like the right thing to do. You know?" Finn shrugged.

"Yeah." Ben did know. You stepped up when you had to.

"Plus, those kids need a dad. A real dad. Not the pathetic excuse for a dad they got in my brother." Finn shook his head. "I loved my brother, man. But I saw him, and I didn't respect him or the choices he made." He scrubbed at his nape. "I don't know how much Poppy has told you, but it was bad. He pretty much screwed around on her from day one. Even before his wedding I caught him with another woman. He'd crawl back long enough to get Poppy to forgive him, and leave her with another child before he got bored with being a family man."

Poppy would stay, too. Like him and Finn when she made a commitment she did everything she could to stick it out. Had there ever come a time when she'd had enough? The thing about people like him, Poppy and Finn, is that they had a shitload of patience and determination, but once they were done, they were done.

"My mother doesn't see it." In one motion Finn peeled the label off the bottle. "Sean was basically a selfish prick. He never did anything for anyone without weighing up how it affected him first."

Ben had a brother like that himself, so he nodded. "You want to make things right."

"Exactly." Finn motioned for another shot. "You sure you won't join me?"

"Nah, I need to watch the drinking."

"Fair enough." Finn changed his order to another beer and one for Ben. "I can watch that drinking with you then."

"What now?" Not being a complete lightweight Ben could risk another beer.

"I told her to think about it." Finn picked at the label on his fresh bottle. "But we both know she's going to keep saying no, because that's Poppy. She'll get it into her head that it's unfair to trap me in a loveless marriage with four kids, and that'll be that."

"Does it bother you?" Ben turned and studied Finn's face. "The four kids thing."

"Nah." Finn shook his head. "But then they're my brother's kids, so maybe it's different."

"Maybe."

Finn met his stare. "Does it bother you?"

He liked the kids, really liked them but liking was a long way from fathering. He gave Finn the truth. "I don't think so."

The silence between them felt comfortable.

"I had the dreams too, you know." Finn finished his beer and clanked the empty down on the bar. "Still do sometimes."

Ben felt his pain. "What do you do?"

Finn grinned. "I'm doing it."

Poppy cleaned on autopilot the next day. The more she thought about Horace's crazy offer, the more she became convinced Horace had had some kind of temporary lapse in judgment. Angry and hurt, he'd made an impulsive offer. If he didn't say anything about it, then neither would she. But he'd opened up a secret corner of her mind and stuff kept coming out of there.

Already she had the kitchen redesigned in her imagination and she hadn't even done the laundry yet.

At noon she picked the girls up and they walked to Dot's to get the boys.

Finn and Maura greeted her when she arrived at Dot's. Well, Maura did, but Finn seemed occupied with chasing Ryan around the garden. His role demanded a lot of growling.

"Poppy." Maura gave her a thin-lipped smile. They hadn't spoken since that last throw down. "Finn and I are leaving tomorrow."

Behind Maura, Dot threw her hands up and thanked the heavens.

Poppy hid her smile. "I'll let you know as soon as we get settled where we are and how to get ahold of us."

"Good." Maura nodded. "As it's my last night, I wanted to take the children for the night. All of them."

Not sure what to do Poppy glanced at Dot. Her gut reaction was a great big hell no. But Maura had offered to take all the children, so it might mean a small step toward some kind of workable future.

Finn walked into the kitchen and scanned all three of their faces before approaching Poppy. "It really is your decision. They're your kids." He held her shoulders. "But I'll be there the entire time, if that helps."

It did help. A lot. Finn never played favorites with the kids. In fact, when Maura did her thing with the boys, Finn always made sure the girls got some special attention from him.

"She really is leaving in the morning," Finn said.

"You too?"

Finn nodded. "To give you a chance to come to your senses."

She laughed, but it was all still awkward. What would Maura make of Finn's proposal if she knew? Then again, Finn handled his mother so much better than Sean had. Sean's idea of handling Maura was to roll over and play dead.

"I'm not going to change my mind." She kept her voice low enough for only Finn to hear.

Finn winked. "You say that now, but I haven't hit you with the my full Irish charm yet."

"Mom." Ryan tugged on her sleeve. "Nana says we're all spending the night with her at the hotel."

Finn closed his eyes and winced. "I'll be there the whole time."

"I'm thinking about it." Poppy cupped Ryan's chin. When Sean was still alive, he'd spent a couple of nights at Maura's. "You want to go?"

"Yeah!" Ryan made a duh face. "She says we can watch movies and eat candy on her big bed."

"Not too much candy." Poppy looked at Finn.

He nodded.

"You want to go?" She turned to Brinn and Ciara who were watching with wide eyes.

The delight on their faces nearly killed her. So quick to forgive and so eager for the attention Maura had never given them.

"I promise," Finn stepped closer and lowered his voice. "And just think, in the morning she'll be on her way."

"Okay then," Poppy said it quickly before she changed her mind.

"Done." Finn went into action. "Let's go and get a bag packed for you guys."

"You sure?" Dot sidled up next to her.

"Nope." Poppy shook her head, but until recently Maura had been the only grandparent they had, and Finn would keep her in line.

"Ben!" Ryan bellowed.

Ripples of excitement washed over Poppy as Ben walked into the kitchen.

"Poppy," he said her name like a caress. Over the children's heads, his dark gaze told her all she needed to know.

Ben hadn't stayed away because he no longer felt this thing between them.

His name escaped her in a breathy whisper. "Ben."

Poppy got lost in the fathomless heat of his eyes. Brain function slowed to a minimum.

Fortunately, Ryan filled any possible silence. "We're going to sleep at Nana's. Me, Brinn, Ciara and Sean. We're all going to sleep at Nana's hotel, and have a big sleepover with movies and candy and chips."

"That's great." Ben glanced at her.

Poppy nodded that she was okay with it.

Four days since she'd seen him and her gaze sucked him in like a missing limb. His T-shirt hid more of his gorgeous chest and arms than displayed them. Ben didn't go in for peacocking of any kind. But she knew what lay underneath that fabric and her fingers twitched to get at it again. Ben's tall, powerful body had done mind-bending things to hers. She needed to get over herself and help her children pack a bag.

"Come on then." Finn upended Ryan over his shoulder. "Let's get your stuff."

Walking beside Ben, Poppy followed Finn and the children to Winters House.

"I couldn't stay away any longer." Ben spoke for her ears only.

The new development left her childless and free tonight. Which was irrelevant. Unless somebody had an idea about how she could spend that time. "You already stayed away too long."

"Hurry, Mom." Brinn bopped onto the porch and gesticulated to her to hurry.

Poppy's packing effort caused even Ryan to accuse her of being clumsy. It took longer than expected to get all four children ready.

Finn loaded their bags into her car. They'd decided to swap cars because of space and car seats and Finn would get his car back in the morning when he dropped the children home.

Standing on the porch with Ben and Dot, Poppy had to suppress the urge to run after the van as it turned the corner.

"Well." Dot made a huge show of stretching and yawning. "I think I'm going to take advantage of a quiet night and have a nice long bath."

Dot trotted back to her own house.

"That was subtle," Ben said.

Laughter eased some of the awkwardness and Poppy relaxed.

"Hey." Ben caught her hand before she could walk into the house. "Why don't you come out for a drink with me?"

"A drink?" Two adults venturing out, without kids in tow, to indulge in an adult pastime.

"Why not?"

Exactly what her silly self had been secretly hoping for and why not indeed! Poppy grinned up at him. "Give me a couple of minutes to get changed."

"You look fine like you are." Ben slipped his arms around her waist. He bent and kissed her. "Hey, how are you?"

The rest of the world rolled back and it was only the two of them. "I'm good." Her life was careening faster and faster into difficult but right now she was good. Great even. "Five minutes, I promise."

Five minutes didn't present much of a challenge when your wardrobe was limited to only slightly ugly shirts and jeans, and almost pretty shirts and jeans. She arrived in the kitchen only a minute late.

As he checked his watch Ben grinned. He took her hand as they walked to the car and opened the door for her.

"Is this a date?" Poppy needed to stop a moment and clarify.

"Should it be?"

"Yes." She slipped into the car on a happy cloud.

He climbed in the driver's seat and started the engine. "Then it is," he said. "But not a proper date. That'll be somewhere we both get dressed up for."

"Really?" She and Ben going somewhere without other people around seemed close to perfect to her. Specifically, without little people who needed lots of attention. "I've never been on that sort of date."

Ben gaped at her.

"I haven't." Poppy tried to shrug it off. "I got pregnant in high school, remember. Since then I've been married, having babies and widowed. It doesn't leave a lot of time for dating."

"We need to fix that." Ben picked up her hand and kissed her knuckles. "A woman like you deserves to be dated right."

That filled Poppy up with all kinds of sweet. "In fact, this is my first date. Ever."

Ben's jaw dropped and he shook his head.

He took her to a local bar. Parking the car outside before turning to her he said, "If I'd known about the date thing, I would have suggested somewhere different."

"This is fine." Poppy hopped out of the car before he could change his mind. A twenty-six-year-old woman on her first date didn't need fancy. She just needed out. On a date. Any date.

Chapter 29

Poppy's excitement only made Ben want to punch himself in the face all the more. She'd never been on a date? What the fuck was up with that? Dickhead husband hadn't even bothered to take her on date nights. Poppy practically danced across the parking lot in her jeans and old shirt.

The clothes didn't bother him. No matter what she wore Poppy was beautiful. When she wore nothing at all, she was even more beautiful. It was the fact that this woman didn't have a pretty dress to wear. His mother had given her the one she'd worn to the dance.

A woman like Poppy should always have pretty dresses to put on. She had the sort of smile that gifted everyone around her. It made you want to make sure she smiled all the time. Everything she had went to her kids first. Who the hell took care of Poppy? Spoiled Poppy? The Bugling Elk did not deserve to be her first date. He caught her before she got to the door. "This is a dumb idea. I'll take you somewhere nice."

She glanced at the door and her face dropped. "Is it horrible in there?"

He shrugged. "It's majorly cheesy."

"Cheesy." Her face lit up with that smile that twisted him into a pretzel. "Please let's go. Please?"

"Seriously?"

Her eyes sparkled. "Oh, yes, I really want to go in."

Then in there they would go. Shaking his head Ben pushed the door open for her.

Poppy skipped across the threshold and stopped. She clasped her hands in front of her and giggled. "It's awful," she said and couldn't sound more pleased about it. "Is that really a collection of Elvis bobbleheads?"

"Yup."

"Right next to a singing carp?"

"Yup."

She tugged his arm and made him stop. Eyes huge she jerked her head at the wall above the entrance to the bathroom. "Are those women's panties?"

Dear God! What had made him think of bringing her here?

"Uh-huh." Let the lightning strike come now. Ben was ready.

"I love it." She crinkled her nose. "It's perfect."

So adorable. The kind of adorable you wanted to roll around in. He pulled her into a hug. "Let's get you a drink."

"Let's." She made for the bar and hopped on a stool. "As this is my first date, I need to establish the ground rules."

"Pretty sure that's not how dating works." He couldn't resist the lure of a laughing Poppy.

"My date, my rules," she said.

Maddison slapped two coasters and a bowl of peanuts in front of them. "What can I get you?"

Poppy looked at him. "What should I have?"

"Two beers." Ben took the stool next to her. "Ground rules?"

"Ah." Poppy spun in her seat and had a good look around. "Are you going to be that date who tries to get me drunk and takes advantage of me?"

Ben winced. "Nope. Consent issue there."

"Good point." Her face fell. Then she perked right up. "What if I give you consent now?"

"Needs to be in the moment." He nodded his thanks to Maddison and poured Poppy's beer for her. "But I could get you a little buzzed and see where that took us."

"That works." Her cheeks went bright red. "Are we okay? About the other night?"

Okay? Ben really didn't know about that. Didn't know if he'd been okay since the day she'd run that stop sign. But he did know that he felt more alive than he had in years.

He was still working on this answer when Heather shoved between them. "Poppy. What are you doing here?"

Poppy stiffened and some of the Poppy-magic drained out of her expression. "Ben and I are having a drink."

"Isn't this place the worst?" Heather leaned forward but her voice carried across the bar. "So totally Hicksville."

Glancing up Maddison raised her brow.

"No offense." Blushing, Heather waved her hand. "Jarryd's here. I am dying for you to meet him. Sweetie!" She stood on her toes and called across the bar. "Jarryd? Over here!"

A tall, slim man turned and gave them a bored look. He sighed, and then made his way over. He'd been at the parade and wearing pretty much the same expression. Poppy's first date had gone from bad to hellish.

Snappy shirt and jeans that probably cost more than Ben's mortgage payment, Jarryd arrived in a waft of aftershave. Ben didn't know aftershave but even he could smell expensive. Jarryd had a straggly goatee dangling on his chin and long hair beneath a knit cap. Gotta love a hipster.

"Jarryd Kennett." He held his hand out to Poppy. "You must be Petal."

"Poppy." Poppy shook the hand.

"And this is the police chief." Heather turned Jarryd his way with a giggle that belonged to a much younger woman. Say a thirteen-year-old girl.

While Ben accepted the limp handshake, Heather launched into *I Fought the Law.*

Yeah, he'd never heard that one before. He'd raise her *Sound of Da Police* and *Bad Boys.* Just to shut her up before Poppy died of embarrassment, he said, "What are you drinking?"

Jarryd grimaced. "I'd say beer but I don't rate my chances of getting a decent microbrew here."

Heather giggled and snuggled closer to Jarryd. "You order for us."

⸻ ♡ ⸻

Poppy worked to keep the irritation off her face. Her nice evening with Ben, and they'd burst her tiny little happy bubble. In a lot of ways, Mom had changed, but the way she treated the men in her life hadn't.

The giggling and simpering brought back a slew of unhappy memories.

While Jarryd went on and on about microbreweries Ben stood by the bar wearing his unreadable face.

Entire being focused on Jarryd, Mom beamed at him as if he represented the font of all wisdom. Mom had fallen deep for this pretentious man. God, her mother had horrible taste in men. Not that Poppy's track record left a stellar impression. Some men had dick written in neon letters above their heads, and everyone could see it but the woman who most needed to. Had Mom watched her with Sean and seen the same inevitable train wreck heading Poppy's way?

"Jarryd's making a movie." Mom stroked Jarryd's arm. "We are on our way to Europe to recruit a European director for the project."

Ben sipped his beer.

"It's a complicated project." Jarryd pulled a face and tugged his wispy goatee. "Not the sort of thing that would interest an American director."

"Uh-huh." Ben nodded.

Had Ben gone to sleep behind that neutral expression? Poppy needed to cultivate a look like that one. A way of being in the room and miles away. When he was with her, Ben focused, intent and a hundred percent with her.

"Jarryd feels he really needs a European touch to this project," Mom said.

What exactly was a European touch?

Poppy glanced at Ben.

He sipped his beer.

"It's a modern retelling of the Marquis de Sade." Mom bounced. "Jarryd is concerned if it's not handled sensitively it will become porn. That's why he wants a European director."

Jarryd winced around his mouthful of beer. "It needs a particular lightness of touch that we can't find here." He glanced at Ben. "Not that the average American knows who the Marquis de Sade was, which is part of the problem."

Ben grunted. He put his beer down on the bar. "You're talking about a man who systematically tortured and killed people for sexual gratification. Don't see how you're going to give that a light touch." He held his hand out to Poppy. "Wanna get out of here?"

Like she wanted nothing else. Poppy hopped off her bar stool and took his hand.

"Poppy." Mom stopped them before they reached the door. "Where are you going? You and Jarryd need to talk about the house."

"I'll call you tomorrow." Poppy wanted this one night without having to think about everything.

Mom glanced at Jarryd and chewed her lip. "We can't wait forever. Jarryd is doing you a favor and I don't want to inconvenience him."

Poppy nearly laughed. If it wasn't so sad, she might have. Mom was still bending her will to the man in her life. Even if she went to California, would she be able to handle that?

Poppy stopped midstride. If she went to California? That little question around the issue had snuck around the corner of her mind. When had she first considered not going?

"What is it?" Ben frowned.

"Nothing." Shoving that thought in the box with the others, she stood on her toes and kissed him. "Let's get out of here."

He leaned his forehead against hers. "I feel like I should insist we be responsible."

"Not tonight." Poppy pressed closer to him. "Tomorrow is soon enough to worry about the future."

Ben opened the truck door. "Fair enough."

They stayed silent on the drive to Ben's house.

He stopped the truck outside and turned to her. "Would you like to come in for a cup of coffee?"

"Coffee?"

"Dating experience," he said. "Ruins the mood if I invite you in for sex."

"Then I would definitely like some coffee."

Ben let himself out, came around the truck, and opened the door for her. He took her hand and led her into the house.

"So how does this work?" Standing in Ben's cabin, a wave of shyness washed over Poppy. At twenty-six it was a sobering realization that she had no game.

With a grin, Ben gave her a quick kiss on the mouth. "I make coffee and figure out when to make my move."

Poppy didn't think he was going to have to do much figuring out. So at ease with their situation, Ben must have had plenty of practice. "You make it sound daunting."

"It is." Loading the coffee maker, fetching cups, Ben moved comfortably around his kitchen. "Too fast and she runs. Too slow, she thinks you're not interested."

"Hmm." Poppy propped her chin on her palm and pretended to give it some thought. "So what sort of clues do you look for?"

Ben shrugged and leaned his elbows on the counter, bringing his face closer to hers. The clean harsh lines of his bone-structure made her want to trace them. It was a great face, one she had grown really attached to. "Does she lean into my space?"

Poppy edged closer to him. He had the perfect kissing mouth. Top lip clearly defined, with a plumper bottom lip. "What else?"

"When I touch her." Ben ran his fingers along the line of her jaw. "Does she move away or does she give me more access?"

Arching her neck, Poppy shivered as he stroked down her neck to her shoulder. "Anything else?"

"Hmm." Ben touched his lips to her throat. "Does she really want coffee?"

"No, she doesn't."

"Good answer." Cupping her nape he tugged her mouth to his.

As if learning how she liked to be kissed Ben took his time.

More than happy to go where he led, Poppy relaxed into him. Familiar and addictive his taste sent a slow, steady burn through her. They kissed like old lovers, content to let the passion build. They had all night

Ben eased out of this kiss. "Stay."

"Yes." Poppy walked to his side of the counter.

With his dark, hungry gaze he watched her come.

Poppy stopped in front of him. Slowly and carefully she unbuttoned his shirt and slid it off his shoulders. He was so beautiful, her breath caught. She touched him, letting her hands learn his chest and shoulders all over again.

Under the slide of her palm Ben's abs tightened.

She unbuckled his belt and then opened the button on his pants.

He stood silent, waiting, his muscles rigid and ready for whatever she wanted.

"You're beautiful." Poppy pressed a kiss to his neck. Opening her mouth, she grazed her teeth over his collar bones and down onto the swell of his pec. She couldn't resist sinking her teeth in. Not enough to hurt, but enough to make Ben groan.

He caught her hips and pulled her pelvis flush with his. Behind his zipper his cock pressed hard and insistent. "What are you doing?"

"Playing." Sinking to her knees, Poppy dragged her tongue down the ladder of his abs. The wonderland of Ben's body all hers for the playing. She slid his zipper down.

Ben went even tenser, staring down at her like a starving man.

She freed him and pushed his pants out of the way. First she explored. She flattened her tongue along the bottom of his shaft until she reached the tip, then she slid her mouth around him. The slightly salty taste of him turned her on even more.

Ben's hands clenched. He dropped his head back and groaned.

The power she had over him was pure aphrodisiac. She learned the shape of him, what amount of pressure made his fists tighten, where he loved the stroke of her tongue. She used her hand with her mouth, her other hand cupping his heavy sac.

Tangling his hands in her hair, Ben exerted enough pressure to keep her doing what she was doing.

Responding to the gentle thrust of his hips she sucked him deeper, going faster as he urged her on.

"Poppy." His voice rasped. "You have to stop that."

She had no intention of stopping.

His voice took on a harsher edge. "Poppy, I'm going to…"

Poppy hollowed her cheeks, then took him deeper. Pumping her hand, she worked him faster.

Ben came with a shout, his fingers digging into her skull.

Poppy took all of him.

Eyes warm, Ben pulled her up. Momentarily sated, he smiled at her. "That was…"

"Good?"

"Better." He kissed her, sliding his tongue into her mouth. Framing her face he kissed her deep and hard. "I want you in my bed."

"Yes, please."

He kicked off his pants. Naked, her hand in his, Ben led her to his bedroom. Reverently he undressed her. He touched her breasts, gaze intent on her nipples as they grew achingly hard under his playing fingers. With a groan he took her nipple into his mouth and sucked.

Poppy arched into his mouth.

He slid his hand between her legs. His fingers slipped through her wet heat.

She bucked into the glide and retreat of his hand, so close that she moaned when he pulled back.

"I want to be inside you." Ben lifted her, thighs around his hips. His cock rubbed against her, sliding through the wetness.

Walking them backwards, Ben dropped her onto the bed. His mouth hit hers, ravenous. He pulled away to put a condom on and then he was back. Lifting her legs he opened her fully and thrust.

He filled her completely and Poppy's spine arched. She wanted him even deeper.

Ben thrust into her, harder this time, pushing her up the bed.

Poppy anchored her hands on the headboard and bore down on him.

His thrusts came faster and faster. Sweat beaded on his face. His torso shone slick as he took her higher, adjusting his angle until he hit the best spot of all.

Beyond caring, Poppy encouraged him. Her thighs gripped him tighter. Her orgasm built.

"Give it to me." Ben looked at her, so intense and demanding, locking her to him.

Her inner walls contracted around his cock, and Poppy let go. She flew. Her body arched off the bed as Ben slammed into her and came.

Ben dropped onto her, his heavy breathing filled the silence. His heart thundered against her chest, reverberating through her.

Poppy wound her legs and arms around him, needing to keep them in this moment for as long as she could.

Ben shifted onto his elbows. Pushing her hair off her face he kissed her forehead, her nose and then her lips. "You're killing me here."

Poppy laughed as pure, sharp joy filled her to overflowing.

Ben's laugher rumbled through her. He rolled off her and got rid of the condom. Loving the sight of him she watched him move naked around the room. A woman could look at this every morning for the rest of her life and never get tired of it.

Except she didn't have the rest of her life, she only had a few stolen moments and this might be her last.

Tonight she refused to get bogged in reality.

He came back to bed and dropped onto his back. Curling his arm around her shoulders he pulled her close to him. "Stay the night?"

"Okay." Poppy tucked her head beneath his chin.

His slid his hand down to her ass. "I can work with that."

Chapter 30

Poppy needed to be home before the kids were. The temptation to stay and make love one more time nearly pulled her back to bed. In the end, her mom side won and Ben dropped her off earlier than either of them would have liked.

He walked her to her door and kissed her goodbye. "Because that was the proper way to end a date," he said.

Still laughing, Poppy let herself into the house and went in search of coffee. Flipping on the light, she leaped back and dropped her purse.

Mom sat at the kitchen table, a mug cradled between her hands. "Hi."

"Shit, Mom, you scared me." Poppy put her hand on her heart, which threatened to pound right out of her chest. "How long have you been sitting there?"

"Not long." Mom shrugged. "Horace let me in, and I made some coffee."

Poppy picked up her purse and put it on the table. She fetched a mug and poured herself a cup. Her mom had to have a reason for chasing the sunrise here. It seemed way too late for a mother-daughter type chat.

"I wanted to talk to you." Mom fiddled with her mug. "About last night."

"Mom." Poppy kept her tone gentle, but she was way too old for a lecture. "I'm a grown woman. What and who—"

"God, no." Mom gaped. "I'm not here about that. Well, not only that but it is kind of part of what I need to talk to you about."

Conversations with her Mom still felt like nails on a chalkboard. Both of them tip-toed around each other, scared to upset the delicate balance of their new relationship. "What is this about then?"

Mom adjusted her shirt, and smoothed her hair down. "Are you still coming to California?"

The question surprised the truth out of her. "I don't know."

Flinching, Mom stared at her mug. "Is it something I did? Is it Jarryd?"

If they were ever going to build the sort of relationship worth having, there needed to be some truth between them. But truth came hard between two women who barely knew how to love each other. Both of them afraid to speak the words that might open the wedge between them again. "Jarryd..." How could she put this? "He's not my sort of man."

Mom looked up.

"But he doesn't have to be my sort of man." Poppy rushed in before Mom could speak. "He has to be your sort of man."

"And he is." Mom nodded. She took a sip of coffee. "This is tough. I've been sitting here thinking how to put this and now I can't seem to find the words."

"Mom." Poppy took her hands. "This is such bullshit. I love you. I've always loved you, even when I didn't like you much or want you in my life."

Jamming her hand against her lips, Mom tried to stop the sob from coming out. "I made so many stupid mistakes." She winced. "And I see you with your children and it makes me realize how much of lousy mother I really was."

"You did your best," Poppy said, because one of the things she'd learned with motherhood was that all a woman could do was her best. Sometimes it was good enough, other times it fell far short. More often it bounced somewhere in between. Like there were no perfect people, there were no perfect mothers. "But we can't keep rehashing the past or we might end up there again." On a deep breath, she took the plunge. "I don't like Jarryd, and the way you are with him reminds me of how you used to be."

"Ouch." Mom stood and went to the coffeemaker. She stood there with the pot in her hand and stared out the window. "I don't know if I can change."

"Are you so sure you should?" Poppy took the pot from her and put it on the counter. "Things between you and Jarryd work for you. They don't have to work for me."

"I couldn't sleep last night." Mom stared into the garden. "I kept wondering if I'd lost you."

"Ah, Mom." Poppy gave into the need to comfort her. "You can't lose me that easily. We're building something here, and we need to go slowly, but neither of us can change who we are."

Mom held her tight. "I want things between us to be better."

"Me too." Poppy blinked back tears. "And that's a good place for both of us to start."

Still wearing a stupid smile, Ben dropped in to see Ma.

The puppy pounced as he walked through the door.

Ma was right behind the dog. "And?"

Helping himself to coffee, he petted the dog while he waited for her to finish that thought.

"You and Poppy went out last night." Ma almost vibrated as she stood next to him. "And I saw you drop her off at Horace's. This morning."

He'd long since stopped reporting to his mother on his dating activities, so he drank his coffee. From the window he had a clear view of Horace's house. Inside Poppy would be getting things ready for the kids to come home. Maybe even making breakfast for Horace.

"Ben!" Ma stamped her foot and came after him. "What is happening with Poppy?"

"She's leaving, Ma." Even saying the words caused a constriction in his chest, but it was still better this way.

"Is she still going to leave?" Ma's face fell.

"You don't want her to go?"

"Do you?" Ma fixed him with a look and got herself a cup of coffee. "The prayer chain is driving me crazy with all their questions. First they say she's leaving with Finn and then her mother. And then everyone is talking about you and her and the way Tara is throwing you and her in Poppy's face."

"Tara's been bothering Poppy?" Maybe it was time to have another come-to-Jesus with his ex?

"I don't care about Tara. That woman is making an idiot of herself." Ma folded her arms. "I want to know why Poppy is still leaving."

"Speak to Poppy."

"I'm talking to you." She slapped his arm. "You like that girl, a lot. And you like her kids too. I bet if you gave her a reason to, she'd stay."

She always saw things through dream lenses. Love conquers all, rah, rah, rah. But love was very rarely enough, and even as Poppy had walked away from him this morning he'd heard that warning bell in his head. *She needs more than you can give.* "Ma."

"No, Ben." Ma slammed her hand on the table. "You need to listen to me. You have it all screwed up in your head. You think you don't deserve to be happy."

"I tried being married." He hated talking about this shit. Like yesterday, he'd remembered that feeling when he'd realized his wife was screwing around on him. The wave of not-good-enough that had nearly sucked him under. "It didn't work for me."

"Because you chose the wrong girl." Ma poked his chest. "Now the right girl is in front of you and you're too scared to do anything about it."

It wasn't as simple as that. Poppy needed more than just a man for her. She needed someone for those kids. He didn't have what it took to be a father, but Finn did.

"I've stayed out of this all this time." Ma gave him another poke. "But I can't do that any longer. I tried to let my boys go and not interfere in their lives.

"This is you not interfering?"

"Ben!" She growled.

"Ma." He held her by the shoulders. It had to end now. "I'm not going to change."

Tears glittered in Ma's eyes. "Well, you damn well should."

Maura brought the children home about half an hour after Poppy got home. Holding a whining Sean, she stood in the kitchen, beaming ice and anger at Poppy. "Ryan insisted on coming home for breakfast."

With the twins hanging on his legs Finn carried the children's overnight bags into the kitchen. His frazzled look made Poppy laugh. "Coffee?"

"Hell, yeah." Finn dropped into a kitchen chair. "You do this every day of your life?"

"Uh-huh." Poppy put coffee in front of him. "It comes with the territory."

"It's not that hard." Maura sniffed but couldn't quite hide the look of relief when Poppy took Sean from her. "You get used to it."

Inhaling coffee Finn shook his head. "I'm sure you do, but I've not been this tired since boot camp."

He was such a good guy, Poppy couldn't resist teasing him. "Want to take back your offer?"

"What offer?" Maura glowered.

"Hell no." Finn's eyes gleamed over his coffee cup. "You don't get off that easy."

Maura inserted herself between them. "What are you talking about?"

"I need to get the children and Horace fed." Poppy put Sean in his highchair and rescued Finn from Brinn tugging him. "Are you staying for breakfast?"

"Thanks, but no." Finn stood. "We've got quite a drive to the airport."

Shoulders collapsing, Maura melted into tears. "I don't know when I'll see them again."

"You'll see them again." Finn put his arm around her shoulders. "Poppy's put up with you this long; she'll probably tolerate you for a bit longer."

"Finn!" Maura scowled.

Finn herded her toward the door. He kissed all four children before stopping in front of Poppy. "Think about what I asked."

"Finn—"

"Think about it." He turned and led Maura back to their car.

Poppy fed the children and even managed to get Sean to eat enough that she could try and put him down for a nap.

While she was upstairs with Sean, Ben came 'round and took Ryan to play ball. As much as she would like to have gone down and spoken to him, Sean was super cranky after his night with Maura, and took all her attention. She and Ben had ended up having a yelled conversation down the stairwell.

The warm look in his eyes still had the power to make her blush.

Also tired, the girls spent a quiet morning coloring in.

Sean woke in time for lunch and after he'd eaten, Poppy took him out with her and sat on the porch. A beautiful day opened around her. Still and warm, the sun struck the green and made it lush and vivid. Still Poppy felt restless.

For the first time in a long time, Poppy had choices, and it scared her. She could return to Philly and take up the life she'd had before Sean had died. A nice house, great neighborhood schools, maybe even pick up some of her old friendships. This time with Finn. He might not love her, or her him, but Finn would take care of them. The downside of Maura didn't seem so daunting with Finn in her corner.

She could carry on her journey to California. Mom had come through for her and the kids. Being close to her mother held a lot of appeal. Just having that blood connection, and building something together that included Mom, her, and the children was something she'd ached for.

Or she could stay in Twin Elks. No way she would accept the ridiculous price for the house Horace had offered. That would be taking advantage of him. But the money she'd saved up for a house down-payment in California needed to be spent on a home. In a short time, Horace had become the grandfather her children would never have otherwise had. In Twin Elks, she had Dot, Kelly and Vince, and a whole host of people who had welcomed them to the town.

Since Sean's death, and maybe even before then, life had pretty much made the decisions for her and Poppy had bobbed along like a cork in its wake. Putting one foot in front of the other, inhaling and exhaling and trying to keep her family together, well, and safe.

The last time she'd made a decision, it hadn't gone that well, and the knowledge haunted her. She'd always wanted to keep the twins, but the decision to marry Sean had been counter to nearly everyone's advice. Mom had tried to talk her out of it, the counselor at the prenatal clinic had gently pointed out her alternatives, even her friends at the time had voiced their concerns.

Yet Poppy, deciding she must be in love, had made the choice to marry Sean. Silenced all opposition to the point of creating a rift between her and her mother, and charged forward.

Horace made his way on to the porch and handed her a beer.

Brinn and Ciara were playing amongst the rose bushes. Sean sat at her feet gumming his teddy bear as he watched his sisters.

"You look like you got a bug up your butt." Groaning, Horace lowered himself onto the porch swing.

"You sound like you need to see a doctor."

"Stop stalling."

"Stop stalling yourself."

"Ha!" Horace nudged a toy car toward Sean. Horace kept it casual but tension crusted up his tone. "You made a decision yet?"

"I'm having some trouble with that." The bitter bite of hops soothed her dry mouth. "Last time I made a decision, I made the wrong one."

"You know how I feel about that," Horace said. "You got where you are today because of the decisions you made. You don't get to cherry-pick isolated events to change. So, what's really bothering you?"

If she wanted sympathy, she needed to talk to Dot. "I'm scared I'll make the wrong decision for me and the children."

"Is there a wrong decision here?"

"Maybe not." Keeping her gaze on Sean she shrugged. "And to be clear, if I do buy your house, I'll pay a fair price for it. And you need to stay in the carriage house."

He looked at her and gave her a toothy grin. His trust took her breath away.

"You know what I want you to decide. I'll even formalize things between us like they were with Hildy," Horace said. "But that's what's right for me. What do you want, Poppy?"

"I don't know."

"Yeah, you do." Horace sipped his beer. "You're just too chicken to grab it."

Sometimes the urge to smack Horace overwhelmed her. "I don't like you much."

"Yeah, you do." Horace chuckled. "Heads up. Here comes Dot like her butt's on fire."

Dot opened the garden gate and hurried up the walk.

Her expression made Poppy go cold.

"Poppy." Dot grabbed her hand. "Ben just called. It's Ryan."

The world tilted around Poppy. "What is it?"

"There's been a small accident. Ryan is okay but he might have broken his arm. Ben says you need to get to the medical center." Dot grabbed her hand and held on, giving Poppy her only grip on reality.

Horace stood. "I'll drive you."

"You go." Dot nudged her. "I'll take care of the others. Call me when you know more."

Horace drove the old Cadillac faster than he should have.

Poppy hung on and tried to reach Ben on his cell. The damn thing kept going to voice mail. A broken arm, just a broken arm, kids broke things and recovered. It didn't matter how many times she said it to herself, the panic kept coming back, rising up her throat and making it hard to breathe.

At the clinic, Horace stopped outside emergency and Poppy leaped out of the car.

Hand at his nape Ben stood in the white, bright hallway. He caught sight of her and hurried forward.

"Where's Ryan?" Poppy needed to see her son, touch him, hold him, count all his fingers and toes.

"The doctors are in with him." Ben took her arm and led her down the hall and into a wide-open bay with cubicles. "I was with him and Ma called to say you were on your way."

"He's all alone." Ryan had nobody with him to hold his hand and tell him everything would be all right.

"There's a very nice nurse with him," Ben said. He stopped at the third cubicle to the left.

Poppy held up her hand to stop him. She took a deep breath. If Ryan saw her panicking it would only make him more frightened. She dragged in a couple of breaths before she was ready, and nodded to Ben.

With a clatter Ben dragged back the curtain.

Ryan. Small in the big bed. His pale face stained with dirty tear tracks. He saw her and fresh tears welled. "M-mommy?"

"Hey, baby." God knew how, but she found a calm voice. She took his precious face in her hands and kissed him, drawing the sticky, sweaty smell of little boy in deep to her lungs. Her baby. Hers.

"My arm hurts." Ryan sniffled and pressed into her chest. "I hurt my arm when I fell."

"I heard." She wanted to pick him up and bundle him close to her heart. She held onto what she could and glanced at Ben. "What happened?"

"He was playing ball with some other kids in the park. He tripped and fell down an embankment."

"He tripped?" Poppy couldn't really make sense of the words. "Where were you?"

"Right there," Ben said. "I was watching them play."

"I wasn't looking where I was going." Ryan raised his head. "I was watching the ball like Ben told me to."

Ben grimaced. "I'm sorry, Poppy. He was only playing football."

"Mrs. Williams?" A young woman in scrubs entered the cubicle. "I'm Doctor Stevens. I'm the doctor in charge of Ryan."

"How is he?" If the damn pounding of her pulse would stop long enough she could hear the doctor. She looked far too young to be a doctor.

"Ryan fractured his arm. But it's a clean break and should heal up nicely." She consulted a bright blue plastic file with dancing teddy bears on the front. "We also think he incurred a mild concussion when he fell. We'd like to keep him overnight, just to be sure, but you can stay with him."

"Okay." Fracture, concussion, the words churned around in her brain.

"We don't expect any problems," Doctor Stevens said. "But given his age, we'd like to keep an eye on him tonight."

"Okay." She nodded. A clean break, the doctor said it would heal up nicely. "His arm will be okay?"

"Sure." Doctor Stevens smiled. "We'll set it for him, give him a cast and he can get all his buddies to write on it."

"A cast?" Ryan perked up. "Can I have a colored one?"

Doctor Stevens chuckled. "Sure you can. I'll get the nurse to let you to choose."

Ryan gave her a goofy grin.

"We gave him something for the pain," Doctor Stevens said. "So he should be quite comfortable."

Breathing labored, Ben found an empty waiting room and sank into a chair before his legs gave out. No matter what he'd seen in the war, and as a police chief, the kids always got to you the worst.

With Ryan it had ricocheted through him so much harder. He couldn't get the picture of Ryan's tear-stained, pale little face out of his mind. Somehow it blurred with other faces. Eyes haunted by pain staring up at him and begging him to save them.

Little Riley Cox the day he'd fallen off his bicycle, broken his leg and scraped one side of his body to hamburger. The nameless kid they'd cut out of the wreckage of a car on the highway. Ben had carried his lifeless body out of the car with the kid's mother screaming out her ragged denial.

They came at him harder and faster until the hard ridge of the plastic chair pressing into his hand provided a tenuous grip on reality.

Private Digby, Digger, drowning on his own blood, coughing out bubbles as he tried to speak. His grip so tight on Ben's hand, as if he could hang on and stop death from taking him. The charred bodies beside the road as their convoy drove through.

More and more faces, hammering on his mind and demanding he look at them and acknowledge them. Demanding he acknowledge how he'd failed them. And Tara crept through them. Her face, the day she'd told him there was no more baby and it was all because of him.

Poppy drew comfort from the calm efficiency of the hospital routine.

Ryan got his cast. Bright yellow, and they settled him in a ward with two beds. The nurse explained that she could spend the night in the other bed, and they would be waking Ryan throughout the night because of his concussion.

Poppy sat by his bedside and watched her baby sleep. Cleaned up, wearing a hospital gown with the hideous yellow cast resting on the covers.

"Mrs. Williams." The Nurse popped her head around the door. "Chief Crowe asked me to tell you not to worry about your other children, as they had it covered."

"Is he still here?"

The nurse nodded. "He's been in the waiting room all this time."

"Does he want to see Ryan?"

"I'll ask." The nurse slipped out of the room.

Ryan flinched in his sleep and Poppy ran a soothing hand over his forehead. Now that the crisis was over, her head ached and exhaustion was creeping in. She wanted to sleep but she didn't think she could take her eyes off Ryan right now.

"Hey." Ben arrived in the doorway. He looked as tired as she felt. His face set in grave lines. "How is he?"

"Fine." Suddenly Poppy had the insane urge to cry. Her voice wobbled as she said, "He's going to be fine."

Needing Ben's comfort she stepped forward.

His big arms came around her and pulled her against his chest. Poppy let go of all the crap she'd been holding inside since Dot had come and told her about Ryan's accident. With Ben she felt safe to let it all go.

"Shit, babe." He pressed his cheek to the top of her head. "I am so goddamn sorry."

"It wasn't your fault." Kids had accidents all the time. Shit happened and especially with active boys. Ben hadn't caused Ryan's accident. "He fell and broke his arm. Kids fall and nine times out of ten they bounce right up again."

Ben tightened his arms about her. "I can stay if you like."

"No." She intended to make use of that spare bed. "You go home and check on the others. Let your mom know Ryan's going to be fine."

"Okay." He stepped away from her. "I'm glad he's okay, Poppy."

She patted his chest. "Me too."

Poppy brought Ryan back home late the next morning. It always took longer to check out of hospital than she would have liked, but eventually she had him loaded in Ben's car and they were on their way.

With Ryan still a little subdued after yesterday and Poppy tired, the drive was quiet. She'd woken up every time the nurse came to check on Ryan during the night.

Dot stood with Horace and the children on the front porch.

Brinn jumped from foot to foot and cheered as Ben helped Ryan out of the car.

Ciara beamed at them.

Ryan wrapped his arms around Dot's legs and clung.

"My, my." Dot rubbed his back. "You have had quite an adventure."

"Did you cry?" Brinn whipped her ponytail back and forth. "Dot said your arm was broken. Did you cry?"

"Ben did." Dot turned Ryan toward the house. "When he broke his arm, he cried because it hurt."

Brinn peered up at Ben and frowned. "You cried?"

Ben nodded. He glanced at his mother and then looked at Poppy. "I'll let you get him settled."

"You're working today?" Dot raised her brow.

Ben shook his head. "See you around." He touched Ryan's shoulder. "Get better."

"What the heck?" Horace scowled as he watched Ben stride away from them. "Did you have a fight?'

"No." Ben couldn't believe any of this was his fault "I'll be right back."

"Mooom." Brinn rolled her eyes. "We're having pancakes because Ryan is home."

"Start without me." She had to put on a burst of speed to catch Ben before he got into his car. "Ben!"

He stopped with the door open.

"Won't you come in and have pancakes with us? I know the kids would love it." Now she was being cowardly. "I would really like it if you did."

"Maybe later."

A warning bell tinkled in her brain. "Is something wrong? I don't blame you for what happened with Ryan. The same thing could have happened if I'd been watching him."

Ben dropped his head and took a deep breath. "Look, you're tired. You've had a helluva night. I'll speak to you later."

"No, speak to me now." She had the weirdest sense that if he left now there wouldn't be a later, which was crazy. Okay, Ben hadn't made her any promises but she couldn't be the only one feeling these things. She'd put money on it. She needed the connection and she touched his arms. "What is it?"

"This." Ben gestured. "I can't do this. Any of it."

Her mind reeled. "What does that mean? You can't do any of what?"

He speared his fingers through his hair. "You need more than me, Poppy. Your kids deserve better."

"What?" She felt stupid, like she was only catching a third of the conversation. "I don't understand."

"Yeah, you do." In his eyes was the implacable truth. Already she could read his withdrawal. "I can't be the man you need. I'm not cut out for this."

"Being with me?" She couldn't believe this. But she had to get her head around it because Ben looked like he was being dead serious. "Being with the kids?"

"You need someone like Finn." Where he gripped the top of the door Ben's knuckles whitened. "Someone who can be a good father to those kids, as well as your man. I'm not that guy."

"Because of what happened to Ryan?" Poppy found it hard to breathe. Her chest ached. "Things like that happen when you have kids. Even the best of parents have things happen to their children. It doesn't mean anything."

"It does to me." He reached for her, pulled his hand back and shook his head. "I can't. I'm no good at this."

Her head nearly exploded. "Who the hell is?" She hauled back on her volume. "Do you think they come with some kind of instruction manual? Nobody is made for this, or cut out for this. We learn as we go along. Even when you plan for children, get all excited about that baby on its way, we're all still learning as we go along."

Ben stood, his face rigid.

"What? You don't think I get scared at times? Feel out of my depth? Inadequate?"

He dropped his gaze.

"Oh, my God." Poppy wanted to hit him, shake him until she could get more out of him. Ben had retreated to that Ben place where nobody got to enter. It wasn't good enough. "I never had you pegged for a coward. You think taking yourself out of our lives is some kind of noble sacrifice you're making."

"Poppy, I—"

"You had your chance to speak and you blew it with that strong, silent bullshit. You can tell yourself that we'll be better off without you. That you're no good at this. But the truth is you're scared." Tears threatened and if she stood here much longer she couldn't keep them inside anymore. "I have four children, Ben. I don't have time or space for scared. I need a man to show up and stick. I've had half-assed and I'm not doing that to myself, or my children, again. So, if you even suspect you might not be able to be that man, then go." She shoved his shoulder. "Get in your car and go, because I need all in. All the time. All the way through. I need that." Her breath sawed through her mouth. "And I fucking deserve that."

Chapter 31

Poppy waited for the children to be asleep before she got her packing underway. For three days she'd drifted around in a haze of hurt. Finally, this afternoon, she'd made her decision. She had gone around to see Dot earlier, but Horace had been out all day and she hadn't had a chance to speak to him yet.

Funny, how she'd spent days dithering about which way to go, what to do and damn Ben had given her the answer. Not the answer she wanted or needed, but an answer.

Yippee!

Her and the children's lives had gotten so tangled up in Horace's. Looking around the front room, the task daunted her. Toys in the chest of drawers. Kids books shoved in amongst Horace's hardcovers. Ryan's sweatshirt tucked down the side of the sofa. Brinn's shoes by the door.

She had to start somewhere. Best way to eat an elephant and all that.

Horace stomped in from the kitchen and leaned his shoulder against the door. "What are you doing?"

"I think I've made my decision." She motioned him to sit. "I need to talk to you."

"Uh-uh." Horace shook his head. "I can hear just as well standing up."

She didn't want to end things with him like this. A hasty conversation conducted with her arms filled with toys and Horace lurking in the doorway. Their time together had meant so much more than that.

"So." Horace sniffed. "Philly or California?"

"California." She gathered up the sweatshirt and the shoes. "I can't go backwards. Even with a man as good as Finn. I want more."

"When?"

"I won't leave right away. Dot says she will come and keep an eye on youYou can put the house on the market and make sure you sell it to someone who's going to love it like I did."

"I see you got it all worked out." Horace stomped to the sofa and dropped into it. Springs creaked in protest.

"I can't stay here." Poppy perched on the far sofa arm. "But because I'm not here, it doesn't mean you have to let the house be torn down and turned into condos. The world has too many condos as it is. Maybe if you had your hip fixed, you'd be able to manage more."

"Don't worry about the house." Horace eased his bum leg out. "Or my creaking bones."

He was going to be reasonable about the house. Relief flooded through her. "It really is a great house. Somebody out there is looking for a house just like it."

"Why?" Horace glanced at her.

"Well, because it's perfect for—"

"Why are you leaving?"

"You know why." Poppy didn't want to get into a long explanation and she didn't think she needed one anyway. "I can't stay here. Not after Ben…"

"Lame." Horace heaved to his feet and limped to the sideboard. He poured two hefty scotches and clomped back and handed her one. "Drink up. It'll make what I'm about to say go down easier."

"I thought it was a spoonful of sugar?" Poppy peered into her scotch.

"Sugar is for pussies. Drink up." Horace downed half of his in one swallow. He grimaced, coughed and smiled. "That's the ticket."

Poppy took a cautious sip. Her windpipe screamed and she wheezed. "What the hell is this?"

"Truth serum." Horace dropped into the sofa. "So you're leaving because of a man?"

"What? No!" Confused. Poppy stared at him.

"Well, as I see it, you must be." Horace sipped the rest of his drink. "You have a place to stay. You could even have a job if you wanted it. You have friends here. People who care for you. Only thing you don't have is Ben Crowe."

She wished she could make him understand. "It's not that simple."

"No?" Horace raised a craggy brow. "So why else are you leaving?"

"I told you. My mother and I have—she has a job for me. Someplace for me to live. I need to build those bridges."

"Ah." Horace nodded. "You didn't tell me your mother would never talk to you again if you didn't go to California."

"What?" Horace was messing with her careful thinking. "She never— it's not like that. Of course she would still talk to me, but we wouldn't get the chance to be close."

"And of course, she would never come and see you here." Horace snorted. "Or you could never take the kids there. Good thing you're going then."

"You don't understand." Poppy felt backed into corner. She needed him to understand. "Things would be very awkward for us if I stayed."

"Because Dot would refuse to have anything to do with you again. She's that kind of coldhearted bitch. She'd probably turn the whole town against you."

"No, she isn't." Poppy wanted to stamp her foot like Ryan. "Dot has been nothing but kind and supportive. Why are you doing this?"

"Because I don't think you should leave," Horace said.

"Of course you don't." Poppy could bust a gut laughing at his hypocrisy. "Because it suits you to have me stay. It fits in with your plan so perfectly."

"Damn straight it does." Horace thumped the sofa. "Having you and those kids here. Best thing that has happened to me since my wife died. If you wanted to stay we could make it a permanent arrangement, put you on a salary."

Poppy softened immediately. "I'm so grateful I met you."

"Grateful-schmateful." Horace heaved himself up. "Me and Cecily, we're the best thing that's happened to you since your no-good husband died as well."

"You're right."

"And you're going to walk away from that because of a man." Horace arced his arm through the air. "Turn away from all you're building here. Friends, family, a place for you and those kids. You're going to walk away from all of that because of a man." Horace drew level with her and glared. "The last time you made a decision because of a man, how'd that work out for you?"

Poppy didn't sleep at all. Not a wink. Horace had a point. Crap! Twin Elks offered her so much, and she wanted all those things. The only thing she couldn't have was Ben Crowe. It was as though she was saying that without Ben she could never be happy, and she truly didn't believe that. You made your mind up to be happy instead of sitting on your butt waiting for Prince Charming to drop happy into your lap.

Great advice, and somebody should take it because she sure as hell wasn't using it.

Dawn found her in the kitchen banging pots and pans around. By seven a.m., she'd baked muffins, cookies and banana bread, had her third pot of coffee going and eggs sizzling in the pan.

"Oh, my." Dot stood in the doorway and blinked. "I—have you—oh, my."

"Coffee?" Poppy grabbed a mug.

"I think so." Dot took a seat.

Poppy poured her coffee, and added cream and sugar the way Dot liked it. "I'm not leaving."

Dot squeaked.

Poppy stared at her. She needed to get this out before Dot said a word.

Dot wrapped her hands around her mug and looked down.

"I like it here." Poppy pushed the eggs around the pan. "The children like it here. We're happy."

"Yes, dear." Dot sipped her coffee.

"I'm going to offer Horace a fair price for the house. I've got money. Not enough for this." She motioned with her spatula. "But enough for a hefty deposit and maybe Horace will let me work off some of the balance."

"I thin—"

Poppy glared at her.

Dot sipped. "Yes, dear."

"I love working with the children at the daycare. I thought I could do something part-time there and then look into getting a qualification. I love growing things. Maybe there's an opportunity for me." Poppy turned the heat off the eggs. Above them came the clumps and bumps of the children stirring. "I'm not sure what I want to do, but I have a place to live, a job if I want it and I can work out the rest."

"Yes, dear."

"The children can start at the elementary school in the fall. They already have friends there, so it makes perfect sense. My mom can come and see them whenever she likes." She got to work on the toast. "She's always offering to lend me money. I might even take her up on that." Not likely, but it was an option if things got desperate.

In the other room, Brinn yelled something at Ciara.

"Even Maura can come and visit when she wants. Finn, too."

"Yes, dear."

Toast popped and she buttered it. "I'm happy to do some shifts for Kelly as well. Just to make a bit of money. It's not much, but it all helps with the groceries." She would need much more than tips. "I haven't gotten it all worked out yet, but if I start with the where then I can make the rest of it happen."

"Yes, dear."

"So there it is. I'm staying." Poppy spooned eggs onto plates. "And if Horace gloats I'm going to toss his eggs in the garbage."

Dot stood and walked to her. She took the spatula out of Poppy's hand and placed it on the counter. Then she hugged Poppy until her ribs creaked. "I am so happy," she whispered. "And I think I'm going to cry now."

On Monday, Peg told Ben she'd seen Poppy at the elementary school. With the registrar. What did Ben think it meant? As Peg stood there looking at him with her head waggling like a mongoose, he chose not to answer.

While he got a coffee from Tuesday, Kelly glared over the counter at him and informed him he may be chief in this town but that didn't mean he could run anyone off. Even Vince chimed in from the back of the store. Something about how stupid letting a good thing go was. Vince was one to talk. Actually, Vince knew all about that, which kind of made them brothers in arms. Or dickheads in denial. Whatever.

Wednesday, he popped into Grover's to grab something for dinner.

Mia crossed her arms and stared down her pug nose at him. Quite a feat considering she was five-two to his six-three. "Can I help you, Chief Crowe?"

"I'm good thanks, Mia."

"Hmph!"

"Evening, Ben." Bart looked mournful. "Got some cold ones in the back if you need them." Bart sidled closer. "Considering everything."

It would take more than a cold beer to ease the gnawing hurt in his gut. "Thanks, Bart."

"Dad, did that lovely Mrs. Williams pick up her grocery order yet?"

Bart went all shades of red. "Not yet, Mia."

Giving Ben the stink-eye over the beets, Mia spoke to her father. "She's such a nice lady that Poppy Williams. I really like her. Such a wonderful mother, and those kids are super adorable. The Williams kids I mean. I think Poppy Williams might be the prettiest lady in the whole town."

Ben couldn't agree more. He paid for his groceries and made tracks to his car.

By Friday, he'd come to the inescapable conclusion that Poppy was here to stay. He couldn't summon up the balls to ask his mother, so he'd gathered up the tiny bits of information tossed his way and put them together.

Tara confirmed it with a vitriolic text over the weekend. Something about him not having the courtesy to tell her he'd moved on with his life. Considering she'd never had the courtesy to keep her legs shut when they were married, he deleted it without answering.

Poppy was staying. In a town this size, he couldn't avoid running into them. The dark cloud hovering over him lifted a tiny bit, which was so stupid it made his teeth ache. All the reasons he couldn't be with her were still there.

Which were?

For starters he'd make a crappy dad. Kids needed someone there all the time, who cared about their lives, guided them, loved them, found time for them.

Damn, he hoped Ryan joined the football team. That kid had an arm on him to beat Cam Rogers. Brinn should certainly get herself into theater group. He'd never met a kid with a better dramatic flair. And Ciara, with her sweet, shy smile had fastened a fist around his heart and squeezed. She didn't talk much, but when she did it was worth listening. With her old soul view of the world, Ciara could end up doing something amazing.

Finn got this about the kids. If Poppy was staying, did it mean Finn would head this way again? Poppy wouldn't find a better guy. Pity, he might have liked Finn if he wasn't Poppy's husband. He forced his fingers to release their stranglehold on his beer. If Poppy and the kids were staying, he needed to get a handle on it. He'd made a choice, a coward's choice. Poppy had called that one right. Maybe in time she'd forgive him enough to let him see the kids.

None of this was his problem. It had nothing to do with him. He'd made his decision and now he needed to stand by it. His footsteps echoed around his house. He chopped vegetables for his dinner but didn't feel like making some sad fucking dinner for one. It didn't make sense to cook everything and sit down at that table, on his own, and eat.

He left the vegetables on the cutting board. Then he sat outside on his porch with a bottle of bourbon and got ass over end drunk.

Poppy could never have imagined herself as a porch sitter. Yet, here she sat, occasionally using her toe to set the porch swing moving again, and keeping an eye on Horace deadheading the roses.

Even the insects kept their buzzing to a subdued murmur as the hot, lazy afternoon settled around them.

Sean had gone down for his afternoon nap, and Ryan sat on the floor beside her dismantling an action figure and putting it back together in anatomically unlikely ways. Brinn and Ciara were having a blanket tea party close to Horace. Ciara had left a place for Cecily.

It was strange that the girls had developed an imaginary friend here in Twin Elks. Of course, Horace played along with it.

Once she'd made her decision, things had dropped into place with surprising ease. Poppy suspected the omnipotent guiding hand of the Twin Elks Prayer Chain at work. Mom cried when Poppy told her the news, but she would be up to visit the week before school started, and help Poppy get the children ready.

Ben had stayed away, and she didn't like to ask Dot about him. He was squatting like the world's fattest elephant between them, but she hoped that would get better with time.

Ryan was enrolled in kindergarten which left her with Sean, and between Dot and the playgroup, they could free enough of her mornings for Poppy to take care of Horace and even look for something else. Dot had some ideas. Poppy chuckled, because of course Dot had an idea or two.

Horace being Horace still stubbornly insisted on not taking money for the house. He reasoned that he intended to will it to her anyway, so why should she pay? Poppy didn't want to be beholden to anyone, and needed to be in control of her future. Horace thought she was full of crap and should take the gift life offered. Negotiations continued. Mostly over beer but sometimes they needed whisky to keep it civil.

A car pulled up on the street and Ryan jerked upright. He was moving before Poppy got out of the porch swing. "It's Uncle Finn."

"Look at you." Finn stopped to greet Ryan. "Tell me that's not your throwing arm?"

Ryan giggled. "It's the other one."

"Whew!" Finn swiped his brow. "Because I plan to make lots and lots of money from that throwing arm of yours."

Brinn and Ciara swooped next.

It took Finn ten minutes to make it up the walkway. He stopped in front of her with his charming smile. "Poppy."

"Finn."

He winked. "Mom's not here."

Good enough news to make anyone smile.

"How's Ryan's arm?"

Poppy had called Maura and let her know about the accident. Then ended the conversation before Maura could launch into hundreds of accusations. "It's fine. A clean break. The cast should be off before he starts school."

"Well, that sucks." Finn ruffled Ryan's hair. "Then again, a cast is a great way to impress the ladies."

Wiping his sweaty face on his arm Horace limped over. "What brings you back?"

"Not really sure." Finn shrugged and looked around him. "I like the town. When I heard Poppy was staying I thought I might come back and offer my services."

"As what?" Horace's brows crinkled over his eyes.

Finn laughed. "I'm pretty handy with a hammer and nails." He kicked at a loose plank. "This old porch could certainly do with some of my attention."

"And that's all?" Horace folded his arms. "You're not thinking that something else here might need your attention?"

Finn mimicked his pose.

Men of all ages had that one in their arsenal. The human male equivalent to peeing on your territory. Poppy rolled her eyes. Ben—

Nope, it still hurt too much to think about Ben. Her gaze strayed to Dot's house, and Poppy yanked it back again. She spent her time on the lookout for Ben's car or his cruiser, then hiding upstairs and peering through the curtains to catch a glimpse of him. Which hurt like hell, so who knew why she did it, but she kept right on doing it anyway.

"Nope." Finn looked at her. "Offer still stands, Poppy, but that's not why I'm here."

She nodded. She got it, but she also knew Finn wouldn't push. "Where are you staying?"

"I hadn't gotten that far in my planning."

Horace snorted. "Thought you military types were all about the planning."

"You should know." Finn raised his eyebrow. "Imagine my surprise when I found a Major Winters in the military database."

"You can't trust those things." Horace clomped up the stairs. "Must be a glitch in it or something."

"You don't say." Finn grinned at Poppy behind his back.

"You can stay here," Poppy said. What the hell, the kids loved Finn and she could use some help with the house.

"Still my house," Horace said.

"Then you invite him."

"Already done." Horace opened the front door. "But I'm a light sleeper so there'll be no middle of night wanderings, if you catch my meaning."

"I don't." Ryan peered up at him.

"You will." Horace winked at him. "Now I'm old, I'm tired, I'm hot and I want to watch some TV. You lot can come and keep me company."

The children trailed Horace into the house.

"There won't be any middle of the night meandering," Finn said.

"I know that." Finn was a good guy. He wouldn't do a thing unless he got some encouragement. "I trust you. We're friends."

Finn winced. "Way to neuter a man, Poppy."

"Let's go in? Horace will start yelling for his coffee soon."

"Poppy." Finn caught her hand. "I'm only gonna ask this once, and then I'm gonna leave it alone. This is what you want, right? Living here with the old guy?"

"Yes." As the days passed she grew more certain. "The children are happy. Horace is actually great company and a good influence on them, and Dot helps me out all the time."

"And you?"

She shrugged. "I'm okay."

"What does Ben think?"

There was so much loaded behind the question it took her a moment to answer. "I don't know what Ben thinks. He hasn't been around."

Finn's gaze searched hers for a long moment. "That's too bad. He's a good guy."

She couldn't talk about it yet, so Poppy shrugged. Yeah, Ben was a good guy with massive commitment issues, and she couldn't go there.

"Poppy." Finn grabbed her hand. "I need to say something to you."

"Okay."

"Sean was one lucky son of a bitch to get you pregnant."

"Huh?" Her face heated.

"Not like that." Finn grinned. Then he chuckled. "Okay, not only like that because any man would be lucky..." Blushing, he cleared his throat. "Let's move on from there. What I meant is that Sean would never have had a chance with a girl like you if you hadn't gotten pregnant."

"I was in love with him."

"Sure you were. At the time." Finn shrugged. "But you wouldn't have hung around. Sooner or later you'd have seen him for what he was, and known you deserved more."

"I'm not so sure," she said. "I was a different woman back then. Horace is always saying how you don't get to change one thing about the past. Even the smallest change would have a knock-on effect."

Finn mulled that over with a small frown. "He's probably right. But still, you need to know, Sean was very lucky to have you. Ben can see that, and if he doesn't get his head outta his ass, it's his loss."

Chapter 32

Ma thunked a cup of coffee on the table and stared out the kitchen window. "Ah, isn't that nice."

All Ben had to do was wait for it.

"That nice Finn is back and helping Poppy fix the porch."

Coffee splashed over his crotch, and Ben leaped to his feet. "Shit!"

"Ben." Ma turned and stared at him. She looked down at his wet pants and giggled. "Having some trouble there, son?"

Sensing a game, Ryan's puppy cocked its head.

Sometimes it paid not to answer. He grabbed up a dish towel and mopped at the damage. Goddamn it, now he had to change pants before he went to work.

Ma went back to her window staring. "Oh, my."

That particular tone bought his hackles up. His mom sounded all breathy and girly. "What?"

"Nothing." Ma turned from the window, her cheeks flushed.

"What?"

"It's nothing. Now why don't you whip those off and I'll wash them for you quickly." She waggled her fingers at him. "Are you hungry? I can make you a sandwich while you wait for them."

"I'm not taking my pants off." How old did she think he was?

"Don't be grouchy, Ben." Ma glanced out the kitchen window again, and stopped and stared with her fingers mid-waggle.

Enough. Ben joined her at the window.

Dammit, Finn Williams really was back. Prick! Who the hell did construction work shirtless? A man could end up with a lost time injury like that. He glanced at Ma. "Are you staring at Finn?"

"No," Ma said, far too quickly. Then she giggled. "Maybe a little. He is very well put together, you know."

No he didn't fucking know. He stomped to the coffee pot and refilled his cup.

"Oh, look, there's Poppy."

Ben's head snapped around like a retriever on a squirrel

"Fuck!" He'd scalded his balls for sure that time.

"Did you spill again?" Ma wrinkled her nose at him. "I'm pretty sure I taught you to put your drinks in your mouth." She got kind of wily looking. "Or maybe it's the idea of Finn being back that's upset you."

He didn't plan to dignify that with a reply. It didn't matter a damn to him whether Finn was back or not. Free country. Finn could come and go as he pleased.

Ma poked his shoulder. "Or is it that Finn is living in the house with Poppy and the kids that has you all in a lather."

He was not in a lather. He was pissed off because he'd spilled coffee all over himself. "Finn is living in the house?"

"Yup." Ma looked altogether too happy about the idea. "Nice and cozy. Poppy tells me he's been a huge help, and you know those kids adore him."

Pretending suddenly got old. "What are you doing, Ma?"

She jammed her hands on her hips. "I'm trying to give you a kick up the ass."

"We've talked about this."

"No, we haven't." Ma rounded the table at a clip and jabbed him. "You spoke and I listened. Now I'm going to talk and you're going to listen."

He tried to stand.

Ma looked. *That* look. The one every mother has in her arsenal and demands instant obedience.

His knees bent and his ass hit the chair before the idea had fully formed in his brain.

"Poppy Williams is the best thing that ever happened to us." She upped the jabbing to a smack. "I love her and those kids, and so do you, you great big lunk."

He did not appreciate the lunk thing, but no way his legs intended to obey him over Ma right now.

"She was yours for the taking and you chickened out. It could be you over there fixing that porch right now. It could be you with your arm around Poppy."

He shot to his feet. Motherfucker!

Finn stood on the porch with his arm over Poppy's shoulder.

Poppy laughed at something he said. Her big beautiful Poppy smile all over her face. The smile that stuck behind his breastbone and set up a constant ache. His smile, and she was giving it to Finn.

"Finn is better for those kids." He hated it, but the truth needed facing.

"Why is that?" Ma cocked her head.

"You know what happened with Ryan."

Ma took a deep breath, and crossed her arms. "When you were two, your father accidentally slammed your fingers in the car door and broke them."

He didn't remember that. "Why?"

"He didn't do it on purpose." Ma rolled her eyes. "But you and Mark were getting out of the car and he didn't realize you still had your hand in the way when he shut the door."

He and Mark used to fight a lot getting in and out of the car.

"When Mark was about four you were playing in the living room and Mark dived off the sofa and onto the coffee table. Knocked his front teeth out. There was blood everywhere."

That Ben remembered. Also how cool all the blood had been and how Dad had put Mark's teeth in a jar for him to keep until his big teeth grew in. "What's your point?"

"My point is parents make mistakes. Even the best parents turn their backs for a second and things happen. I don't blame you for what happened to Ryan and neither does Poppy. The only person who blames you is you."

He had to say this before he lost the nerve. "And the baby?"

"Sweetheart." Ma's face softened and she leaned over and cupped his cheek. "Babies don't make it. It happens all the time. No, it's not right or fair, but it's life."

He knew all this, had known it for a while but the thing with Ryan had dredged up the doubt again. His counselor reckoned he was scared of making another mistake so had chosen to insulate himself instead. She didn't think a whole helluva lot of his strategy either. Come to think on it, neither did he. "Ma. I'm no good at the marriage thing. You know that."

Ma slammed her hand down on the counter. "Tara was no good at marriage. As far as I can see, you did fine."

"I made a shit choice."

"Can't argue with you there."

"What if I make another shit choice?"

Ma pointed out the window. "Look outside that window and tell me that's a bad choice."

On the porch, Ryan sat on a piece of lumber while Finn was hammering.

"Ben!" The twins had slipped into the kitchen without him seeing them approach.

Ma's huge puppy writhed and gamboled around them. That thing was going to be a horse. It needed children to play with.

Ciara stood behind Brinn, a shy smile on her face. It ate right into his heart until he wanted to bawl like a...well, a little girl.

"Where have you been, Ben?" Brinn shoved a hand on her outthrust hip. "Ryan's arm is so itchy now and Sean lost another tooth."

"Hey, sweetheart." Ben couldn't resist touching her sweet face. "You doing good?"

"I'm great." Brinn grinned at him. "I'm starting at the elementary school at the end of the summer. Ciara too."

Ciara tugged on his sleeve. "You should come back. To the family, you should come back."

Damn. Didn't that just carve a crater right through the middle of him. Kids saw things so simply. "I'll visit. Soon." As soon as it didn't cost him a vital organ to be around Poppy.

"It's okay, Ciara." Brinn put her arm around her twin. "We have Uncle Finn now. He is helping us fix up the house. And he really, really likes our mom."

What the hell did that mean? Ben gripped his coffee mug as he kept the question inside.

"Anywho." Brinn smoothed down her shorts. "Mom asked me to come and ask Dot if she wanted to come for pizza tonight." She nudged him. "We're making our own. Uncle Finn says it's so much better for you than the stuff you get in the store."

"That does sound like fun." Ma lit up like a sparkler. "I even saw this YouTube thing on how to make a dessert pizza."

Dessert pizza. Ben wanted to curl his lip. Who the hell made dessert pizza?

"Yeah." Brinn high-fived Ma. "We're going now. Back to our house, Ben."

He managed a tight smile "See ya."

"Yup." Brinn rocked on her sparkly Converses. "Our house across the road where our Uncle Finn is having a long sleepover."

The thing about being manipulated was that even though you saw it coming, sometimes the arrow shot true.

"With him there, with out mom, it's like having a dad."

Why the hell was he standing here while Finn played house with Ben's family? And they were his family. He sure as hell didn't deserve to get so lucky, and it would take him a lifetime to let them know it, but they were his.

Ben shot out the door ahead of the twins, and got halfway to the house before he even realized his feet were moving.

Finn stopped hammering and stood. "Ben."

"Finn. Poppy about?"

"Maybe." Finn flipped the hammer in his hand.

The door opened.

Ben tensed.

Horace walked out. "Ben."

"Horace."

"Poppy here?"

Horace scowled at him. "Could be."

"Why are you all standing here and glaring?" Brinn inserted herself between them.

Ma came up behind him. "Good question. Why are you all standing around staring at each other?"

With a nod, Ryan told her, "It's a guy thing."

"Mom," Brinn yelled. "Ben's here to see you but Horace and Finn won't let him in."

He owed Brinn big for the next fifty birthdays, and he planned to be around for most of those.

His skin prickled and Poppy stepped out on the porch. It hit him again how beautiful she was. Not just her pretty face and gorgeous body, but the light of Poppy that eked out of her.

"Ben." She didn't meet his eye.

He wanted to reach inside her and find her smile for her. "Can we talk?"

"Haven't you said enough?" Finn and his hammer took a step closer.

Poppy crossed her arms. "I don't think so."

"You heard the lady." Horace tapped his cane on the porch.

"Just to talk." Ma stepped in closer to him. "What harm can it do for them to talk?"

"Plenty." Horace huffed.

Poppy stared at his feet. "I think you said everything you needed to say."

Finn and Horace kept on glaring.

Ma nudged him.

The twins and Ryan stared at him.

Only Poppy wouldn't give him her eyes, and he desperately wanted them. "I said a lot when we last spoke." Fine, if Poppy's posse insisted on riding shotgun, they could hear this right along with her. "Most of it a load of bull...rubbish."

That got her attention. Her beautiful big brown eyes finally turned his way.

"I got scared, Poppy. I thought I couldn't do this." He waved a hand at the house and the kids. "I thought I wasn't good enough for this."

Ma snorted. "You're a wonderful man."

Just like Ma to have his back, even when he screwed up. "I'm not so sure about that. I didn't behave that way."

"Maybe not." Ma poked him. "But we all make mistakes."

Poppy's big eyes carried a world of wary, and he hated that. "What are you saying?"

"Come on." Finn gathered the twins and Ryan. "I think we should let Mom and Ben chat."

Horace jabbed his finger at Ma. "That means us as well, Dotty."

Footsteps thudded across the boards. Kids argued, adults answered, but Ben didn't want to look away from Poppy.

Someone shut the front door and they were alone.

Ben climbed the first step. "I'm saying I'm a dickhead. I love you, Poppy, and I love your kids." He took the next stair. "I panicked when Ryan got hurt and ran scared. But if you'll still have me, I'm not running anymore."

She hunched her shoulders. "How do I know you won't run again?"

An excellent question. And a more than fair one considering Poppy had more than herself to keep in mind. "I'll do whatever you need me to do to make sure you know it."

"Like what?"

"I hadn't gotten to the details yet." He'd charged over with a pterodactyl up his ass. "I love you. I want you and the kids to be part of my life. You tell me what you need to make that happen."

"I need a man who stands by us."

"Done."

"I need a partner who steps up."

"Done."

"I need someone who has my back and my children's back."

"Done."

"Faithful."

"There's nobody else. There couldn't be."

"And I need you to kiss me now."

"Done." Ben took the last step. "But that's gonna be more like a work in progress."

Epilogue

In the middle of the night, the Twin Elks Public Library was a place full of creepy shadows and large, hulking shapes. Built square and solid in the fifties, it provided the perfect venue for clandestine meetings. Beyond the stacks, and behind the small reading nook where every Thursday librarian Sally Klemper read a story to the town's children, lay the meeting room.

As Chairperson called the meeting to order, the murmur of conversation stopped. "Good evening," she said. "Thank you for being here. The chair recognizes the secretary for a report on last month's action items."

"Thank you, Madam Chairperson. Members." The secretary rapped her sheaf of papers on the shiny laminate tabletop. "As you are, no doubt aware, we made great progress on last month's action items."

"Hear, hear." Member without portfolio clapped enthusiastically.

"Can we get on with it," grumbled Treasurer. "It's late and my hip is killing me."

All eight members glared at him.

He subsided into a muttered silence.

"Item one." Secretary consulted her paperwork. "We can report a very successful conclusion to the resolution of this committee to see Ben Crowe settled. Can you confirm that that all is well, Mr. Treasurer?"

"You know it is." Treasurer couldn't quite suppress his smile. "Now, don't get all a-twitter or anything and start up with your clucking, but I might have heard mention of a ring in the future."

An excited chorus followed his statement.

"Madam Chairman?" Secretary turned to the head of the table.

Madam Chairman mimed locking up her lips and tossing her key over her shoulder.

The committee broke into applause.

"Right. Item two." Secretary had to rap her papers on the table for a few seconds to call the meeting to order again. "Item two also saw a very successful conclusion in that Winters House is once more inhabited and the threat has been neutralized."

"For the moment," said Treasurer. "But the threat could return."

A stiff breeze ruffled through the meeting room. Secretary snatched at her papers and glared at the empty ninth place at the table. "Stop that?" She looked at Treasurer. "We only agreed she could come if she didn't do her"—Secretary wheeled her hands in the air—"stuff."

"It's not like we can keep her out," said Treasurer.

The breeze died down.

"Noted." Madam Chairperson tapped Secretary's paperwork.

Secretary made a note in the monthly minutes.

"Item three remains in progress." Secretary turned to a woman seated on her left. "Can we get a report on that?"

Communications straightened in her chair. "Although there has been some progress, neither Kelly nor Vince show any sign of moving closer."

Madam Chairman shook her head. "That is disappointing. We may have to step up our efforts in that area."

Treasurer tapped his knuckles on the table. "With respect, fellow committee members, Vince is newly divorced."

"Yes, dear." Catering put her hand over his. "But he's was married to the wrong woman."

Treasurer snatched his hand away. "A man needs time."

"Of course he does," murmured Counter Intelligence with a kind smile from behind her knitting needles.

"Noted." Secretary scribbled on her notepad. "Which brings us to our purpose."

The entire meeting straightened in their chairs.

Secretary took a deep breath. "The revitalization of Twin Elks through the active encouragement of growing our community."

"Young blood," muttered Treasurer. "We need more young blood."

"I have an idea." Member without portfolio stuck her hand in the air.

All eyes swung in her direction.

"I think we should launch a social media campaign to appeal to younger people across the country."

Counter Intelligence dropped her knitting. "We can't advertise."

"No, nothing like that." Member without portfolio giggled. "I'm talking about a subtle campaign that details Twin Elks as a lovely place to live, build a career and later raise a family. We appeal to people on a more subconscious level."

"Subconscious is good." Counter Intelligence gathered up her knitting and resumed her purl row. "Just nothing too obvious."

"What the hell is social media?" Treasurer looked to Catering, who shrugged.

"Facebook," said Member without portfolio. "Twitter, Instagram, Pinterest, Tumblr." She tapped her chin. "Although Tumblr can be a bit dark and twisted. You have no idea what you will find there." She flushed and cleared her throat. "I could be in charge of that."

Secretary rapped the table. "All in favor of the creation of a social media campaign say aye."

A chorus of ayes followed. Secretary's papers rustled and settled down. "Motion passed," Secretary said. "Member without portfolio shall now be referred to as Social Media." She checked her agenda. "New business?"

Madam Chairman looked smug. "I had a very interesting phone call the other night. From my son."

Sarah Hegger

Born British and raised in South Africa, Sarah Hegger suffers from an incurable case of wanderlust. Her match? A hot Canadian engineer, whose marriage proposal she accepted six short weeks after they first met. Together they've made homes in seven different cities across three different continents (and back again once or twice). If only it made her multilingual, but the best she can manage is idiosyncratic English, fluent Afrikaans, conversant Russian, pigeon Portuguese, even worse Zulu and enough French to get herself into trouble.

Mimicking her globe trotting adventures, Sarah's career path began as a gainfully employed actress, drifted into public relations, settled a moment in advertising, and eventually took root in the fertile soil of her first love, writing. She also moonlights as a wife and mother. She currently lives in Littleton, Colorado, with her teenage daughters, two retrievers and aforementioned husband. Part footloose buccaneer, part quixotic observer of life, Sarah's restless heart is most content when reading or writing books.

Sign up to receive up to date information, sneak peeks, giveaways and special offers. Including an exclusive free read of the contemporary novella *Wild Honey*.

Turn the page to visit my website and find me on social media!

Website	Tumbler
Facebook	**Pinterest**
Twitter	**Instagram**
Amazon	**Goodreads**

Read on for an excerpt of Positively Pippa, #1 Ghost Falls Series!

Positively Pippa

From author Sarah Hegger comes an exciting new series set in small-town Utah, where secrets don't keep for long—and love turns up in the most unexpected places.

For Pippa Turner there's only one place to go when her life self-destructs on national TV—home to Ghost Falls, and her heavily perfumed, overly dramatic, but supremely loving grandmother, Philomene. If anyone will understand how Pippa's hit makeover show was sabotaged by her vengeful ex, it's Phi. But she's not the only one who's happy to see her—and Pippa can't help but wonder if Matt Evans, her gorgeous high-school crush turned Phi's contractor, is game for a steamy close-up…

Matt owes his whole career to Phi and her constant demands to embellish the gothically ridiculous house he built for her. Getting to see red-headed, red-hot Pippa is a bonus, especially now that she's no longer the troublesome teenager he remembers. He's willing to stay behind the scenes while she gives her own life a much-needed makeover, but not forever. As far as he's concerned, their connection is too electric to ignore. And the chance to build something lasting between them—before she can high-tail it back to Hollywood—is going to the top of his to-do list…

Chapter 1

"Aren't you—?"

"No." Not anymore she wasn't. Pippa snatched her boarding pass from the check-in attendant and tugged her baseball cap lower over her eyes. Couldn't Kim Kardashian help a girl out and release another sex tape or something? Anything to get Pippa away from the social media lynch mob. She kept her head down until she found her gate, and chose the seat farthest away from the other passengers waiting to board the flight to Salt Lake City. Latest copy of *Vogue* blocking her face, she flipped through the glossy pages.

Peeping over the top of her magazine she slammed straight into the narrowed gaze of a woman three rows over. *Shit!* Pippa dropped the woman's gaze and went back to Vivienne Westwood bucking the trend.

Across the airport lounge the woman's glare beamed into the top of her head like those laser tracking things you saw in spy movies. Pippa buckled under the burn and slouched lower into her seat.

Look at that, Fendi was doing fabulous separates this season. And really, Ralph Lauren, that's your idea of a plus-size model? Stuff like this made her job so much harder.

Her former job.

Losing her show still clawed at her. Losing? Like she'd left the damn thing at Starbucks as she picked up her morning latte. More like her jackass ex with zero conscience had knocked it out of her hand. Framed, stitched up, wrongfully accused—judged, found guilty, and sentenced to a plethora of public loathing wiping out all the years spent building her career. Burning sense of injustice aside, she was stuck in this thing until it went away.

Angry Woman lurked in her peripheral vision. As sweat slid down her sides, Pippa tucked her elbows in tight and risked another glance.

Under an iron-gray row of rigidly permed bangs, the woman's mouth puckered up.

Back to *Vogue*. The knot in her stomach twisted tighter, and she checked her cap. What the hell? A baseball cap and shades always worked for other celebrities. Why not her?

Angry Woman squared her shoulders and huffed.

This could go one of two ways. Either Angry Woman would come over and give her a piece of her mind on behalf of women everywhere, or she'd confine her anger to vicious staring and muttering. Maybe some head shaking. *Please don't let her be a crusader for women. Please, please, please.* After two weeks of glares, stares and condemnation, Pippa had gotten the message:

Pippa St. Amor, the woman America loves to hate.

Right now, all she wanted was to sneak home and stay there until someone else topped her scandal. God, didn't *Vogue* have anything fresh? She'd make a list. Lists were good. Soothing. *Item one, run away from Angry Woman and hide in the bathroom. Item two, get your career back.* She moved *item two* up to first place, where it had been since she left home at eighteen, and gauged the distance between her and the bathroom door. She'd never make it.

Angry Woman lifted her phone and snapped a shot of Pippa.

Damn, she'd forgotten that option; this one by *far* the worst. God, she hated Twitter. And Facebook. And Instagram, and Snapchat, and whatever-the-hell new social torment site some asshat was thinking up right this minute. The ongoing public derision chipped off bits of her until she felt like an open nerve ending.

A friend huddled next to Angry Woman, long hair that was totally the wrong shade of brown and aged her by ten years at least. If Pippa had her on the show, Long Hair would be wearing a cute, hip cut, a fresh new makeup look, and mile-wide smile with her new sense of self.

The reveals never got old. There was something about a woman finally seeing her own beauty that made all the other crap that went with a television career worth it. Ray had ripped that away from her too.

Pippa was getting it with double barrels now. Lips tight, matching twin spots of outraged color staining their cheeks as they whispered over Angry Woman's phone. They both wore mom jeans. Up until two weeks ago it had been her mission to deliver moms everywhere from jeans like that. Along with those nasty, out of shape T-shirts they sold in three-packs of meh colors that had no business existing on the color spectrum. Angry and Long Hair were so her demographic. They'd probably seen the original episode live and watched it over and over again on demand or something. Maybe even watching it right this minute on YouTube.

YouTube! She hated YouTube, too.

Why didn't they call her flight already and get her the hell out of here?

You didn't sleep with the boss, and especially not in television. For four years. Ray had always been a bit sneaky, but to annihilate her career to boost his own? She hadn't seen it coming. But you couldn't rely on a man. How did she not get this by now?

Three minutes until boarding.

"Excuse me?"

Ah, shit, shit, shit, double damned shit in a bucket. So close, two minutes and fifty-five seconds. Smile and look friendly. "Yes."

Try not to look like you.

"You're that woman, aren't you?" Angry Woman narrowed her eyes, and Pippa leaned back in her chair, out of striking range.

"Hmm?"

"It is you." Long Hair planted her legs akimbo like a prizefighter. "I watched every single one of your shows. I can't believe you said those things, and I—"

Two minutes, thirty seconds.

"—should be ashamed of yourself. What you said is a crime against women everywhere. You made that poor woman cry."

Of course they cried. They were supposed to cry. The shows were edited to make them cry even more, but not the time to point it out.

"Shocking. And cruel. You're just a . . . a nasty bitch." Angry Woman got the last word in. She'd been called worse. Recently, too, and it still stung.

A man in the row opposite turned to watch the action. The three teens beside him openly stared and giggled.

I didn't say it, people. Okay, she'd said it, but not like that. *Editing, people.* Creative editing—the scourge and savior of television celebrities worldwide. She could shout it across LAX and it still wouldn't do any good. Until the next scandal broke and hers was forgotten.

"This is a boarding call . . ."

Thank you, Jesus!

"I'm sorry, that's my flight." Pippa creaked a smile and gathered her things. Handbag, phone, iPad, and coat. Her hands shook under the combined weight of several sets of eyes and she nearly dropped her phone.

No cabin baggage, not on this flight. Nope, this flight she'd packed just about everything she owned into the two heaviest suitcases on the planet. Paid extra weight without an argument. Anything to get the hell out of LA and home to Philomene.

Phi would know what to do.

Chapter 2

"Shit, Isaac. If the plumber needs quarter-inch pipe, get him quarter-inch pipe." Matt threw open the door to his truck as he half listened to another lame excuse. He could recite them by heart at this point anyway.

"No, I can't get the pipe. I'm at Phi's house now." He sighed as Isaac went with the predictable. "Yes, again, and I can't come now. You're going to have to fix this yourself."

He slammed his door and keyed off his phone. Smartphones! He missed the days of being able to slam a receiver down. Jabbing your finger at those little icons didn't have the same release.

When God handed out brains to the Evans clan, he must have realized he was running low for the family allotment and been stingier with the youngest members. Between Isaac and their sister, Jo, there could only be a couple of functioning neurons left. And their performance, like a faulty electrical circuit, flickered in and out.

He grabbed his toolbox from the back of the truck. This had to be the ugliest house in history, as if Hogwarts and the Addams family mansion had a midair collision and vomited up Philomene's Folly.

His chest swelled with pride as he stared at it. He'd built every ugly, over-the-top, theatrical inch of this heap of stone. He'd bet he was the only man alive who could find real, honest to God, stone gargoyles for downspouts. Not the plaster molding kind. Not for Diva Philomene St. Amor. Nope, she wanted them carved out of stone and mounted across the eaves like the front row of a freak show.

"Hey, Matt," a kid called from the stables forming one side of the semicircular kitchen yard.

"Hey, yourself." He couldn't remember the name of Phi's latest rescue kid doing time in her kitchen yard. Kitchen yard! In this century. Diva Philomene wanted a kitchen yard, so a kitchen yard she got, along with her stables.

"I want a building to capture the nobility of their Arabian ancestors thundering across the desert." She'd got it. Heated floors, vaulted ceilings, and pure cedar stalls—now housing every ratty, mismatched, swaybacked nag the local humane society couldn't house and didn't want to waste a bullet on. A smile crept onto his face. You had to love the crazy old broad.

He skirted the circular herb garden eating up the center of the kitchen yard. A fountain in the shape of a stone horse trough trickled happily. He'd have to remind her to drain it and blow the pipes before winter. He didn't want to replace the piping again next spring.

The top half of the kitchen door stood open and he unlatched the bottom half before stepping into the kitchen. The AGA range gave off enough heat to have sweat sliding down his sides before he took two steps. He opened the baize door to the rest of the house and yelled, "Phi!"

He hadn't even known what a baize door was at nineteen, but the Diva had educated him because she wanted one and it became his headache to get her one.

"Mathieu!" The Frenchifying of his name was all the warming he got before Philomene appeared at the top of her grand, curving walnut staircase. Thirty-two rises, each six feet wide and two feet deep leading from the marble entrance hall to the gallery above.

The soft pink of the sun bled through the stained-glass windows and bathed the old broad in magic. Her purple muumuu made a swishing noise as she descended, hands outstretched, rings glittering in the bejeweled light. "Darling."

She made his teeth ache. "Hold on to the railing, Phi, before you break your neck." It had taken a crew of eight men to put that railing in, and nearly killed the carpenter to carve a dragon into every inch of it.

She pressed a kiss on both his cheeks with a waft of the same heavy, musky perfume she'd always worn. She smelled like home. "You came."

"Of course, I came." He bent and returned her embrace. "That's how this works. You call, I drop everything and come."

A wicked light danced in her grass green eyes, still bright and brilliant beneath the layers and layers of purple goo and glitter. She'd been a knockout in her youth, still had some of that beautiful woman voodoo clinging to her. If you doubted that for an instant, there were eight portraits and four times that many photos in this house to set you right. Or you could just take a look at Pippa—if you could catch a quick glance as she flew through town. He made it his business to grab an eyeful when he could.

"I am overset, Mathieu, darling." She pressed her hand to her gem-encrusted bosom.

"Of course you are." The Diva never had a bad day or a problem. Nope, she was overset, dismayed, perturbed, discomposed and on the occasion her dishwasher broke down, discombobulated.

"It is that thing in the kitchen." She narrowly missed taking his eye out with her talons as she threw her hand at the baize door.

Her kitchen might look like a medieval reenactment, but it was loaded for bear with every toy and time-saving device money could buy—all top of the line. "What thing, Phi?"

"The water thingy."

"The faucet?"

She swept in front him, leading the way into the kitchen like Caesar entering Rome in triumph. "See." He dodged her hand just in time. "It drips incessantly and disturbs my beauty rest."

He clenched his teeth together so hard his jaw ached. He ran a construction company big enough to put together four separate crews and she called him for a dripping faucet. "I could have sent one of my men around to fix that. A plumber."

"But I don't want one of your men, darling." She beamed her megawatt smile at him. "I want you."

There you had it. She wanted him and he came. Why? Because he owed this crazy, demanding, amazing woman everything, and the manipulative witch knew it. He shrugged out of his button-down shirt and pulled his undershirt out of his jeans. He was going to get wet and he'd be damned if he got faucet grunge all over his smart shirt.

Phi took the shirt from him and laid it tenderly over the back of one of her kitchen chairs. "This is a very beautiful shirt, Matt."

"I'm a busy and important man now, Phi. A man with lots of smart shirts."

She grinned at him, and stroked the shirt. "I am very proud of you, Matt."

Damn it all to hell, if that didn't make him want to stick out his chest like the barnyard rooster strutting across Phi's kitchen yard. He turned the faucet on and then off again. No drip. "Phi?"

"It's underneath." She wiggled her fingers at the cabinet.

He got to his knees and opened the doors. Sure enough, a small puddle of water gathered on the stone flags beneath the down pipe. Good thing Phi had insisted on no bottoms to her kitchen cabinets. It had made it a bitch to get the doors to close without jamming on the stone floor, but right now it meant he wouldn't be replacing cabinets in his spare time.

"You should be out on a date," Phi said from behind him.

"If I was out on a date, Phi, I wouldn't be here fixing your sink."

"Yes, you would."

Yeah, he would. He turned off the water to the sink. "Have you got some towels or something?"

She bustled into the attached laundry and reappeared with an armload of fluffy pink towels.

Wheels crunched on the gravel outside the kitchen and Phi dropped the towels on the floor next to him. She tottered over to the window to stare. A huge smile lit her face and she gave off one of those ear-splitting trills that had made her the world's greatest dramatic soprano. Everyone, from the mailman to a visiting conductor, got the same happy reception.

He leaned closer to get a better look at the pipes beneath the sink. Were those scratch marks on the elbow joint? Neat furrows all lined up like someone had done that on purpose. He crawled into the cabinet and wriggled onto his back. They didn't make these spaces for men his size.

"Mathieu?" Phi craned down until her face entered his field of vision. Her painted-on eyebrows arched across her parchment-pale face. "I have a visitor."

"Is that so?" What the hell, he always played along.

"Indeed." Her grin was evil enough to have him stop his tinkering with the wrench in midair. "I thought you might like to know about this visitor."

The kitchen door opened. A pair of black heels tapped into view. The sort of shoes a man wanted to see wrapped around his head, and at the end of a set of legs he hadn't seen since her last trip to Ghost Falls—Christmas for a fly-by visit. His day bloomed into one of those eye-aching blue sky and bright sunlight trips into happy.

Welcome home, Pippa Turner.

Pippa wrapped her arms around her grandmother and held on for dear life. Thank you, God, she was home. She'd made it in one piece. Missing the bits taken off her by the women at the airport, the car rental lady, and a group glare from a bunch of tourists at the baggage carousel of Salt Lake City Airport.

Phi tightened her arms around Pippa, as if she knew. Of course she knew, Phi always knew. The ache inside her chest unraveled and unlocked the tears. Not once in this whole ghastly two weeks had Pippa cried. But the smell of patchouli oil wiggled underneath her defenses and opened the floodgates. Home. Safe.

"*Ma petite.*" Phi stroked her back in long, soothing strokes. The jewels encrusting her bodice pressed into Pippa's chest, like they had all through her childhood. "My poor, sweet girl."

The tears came thicker and faster, gumming up her throat and blocking her nose until they roared out in great gasping sobs.

Phi absorbed it all, like Pippa knew she would. Quiet murmurs and calming pats that eventually calmed the storm enough for her to speak.

"Now." Phi cupped Pippa's face between her pampered palms. "You will tell me all the dreadful things that man did to you."

The relief almost got her crying again, but Pippa dragged in a deep breath. She could tell Phi everything, about Ray, the vapid blond thing he was boning, her meltdown, the lies—all of it. She had a list of every last one. And Phi would believe her. Not like those sharks surrounding her in LA. "Did you see it?"

Phi's eyes clouded and her mouth dropped. "I did, my love, and it did not look good."

"I only watched it once, and I haven't had the guts to watch it since then." Pippa's stomach clenched up so tight she thought she might puke. She hadn't been able to bring herself to watch the footage a second time, and that one blurred nightmare viewing was enough to know it had to be bad. Plus, the angry women mobbing her everywhere she went pretty much gave the game away.

Phi's droopy mouth confirmed how bad.

"It was Ray." Her legs collapsed like overcooked green beans and she needed to sit. The heavy kitchen chair screeched across the stone floor as she pulled it out. "He wanted me gone and used the show to make sure it happened."

"But why?" Phi threw her shoulders back, looking ready to do battle for Odin. It was the same pose she'd been photographed in while singing Wagner in Milan.

For the first time since Christmas, a real smile curled around the corners of Pippa's mouth. Drama was hardwired into her grandmother. Her mother hated it, and her sister, Laura, did her best to flatten Phi's flare. Pippa loved it. It warmed her from the inside and gave her that bit of driftwood she desperately needed. When you were with Phi, you had to go with it.

"Ray wanted a younger piece of ass." Saying it out loud brought the slow simmer up to the boil again. She'd only turned thirty-two three months ago. How much younger ass did Ray want? The answer stuck like a phlegm ball in the back of her throat. Twentysomething and fresh out of journalism college. Probably Debbie Does Dallas U.

"Men." Phi snorted and thrust her chin out. The Aida angle, a touch of defiance and high enough to catch the glitter of the follow spot. The expression crumpled and Phi glanced down at the floor. "It's all about sex for them."

A grunt sounded from under the sink. Pippa's nape crawled as her brain sorted this new information. "Phi?" She was afraid to ask. "Is there someone here?"

Phi waved a hand toward the sink, looking way too arch to be innocent. "It is just Mathieu."

"Thanks, Phi." A deep, dark country-boy rumble from under the sink.

Just Mathieu! An hysterical scream of laughter gathered in Pippa's throat. Matt Evans wasn't *just* anything, and he was under Phi's sink listening to every word of this.

"Hey, Agrippina," said the voice from the floor.

Only one person, other than Phi, called her Agrippina and lived to tell the tale. Sonofabitch, and she'd thought her day was done messing with her. "Hey, Meat."

"Matt is fixing my sink," Phi said.

Useful information she might have appreciated . . . say . . . five minutes ago. She leaned back and peered around the side of the table. Sure enough, a set of jeaned legs stuck out from the cupboard. His white T-shirt rode up exposing a couple of inches of tanned, smooth stomach. Matt Evans still had a little something-something going on. A too good looking, seriously charming, hot as hell, cocksure son of a bitch. Seriously nice thighs under those jeans.

"Don't mind me," he said.

With Phi listening she might have launched into her men and sex theories.

"We need champagne." Phi leaped to her feet.

"Champagne?" Pippa dragged her eyes away from the sizeable bulge at the top of those thighs. Matt Evans was packing. "I don't think I'm in much mood for celebrating."

"Darling." Phi flung her hands out in front of her. "Never let them see you bleed. Tonight we drink to your homecoming, and poor, single Matt eventually getting a date. Tomorrow we plot our revenge."

In Phi's wake the baize door swung shut with a whisper across the stone floor. Tools clinked from under the sink.

"Are you going to come out from under there?" Pippa craned her neck and caught a glimpse of his firm chin, dotted with stubble.

"Is it safe?"

The edge of another weeping storm swept through her. "Probably not."

"Younger piece of ass, huh?" Matt chuckled softly. *Go ahead, rub it in, you smug shit.*

"Dateless, huh?" Hard to believe the man who girls ripped one another's hair out for in high school was dateless.

Matt snorted a laugh. "Damn, it looks like someone cut this pipe."

Phi! Pippa dropped her head to the table with a thud that reverberated all the way to the back of her aching skull. The timing was too convenient to be believed. Not to mention the super-subtle way she'd worked into the conversation how unattached Matt Evans was.

"If you're done with the crying thing, could you hand me a wrench?"

Was she done with the crying thing? Tears stung her eyes and made her blink. Nope, she had a few tons of water left to shed.

"Wrench." A tanned hand emerged from the cupboard and curled his fingers in her direction. Oh no, he didn't. The last man to crook his fingers at her . . . had been Matt Evans. She hadn't responded that time, either.

She was done with taking crap. *Hello, Mr. Leg Man, here comes trouble, sashaying over the kitchen floor right at you.* Matt and his ogling were one of the best parts of coming home to Ghost Falls. Nothing like steady appreciation to lift a girl's spirits. Matt didn't do subtlety, either. Hot, naughty twinkle in his eye, small smile playing on his mouth, he'd hand out that sexy attitude in bucketloads. Her heels rang against the stone floor. She parked a four-inch heel right next to his hip, pressing her ankle in to get his attention. She lifted the other over and trapped him between her legs. Her pencil skirt pulled tight across her thighs.

The man between her thighs stilled. He loaded his voice with enough warning to tell her he was onto her. "Agrippina."

Through the opening where the sink trap had been she caught his eye, twinkle still there, daring her to do her worst. "Meat."

His eyes widened as he read her intention a split second before she opened the faucet to max. Water gushed out, straight down the downpipe. His body tensed.

Pippa leaped out of the way as he uncoiled from under the sink. Damn that felt good. Absolutely childish but so good. Turns out, Matt knew some very nasty words. She sprang back as he emerged, shaking his head like a big, wet dog.

"You think that's funny, do you?" She did. She totally did, and her grin said so. Strong hands fastened around her hips, whipped her right off her feet, and slammed her into a rock-hard, very wet chest. Her feet dangled a foot off the ground. Water spiked his eyelashes and dripped off the end of his nose. "That was not very nice."

Her blouse clung to her in a sodden mess as he held her in place. She wriggled to get free, mashing her breasts against him. The damp cloth between them vanished against the blaze of warmth coming off his chest. "You can put me down now." Damn, her voice got all breathy and girly.

He gave her an evil grin and lowered her to the ground, chest rubbing all the way. It felt so good, her little old toes curled in her kick-ass shoes. The smug shit knew it.

Matt stepped back and she got a good eyeful of him. Matt in his twenties had been hot, hot, hot. Today's Matt was a supercharged version with hard angles and sinewy muscle. He fisted the back of his T-shirt and dragged it over his head.

Holy shit! Hard ridges marched up his belly from his belt to expand into the hard slabs of his pecs. Those shoulders begged to have her sink her teeth into the muscle. Her mouth dried and her tongue stuck to the roof of her mouth.

He raised one dark eyebrow at her. "Well."

She folded her arms over her see-through blouse. "I see you've let yourself go."

"Liar. You were so checking me out." He laughed, a flash of white teeth that softened his harsh features.

The sound tugged at something buried deep inside her. It bubbled up under her chest and turned her mouth up at the corners.

The look in his topaz eyes warmed into hot, melty chocolate, and reminded her who was the girl here and who was the boy. God, it must be years since a man had looked at her like that. A look like that could make a girl's day a whole lot better.

Books by Sarah Hegger

Contemporary Romance
Passing Through Series
Drove All Night
Ticket To Ride
(Releases June 19th 2019)
Walk On By
(Releases July 10th, 2019)

Ghost Falls Series
Positively Pippa
Becoming Bella
Blatantly Blythe
(Releases March 6th, 2019)

Willow Park Romances
Nobody's Angel
Nobody's Fool
Nobody's Princess

Medieval Romance
Sir Arthur's Legacy Series
Sweet Bea
My Lady Faye
Conquering William
Roger's Bride
Releasing Henry

WITHDRAWN
HOWARD COUNTY LIBRARY

CPSIA information can be obtained
at www.ICGtesting.com
Printed in the USA
LVHW011751220519
618750LV00013B/618/P